Moscow Lost

Moscow Lost

Book 5 of the Moscow Nights Series

By Beth H. Macy

Edited by Dori Harrell

Moscow Lost ebook ISBN: 979-8-9908250-2-4

Moscow Lost paperback ISBN: 979-8-9908250-3-1

Moscow Lost hardback ISBN: 979-8-9908250-4-8

Book Cover Design by ebooklaunch.com

Edited by Dori Harrell, of Breakout Editing

Interior Design by Colleen Jones, of Breakout Editing

Acknowledgments

Thanks to Robert Browning for his poem "Andrea del Sarto." "Ah, but a man's reach should exceed his grasp, or what's a heaven for?" has guided my life.

I want to thank my partner, Chris, who cheerleads as I work on my goal to master my craft.

I thank my good friend Corinne for allowing me to continue having fun with Korinna.

My appreciation for my loyal followers who ask, "When's the next book coming out?" and my friends who cheer me on in this endeavor.

I am grateful to my wonderful editor, Dori Harrell, who mentors me to be a better writer.

Chapter One

Elda Ainsworth froze in place. Was that a footstep? Had she been detected?

Her fingers were numb from the cold, despite her insulated gloves. She snugged her gaiter up over her nose and mouth to conceal any signs of breath. She crouched down behind the dumpster. The frigid wind whirled around her. She pulled up the collar of her jacket and tugged her watch cap down low over her curly salt-and-pepper hair.

Thankfully, the Russian factory she was next to didn't have guard dogs, and the security detail was civilian, much like what she would call rent-a-cops in the United States. She held her breath and listened.

Nothing.

She consulted her Garmin watch. He was late. She would give her contact two more minutes. After that she would catch her ride out.

Elda had been in the Yelabuga region of Russia for three days now, gathering intel on the drone factory and shipping schedules. She existed in the shadows of the night and was dressed entirely in black, carrying a black backpack and a fifteen-round semiautomatic compact Udav Poloz pistol, complete with a silencer. In a sheath on her belt, she stowed a Shaitan throwing knife.

Crunch. A footstep in the ice-covered snow.

Elda whirled. Someone was here. She screwed the silencer onto her gun. Waited.

Voices floated to her hiding place.

"*Da.* She told me to meet her by this factory."

Damn. She had been sold out. That was her contact's voice.

"It appears as if you have been stood up, little man. If you are telling the truth."

Elda didn't recognize that voice.

Her contact spoke again. "I am. I swear to it. I would not lie to the FSB."

"I think you have lied to me to save your skin from your own charges. This was your last chance."

FSB. Damn, that's not good. Elda willed her heartbeat and breathing to slow. Her leg muscles tensed. She shifted her weight onto her front foot in case she needed to run. She prayed she wouldn't have to. She was slowing down as she got older. Her hand thumbed the safety on her pistol to off.

Elda heard a soft pop and the crash of a body falling over. Footsteps headed her way. She readied her aim.

The man rounded the corner of the dumpster. He spotted her and startled. He raised his hand to fire at Elda, but before he could shoot, Elda planted a bullet between his eyes. He fell over, landing facedown at her feet. His SR-1 Vektor pistol clattered to a stop a few feet ahead of his body. Elda returned it to his hand.

She picked his P-96 pistol from his belt holster, rolled him over, and shot him a second time in the same hole in his head. She wiped his and her prints off the gun and deposited it into the other dead man's hand, curling his fingers around it. "Sergey, you have been a bad man. You killed an FSB agent."

She waited, listening.

No sounds. Good.

She consulted her watch. Damn. She was running behind. She hoped her ride would still be on the river. It was a long walk to Kazakhstan.

Damn again. No boat.

Elda lay near the bank of the Kama River. The snow muted the aroma of the earth. Cold tendrils poked through her layers and wrapped around her chest. She needed to move soon. Her boat was to be at the dock at 0200 sharp. It was now 0205. She had literally missed the boat. What now?

Any communication might be intercepted. Once the FSB officer was discovered missing, the place would swarm with enemy agents. She wondered if the pickup boat would make another pass. The pier was deserted.

She took out her Steiner Military/Marine binoculars and scanned the riverbanks. She had a difficult time discerning shapes. The blackness of the shore and water blended together. Was there a boat on the other side, about one-third of a mile upriver?

Taking a chance, she took out a penlight and clicked two flashes. She received two in return from the vessel. Then three blinks—short, short, long. Elda struggled to recall her Morse code. "U?"

A long pause, followed by blinks: short, short, long, long, long. Another lengthy pause. "Two?" Then long, long, and a short pause. "M?" A short blink and then nothing. "E?"

U 2 ME.

Elda clicked back two flashes. She wore neoprene shorts and a neoprene top under her clothing, but damn, that water looked cold. She reached into her pack and put on a neoprene cap and gloves. She regretted not having any flippers, but on the up side, she'd find out how waterproof her shoes were.

She detached her knife from her belt, strapping it to her leg, and bagged the pistol. She removed her jacket, balled it up, and shoved it into her pack, along with her sidearm. She wrapped her backpack in a waterproof sack and tied it around her waist. The weight would drag her down, but the river was narrow at this spot, and all she needed to do was swim across to the other bank. She shivered.

Elda slithered to the edge and slipped into the shockingly cold water. Her muscles seized and her breath was ragged. She powered through it, reminding herself she had three choices: stay on the Yelabuga side and receive life in prison or death, die swimming across, or make it to the other side. She forced her arms and legs to move, filling her lungs with air for buoyancy and power. *Stroke, stroke, go, go, swim, survive.* Her mind pushed her body to its limits. She did not allow any other thoughts to deter her.

Her hand hit bottom. She crawled out of the water and lay on her back, gasping for breath. She told herself to move before she froze in place. She staggered to her feet and glanced upriver. The boat was still there.

A thought hit her. What if they were also compromised? Her chest tightened. She told herself Siberia couldn't be much colder than she was right now. She had to get to warmth before hypothermia set in. She willed her feet to move her to the boat and warmth—or death.

Despite the overwhelming sound of buses, mopeds, and car horns in Kolkata, India, Charlie Burlamachi perceived a sound behind her—the same cadence of footsteps she had heard earlier.

Suspecting someone was following her, she darted across lanes of traffic into the Foley open-air marketplace, where she was absorbed into a sea of humanity, produce, products, color, and noise. She squeezed between people and under outstretched arms to maneuver through the market, stopping to admire wares and check for her tail. The smells of cardamom, coriander, and peanuts reminded her she had not eaten lunch. Her stomach growled to confirm her thoughts.

Charlie purchased a pair of ginger-colored drawstring pants and a few brightly patterned shawls, which she layered over her head and clothing. While moving, she darkened her face and hands with a quick-dry liquid makeup and added a bindi to her forehead, completing her outfit. The layers hid her muscular build and closely cropped hair.

Charlie danced a twisted path, leading her back to where she'd entered the market. With a shawl over her head, obscuring her face from the sides, she exited. Alert to each sound around her, she listened for those footsteps. Absent.

Charlie continued onward, to locate the technology company the US suspected was running troll farms and hacking into government servers. Her job was to plant software on at least one of those servers, to allow Ashok Bhatt and others back in the States to remote in and take down the farms.

The other part of Charlie's assignment was to eliminate the man behind the hacking espionage.

The night was pitch black. Charlie, now dressed in tactical clothing to match the night sky, with camouflage paint on her face, blended into the darkness. She drew out and unfolded her steel-bladed Benchmade dagger and wiggled the sharp spear end into the bottom of the window, slicing off enough wood to insert a slender, angle-tipped pry bar. Inch by inch she lifted the window, wincing at each small noise it made. She waited.

No alarms sounded. No lights went on.

She slipped in through the window and found herself near a wooden stairway. The area hummed. Computers sat everywhere—stacked under the stairs, on and under folding tables. The wiring would make any electrician shudder and firefighters run for their gear. The layers of dust indicated no one had swept for weeks.

Charlie wove in among the computers on the floor, moving them forward in order to access the back ports. She inserted a thumb drive into one USB port on the closest computer and waited ninety seconds, as instructed. She repeated those steps three more times to ensure redundancy in infecting their network.

Done.

Charlie slid out and viewed her dust trail. She could do nothing to eliminate it, shy of cleaning the entire floor, so she scuffed around to make more paths among the computers. Satisfied, she tiptoed up the stairs. According to the intelligence she'd received, the leader, a Russian expat, slept in a makeshift bedroom on the top floor during the week. On weekends he lived the high life in his own mansion.

When Charlie reached the top floor, she spotted a body outside a doorway. The wooden door was closed. She stopped, crouched, and analyzed. She smelled the acrid scent of unwashed male and not the putrid decomposing smell of a dead body. *Was that snoring?* She crept up to the sleeping guard and, before he could awake, stuck him in the neck with a heavy sedative.

Charlie took out a small electronic listening device, pressed it against the door. More snoring from within. She opened the door a few inches and viewed an old canvas cot with a sleeping man on it. She slipped into the room, closing the door behind her.

Keeping her back against the wall, she scanned the space. They were alone.

Once at the cot, she looked down at his face. Although his mouth was wide open, she recognized him as her mark. He made appalling noises, covering any sound from her footsteps. She sniffed a glass with amber liquid in it on the table next to the cot and a half-empty brandy bottle sitting on the floor. They were the same.

Charlie threw two pills into the back of his mouth and poured the brandy in after them. She clamped his mouth shut. He struggled, gasped, and sputtered. Charlie implored the pills to take effect. Her thoughts answered, he abruptly stopped coughing and wheezed, staring at Charlie with watery eyes.

Charlie found it hard to breathe. She forced her thoughts to the background to be dealt with later.

She pulled his pillow out from under his head and propped his arm on it. She took his hand to straighten the arm and tapped with two fingers on the inside of his elbow. Finding a prominent vein, she injected a chemical into his system. This, combined with the pills, would mimic an opioid overdose.

His eyes closed and his breathing became shallow. He jerked and was still. Charlie felt his pulse and held her hand under his nose.

He was gone.

Charlie's limbs felt heavy and her feet glued to the floor. She shook herself like a dog coming out of the water. Time to move. She had accomplished her mission. She must focus on how to escape back to the States.

Chapter Two

N HIS SPARSE, UNDECORATED DC OFFICE,
Ed Wilson slammed down his desk phone. He crumpled up papers and hurled them at the basketball hoop on his metal wastebasket.

They all missed.

He thrust his chair back and snatched his black suit jacket from the back of the chair. He tightened his dark-blue tie, buttoned his jacket, and spit on his hand to slick his cowlick back. He polished each patent leather shoe on the back of a pant leg before storming out the door. He yearned for the old Corfam shoes. They held a shine.

Ed marched down the hallway and stopped outside his boss's office. He felt his temples tense. He took a moment to breathe and compose himself, then rapped on the door.

"Come in."

Ed entered and studied his boss, Jack Stone. Jack was in his mid-forties, a well-built man with muscular forearms, often displayed below rolled-up shirtsleeves. His dark-brown hair was slicked back, his face clean shaven.

He wore a gray suit, with the jacket slung casually over the back of his chair. He rarely wore a tie and preferred his top shirt button to be open.

The grapevine said Jack considered himself hard to read, but Ed's experience with Jack proved otherwise. Today Jack was fidgety and did not meet Ed's eyes. A sure sign of bad news coming. Jack was political, so it could be anything. This, however, was something Jack himself was uncomfortable with. Budget cuts weren't in *that* category. Rather than guess, Ed waited to be told.

Jack cleared his throat and tapped his pen on his desk. "The Oversight Committee has informed me they can't fund your black-ops group. They have learned we are focusing on Russia and don't believe that is necessary anymore. They claim China is where we need to concentrate."

"You know that's not true, Jack."

"I know, Ed." Jack shrugged, indicating he could do nothing more for Ed.

Ed's heart sank. What would this mean to Elda and the rest of her crew? Would *he* have a job? "How did they discover us?"

"Kevin Ball, may he rest in peace, informed them there was too much money in your budget, and he suspected the existence of at least one black-ops operative, Elda Ainsworth, working for you."

Ed rubbed the back of his neck. "But you know Elda was killed by the Russian agent Toshchiy Chelovek."

"Yes, I know you told me she was dead. But I'm sure you have replaced her by now."

Ed opened his mouth, when Jack held up his hand, "You know I'd rather not know. As long as my requests are taken care of and traitors to the United States become extinct, I am happy your organization is doing the job it should. Plausible deniability."

Ed clenched his fists and then relaxed them. His head

pounded. "Where does the funding come from now?"

Jack shrugged. "It doesn't. I informed the Oversight Committee only two operatives worked for you and I would fire them and reassign you."

Ed stood speechless. His worst-case scenario.

Jack continued. "That said, you know you worked at the discretion of the president, not of the committee. So if you go to him, I am fine with that. I have informed him of the small problem we have here. As far as I'll be concerned, you won't be working on Russian issues for me. I will slot you into a NO-OP desk job to cover pay and organizational structure needs."

Ed rubbed his forehead. He had to turn this around. He'd had a good relationship with the previous president but no track record with the current one. Being an unknown might work in his favor.

Jack cleared his throat. "I'd advise you to get on his calendar immediately."

Ed frowned. "What's driving the time urgency?"

"Well . . ." Jack shifted side to side and scratched his brow, careful not to disturb his hair. "The Oversight Committee said they feel strongly your team cannot be disbanded, that each member must be eliminated. They cannot risk having rogue agents working against the new administration's agenda. Your group is too skilled and known to ignore orders and instead do what they think is right."

Ed's feeble hope crashed into despair. "What!? They are United States citizens. The committee can't put a hit out on them."

Jack studied his floor. "Apparently they can. They hired a man to do this. It's unusual but not unprecedented. I fear this type of thing may happen more, depending on which way this upcoming election goes. You will need to give the hit man a name, to keep yours off the list."

I hope he's got a good mission for me. Elda ran her fingers through her hair to fluff up her curls. She looked down to check her gig line. Satisfied her shirt buttons, fly, and belt buckle were aligned, she rapped her knuckles on Ed's door. Bump-bump-de bump-bump . . . bump-bump.

"Come in."

Elda pranced into Ed's office and stopped short. Ed wasn't smiling, not even at her comical knock. His short black hair stuck up at all angles. His tie was loose and crooked. Something big was up. She strode up to his desk. "Hello, Mister Ed," she joked, and whinnied.

Elda didn't hear the expected laugh in response, though Ed's lips did threaten to curl into a smile. She spotted the pile of crumpled papers around his wastebasket. *Not one* had gone in through the basketball hoop perched on the rim. Whew, this was serious. She calculated it wasn't a good time to brief him on her trip to Yelabuga. She plopped into his guest chair. "What's up, Ed?"

Ed frowned, sighed. "We have a problem. The Oversight Committee has learned of our black-ops team and demanded it be disbanded. The noise around the budget Kevin Ball made alerted them to your existence. Plus, they don't believe any resources should be targeting Russia at this time. They want everything focused on China."

Elda exhaled. This *was* big. "Whew. So what's that mean?"

Ed looked down at his shoes. "I obtained a private meeting with the president. He does believe Russia is still a threat. We arranged other funding for your team, but you'll have to go underground and not be associated with my organization."

Elda furrowed her brows. It wasn't like Ed to avoid

looking at her. "For how long?"

Ed lifted his foot, inspected his gleaming right shoe, and polished it on the back of his slacks. "I don't know. I have the account with your funding. After this meeting I know nothing of you or your employees, Charlie Burlamachi and Ashok Bhatt." He paused and passed her a purple sticky note with an account number on it.

Elda memorized the number, "What flavor?"

"Blackberry, I think." Ed bit his bottom lip. He was not telling her *something*.

Elda popped the note into her mouth and chewed. Ed passed her a bottle of water. She took a large gulp, swallowed, and made a face. "Yuck, blackberry, my ass. Same bank and access as in Operation Bittman? We had to keep the funding for that project hidden, since the Russians and the Brits worked with us and we weren't sure who to trust."

"Yes." Ed's eyes were unfocused and watery. He chewed on his lower lip.

Usually Ed perked up when she mentioned the successful Operation Bittman—after all, they had saved the president's life. This time Ed didn't react. Elda cocked her head. "Anything else up, Ed?"

"Unfortunately, yes." He grimaced.

Elda waited. She could feel her heart beating in her chest.

Ed rubbed his temples. He looked at her for the first time in their conversation. "They also said that as well as getting rid of the covert organization, they will eliminate each member of the team, and I need to supply at least one name."

"So did you spike my water?" Peeking at Ed's face, she checked her pulse.

Ed was sad to see Elda stride out of his office door for perhaps the last time. They'd worked together for years and were close friends. He'd met her many years ago in Wales, where he'd been on a task for his CIA officer father, Ed Senior. Impressed by Elda's demeanor under lack of sleep and pressure, Ed had passed her his father's card. Years later she'd called Ed's dad and was recruited to work for the agency. Now Ed Junior was her handler.

Before she'd left, Ed had given Elda instructions and files on the operations he required she accomplish for him and America. They agreed on a secret encrypted communication channel to use going forward. He was confident Elda would accomplish the jobs. Nevertheless, he felt sick to his stomach. His jaw hurt from clenching his teeth.

He chewed two Tums and washed them down with an Excedrin followed by one-half a bottle of water. Ashok and Charlie would go with her. After transferring their files to Elda, he'd deleted all mentions of them from the server and his computer. He now searched for and deleted all remaining files on Elda, the black-ops group, and any past missions from his computer and the database. There would be no trace back to her.

"Damn it, the backups." He spun to verify his door was closed and no one could hear him. He texted Elda on their secure messaging channel to have Ashok take care of the backups. Knowing Elda, she'd archive them in a secure location so that no data would be lost.

Ed had promised Elda he would keep her informed and help her stay ahead of any assassin. He hoped he could. The Oversight Committee had promised him they would send him the background on the assigned killer today.

His office phone rang. Ed waited until the third ring to pick up. "Yes?"

The voice on the other end sounded like fingernails on a blackboard. Ed detested this man. He had celebrated when Elda and Charlie had caught Ronald Glass passing American confidential material to the Russians. The man was a traitor. But due to his political connections, he had received a full pardon, was released from prison, and was back in the Senate, assigned to the Oversight Committee.

"We have a new employee for you. You understand what duties he is to perform, yes?" Ron informed Ed in a snide twitter.

Ed gnashed his teeth. "Yes, I do. How was this employee sourced, and may I have his résumé?" He closed his eyes and rubbed his temples. Molten lava poured onto his head could not be more painful.

"His name is Butch Steele. He is someone who once did a job for Frank Garcia, and Frank recommended Butch. Unfortunately, Frank's early demise prevents us from finding out more, so you will need to find out yourself." Ronald snickered.

"Ah . . . I see." Frank Garcia had been on Moscow's payroll. Ed reached for his keyboard and searched online for stats about the assassin. He frowned. "When will I meet him?"

"He should be showing up at your office door momentarily."

Ed's office door slammed open, and a squat, muscular man, about fifteen pounds over his fighting weight, wearing faded jeans and a white T-shirt ripped at the throat, and stomped in.

Ed took off his glasses, polished them, and replaced them on his face. "And you are?"

The man cupped his hand and examined his fingernails. "Butch Steele. Just wind me up and point me in the right direction, and your troubles will be gone." Butch glanced around, spotted the guest chair, and pulled it over to Ed's desk. He turned the metal and plastic chair backward and plopped himself on it, arms draped over the back of the chair.

Ed ground his teeth together and inhaled, blowing the air out through clenched teeth. "Did they tell you what you are going to do?"

Butch yawned. "Yup. And they said you'd give me the names."

Ed appraised the man. "Do you have experience in this type of job?" From what Ed could glean in his short research, Butch was a petty thief. A string of prison sentences attested to his lack of skill at that job.

Butch shrugged, "I've done some things."

Ed glared over the top of his glasses at Butch. He pushed his glasses back up his nose and took a deep breath in. His head was in a vise. Pain radiated down his neck. "Do you own a gun?"

"They said you'd kit me out for the job."

In their dreams he'd give this ex-con a weapon. He gnashed his teeth. He decided to add investigating the Oversight Committee to Elda's project list.

If Ed was a betting man, he'd give Butch five days max left to live. He drummed his fingers on his desk. Who should he send him after first? Elda. She'd be able to figure out the best disposition for this overconfident punk.

Ed tossed Butch a pad of paper and pen. "Give me your contact information and come back here tomorrow at 0900 for your gear. Include where you are staying, in case we decide to deliver anything to you."

"Yes!" Butch jumped up and pumped his fist. He scribbled his number and address, chucked the pad onto Ed's desk, and paraded out of the office.

Ed swallowed two extra-strength Excedrin, followed by a healthy swig of water. He logged on to the secure comms and sent a message to Elda with Butch's background, address, and phone number. He received an affirmative and logged off.

Elda would teach Butch a lesson. This might even be fun.

Elda slipped into Butch's basement Georgetown apartment and wiggled her nose. An array of smells assaulted her. Decaying food in the garbage, unwashed dishes, dirty clothes, stale cigarette smoke. This man was a pig.

Wearing latex gloves, she gathered a few cigarette butts from his ashtray into a plastic bag. She removed hairs from his hairbrush and put them into a second container. She found a pair of old sneakers thrown in his closet and tossed them into a larger plastic bag. She hid a small camera on the finial at the top of a side lamp. Satisfied, she added the items to her backpack and stole away.

A few minutes later, Elda, dressed in black from head to toe, sat a short distance away at the Blue Bottle Café, sipping a mug of coffee and watching the inside of Butch's apartment on her phone.

Butch staggered in, holding a six-pack of Bud Light. He burped and slid onto his couch, turned on the TV, and opened the first beer. Within an hour he was passed out.

Elda glanced at her watch: 2000 and the café was closing. She left a large tip and nipped around the corner, fading into the shadows. Ten minutes later, wearing oversized sneakers, she reappeared inside the James Allen jewelry store. Lifting a few of the semiprecious pieces not been deemed worthy of locking up in the safe for the night, Elda scattered about enough DNA evidence for Butch to be sent away for a long while. She inserted a device into the door lock that would pop it open and trigger the alarm upon command. She stepped with force onto a patch of dirt outside the door, then hastened back to Butch's place and tiptoed in and out, leaving the loot under the kitchen sink and returning his sneakers to his closet.

Once well enough away, Elda activated the alarm. Within minutes, police sirens and blue lights abounded.

That takes care of him. Let's see who else they send.

Chapter Three

OUTSIDE ELDA'S HOUSE IN A PRIVATE COVE in Maine, the wind howled and the waves crashed against the rocks below. Inside, a different storm blew.

"Damn it!" She ran her fingers through her hair. Papers were strewn across her wooden desk in her tiny windowless office in her Down East Maine home. She gnawed the sides of her fingers. "Everything is running behind schedule!" she complained to the air.

Vee, lying by her feet, looked up at her with large brown eyes and wagged her tail.

"Sorry, Vee." Elda reached down and patted her little black-and-white Coton de Tulear dog. "Mommy's frustrated. I hate paperwork. I'd much rather be out in the field with Charlie, but I have to set up our new office. That's going to take me forever. And without the support that Ed's office gave me, I will be more involved with the administrative duties. Plus, I need the operational bandwidth that working with Tosh's team gave me. I have to hire at least one more, perhaps two agents. Fuck."

She drummed her fingers on her desk, then tapped on her Macintosh keyboard to view her budget. "That's it!" She seized her phone and pressed one of her FAVORITES. The call connected.

"Hey, Korinna. Are you bored without a job yet? I need to hire you."

Korinna Federov switched off her phone and sighed. She folded her long legs into the lotus pose to return to her meditation. Her intrusive thoughts kept barging into her brain.

Why had she agreed to work for Elda? She was enjoying Maine and her retirement. Her drawing and basket-weaving classes were such fun. And she loved spending time with her husband, Egor, and going for long walks with him and their two small dogs, Dasha and Sasha. Their dogs were thriving in the large house, with a fenced in yard to romp around in. So different from being in a tiny flat in Moscow and only taking short jaunts to the park across the street.

Korinna tossed her hair. She relished the feel her newly bobbed and dyed-blond hair made on her cheeks as it swayed with her head movement. She inhaled into her abdomen and shut her eyes.

Her mind would not quiet.

On one hand, she missed the excitement and interactions of her old job translating for the Kremlin bigwigs. She'd thrived on having her finger on the pulse of international interactions. Plus, the job for Elda's would be part time. Korinna could pick her own days and hours, and through helping organize and plan Elda's jobs, she would again be witness to background covert operations. After years of traveling on planes to translate for Russian dignitaries, she'd thought she'd be happy staying in one place, but she itched to travel.

Korinna opened her eyes.

The Kremlin believed she was dead. This home Elda had selected for her was secure in a protected enclave in Down East Maine, where Elda herself lived. Korinna wondered if she could safely travel again.

She rose to her feet. Today's meditation was not happening.

Egor, her clean-shaven, tall, and lanky husband, with a full head of gray hair, lumbered into the living room and gave Korinna a bear hug. Her six-foot frame felt dainty and small in his embrace. She snuggled in.

Egor held her at arm's length. "What's up, honey?" He led her into the spotless kitchen and put the kettle on to boil. They sat at the white wooden breakfast table.

Korinna explained over her tea, ending with, "Elda said I could quit at any time."

"So take the job, hon. You've reorganized the house, cleaned out all the closets and cupboards, and have worked through most of the classes offered at the local center. You're a great planner and organizer, as well as a superior translator. Why let all that talent go to waste? Besides, Elda asked. She must need you."

Korinna looked at her husband with her blue eyes. "Will you be okay while I'm working?"

Egor laughed. "I could use the time to practice my violin. I'm thinking of getting together with some other musicians and giving concerts at the center. I've spoken with other talented musicians in this town. Don't worry about me."

Korinna nodded. Her mind was made up. "Although I'm still pissed at her mode of transportation for me when spiriting me out of Russia—being locked in a swaying pitch-dark cargo container has left me with PTSD—I do owe her for saving my life."

The rapid beeping startled Elda. Someone had breached her outside perimeter and was on her land, nearing the house. She snagged her Smith & Wesson 9mm revolver and scanned her security monitors. She slipped her gun into her well-worn brown leather underarm holster and strode to her front door, unlocked it, and swung it open. A tired looking Charlie stomped into the Maine house.

Elda poked her head out. "Thank you, Jim."

He waved back. Jim was an old friend. Retired, he helped Elda out. He'd picked Charlie up from the airport, blindfolded her for the trip, and delivered her to Elda's door.

"You look like hell, Grasshopper."

Charlie glared at Elda.

Elda took Charlie by an arm and steered her across the worn wide-planked floors into the kitchen and deposited her at the table. "Let's get you some coffee. When did you land?"

Charlie yawned. "Yesterday."

Elda watched Charlie rub her eyes and shake her head. Charlie was obviously asleep on her feet.

Charlie looked around through red-rimmed eyes. "Weren't we supposed to be in an office in the DC area by now?"

Elda sighed. "Yes we were. Things are behind schedule. So how did your mission go?" She handed Charlie a large ceramic mug of black coffee.

Charlie held her coffee under her nose and breathed deeply. "I'm glad that's the last job for Ed. I don't relish being an assassin." She gulped her coffee. "I realize it was important to remove this guy, but isn't that what the FBI and CIA are for?" Charlie stood, reached for the pot, and topped off her mug.

"If you want, Charlie, I may have a syringe around and you can mainline the caffeine." Elda ducked as Charlie's hand slapped the air where Elda's head had been. "To answer your question, yes, it has been their role, but they are under a lot of scrutiny lately. Thus, the need for a black-ops team."

Looking perkier, Charlie asked, "So do we have something juicy on our radar?"

Elda squashed Charlie's hope. "Unfortunately, we first have to pay our debt to Ed for letting us go and for hiding our existence. That means more roles like the one you just accomplished."

"Ugh."

Korinna rolled a large whiteboard into her well-organized study. She slapped down a stack of various colored sticky notes on her desk. She selected the pile of vendor and construction contracts Elda had given her and sorted them by action date. She laid out different-colored whiteboard pens and drew swim lanes on the board. Soon a list of action items on stickies cascaded down and through the swim lanes.

Korinna referred to one note and lifted her phone to call the vendor. "Hello, is Mr. Gunn there?"

"Who's calling?"

Korinna rolled her eyes. She hated that answer. "I'm calling for Elda Ainsworth."

The man on the other end yelled in Spanish. "It's that annoying woman again. She's probably pissed because we're behind schedule."

Korinna heard a man answer him, in Spanish, "Give her the brushoff. We have more important jobs to finish. She's too stupid to realize ACE Construction has better product and is cheaper."

"He can't come to the phone right now."

Korinna said in Spanish, "Please tell Mr. Gunn, since he is in default, I will be exercising the escape clause in the contract. That means he will owe us ninety thousand dollars, as well as another eighteen K in penalty fees. Oh, and I expect it to be paid within thirty days, or he will hear from our lawyers. Thank him, too, for the referral to the other vendor."

Korinna hung up. It felt good to be working again.

She looked up ACE, called, explained the job, and negotiated the price. Within minutes an agreement via email for sixty-five thousand dollars for the remainder of the retrofit was in her inbox.

She dialed again. The sound of the phone ringing floated from across the cove and through her open window.

Elda's jaunty voice came through. "Hey, Korinna, what's up?"

"I have a handle on your project, Elda, but I will need to go to DC to meet with some of these guys."

"A handle? Already? You're amazing. Okay, I can deck you out with a disguise that will fool facial recognition, and I'll snag you a fake ID. Can you wait a day?"

"If we can obtain an outfit that fits me this time," Korinna stated in a flat tone.

Elda guffawed. "No worries, Korinna. You can wear your own clothing. We'll make you a tad taller and change the contours of your face."

"Am I allowed to fly, or are you going to shove me into a shipping container again?" Korinna could envision Elda's grimace.

"Gads, Korinna, when will you forgive me for that?"

It was hard for Korinna to not laugh at Elda's plaintive tone. "Never?"

Korinna laughed at Elda's exaggerated sigh. She would let Elda off the hook soon, but for now payback was enjoyable.

Chapter Four

A SHOK BHATT, ED'S COMPUTER WHIZ, NOW assigned to Elda, stood in his makeshift office, carved out of the living room in his small DC apartment. He packed his ASUS ROG Strix G18 with the Intel Core i9-13980HX processor, 64 GB RAM, 8T disk drive, facial recognition, and a max turbo speed of 5.6GHz, souped-up laptop into his canvas backpack. He darted into his tiny bedroom, seized the remaining clothing from his bureau, and threw it into a medium-sized leather go bag that had been his Christmas gift from Elda.

Ashok padded into his kitchen, admiring how empty and clean it was. Gone were the dirty dishes piled up in the sink, and wrappers and sports-drink cans overflowing the wastebasket. All he required was stacked, waiting for him to grab from the kitchen counter. He took the Clif chocolate energy bars, Monster energy drinks, and two bottles of water, dropped them on top of the clothing, and zipped up the bag, which he slung over his shoulder. He pulled his backpack over his other shoulder. He swayed as he adjusted to the weight of both pieces of luggage.

At five foot eight inches, Ashok was not a large man, but for the amount of time he spent sitting at his computer, he was in surprisingly good shape. Working with Elda on various gigs built some muscles. Plus, she constantly needled him about maintaining them.

Elda had asked him to head to Maine to join the rest of the team. She'd promised him a home within walking distance of their new DC office, when all was built out, but for now she needed her folks together in a secure, untraceable place. No one, except Ed, knew of Elda's home up north, or rather, "down east," and even Ed didn't know her exact location. Ashok booked a flight into Bangor under an assumed name. Elda's friend Jim would pick him up at the Bangor airport.

The sounds of his footsteps echoed in the near empty DC apartment. The rest of his belongings sat in storage. He looked around to ensure he had everything of importance, and locked the door behind him. The lock tumblers falling in place gave him a strange feeling of finality, the sadness of an ending before the beginning.

Ashok detoured to say goodbye to a neighbor. This elderly woman, Florence, had been kind to him, often leaving casseroles in his refrigerator to encourage him to eat when blasting through the night on a project.

He knocked on her door and was bustled in by a stout bundle and enveloped in a Lily of the Valley hug. "Where are you going now? Would you like something to eat, dear?"

Ashok smiled. "No thank you, Miss Florence, ma'am. I only wanted to say farewell for now. I am moving."

Florence's face fell. "Oh dear boy, I will miss you."

Ashok patted her arm. "And I you, Miss Florence. I will try to return here to see you though."

From within her apartment, Ashok heard footsteps in the hallway, heading toward his old place. He cracked the door and peeked out to view a large man with square shoulders entering his flat. *Darn, that's not good.* He was sure he had locked up. He closed her door and locked it. He treaded to the window, where he saw a black sedan idling at the curb, with a man behind the wheel.

He scanned for exits.

"Is something amiss, dear?" Florence inquired.

"Miss Florence, ma'am, I hate to admit this, but I owe some money, and I think they have sent some folks to collect." He gave her his best innocent doe-eyed look. "I'm afraid I'm going to have to cut this visit short and leave via the fire escape." The fire escape terminated in the alley, which had an egress to another side street and would allow him to avoid the car parked in front of the building.

Florence hustled to the kitchen and back and shoved a Saran baggy of chocolate chip cookies into Ashok's hand. He gratefully took it. Miss Florence's cookies were the best.

"Tut, tut, dear boy. I have been low on funds myself when I was young. I wish you had asked me for help."

"I didn't want to impose on you, Miss Florence. But I must run now." He opened the window and headed out to the landing. Florence started to say something, but Ashok held his finger to his lips. Ensuring no one was in the alley below, he raced down the fire escape.

A man with a crew cut, dressed in a navy T-shirt, gray corduroy jacket, and black jeans, knocked politely at Ed's open door and snapped into attention.

What now? Ed looked at his online calendar. He wasn't expecting anyone. "Yes?"

"Mark Slaughter at your service, sir."

"And why are you here?" Ed typed the name into his database search engine, and a profile of the man appeared on his screen. An ex-marine, sniper duties, honorably discharged, currently unemployed. He sighed. They'd sent another assassin, only this one could shoot.

"May I come in, sir?"

Ed motioned for the man to take a chair. He felt his temples tighten.

Mark remained standing.

"Please sit." Ed wondered what he had done wrong to deserve this. A drumming of pulsing pain started in his forehead.

Mark sat, his back ramrod straight, his hands resting lightly on his thighs.

"Who sent you?" Ed reached into his desk drawer and slipped an Excedrin into his hand.

"The Oversight Committee, sir."

Ed popped the pill into his mouth and chewed. Talking to this man was like pulling teeth. "Who on the committee specifically?" Ed expected the answer and was not surprised when Mark informed him, "Mr. Ronald Glass."

"Did Mr. Glass tell you what he wanted you to do?"

"Yes, sir. I'm to take out one or two people. You're to give me their names and locations. I'm looking forward to using my military skills again, and I've been paid well to do this."

My God. That was positively garrulous for the man. "Let's start with one person and see how you do, okay?"

"Yes, sir."

Ed scribbled Elda's name on a Post-it Note and passed the paper to Mark. Mark read it and was handing it back, when Ed said, "No, no. That's edible paper. Just chew and swallow."

Mark's eyes grew large, but he crumpled up the paper and obediently chewed. He passed it from side to side in his mouth and spoke around it. "It doesn't appear to be dissolving, sir."

Ed frowned. "Really? It should have melted to half its size by now." Ed offered him a bottle of water.

Mark gagged as he forced the paper down. He wiped the tears from his eyes. "Fucking horrible, sir." He coughed. "Where would I find Elda? Do you have an address?"

"No, I don't. In fact, last I heard she was reported as having been killed, but we never found the body. And she never reported back. So if she is alive, she is a traitor, and you'll take her out. Otherwise she's dead and your job is done."

"Do you have a picture of her at least?" Mark cleared his throat, swallowed a few times, and gulped a large swig of water. He blinked as his eyes welled with tears.

"Ah yes, here's the only one on file. It's from her Bureau of Navy Personnel, BUPERS, file when she joined the United States Navy." Ed gave Mark an old photograph of a much younger Elda.

"Thank you, sir. Consider it done." Mark, looking green, still clearing his throat, marched out the door.

Ed grinned, hearing the door of the nearby men's room open and swing shut. Perhaps that pad of paper wasn't the edible type after all. He felt his headache receding.

He closed his office door, opened the bottom drawer of his desk, and took out a burner phone.

Chapter Five

BORIS SIDEROV SAT BEHIND HIS MAHOGANY desk in his Kremlin office and traced the deep fingernail scratches with his hand. He cursed. The memory of that insane assassin, Nyoka Morozov, scratching his desk made his blood boil. His square face, already blotchy from too many shots of Russian Standard, reddened. He breathed in a few times to calm himself.

Boris was a large man, but not fat. He worked out daily in his home gym, not trusting the security in any other gym. He was not a fitness buff, but he believed that muscles made one look more powerful, and therefore more likely to be obeyed. He ruled by intimidation, force, and blackmail.

Tosh, a slender but fit man, about five foot ten inches tall, with piercing gray eyes, stood at attention in the doorway, waiting for his boss to tell him the reason behind the summons.

Boris looked up from his desk. "I need you to eliminate someone."

Tosh nodded and put himself in a relaxed stance.

"He is an enemy of the state," Boris continued.

"Is he dangerous, *ser*?"

"*Net*. The man is a pushover. I doubt he's ever held a gun."

Tosh arched his eyebrow. "May I ask, *ser*, what he has done?"

Tosh's eyes bored through Boris, who felt as if Tosh had read his innermost thoughts. He studied his fingernails. "He is disloyal."

"To whom, *ser*?"

Boris glared at Tosh. He sniffed, as if something in the room smelled. "To Mother Russia. He speaks ill of our leader."

Tosh stood in silence.

Boris said no more.

Tosh pressed on. "Is he in Russia?"

"*Da*. He lives in Moscow. This is an easy assignment." Boris rested both elbows on his desk.

"He is a Russian?"

Boris noticed a frown flicker across Tosh's face. Killing a Russian citizen was, apparently, to Tosh, outside his role as an agent. Boris slapped his desk. "Of course he is. Why all the questions? Our leader wishes to send a message to anyone who may think of speaking out against his policies. This man's death will be well publicized and must have all the earmarks of a Russian execution. *Vy ponimayete*?" His voice rose in pitch and cracked.

Tosh snapped to attention. "*Da, ser. YA ponimayu.* It *is* clear."

"Good. Now go see Gorky. He will have all that you need."

Tosh marched into the poison lab. His nose twitched at the variety of smells, some acrid, some sweet, floating through the room. He hoped that nothing in the air was harmful. He trusted Gorky Krovopuskov's professionalism of using the hood for anything that might be poisonous. He waited for Gorky to finish his work.

"Tosh!" Gorky cackled. "It has been far too long. What can I mix up for you today? Something that explodes? Or perhaps a flavoring to enhance a deadly drink?"

Tosh gave Gorky a warm pat on his back. "Gorky, my old friend. It has been too long. I am here on behalf of Boris, but also myself. I understand Boris requested you to mix up something special?"

Gorky's eyes lit up. He rubbed his hands together. "Ah yes, a lovely combination of Tetrodotoxin and Polonium-210. The two together can be overkill . . ." He crowed at his joke and wiped the drool from the corner of his mouth. "Polonium 210 will send a definitive message of a Russian hit. But as we know, it can be fatal to anyone who handles it, and it's slow acting and sometimes doesn't do the job. Thus, the Tetrodotoxin. It's a paralytic that, in the right dose, will have a rapid onset and kill within hours. Boris must really want this person dead." He leered at Tosh.

"That's why I'm here. I've decided my niece, your god-daughter Snezhana, will be handling it. How can we protect her?

"Hmmmm . . ." Gorky paced. "No, no . . . ah . . . no . . . aha!" He grabbed a pen and scribbled at a rapid pace. "Yes. That's it. Give me one day and I can have it ready for you. Not to worry—I will protect Snezhana, and the target will be very dead. Double dead." He cackled. "Hummmm, yes, *otlichnyy*, yes, excellent . . ." He hummed, trotted to a cabinet, and pulled out potions.

Tosh retreated before anything noxious escaped from the stoppered beakers in front of Gorky. "Thank you. I'll be back tomorrow afternoon."

"She will be well taken care of. Do not worry."

"*Spasibo, moy drug.*"

That sent Gorky off into laughter. "*Moy drug.* My friend. My *drug.* Drugs! Poisons. It all is so fitting, isn't it? They are my friends."

———

Anatoly Petrov lowered his scope and whispered to Snezhana Chelovek. "*Der'mo.* Why are we killing this person? We have watched him for days, and he is just an innocent." Anatoly scowled and narrowed his blue eyes.

Snezhana chose her words. She suspected their own lives would be in jeopardy if they didn't carry out the Kremlin's orders. "He has, through his words and writing, angered powerful people in our government."

Anatoly pounded his fist on his thigh. "That's it? *Words?* We are assassinating him because someone didn't like what he said? *Der'mo.* That's the reaction of a weakling."

"He'll be inside for the night. Let's get this over and eliminate him."

Anatoly stood his ground. "Why?"

Snezhana understood his hesitation. She didn't like this job either. "Because Uncle Tosh's life will be in danger, as will ours, if we refuse this job."

"*Der'mo!* And we have to poison him? Why? I had him in my sights. One bullet and we'd be done."

Snezhana put a hand on his arm to stave off the pending explosion. "They want to send a message. I'll take care of him. You keep an eye out. You never know who they may have sent to watch us."

Veins stood out on Anatoly's neck. "Watch us?"

"Yes, to ensure we can be trusted to carry out the orders. Times have changed, Anatoly. What was that Moscow rule Elda told us about—always assume you are being watched?"

"Do not look back. You are never completely alone."

They were crouched in an empty apartment across the street from their mark's. Snezhana stretched her long legs and stood. She opened her shoulder bag and viewed the metal, lead-lined container within. Next to it lay special gloves Gorky had instructed her to wear at all times when handling the container's contents. She hoped they worked.

Wearing dark-colored running gear, Anatoly and Snezhana jogged side by side up the street where their target lived. It was a few minutes after dawn, and the area was deserted. Their quarry had left yesterday, and reports placed him in St. Petersburg, where he was participating in an anti-government protest. If he stayed on schedule, he'd be home tomorrow.

"How good is your intel, Snezhana?"

"As good as anything Boris's organization gives us. Keep your weapon handy just in case."

Anatoly adjusted the straps of his hydration pack. He hid his weapons in the main compartment, with a smaller water bladder in a secondary compartment, connected to the hose. He could access his pistol through a Velcro side flap.

They reached the apartment complex and slipped in as a tenant exited the main door. They paused to ascertain the tenant was not returning, then took the stairs two at a time to their destination floor.

Anatoly stood watch while Snezhana picked her way in. He heard the click of success and backed in behind her. The stillness and stale smell of an unoccupied apartment met them.

Drawing his gun, Anatoly cleared all the rooms. Snezhana followed, installing monitoring devices along the way. Her inherited photographic memory captured the layout.

Anatoly checked his watch. "Eight minutes. We have to go."

Snezhana nodded. They reversed their running shirts to display the bright-red insides. Snezhana took crimson shoe covers out of her tights pocket and covered her running shoes. Anatoly drew on a hunter's orange watch cap. Snezhana tucked her hair underneath a cobalt-blue cap. To a casual observer, they would look different from the runners who'd entered the building. They sprinted down the stairs and up the street.

The following day, with a black cape wrapped around her shoulders and billowing behind her, Snezhana flowed across the street toward the target's apartment. A man in a gray suit and red tie approached from the other direction. She sashayed past him and did not look back.

Anatoly's voice came over her earpiece. "Good call."

"Remember the tenant we passed yesterday? It was the same man."

"It could be a coincidence."

"You know what Tosh and Elda say about coincidences . . ."

"*Da*. There is no such thing. *Khorosho*. He jumped into the black sedan. They've disappeared around the corner. Go quickly."

Snezhana strode up to the building's front door. Her actions hidden by the cape, she drew out her locksmith kit and slipped inside in less than a minute.

She bounded up the wooden stairs. Although Snezhana was a light woman, each step complained at her footsteps. She stopped at the first landing to tighten her earpiece and ensure she was not being observed.

Snezhana picked up her pace and soon reached the fifth floor. She cracked the hallway door and looked up and down, listening. The hum of the old building was the only sound.

She stepped into the hall. She was the only living thing, if you didn't count the cockroaches. She dashed to the apartment door and clicked her earpiece.

"He is in the living room watching TV," Anatoly said.

With a lightweight pair of gloves on, Snezhana applied her tools to the lock and crept inside. Dropping her cape inside the door, she slipped out of her shoes and padded across the linoleum floor.

His back was to her as she entered the living room. The volume of the TV show obscured any sound of her entry.

She stopped, drew on her protective gloves, and extracted the glass container with the poison mix. Advancing, she reached over the back of the couch, pulled his forehead back with one hand, and with the other shoved the vial between his teeth and poured the contents into his mouth. She dropped the empty poison container. She clamped his mouth closed while twisting his hair in her hand, pulling his head farther back.

He fought her and tried to remove her hand from his mouth.

She yanked his hair and stroked his throat.

He swallowed.

Snezhana let go, gathered the vial, and shoved it back into its case.

He rose, but his legs wobbled beneath him. He pitched forward onto the coffee table, breaking the cheap piece of furniture in two as he collapsed onto the floor. He spasmed in his futile efforts to stand up.

Snezhana watched his movements slow.

His breathing became more labored, stopped, started again, rattled, stopped, and with one last attempt to draw air into paralyzed lungs, he lay still.

Snezhana probed for his pulse.

He was gone.

She clicked her earpiece. Anatoly clicked back. Mission accomplished.

Now to leave undetected. She lifted her cape from the

floor and wrapped it around her waist as a skirt. She put the poison case and gloves into a handbag she'd carried in under the cape. She removed a long blond wig and a formfitting black jacket from the purse. She also extracted two-inch square heels that she affixed to the bottom of her black pumps. Dark sunglasses completed her transformation. She sent a silent thanks to Elda for having taught her so much about disguises.

She stopped at the door and listened. All was quiet. She used a handkerchief to open the door, hearing it lock shut behind her. She sauntered down the hall to the elevator. Once in, she sprayed a strong perfume on her neck. Elda had also taught her that being obvious helped one hide in plain sight. Snezhana would now be associated with that scent, which would not be in the apartment.

Snezhana strolled down the street, accenting the swing of her hips, as she passed the black sedan. Her heart beat faster. She forced herself to continue at her leisurely pace. She turned onto a side street. Anatoly waited at the curb in a beat-up baby-blue Lada. Snezhana opened the passenger-side door and glided in. "Drive off as if you have no place to be."

Anatoly growled and put the car into gear.

Boris's phone rang. His secretary poked her head into his office. "*Isveniti ser*, this is the third time today his coworker Emil Bychkov has called you. He is sounding increasingly angry and demands I find you. He is on line two."

"*Blyad*." He picked up the receiver and punched a button on his desk phone. "What is it, Emil?"

"Where is Nyoka? I didn't give her to you—I *lent* her to you, and I need her back."

As far as Boris was concerned, Emil could have the bitch. "She's still on a job for me. I'll send her to you the moment she gets back."

"You better."

"*Khuy tebe!*" Boris said to the disconnected phone. He swore he'd get even with Emil for sending Boris his trash. He put the receiver back on its cradle. He wondered what task Emil had that would require Nyoka and made a mental note to research that at another time. Perhaps it would be something Boris could get a piece of.

Where was Nyoka? Never mind where was Nyoka, but where were all *his* assassins? Dmitri Smirnov and Murka Mikhailov were also missing. If his superiors found out he'd lost three operatives . . . well, it would go poorly for him. He needed to find them.

He reached for his receiver and dialed. "Tosh? I have a job for you."

Tosh considered his crew. He had to give them a decent mission before they fell apart. Anatoly desired an honest kill. Snezhana required an op that would challenge her active mind. They both seemed to be struggling with the ethics behind taking out their recent target. He remembered when that wasn't an issue.

"*Der'mo!*" Anatoly Petrov slammed his massive fist into his thigh.

Snezhana winced and rolled the back of her hair around her forefinger, her hand slipping downward to caress the long-gone brown ponytail. She swirled in her chair.

Tosh, her handler bend uncle, narrowed his steely-gray eyes. "Snezhana, stop that." He snapped at Anatoly, "Anatoly, control yourself."

Snezhana came to a stop.

"*Ochen' zhal'*, *ser*. I am angry," Anatoly explained. "I guess it, from what you have told me, is from frustration. I am sick of the type of assignments we have been given. And when we get one, we have to tread lightly." He snorted. "Be politically correct. *Der'mo*. This job is not what it once was. Our missions were clear and our kills were clean. We worked for the good of Mother Russia, not to advance some bigwig or to line someone's pockets."

The three sat in Tosh's office in the Kremlin. Gone were the wooden file cabinets containing Tosh's off-computer records. When he'd been reinstated to his job in the Kremlin, after a stint of being declared missing and presumed dead, Tosh had decided to leave his important files off site and off his computer. He had little trust for others around him and no trust in computer network security. The FSB cyber organizations in Russia could breach any security he put in place.

The fourth member of his team, Stas Garin, was situated at their off-site office, his computer here at the Kremlin pumping along, the rolling display of lines of code compiling, giving the illusion Stas had stepped out for only a moment.

Tosh sighed deeply. "*Da*. I understand, Anatoly. I'm sick of the infighting and politics too. And the poisoning and imprisonment of good people, who happened to pick the wrong side, does not sit well with me either."

Snezhana brought her hand up to her hair and dropped it. "What shall we do, *dyadya*?"

"I have an idea . . ." The phone rang. "*Da?*" Tosh answered.

The voice on the other end was Boris's secretary. "He wishes to see you now."

Now was the time to win at Boris's game or lose everything. "Very well. Tell Boris I'll be right down." Tosh hung up with a thin smile. "It's time to see if my idea works. If

I don't return, leave immediately. Do not come back here." Shoulders squared, he marched out and then knocked on Boris's door

"Enter."

Tosh stood at attention a few feet inside the doorway of Boris's office.

"Tosh."

"*Dobroye utro, ser.*"

Boris indicated his guest chair. "Come in and sit down."

Tosh did as he was instructed.

Boris stared at Tosh.

The silence grew.

Boris threw the *Rossiiskaia Gazeta* newspaper across his desk to Tosh. "Congratulations on your last mission. The story has been leaked to many media outlets and protest organizations. The president is pleased."

Tosh leafed through the coverage on the civilian's death. He looked up at Boris. "*Spasibo, ser.*"

"I have a few other things I need you to do."

Tosh noted Boris stroked the deep scratches on his desk. "*Da ser?*"

Boris's left eye twitched. "During one of my previous operations, I was dealing with a man called Kevin Ball, a mole in the United States government in DC." He put a finger on the side of his eye, sighed, brought his finger back to the desk, and continued. "Kevin moved some money for me to offshore accounts. Unfortunately, he was eliminated before I could obtain the account numbers from him. I will give you all the data on him and that operation. I want the money found and transferred to this account." Boris passed Tosh an account number written on a pad of paper.

Tosh memorized the number and returned the pad. He rubbed his chin with his hand but gave no sign of his own knowledge of Kevin and the missing money.

Boris rubbed the scratches, as if to erase them with his

fingertips. He ground his teeth before going on. "During that operation, three of my operatives went dark. They were all new to my organization, so I have no history on their abilities or where they might go. However, their résumés were stellar. It's hard to believe someone took out all three of them."

"Where were they last, *ser*?" Tosh kept his face impassive. He wondered why Boris cared. From what Tosh had gleaned, those operatives were novices and possessed no record of success as agents.

"Nyoka Morozov and Murka Mikhailov were last seen in Wales." Boris tossed the files on the two assassins to Tosh, who flipped through them and put them to one side. Boris narrowed his eyes.

Tosh nodded for Boris to provide more details.

"Dmitri Smirnov was last viewed on DC Metro webcams." Boris slid Dmitri's file across to Tosh.

Tosh scanned and memorized it. His photographic memory had gotten better with age.

"And if I find them, *ser*?" He hoped Boris wouldn't ask him to drag them back to Moscow.

"*When* you find them, if they are alive, you can make your own determination about their disposal. I only need verification of life or death. I would prefer they not return, since they have shown such disrespect by not informing me of their whereabouts."

Good. Perhaps Tosh could use them in some way. He'd see what they were made of. "Anything else, *ser*?"

Boris punched his fist into the palm of his other hand. "*Da*. There are major leaks from our cyber teams, allowing the Americans to target them. We need to find these leaks and plug them—by whatever means possible."

Boris passed Tosh a sheet of paper with a name and an address in Moscow written on it. He placed a picture down on his desk and tapped it with his forefinger. "We have evidence that this man is an American spy. Capture him, find out what he knows, especially who else is in his network, and eliminate him."

"*Spasibo, ser.* Consider it done."

Boris waved his hand to dismiss Tosh.

Tosh remained seated. "I have one matter to talk to you about, if I may, *ser.*"

Boris's eyes narrowed. His lips pursed together. "*Da?*"

Chapter Six

E**LDA KNELT NEXT TO C**HARLIE ON THE DUSTY floor of a second-story flat in an abandoned building outside Moscow. She set up a telescoping tripod and slid a laser directional microphone and a telescopic infra-red camera onto the dual-mount adapter. She plugged in earphones to the listening device. She assembled the black metal sniper rifle, unfolded the bipod, and positioned the top PSO-1 sight on the VSS Vintorez to aim at an upper window of the building across the street. She fed 9x39mm cartridges into the magazine and rammed it home.

Charlie loaded her belt and pockets with flash bangs, grenades, and magazines. She slung the strap of a black OTS-02 Kiparis machine gun over her shoulder and slipped a semiautomatic Makarov pistol into her shoulder holster.

Elda knew Charlie lusted after the Makarov, loving the simplicity and the reliability of it as well as the size and feel of the grip. Depending on how the op went, and how they left Russia, perhaps she could let Charlie keep the firearm.

Charlie reached into the kit bag they'd acquired after entering Russia, and clipped a gas mask onto her bulletproof vest.

Elda put on her own vest and filled her pockets with incendiaries and smoke bombs. She selected a PP-2000 submachine gun and slammed a spare 44-round magazine into its rear stock. At about two feet in length, with an enlarged trigger guard to function as an additional handhold, it was often termed a machine pistol. Elda admired its versatility, with the folding buttstock and add-on laser and tactical lights. A mean-looking weapon. She should arrange to have these weapons smuggled to her new office. She put on the earphones and listened.

"According to the intel that Ed gave us, this is the cyber farm. And our informant is right on schedule. He's saying how he needs a vacation. That's our go-ahead code. We should be able to extract him and burn the place down."

Charlie nodded and headed for the stairs.

Elda saw an unmarked dirty white van drive up. Out spilled Anatoly and Snezhana. "What the fuck? Hold it, Charlie!"

Anatoly and Snezhana entered the building. Shots rang out. Screams. Anatoly and Snezhana appeared at the doorway, dragging a crying man, begging for his life. They hog-tied him and threw him in the back of the van.

"On it!" Charlie flew out the door.

Elda bagged up their gear, and left by the back door, where the beat-up beige VAZ 2105 sedan was parked. Elda required transportation that would blend in with the rest of the vehicles on the road and not stand out as something the authorities or oligarchs would drive. Elda had selected this car from a short-term parking lot at the airport and had negotiated a price with the owner, with the added promise if he would give Elda his address, she would mail him instructions on how to retrieve it once she was done with it. Elda doubted he would bother to retrieve the car, since she'd given him enough money for a much better one.

She scanned back and forth for it now.

Gone.

No one would steal that wreck of a car. It had to have been Charlie. She would need it to follow the van.

Elda stashed her gear in her trusty backpack behind a dumpster, jogged around the side of the building, and ran across the street to hug the wall of the other building. Back sliding against the wall, gun in hand, she sidled up to the door and flung it open. No response. She heard chaos upstairs, where people yelled in Russian.

The first floor was an empty large space.

Elda took the steps two at a time and inspected the door at the second-floor landing. A keypad entry system was no challenge to Elda's equipment. She slapped a device on the keys. It ran through multiple combinations of possible numbers, and after a couple of minutes, it stopped and the door swung open. Elda viewed a room packed with humming servers. She threw in a smoke bomb, to evacuate anyone tending the machines, and dashed up the stairs.

The door to the third, and top, floor was broken and hung on one hinge. Anatoly had been here.

The open-concept layout presented numerous tables, desks, and chairs, with pieces of ceiling tiles scattered about—most likely from Anatoly firing warning shots. People were whimpering and hiding under their workstations. Placing a gas mask over her nose and mouth, Elda jumped into the room, behind three tossed smoke bombs. She dove to the floor and rolled away from the doorway as the fire alarm went off and the employees scrambled for the exit.

She headed for the back wall and started attaching incendiary devices, with timers, where they would best burn the building down. She slapped C4 on a support beam and started its timer. As she worked her way out, she cleared each room so no one would be trapped inside.

Bounding down the steps, she popped into the second floor and installed more charges and incendiary devices. She glanced at her watch and told herself to move faster.

On the first floor, as she was setting the timer for the explosive on the last support beam, she heard a charge go off upstairs. *Crap, that's too early.*

The car was smoking and overheating by the time Charlie pulled it into an alley. She saw Anatoly and Snezhana drag the informant into a nearby building. She scanned her surroundings. There! That building on the opposite side of the street looked like it had empty offices. And from a window, she could obtain a sightline on the building the two Russians entered. Perhaps she would be lucky enough to see inside and catch a glimpse of them.

She ran low across the street and tried the front door. Locked. No time to pick it. She had to get upstairs. She unclipped her pocket pry bar from her belt and inserted the tip in the doorjamb by the lock. Grabbing her stubby claw hammer, she drove the pry bar in and broke the wood off by the strike plate. With a strong kick, she was in.

The cobwebs and broken glass in the entryway said it all. The building was deserted. She took the stairs two at a time, stopping at the first floor to check if she could see into the other building.

Nothing.

She scrambled to the second floor and broke into an empty office. She peered out the dusty cracked window. Score! They were in the second floor of the building directly across the street. The informant was zip-tied to a chair. Anatoly was yelling and slapping him. Slap. The chair fell over. Anatoly righted it and its occupant, who sat slumped, with his head down.

Charlie opened the window. She put a small camera on the sill and positioned her sniper rifle.

Anatoly stomped away and returned with a bucket of water, which he flung over the man's head. He put a hand under the man's chin and lifted his head. The man spat on Anatoly. Anatoly stepped back, reaching for his pistol. Snezhana grabbed his arm, pulling him farther away.

Charlie squeezed the trigger, then turned and sped out of the building to the still-smoking dilapidated car. Flames licked at the bottom of the oil-caked engine.

Damn. That wasn't going anywhere.

Charlie slinked to the end of the alley and looked up and down the street to locate a car she could steal. A royal-blue Marusia B2 sports car squealed to a stop at the end of the alley. Charlie stared at the lines of a car that could go 190 miles per hour and reached out her hand to stroke it.

The passenger-side door swung open. "Stop gawking. Get in!"

Charlie settled into the low-slung passenger seat and gazed at Elda. She had soot on her face, cuts on her hands, and bruises and dirt on her arms. Charlie looked at the backseat and saw their packs.

"How?"

Elda pressed the accelerator to the floor. "It was easy, Grasshopper. I have a tracking device on your phone."

Charlie ran her hand over the side of her dark-gray leather seat. "And where did you steal this lovely set of wheels?"

"Apparently there is a lot of money in disinformation nowadays. Especially if you are the top dog. However, I don't think he'll want to return to that industry anytime soon. He was standing crying outside the building as it collapsed. After I crawled out of the rubble, I persuaded him he would be better off giving me his car, then taking his money and getting the hell out of Russia while he still could. I may have implied I had enough on him to turn him in as the informant to his bosses."

"May have?"

Elda beamed at Charlie. "And you, Grasshopper?"

"I put a bullet into the informant."

"Confirmed?"

"Yes." Charlie displayed on her phone a picture of a corpse tied to a chair with a bullet neatly centered in his forehead.

"Nice shooting. How did you manage to snap that picture and get away?"

"I turned tail after taking the shot, but before I left, I positioned a camera that took and transmitted these stills, and then it self-destructed."

"Well done, Grasshopper. I'm impressed."

Anatoly and Snezhana ran down the concrete steps and out into the street, weapons drawn. They spotted the back of the low-slung blue car fishtailing as it disappeared around the corner.

Anatoly slammed his fist on his thigh. "*Der'mo*! They got away. Did you get a glimpse of them, Snezhana?"

"*Net*. Only the back of their heads. I can guesstimate how tall they are from the position of their heads in the car seats. I can think of two people with those haircuts and heights who would fit that profile."

"Who?" Anatoly growled.

"Elda and Charlie." Snezhana reached up for her ponytail.

Anatoly shook his head. "*Net*. It can't be them. They don't assassinate people. And, Snezhana, that ponytail is long gone. Elda probably wanted to frame it for you after she cut it off."

Snezhana glared at Anatoly, then raised her hands, palms up. "That's my point, Anatoly. I may be comparing the glimpse I had to them only because we know them."

Anatoly narrowed his eyes. "Can you think of a reason they would be here?"

Snezhana shrugged. "Do we know why *we* are here? Snatching and interrogating prisoners is not what we do."

"Tosh told us to find out who this man is working for."

"I know that." Snezhana slapped Anatoly on the arm. He made a fist but restrained from punching back. Snezhana went on. "Tosh told us that all he knew was this mission had to do with the disinformation campaigns targeting the United States during this election year. That unknown Russians are helping the West take down our server farms, here in Russia and in India. He implied the directive to stop the leaks was straight from the top. If so, it's not going to go well that we have nothing to give Tosh."

"So . . ." Anatoly scratched his buzz cut. He was not clear where Snezhana was going with this conversation.

"*So* we don't want to be among those who are suddenly made obsolete in their jobs in Russia."

Anatoly stared wide eyed at Snezhana. "*Der'mo!*"

CHAPTER SEVEN

TOSH BRACED HIMSELF FOR BORIS'S REACTION. Boris tapped his fingers on his mahogany desk and glared at Tosh. "Your people got the target, but he was shot by a sniper?"

"*Da, ser.*" Tosh stood expressionless.

Boris narrowed his eyes. "Who was the sniper?"

"We have no findings on that, *ser*. They drove a blue Marusia B2 sports car. We got a partial plate, and it appears it may have belonged to Ignatiy Lawless, the man in charge of the cyber farm that burned down."

Boris cocked his head. "*Interesnyy.* Was the man found at the scene?"

"*Net.*"

Boris put his forefinger on his chin and squinted at Tosh. "What do you make of that?"

Tosh did not flinch. "Perhaps Ignatiy ordered one of his people to kill the informant so we wouldn't find out his *own* implication in the leaks. We need to locate him."

"Do that. But before you do, find my other assassins.

I've changed my mind about eliminating them. I could use the bandwidth." Boris traced the scratches on his desk.

"*Da, ser.*"

Boris stared at Tosh, who cleared his throat and mentioned, "About the other matter we discussed last time, *ser?*"

Boris waved his hand dismissively. "After you do those tasks for me, you will be free to work in the darkness."

"*Ser?*"

"What, Tosh? You are starting to be a bother here."

"If I may say so, *ser*, if we are allowed to work *now* as a black-ops unit, we could be more efficient and *no one* would need to know what you have us working on."

"Good point. *Khorosho.* But I may on occasion tap you for missions."

"Effective immediately, *ser?*"

"*Da.*" He waved Tosh out.

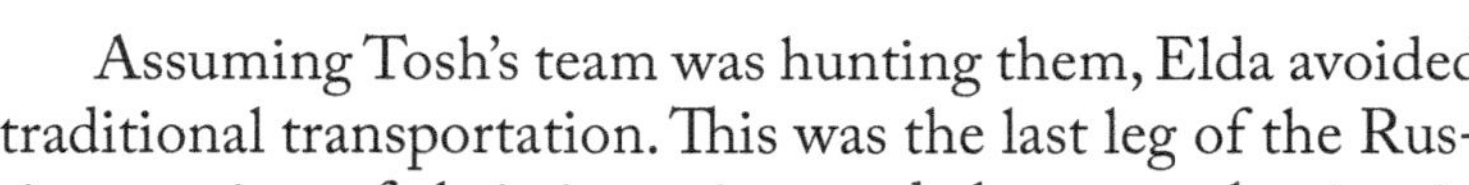

Assuming Tosh's team was hunting them, Elda avoided traditional transportation. This was the last leg of the Russian portion of their incursion, and they were leaving in style under a pile of hay.

The man who owned the hay cart had agreed to bring them as close as possible to Ivangorod on the Russian side of the Estonian border. There, they would slip into wet suits with traditional fishing outfits beneath the suits. Elda wished the Friendship Bridge was open to foot traffic. The only way to cross now had to be done underwater.

The Russian border guards patrolled on a predictable schedule, and timing was tight. Elda had alerted the Estonian border police to their arrival, but she hadn't received confirmation of permission to enter the country. This was not a cakewalk.

"Elda?" Charlie whispered, from under the hay.

Elda sneezed and sputtered. The hay made her allergies run wild. "Yes, Charlie?"

"I'm not an assassin."

"No, you are not," Elda coughed out,

"But I just killed an un-armed man in cold blood. My other kills were in war or in self-defense."

Elda detected a note of pleading in Charlie's voice. Did she want absolution or an explanation? "Yes, you did."

"That makes two in a short time," Charlie added.

The cart jostled along the dirt road. Elda sneezed again. "Damn, it's a good thing we're in the middle of nowhere and don't need to be quiet."

"Darned good, Elda. Your wheezing is enough to give us away." Charlie's laugh was halfhearted.

"What do you need, Charlie?" Elda asked.

"Did he have a name?"

"Vadim Popov. He was Russian American living in Moscow."

Elda strained to hear Charlie's repl. "Why did we have to kill him? What did he have that was so dangerous for the Russians to know?"

Elda blew her nose loudly. "Good question. The man you shot was our lead informant in our campaign to shutter the Russian disinformation cyber farms in Russia and India. He was the connection between all our cyber-farm moles, and had he been captured, we would have lost many more people, as well as lost the progress we've made in shutting them down."

"But how can that be important? Who would believe the stuff they send out anyway?"

"Ah . . . ah . . . choo. Sorry. This damned hay. Grasshopper, they are clever and send out broadcasts with enough kernels of truth in it to be somewhat believable. And they are not relying on individuals to believe what they read. They have media sources within the States and other countries who receive this news from Russia and send it back out, which increases the believability factor." Elda reached behind her neck and pulled straw from the inside of her shirt.

"Is this the new Cold War?"

The hay above Elda shifted as she scratched her back against the floorboards of the cart. "It's hard to compare the two. The main thread between then and now is a continued effort to infiltrate and discredit the American and Western governments and intelligence services, but now they also intend to fracture the population and create wars and destruction within. With the assistance of AI and social media, they are able to reach so many more people at once than they ever could."

"I'm not sure I'm prepared to fight this type of war."

Elda snorted. "I know I'm not. But they are also still waging the older type of conflict where, in addition to using blackmail and outright purchase of an individual's loyalty, they bury moles within, often by obtaining birth certificate of children who have died, replacing the children with Russians, who will grow up and wait to be activated to serve their country."

"Won't the death show up when they do a background check?"

"No. They were clever enough to have destroyed all records of the death."

"Damn."

Silence.

Elda was discouraged at the enormity of all that they faced. If she felt this way with all that she had seen and understood, she could only imagine how horrible it was to Charlie.

"Elda?"

"Yes?" How could Elda silence Charlie's discomfort about their new roles?

"Did we have to leave that lovely set of wheels behind for *this*?"

Elda chortled and coughed. "You're killing me, Charlie." Wheeze, the sound of her inhaler, then silence again.

"Elda?"

"Yes, Charlie?"

"What do we do?"

"Damned if I know, except to use whatever tools we have to stop them by whatever means possible."

"Fuck."

The cart stopped. Elda saw nothing but fallowed fields. The surrounding trees and shrubs would give them some cover, but they would have to stay low and move fast.

Elda paid the driver the rest of his money plus a sizable tip. "*Spasibo.*"

He nodded and drove off.

Elda stripped off her clothes, replaced them with baggy old-man's fishing garment, and pulled on a wet suit. She shoved her backpack and clothes into a fishing sack, slung it over one shoulder, tied a bait bag of worms onto it, along with a foldable fishing rod and net. She glanced behind her and saw that Charlie was following her lead.

Elda handed Charlie an envelope. "Here are your papers. Memorize your new identity."

"Yes, ma'am. So where are we going?"

Elda drew a map in the dirt. "We are going to zigzag our way to Ivangorod. According to the satellite footage I've been studying, the border is heavily patrolled and has electronic surveillance to boot. They have been building a steel wall along the banks on the Russian side. However, there is an spot, a tad after the falls, where we can slip into the river." After Charlie absorbed the information, Elda scuffed out the drawing.

She tossed a cameo-colored cape to Charlie. "Throw this over your shoulders. We need to avoid being spotted by the drones, and we don't have much cover between here and the river. To get north of the waterfall, we have to pass by a populated region. There are some wooded areas south of the railroad tracks. The tracks lead to a bridge over the river. It's too heavily guarded at that point to cross."

Charlie looked at the cape. "This wouldn't be any chance be a cloak of invisibility?"

"Wishful thinking, Grasshopper."

"What's the plan, Master?"

"Our cart driver has a cousin with a panel truck. He will drive by on Narovskaya Ulitsa. If we can meet him at the curve in the road near the building with the blue roof at noon sharp, he will stop for thirty seconds for us to jump into the back of the truck. That will avoid us being seen on the regularly scheduled drone pass."

Charlie glanced at her watch. "It's ten after eleven. Do we have enough time?"

"We should. If nothing stops us along the way. We have no time to spare. Move fast and stay down."

They crouched under their capes and ran northwest. Elda felt the ground under her feet tremble. She held her arm up and dropped to the ground. "Down! A train is coming!"

She and Charlie lay behind a small stand of bushes, hoping that the train conductor would not spot them. The train passed. Charlie started to rise.

"No. Wait. Make sure you are completely covered and stay silent."

They froze. A small drone flew overhead behind the train.

Elda waited a heartbeat and then rose. "All clear, Grasshopper. Hurry though. We lost precious minutes." They fast-walked toward a stand of trees.

Elda and Charlie hunkered low beneath a large branch. The building with the blue roof was north of them, and the curve in the road lay to their west.

"This is the place. Time check, Charlie."

"Eleven fifty-eight."

"I hope his watch isn't fast and he's been and gone. I'm not sure what we'll do if we miss him. It's heavily populated from here to the river." Elda looked at her own watch. The long hand moved to 11:59. She clicked the settings to digital, confirming the time. She chewed on the sides of her fingers. They should be able to hear the sounds of the van approaching by now. "Let's crawl to the edge of the road so we can quickly board, in case he's late. We can't get caught by the next drone pass. We should be able to stay hidden in the tall grass."

They slithered through the undergrowth, stopping at about five feet from the road. Elda checked the time again. Noon on the dot.

"Damn. Where is he?" Elda could feel her heart beating in her chest. She breathed, filling her chest, and rubbed her ears to slow her pulse. She sensed, rather than heard, a vehicle approaching. "Keep your head down. Someone's coming. Wait to ensure it's our ride before jumping up. Follow my lead." Elda peered through the blades of grass. A dirty white panel truck headed north toward the left curve. "That's got to be it. Go, go."

They hopped up and dashed to the road as the truck slowed to a stop.

"Well done, Grasshopper. We made it," Elda whispered to Charlie in the back of the van.

"What's next?"

Elda folded up the capes and stowed them in her backpack. She passed to Charlie a mask and a small oxygen tank and a weight belt. "Do you know how to use this gear?"

Charlie turned the mask over and inspected the tank. "Yes, ma'am. How many minutes of O2 do we have?"

"You have ten minutes, *if* you conserve. Eight minutes on average."

"How far are we swimming?"

"One tenth a mile, give or take . . ."

"That could be tight. Is there a current?"

"Yup. There will be. We're about three kilometers north of the waterfall. The river flows north into the Baltic Sea. I expect the crossing could be dicey. The van will stop for thirty seconds, no more, no less. We'll jump out and dash to the bank of the river. The next drone overpass will be five minutes after we arrive, so we have to be efficient with our time. When I say go, dive in and sink to the bottom. Then swim like hell over to the other side."

"I can do that."

"Do *not* surface or you may be shot."

Elda slid down the embankment and sank into the river.

Charlie hastened to follow her. She hit the water. The chill of the river on her exposed head and hands shocked her, and she struggled to regain her breath. Her weight belt drew her under. She resisted the urge to surface. She drew in a breath from her air tank. Shit. She was using up oxygen already and hadn't made any progress across the river.

Charlie fell into a natural rhythm of swimming. She had no way of knowing if she was heading across or going sideways. Her only bearing was the light filtering down from above. She fought her need to know and trusted her instinctive sense of direction. She slowed her breathing to conserve the little oxygen she had.

The air wasn't flowing well. Charlie found herself sucking for the last air out of the small canister. She must surface soon. Where was she? Was she far enough across to not get shot? Or would she surface and float the remaining way with a bullet in her head?

She sucked at the air again. She held her breath after filling her lungs with what was left. She glanced at the gauge.

Out. Damn.

Was that the bank ahead of her? Her chest muscles strained, and she swallowed hard and pinched her nose closed, to not inhale.

No matter what, she had to surface, *now*.

Dripping wet, Elda climbed out of the Narva River and stashed her swim gear in her fishing bag. It had started pouring while they were underwater, a fact that she rejoiced in, since it churned up the water, hiding any escaping bubbles.

Elda stripped off and dressed in her fishing clothes, hoisted a bunch of the fish left tied together on the bank, and started walking. She prayed that Charlie would soon surface. She relaxed when she heard splashing, coughing, and cursing behind her.

"Put your swim togs in your pack. Here, catch." Elda tossed Charlie a dead fish hanging on a line.

Charlie fielded it as it slapped her on the arm, leaving a slimy trail. "Ugh. Where did you get that? It stinks."

"Hang it on your bag and follow me. It's a good thing it's raining, Grasshopper. It helps cover up the fact that we're drenched from our swim."

The two of them strolled along the path, when they spotted two Estonian border patrol agents. Elda's heart pounded in her chest. She hoped these sentries knew they were coming.

"Nice day for a swim." the woman in the pair said in English.

"The fish are better on this side of the river," Elda replied.

"As are the people," the guard retorted.

Elda finished the password banter with, "I have heard they are very helpful."

The patrolman nodded. "Come with us. Your Korinna has told us to let you know she has made first-class travel arrangements for you. It's not safe to stay too long here along the border. There are too many Russian eyes and ears. We will get you on the train to Tallinn, and from there you will fly to Helsinki. *There* you will be safe."

"*Tänan teid.*"

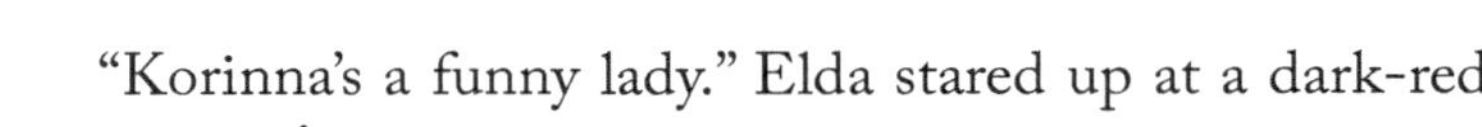

"Korinna's a funny lady." Elda stared up at a dark-red cargo container.

Their police escort keyed in a combination. The container clicked open, and the latch smoothly slid to one side. Elda saw an identical keypad inside, in case they needed to escape.

The policewoman leaned in and touched the corner of a large box. A section of the wooden-slatted front slid into the box, curving at the corner, to lie flat along the inside wall. She handed the two women headlamps. "Go through there. Good luck. Safe travels. I will close the container after you crawl through."

Elda threw her body into the opening and saw that it led to a small corridor. Once she stood, she noted that the front boxes were separated from the rear by solid beams to avoid shifting. On the left was a crate approximately eight feet tall by four feet wide and an unknown length. An identical one butted up against it on the right. She ran her hand along the outside until she felt the pressure sensitive keypad and keyed in the code Korinna had texted her.

"Hey, nicely done, Korinna! This is an upgrade." In front of Elda was a small room with handholds along the side, a mattress bolted down in one corner with straps to hold the sleeper in, a chemical toilet in the other, with handholds, a seat belt, and a wooden box with water and food screwed into the side wall. The entire inside was covered with soundproof padding. A battery powered lantern hung near the door. She heard Charlie thump down onto the floor from the crawlspace.

"Ouch! Where are we?"

The clang of the container door closing made Elda flinch. She nudged Charlie over to the opened room on the left. "Welcome to your new home for the next perhaps twelve hours. With loading onto the train and unloading, there's at least four hours of travel time for that section of the journey to Tallinn. The flight from Tallinn to Helsinki will be just over one-half hour, but who knows how long unloading and loading will take. Or if we'll even be shipped out that same day."

Charlie looked at her accommodations with a grimace.

Elda reached past her and shone her headlamp on a keypad inside the door. "The combo is 5-2-3-9-8-3-3. That will both shut and open your door." She handed the open-mouthed, mute Charlie an earpiece. "Comms. Although these containers do have some soundproofing, we will have to keep quiet and communicate only when necessary."

Charlie inserted her earpiece.

Elda patted her on the arm and said in her best airline captain's voice, "Please do enjoy your journey. You may experience some turbulence, so please stay buckled in at all times. I'll be in the suite next door."

Elda entered her crate and closed the door. She inhaled and closed her eyes to fend off an attack of claustrophobia. "I'm so sorry, Korinna. This is a good lesson for me," she whispered to herself.

She used the toilet, snatched a water and a chunk of cheese, and sat on the mattress. "Get a few hours of rack time," she told herself. She finished her snack, covered up with a blanket, and buckled herself in.

The container swinging side to side woke her. She heard a faint crash from next door and keyed the comms. "You okay?"

"Shit. I had to pee and got cocky, so I wasn't using the handholds on the way back. Except for my ego, I'm unharmed."

Elda chuckled and terminated the transmission. Perhaps more than one person had learned a lesson today. She tightened her belt. She sure hoped those guards were on the up and up and they were on their way to Helsinki, not Siberia.

CHAPTER EIGHT

CHARLIE SETTLED BACK IN THE PASSENGER seat with a contented sigh. "It sure is good to be back in DC."

Elda swerved her Honda Acura hybrid around a lost tourist and continued on her way to the airport. She shivered and flicked her seat heat indicator to high. "Yes, Grasshopper, it *is*."

"You *already* have the air on your side up to max heat, Elda. Are you *that* cold?"

"I am. I can't get the cold of Russia out of my bones. I'm glad you agreed to come with me to pick up Korinna. We can debrief a bit, and it will be good for the two of you to get to know each other better. You haven't had the chance to work with her yet."

"No worries, Elda. I also want to see the construction on the new office."

Elda's phone rang. "Hi, Korinna. You're on speaker. Charlie and I are on our way to pick you up."

Korinna's voice came over the car's speaker system.

"*Mne zhal'* Elda. I won't be there. A sudden family emergency came up for my doggie daycare, and they closed for today. Egor caught me with the news as I was in line to board. I managed to reticket for tomorrow."

"*Khorosho*, Korinna. I'm happy to be riding around in comfort with heated seats. When you arrive, I'll tell you my idea for container transport three point oh."

Korinna chuckled. "What's that?"

"Heat." Elda rang off to Korinna's laughter.

Charlie tucked a foot under her butt and swiveled to Elda. "What now? Can we still visit the site?"

Elda shook her head. "Let's save that for tomorrow. I'd like to stake out Mark Slaughter's apartment and see if he has any habits we can exploit."

Elda smoothly pulled the car into a parking space. "There he is." She reached into her backpack and drew out a small disguise kit. She quickly lengthened her nose and widened her face with the latex appliqués. A small amount of makeup blended the changes in. She inserted blue contacts to change her eye color and slipped veneers over her front teeth, making them large and whiter. She was ready to face Mark.

They jumped out. Charlie reached into her bag and slapped a different license plate over Elda's front and back plates.

Elda raised an eyebrow.

Charlie shrugged, then took the front tail. Elda fell into the rear.

They followed Mark to a local coffee shop, where he ordered a donut and black coffee and sat at a table with his back to the counter, facing the door.

Charlie grabbed a double espresso and took station at an outdoor table.

Elda strode in and requested an espresso. She stood next to Mark's table while the woman behind the counter made the order.

"Mark. Your coffee's up. Sorry you had to wait for a new pot. I know you're anxious to get a jump start in the mornings."

Mark walked up to the charming young female barista and flashed her a white-toothed smile. She handed him his coffee with a flirty wink.

Elda appraised their interaction and concluded Mark was a regular here. The barista plunked Elda's drink in front of her. Elda sat at a table across the way from Mark. He held his phone up with the camera facing her, typed, and shook his head.

Elda looked down at her clone of Mark's phone, which she'd obtained while standing next to him. The facial recognition software rejected her as a match to her BUPERS photo. She silently thanked her Hollywood makeup-artist friend, who'd taught her so much. She also blessed Ashok for his technology, which allowed a brush-pass clone of someone's phone.

When Mark rose to bring his cup and plate to the barista and flirt one more time, Charlie left, resuming the front tail. When he exited, Elda reversed her jacket and wound a scarf around her neck and head. Elda and Charlie switched off leading.

Elda removed her jacket and scarf and put them in her backpack. While Mark ate lunch, Elda dashed into a nearby shop's ladies' room and emerged wearing gray sweats. Underneath she wore black Spandex running tights and a bright-orange long-sleeved tee. Later on, the sweats went into the pack, and a re-disguised Elda ran a few laps, keeping him in sight. Elda knew Charlie carried a similar backpack of disguises and tried to spot her too. Charlie's costume abilities had improved from their early days of working together.

They trailed Mark back to his apartment complex. Once

he was inside, they returned to their hotel room to compare notes and bring Ashok in, to research Mark's stops. Ashok was still up in Maine, entrenched in Elda's spare room. Elda made the secure connection and sent Ashok the data. Charlie popped out for sandwiches and returned as Ashok appeared on Elda's laptop screen.

"I have researched the coordinates and addresses you sent me, Miss Elda. Oh, hello, Miss Charlie. You will most definitely be pleased with what I found."

Charlie waved and tossed Elda a white paper bag.

Elda ripped it open and unwrapped the wax paper and peeked at the sandwich. "Chicken salad, no pickle." She spilled the rest from the tattered sack. Chips and box of milk. "Yum, Charlie! Thanks." She looked at Ashok who appeared to be pouting. "So sorry, Ashok. I didn't want the food to interrupt your story. Go ahead and delight us."

"Yes, yes. It is most interesting. It appears as if Mister Mark has some underhanded connections and activities."

Elda glanced up from her food to the monitor. "What do you mean?"

"This address he stopped at is connected with an international arms dealer."

Ashok darted back down into Elda's basement. "I certainly hope Miss Elda will like the most excellent improvements." He climbed up onto a stepladder and reached for a cable sticking out near the ceiling. Popping ceiling panels off to one side as he advanced, he pulled the cable over to the other side, where a collapsible table lay propped against the wall. He stepped down and paused to grab a drink of water, while eyeing the job in front of him.

Ashok had decided to turn Elda's finished basement into an office for him. He needed to pull the internet cable over to the computer he was setting up, and he also required a power source. He opened the electrical panel and smiled. It was a modern system and there was room for more circuit breakers. He turned off the main power to the box and switched on a headlamp. He kept a running commentary while he attacked the wires. "Take off the front panel. Check. Main power off. Check. Remove front cover. Check. Turn the new breaker off, slide it in, and seat it. Check. Connect the wires. Check. Pop out the knockout plate and replace the cover. Check."

Ashok took a deep breath. "Well, now I hope Miss Elda doesn't come home to find the place burned down or me very much so fried in the basement." He switched the power on.

Nothing sparked.

The basement lights came back on. Satisfied, he labeled the circuit breaker. "I am most delighted that my basic electrical skills are still intact."

Ashok trotted to the table and muscled it up and into place. He unpacked a modem and installed it on the wall. Grabbing the internet cable, he connected that to his modem. "I will run a wire from here to upstairs. Miss Elda should not be using Wi-Fi, no matter how secure she may think it is. Sometimes old school is best. Miss Elda would agree." He reached into another box and extracted a Dell PowerEdge R760 with two 5th Generation Intel Xeon Scalable processors with up to 64 cores. He patted the server. "This will be most satisfactory. I must order a rack and additional servers once I am settled in our new office. For now . . ." He scanned the basement. "Aha—that will do!" He darted to Elda's workbench and selected two square metal rods and two pieces of wood. He placed the wood on his table and lay the rods over the wood at a right angle, making a small rack with airflow beneath it for his server. Unpacking a small fan, he positioned it on the far end of the table, so it could blow air around the equipment. Now he must install an electrical outlet and power strips. Grabbing his screw driver, he returned to the electrical box.

Where was she? Korinna was always on time. Did something happen to her? Elda sat idling in the Terminal 2 passenger pickup zone. She scrolled through her messages on her phone and spied the text from Korinna: LANDED. Sent ten minutes ago.

Elda started to type that she had to move her car to short-term parking, when she spotted Korinna across the street, wheeling a roller tote. Although Korinna was over an inch taller from shoe inserts, wore a brown wig, had contacts that changed her eye color from blue to brown, and applied various cosmetic changes to her facial structure, that red greatcoat Korinna loved to wear was easy to spot. Elda would break the news to Korinna that the red coat must stay in Maine.

Elda waved at Korinna, who increased her stride, threw her luggage into the opened truck, shut it, and scooted in.

Elda sped away. "Whew, Korinna. I thought something happened to you."

Korinna grimaced. "I doubt my own mother could have recognized me with this stuff you made me put on my face."

Elda studied Korinna's face. Elda had designed a good disguise for Korinna. However, she should not use any one cover for too long. "I'll give you another identity to fly back with. I have a kit here. Oh, and thank you for making the travel arrangements from Estonia. Was it not possible to fly directly from there?"

Korinna giggled.

Elda wagged her forefinger at her. "Are we even now?"

Korinna winked at Elda. "Perhaps . . ."

"I will remember never to piss you off again. Enough said. Where to?"

Korinna referenced her notes. "Let's drop by and visit ACE Construction. I want to make sure they know who's in charge, and I want to go over the work details with them. After ACE, we go eat lunch, and then you can drop me off at my lodgings so I can nap before dinner."

Elda smiled. As usual Korinna had planned out everything in detail. They'd be able to move into the DC office soon.

Splash. The remainder of the pot of coffee went down the drain. The barista started a new pot.

Sitting at a table in the DC coffee shop, Charlie noted the time. Right on schedule. If she was correct in her calculations about Mark's timeline, he would be walking into the café in a few minutes.

Five minutes later, with the aroma of fresh coffee wafting through the air, Mark strode through the front door. The barista poured his cup.

"Thanks, gorgeous."

The barista blushed.

Mark grinned and winked. "Sorry I can't hang around, but I've got a busy day today." He spun and almost collided with Charlie, who was returning her empty cup and plate.

"So sorry, sir." Charlie—disguised with a motorcycle helmet on her head, a mustache and well-trimmed beard, and a leather jacket with angels' wings and GOD'S MESSENGERS stenciled on it—set her dishes down. "God be with you," she said, and ambled out.

Mark didn't give Charlie a second look. He was too engrossed in flirting with his barista.

Outside, Charlie opened an app on her cell phone. Good. The pinhead-sized tracker she'd slipped into Mark's jacket pocket was working. That should make it easy to follow him. She mentally thanked Elda for teaching her the tricks of the trade.

Charlie sprinted around the corner to her red-and-black Softail Deluxe Harley-Davidson, switched out helmets, placing the first helmet into the HogWorkz Black Magic King Tour Pack. She reversed her jacket, displaying a plain black exterior. "Ouch." She looked around for anyone who could have heard her or witnessed her removing the beard. She rubbed a dab of aloe on to calm down any redness on her chin from ripping off the adhesive. She glanced at her watch. Good. She was getting faster at these disguise changes.

She activated the Transmit function on the tracker to send the locations to Ashok and would do a ride-by after Mark, to view each stop herself. The bike was too enjoyable to not take advantage of having it for a day. She wondered if Elda would let her keep the bike. It was an awesome ride.

She started it up and rode away with the deep, throaty rumble of the Vance & Hines pipes surrounding her. After her circuit, she headed to her meeting with Elda.

At the Hilton Hotel's suite, Charlie tossed her helmet and jacket onto the couch.

"Good work, Grasshopper." Elda waved a hand, indicating that Charlie should join her on the meeting. Elda and Ashok were on a secure video chat and analyzing the location feeds that came in from Mark's tracker.

Charlie peered at the screen. "Is this a map of where he went today?"

From one of the windows tiled on the screen, Ashok answered, "Yes, Miss Charlie, and the list of places with description are in the second window."

"He's a creature of habit, isn't he?"

Yes," Elda agreed. "Morning coffee and lunch at the same place at the same time."

"And, Miss Charlie and Miss Elda, you will find this most interesting." Ashok overlayed another window onto the chat view. "One of the places Mister Mark visited is owned by Mister Gunn."

"Elda, isn't he the construction guy that you hired and Korinna fired?"

Elda scowled at Charlie. "He is. I wonder what business that man is really in . . . Ashok, can you trace all businesses and buildings he owns?"

"Certainly, Miss Elda." Ashok's fingers moved over the keyboard. "He visited the international arms dealer again and a warehouse."

"A warehouse? Do you have any information about what it's used for?"

"No, Miss Elda."

"I think, Charlie, once we're done with checking out the inside of Mark's apartment, we might want to scope out the warehouse and determine if it warrants a nocturnal visit before we turn all this over to the FBI. Oh, and Ashok . . ."

"Yes, Miss Elda."

"Why don't you come to DC and we'll set you up an office here in the hotel. Our permanent office space should be ready soon, and you can grab any computing equipment you need out of storage."

"That would be most helpful, Miss Elda. One computer is limiting and slow."

Elda took a deep breath. They had to execute this operation down to the second. She was used to operating on her own, and although she had great confidence in Charlie, Charlie didn't have the years of experience that

Elda had. Elda reminded herself that Charlie had grown into a skilled agent and Elda could depend on her. "Start your stopwatch, Charlie. We have no more than forty-five minutes, if we count the time it takes to drive here from his lunch location. I want us out in thirty."

Charlie and Elda wore the uniforms of electrical contractors from Union Electrical Company, often referred to as UEC. Ashok determined that UEC had an exclusive service contract with the owners of Big Property apartments, who owned Mark's complex. Ashok had broken into their database and obtained the passcodes for the gates. Elda printed up a large magnetic sign that closely approximated the one the firm used on their vans. Charlie rented a white Ford panel van and slapped the sign on the side.

Slipping on latex gloves, Elda stood in front of Mark's door and picked the lock while Charlie kept lookout. "Twenty-eight minutes left," Elda reminded Charlie as they slipped in.

They split up and met back at the front door. "All clear. Twenty-five minutes left. Look for wall safes, hidden panels, large boxes in closets."

Charlie gave Elda a thumbs-up, and they went in separate directions again.

Elda opened the door to the hall closet. Neat and tidy. And small. Dust couldn't hide in there. Too small. She stepped inside and felt around the left-hand wall until she located a button. When she pressed it, a door popped open. Inside was a stash of XM7 US Army–brown assault rifles, with 25-round box magazines piled against the wall, and a wooden box with the word GRENADES stenciled on top. Elda snapped a picture but decided against opening the box, for fear of leaving wood chips.

Charlie walked up behind Elda and peered into the inner chamber. "Wow, Master. That's some haul."

Elda nodded and checked her watch. "Fifteen minutes

left. What did you find?"

"The bedspring is solid and has a fake side that opens." Charlie showed Elda a photo of boxes of ammunition stashed inside.

"Hmm, bedroom, hallway . . . look in the kitchen. I'm going to double-check the bedroom and bathroom."

A knock on the door froze them in place. A quavering, elderly female voice entreated, "Mark, are you in there?" They stood breathing shallowly until the footsteps retreated.

"I'm shortening the timeline," Elda whispered. "Ten minutes tops. *Go.*" She dashed to the bedroom.

Elda scanned the space and found a stack of ten shoeboxes. *Mark wasn't that fancy a dresser that he wore all those shoes. What's he hiding?* The top box contained black wingtip shoes, as did the next box, but the third box down and the five under that contained US Army SIG Sauer pistols. After taking photos, she moved to his desk, lifted the keyboard of his computer, and found a sticky note with thirty-four alphanumeric characters on it. Interesting. Too long for a password, but perhaps an account number? She turned the keyboard over and spied another sticky with a seven-digit alphanumeric code. Now that could be the password. She snapped pictures of both and hurried to meet Charlie at the front door. "Anything?"

"There are a lot of cleaning supplies for a man who most likely has a cleaning service."

"Good observation, Charlie. Mark does not appear to be the type who obsessively cleans." Elda hurried into the kitchen. Careful not to disturb anything under the sink, she selected a can from the back and unscrewed the bottom. A plastic bag of white powder was crammed into the can. She screwed it back and placed it in the ring of dust, exactly where it came from. She and Charlie wore gloves, in order to not leave prints.

"Two minutes. Go!"

Charlie opened the door and scanned up and down the hallway. "The coast is clear."

Elda followed her out and removed her gloves, shoving them into her cargo pants pocket.

"You two . . . please, I need help."

Elda whirled around to see a woman with white hair leaning on a cane, peeking out her apartment. "What is it, ma'am?"

"My computer isn't working. Can you help me with it?"

Charlie turned away from the woman. Elda sighed and motioned for Charlie to go on to the van. "That's not what we do. Are you sure it's plugged in and turned on?"

"I never turn it off, dear."

Was this a trap, or was this a befuddled woman needing some help? If it was a trap, someone was on to them and they were toast anyway. If not, what could it hurt to give the woman a couple of minutes? If anyone was on to Elda and Charlie, they would have already taken both of them out.

Elda followed the woman into her rooms.

A few minutes later, Elda hopped into the passenger seat. "Let's get out of here."

"That was quick. I was wondering if I should send the cavalry after you." Charlie started the van and drove off the property. "So what's the scoop?"

"She was a harmless little old lady with cataracts, who couldn't see that the plug in the back of her computer wasn't firmly seated. She told me the computer kept going on and off, so I looked at all the connections. Sure enough, the power cord was almost half out. I pushed it in and screwed the monitor connector in so that it wouldn't slip out. She thought I was a miracle worker and tried to pay me." Elda swung a quart-sized ziplock baggy full of cookies. "I refused to take money, so she gave me this bag of cookies instead."

Charlie reached for the treats. "Yum! They look like homemade chocolate chip!"

Elda snatched it away. "Lesson, Grasshopper. What if that woman wasn't a kindly old dodger and the cookies are poisoned?"

"Crap! Who would poison chocolate chip cookies? Sadist!"

"I'm going to throw them out. Sorry." Elda tossed them onto the floor.

"Damn! Where are the perks in this job?"

"What about that lovely Makarov you're carrying?"

Charlie chuckled. "True. What's next?"

"We go inspect the warehouse over in Ivy City." Elda checked the street signs. "Turn right at the next intersection then drive straight until Sixteenth Street Northeast. Turn left there."

Charlie cruised past the warehouse, with Elda holding up a written note, referring to it, and looking around in confusion. Elda spotted a man patrolling outside the warehouse, with an obvious gun-shaped lump low under his jacket. "Hey, mister," she yelled at the man. "Is the Watermelon House near here?"

The man patted his hip, confirming his weapon, and strode to the van. Elda held out the notepaper, displaying an address.

He took it, read it, and thrust it back. "Jesus, no. You guys are way lost. Don't you have a GPS?"

"We did, but it crapped out on us." As she spoke, the warehouse door opened. A guard stood in the opening, with a black eighteen-inch Croatian Agram 2000 machine gun slung over his shoulder.

The first man pointed behind them. "Well, that's on the other side of town."

Elda grimaced. "Damn. Well, we can at least go there and scope out what needs to be done."

A German shepherd's head poked out the doorway. He growled at the van. His handler planted his feet and held the dog back with two hands.

"Thanks for your time." Elda waved at the man as they pulled away. She slipped the paper into a plastic bag. "We'll run his fingerprints."

Charlie wrinkled her forehead. "Damn. Did you see those weapons? Plus, a dog."

"Yup. He's got a piece-of-shit submachine gun, but with the dog, this will be tricky."

At the hotel, Elda clapped her hands and called Charlie to the suite's living room, where Ashok now had his equipment, daisy-chained across the table in front of the couch. Elda pulled two chairs up on the other side of the table and plopped down onto one. Charlie trotted in and took the other.

"This is a larger operation than I expected. Gun running and drug smuggling combined. We need to get some evidence to give to the FBI, DEA and ATF in order to have them raid the warehouse. That means we'll be paying it another visit."

"But the dog . . ."

"Don't worry, Charlie. I have a plan. First, Ashok, what did the numbers mean? Can we send Ed enough facts to put this guy away for a while?"

"Miss Elda, I traced the account number you gave me to an offshore bank. The security precautions were most excellent around the accounts, but Miss Charlie solved that problem."

"Really?" Elda stared at Charlie. "What did you do?"

Charlie shrugged. "I know someone who works at that bank."

"Say what? We find an obscure offshore bank and you know someone who works there?"

Charlie grinned. "He and I served together. He was

a finance major and interested in how money was being laundered, so after the military he started working in various banks. We tried to recruit him for the agency, but he refused. Nevertheless, he does a favor for me every once and a while." Charlie passed Elda a printout showing the deposits into the account.

Elda scanned the list. "Very well done, Charlie. I'm impressed. How were these deposits made?"

"Electronic transfer, but I obtained the other banks and a full list of accounts and routing numbers. Ashok is tracing them now."

"Good job."

The overcast night was pitch black. Elda turned off the 2020 Porsche Taycan lights and rolled into the parking area adjourning the warehouse. She cut the engine and brought the car to a stop by short bursts of the parking brake.

"Do all B and E experts drive expensive wheels?"

"No, that's the point. No one will suspect that this is a getaway car. And it has the power under the hood to get away."

"I suppose we have to return *this one* too?"

"Yes. Life is made of brief moments of pleasure. Enjoy the transitory moments."

Charlie made a gagging sound.

The two spies were dressed in black, with black masks and gloves. Both strapped a variety of weapons to their bodies and a black backpack sat on Elda's shoulders. They exited the car and ran to the back wall of the warehouse.

The building was windowless, but security cameras hung over the front door. The small red lights ringing the lens informed Elda that the night-vision camera was on. In their drive-by, Elda had identified a power panel in the back. She located it, took out a screwdriver, and opened the panel, exposing the switch to power everything off. She held up ten fingers and nodded to Charlie, who scuttled around the side of the building to position herself outside the range of the cameras. Elda counted to ten and threw the switch. She ran to join Charlie.

The door to the warehouse swung open. A sentry came out leading a ferocious-looking German shepherd. Elda broke out in a cold sweat. She hoped the dog was hungry. However, she didn't relish being his meal. She placed something on the ground, tapped Charlie on the shoulder, and signaled for her to follow back around to the other side of the building. Once there, she whispered to Charlie to reposition herself on the corner of the building, next to the door.

Elda counted to thirty and peered around the corner. The dog stood drooling and wobbly legged. The guard was trying to get something out of his mouth, but the dog resisted, until it toppled over onto its side. The man leaned over his dog. Charlie leapt onto the guard's back, covering his mouth with one hand, stabbing him in the neck with a syringe in her other hand. He collapsed on top of his dog.

Elda jogged up and checked the dog's pulse and the guard's. She signaled to Charlie to help her drag both bodies into the building so no one would discover them. They lugged the two to the door and dropped them. Elda signaled for Charlie to enter the building, and sidearm drawn, followed her. They stooped low, listening for the faintest sound. All around them lay loaded shipping pallets. Piled on one pallet were boxes labeled *Ajax*, another pallet with *Bleach* wipes, and on went the cleaning supplies.

Elda bet they had drugs hidden in them.

No one else was present. They dragged the guard, dumping him inside, and carried the dog, placing him next to his handler. Elda felt their pulses. Slow and steady. They would be out for a while.

Charlie circled the pallets, discovering a desk with a logbook on it, and penlight in her mouth, she snapped pictures of each page.

All Elda could hear was the clicking of Charlie's camera and the dog snoring. She took out her flashlight and shot pictures of the pallets. Selecting one, she slit the shrink wrap and the box with her knife, enough to sneak out a can. She took clear tape out of her backpack and taped the box and shrink wrap back up so the breech would only show from a close inspection. If everything disappeared from the warehouse before the FBI arrived, at least she could give them this piece of evidence. Inadmissible in court, of course, but that wouldn't stop the FBI from pressing their lead.

Wooden boxes were piled on another pallet, and from the sizes, Elda surmised each box was full of weapons.

Satisfied they'd obtained enough to justify the FBI investigating, she sent the pictures to Ashok and Ed, asking Ashok to send the rest of the evidence on Mark to Ed and the FBI. She requested that they pick up within the hour

The noise of a vehicle driving toward the warehouse alerted her. She and Charlie simultaneously doused their lights and ducked down with their guns drawn, aimed at the door.

The car drove by.

"We have to leave *now*." Elda scratched her head. What to do with the dog and the guard?

Charlie, assisted by Elda, flung the alcohol-sodden, unconscious guard into the dumpster. He was minus his weapon, wallet, cell phone, and shoes. Charlie had selected this location across town because it would be difficult for him to get back to the warehouse. He'd also be out for three

or four more hours, which gave them a good lead. It would take other drug smugglers a while to raise an alarm, since the guard could be off on rounds with the dog. Everything was in place, door locked, lights on, minus only a sentry and a dog.

"Can we take the dog to a shelter, Elda? I'd rather not leave him abandoned on the streets of DC."

"Good idea, Charlie. I know some of the handlers at the K9 training center. He'd fit in well there. And they have the experience to handle him."

After dropping off the dog and returning the van, Charlie slid into the car and stroked the soft leather seats. "Elda?"

"Yes, Charlie?"

"Do we really, really have to return *this* beauty of a car?"

"Sorry, Charlie. We do."

"Damn."

Elda dialed Ed on her burner phone. "Ashok is going to send you some information. The FBI will be interested in it and should move on it within the next few hours. I have sent you both the pictures from the warehouse, and I also nabbed some physical evidence, in case the FBI arrives too late. It's a large drugs and weapon smuggling op."

"Oh, *hi*, Elda. I'll get that done immediately. And, Elda—"

Elda hung up. No time for pleasantries. The less time she was on the air with Ed, the better.

"What now, Master?"

"We return—" Elda's burner cell rang. She glanced at it and frowned. She had only given that number to Ed, but this caller's number wasn't Ed's. That could only mean . . .

"Hello, Tosh."

"*Pryvet*, Elda"

"*Pryvet*, Tosh. To what do I owe the pleasure? And *how* did you get this number?"

Chapter Nine

AURELIO AINSWORTH YANKED THE MIRROR off the wall and heaved it onto the bed, then sat in his Cancun resort room's stuffed armchair, panting from the exertion. A knock sounded on his door.

"Eeek!" Aurelio screamed and dove under the bed. His bare feet and legs stuck out into the room.

He heard a shout from outside the door, "Aurelio, it is I, Stanislav. I am here with Yevgeni. Please let us in. It is not safe in the hallway."

Aurelio crawled out from under the bed, tiptoed forward, and put his ear to the door. "How do I know it is you two gentlemen and not someone pretending to be you?"

"You are right to ask that question," the main claiming to be Stanislav replied. "The darkness is all around us. We know how special you are, and you know we are kindred spirits. Search your heart, and if you find the answer, let your comrades in."

Aurelio grabbed his crotch to comfort himself. He rocked forward and back on his feet. Finally he reached out and opened the door. Stanislav and Yevgeni rushed in with their luggage and slammed the door shut behind them. They engaged the security lock.

"Have you swept the room, Aurelio?"

Aurelio looked around in confusion. "Why? Is it dirty?" Peering at the two men, Aurelio wondered if they were real, and he touched Stanislav's face.

"Yes, Aurelio, we are real. We came here on your invitation. Do you not remember?"

Aurelio stuck out his flabby chest. "Of course I remember. I am honored to have you here, Stanislav. You are the ruler of the world, after all. I can't wait to explore this resort. I have already scored some excellent hash. Would you like some?" Aurelio led his two guests out onto his balcony to smoke hash.

They looked out over the white sand and turquoise water.

Yevgeni ran his hands around the railing. "No bugs, *ser.*" He sat at the small table on the balcony, took out a deck of cards, removed the numbered cards two through five, dealt two hands of six cards, and started playing Durak by himself.

Stanislav took a hit off the bong. "Are our rooms nearby, Aurelio?"

"Yes, Stanislov. This room expands to a huge suite by connecting to suites on either side. I reserved them both." Aurelio looked with watering eyes for approval from Stanislav.

Stanislav blew smoke out his nose and nodded at Aurelio. "Smart move, Aurelio."

Aurelio puffed up with pleasure. He pushed back a lock of his thinning hair from his face and adjusted his wire-frame glasses on his nose.

"So how long have you been here?" Stanislav passed the bong to Aurelio.

Aurelio inhaled all the smoke and drew in again. "I arrived this afternoon."

"Are there watchers?" Stanislav held out his hand for the bong.

"You know there are always watchers." Aurelio took another hit and exhaled as he pointed. "See that man walking with that woman?" He took a third hit before he passed the bong to Stanislov.

Stanislav looked down at a rugged-looking man in his late twenties, alongside a woman with shoulder-length blond hair and stunning deep-blue eyes. "Those two?"

"Yes. They have been sent by my half sister to spy on me."

"You are very wise, Aurelio. He looks military. We will watch them." Stanislav passed the bong to Yevgeni and tapped the cards. "Move the two of spades there."

Aurelio giggled. "Let's snag some food and see if we can score some cocaine."

"Get some clothes on first, Aurelio."

Dmitri plopped down onto a lounger on the resort's beach. He took a moment to adjust himself in his beach trunks and smoothed sunscreen onto his taut abdomen.

"We can't stay in Cancun forever, Dmitri."

Dmitri glanced up at the speaker. "Why not?"

"Well, we can't very well go waltzing back to Boris after all this time." Murka, a stunning woman, with shoulder-length blond hair and deep-blue eyes, threw a handful of sand on Dmitri's stomach and sank down into the chair next to him.

Dmitri grimaced, brushing the sand, which was embedded in his Hawaiian Tropic coconut sunscreen. "I don't trust Boris anyway. I can do better freelancing. Want to join me, Murka?" Dmitri glanced over at the sound of giggling and spotted a group of three men sitting nearby, staring at them.

They whipped their books up to their faces. One lowered his book so his eyes peeked over.

"*Kakogo khrena* is that?"

Murka turned to the rowdy group and patted Dmitri's arm. "Ignore them, Dmitri. They are high on drugs." She adjusted her sunglasses, which reflected the glare of the midmorning sun.

Dmitri turned on his lounger, planted his feet in the sand, and looked Murka up and down. She was dressed in a formfitting tank top, shorts, and leather sandals. The blue of the tank top matched her eyes and accented her tanned and shapely arms and well-built shoulders. Her skin glistened with sunscreen.

She reached to her left and adjusted the hidden gun in her belt holster. Dmitri felt certain he could turn her from being gay. After all, what could two women do to satisfy each other? The more she knew him, the more she would want him. "What about going in with me on finding some gigs? There's plenty of Russian expats here who could use us."

Murka shrugged. "If you find something, let me know. I'll consider each job."

He snorted. "What's there to consider? Money is money."

"Not all jobs are created equal. Some money would be nice though. I just bought a house."

Dmitri startled and frowned. "What? When did you do that?"

"Yesterday. I was thinking of getting a roommate. Interested?"

"I could be. How many bedrooms? One?" Dmitri leered.

Murka stared at Dmitri over her glasses and raised her

eyebrows. "I thought we settled that. Calm your hormones. Three bedrooms. We can use one as an office."

"What about Nyoka?"

Murka waved her hand dismissively. "She's crazy. We're well rid of her."

The talking and giggling from the nearby men grew louder as they sipped their drinks. Dmitri saw one of them pointing at him. "I'll be right back."

Aurelio tapped an article in the local paper and passed it, folded to the article, to Stanislav and Yevgeni. "That's it! A goddess will protect me from my siblings and the man in the black truck. We must go see her." A shadow fell over him. He yelped.

Stanislav and Yevgeni hopped up, Stanislav saying, "We'll be right back. Must reserve the trip!" They ran toward the lobby and concierge.

A man loomed over Aurelio. "What's your problem, little man?"

"No-no-nothing," Aurelio stammered.

"Mind your own business. Understand?" The man reached into his pocket and flashed a switchblade at Aurelio.

"Y-y-y-es"

"Remember my name. Dmitri. You will answer to me." The man turned and marched away.

Aurelio fell off his chair and landed facedown into the sand. Stanislav and Yevgeni returned and helped him up, wiping the sand, tears, and snot from his face with a towel. Aurelio saw his drink on the ground and grabbed Stanislav's, downing the scotch in a gulp.

He drew himself up. "Let us go and plan our excursion to Calakmul. I think perhaps the inside bar might be a better venue for us." He minced his way toward the bar.

"Nothing? Someone comes into Moscow and kills your captive while you are interrogating him, and you have nothing to go on?" Tosh's voice was low and cut like steel.

He, Anatoly, Snezhana, Yuri, and Stas had gathered in their new office in Moscow. Tosh paced while the others sat.

Stas, already pale from hours at his computer, turned even whiter and shrank into his chair.

Yuri raised his hand.

"Yes, Yuri?" Tosh barked.

"Did you mean to invite me here for this?" Yuri Kuznetsov was a large man, often mistaken for Anatoly's younger brother. However, where Anatoly was hardened inside, Yuri had a soft heart and would never be an assassin. His skills lay in networking and logistics. When Tosh had re-formed his team, he hadn't rehired Yuri but instead used him on a case-by-case contract basis.

"Yes, Yuri, I did. I'll need you for the next mission. Before we get to that, I must find out what went wrong in *this* one."

Anatoly pounded one fist into the other hand. Snezhana cleared her throat.

Tosh glared at her. "Do you have something to add, Snezhana?"

"*Da, ser.* I do." She twirled her fingers of one hand into the back of her hair.

"What is it?" Tosh checked his pulse and inhaled, willing himself to relax and listen. Snezhana often had valuable insights.

She squared her shoulders and looked directly at Tosh. "The main goal of the cyber farm in that location was political disinformation aimed at the United States, correct?"

"Correct." Tosh already had wandered down this thread and hoped Snezhana reached a similar conclusion.

"Unlike 2016, when the goal was to elect Russian friendly candidates, this disinformation is targeted at all parties, creating random chaos. Therefore, the United States would most want it stopped." She halted.

Tosh nodded. He was proud of his niece. She was spot on, as usual. "Correct. So you are inferring the person who shot the informant was from the US?"

"*Da, ser*. My initial impression was that Charlie and Elda drove away in the getaway car."

Tosh lifted one eyebrow, but he waited for Snezhana to finish.

"And a wonderful piece of machinery that was." Anatoly growled.

"So we need to find that car," Snezhana concluded.

"I have." Stas spoke in a timid voice.

"Where?" All three chimed together.

"There is a small farming village not too far away from where you held the man they shot. Satellite imagery shows this village built a dirt racetrack and is making money winning races with a blue sports car that meets your description." Stas turned his laptop around so they could see the images tiled on his screen. "See this picture before you were there? And this one after? New track. And the timing fits."

Tosh narrowed his eyes. "*Govno*. Any DNA they may have left is long gone from that car. This does have Elda's fingerprints on it."

Snezhana raised her hand.

"What!"

Snezhana dropped her hand down by her side. "Elda and Charlie are spies, not assassins. What makes you accept it's Elda, past my assuming the two women looked like them?"

Tosh pumped up his blood pressure cuff and read it

while the rest waited. He nodded he was okay. "Think, people. The Cold War is over. The new war is creating chaos and division through misinformation. As you correctly surmised, Snezhana, the United States would most want to shut that farm down. Why not repurpose the otherwise useless Cold War spies to fight this new war? Especially if one of the spies was an expert on Russia, as Elda is. The two operatives were professional. That fits. Giving an expensive car to a small farming village has an Elda flair to the operation."

Snezhana nodded. "*Spasibo, ser.*"

"Let's put it on our list to follow up with, but by now they are far away." He spoke to Stas. "Do you have any intelligence on where the three assassins may be?"

"*Da.* Mexico. Specifically, Cancun."

"What makes you think that?"

"I asked Ashok if he had anything."

Tosh raised an eyebrow.

"He last spotted them at a resort in Cancun,"

"All of them?" Tosh queried.

"Dmitri and Murka. He didn't know where Nyoka was. However, I have found reports of a new Mayan goddess over in Calakmul, Mexico. Her description fits Nyoka's." Stas turned his laptop to show a picture of a woman with long black hair and spiked nails. She wore a headdress of snakeskins woven into her hair.

Snezhana rubbed the goosebumps that appeared on her forearms and studied the face in the picture. "Yes, that's her. How far away is this place from Cancun?"

Stas typed on his computer. "About eight to nine hours."

"Yuri . . ."

Yuri turned to face Tosh. "*Da, ser?*"

"You've worked for Elda in the past. Try to think on any way she operated then, that we have not yet seen in our dealings with her. I can't let her interfere with my operations in Russia."

"*Da, ser.*"

Tosh clapped his hands together once. "Yuri, Anatoly, Snezhana, go now."

The three stood.

Tosh slapped his hands together once more, urging them along. "*Itdi, itdi, itdi. Seychas!*"

Having left his luggage in his room at the resort in Cancun, Yuri strode outside. He stopped in surprise. "Michael Smith?"

A man in a hotel uniform marched up to Yuri and hugged him.

"What are you doing here? Last time I saw you, you worked for the US government at a Bermuda resort."

Michael put his finger to his lips and winked at Yuri. "The money and perks are quite good, so when they began this operation, I volunteered."

"Well, it's good to see you at a time when I'm free to come and go as I please."

Michael laughed. "Keep it that way, my good man. I must return to work." With a wave he was gone.

Yuri smiled at the good memories of his forced Bermuda stay. *I do owe Elda a thank-you for not killing me and instead stashing me away at that resort.* Of course, Elda and he had been good friends when Yuri worked for her, spying on her drug-addled half brother.

His smile dropped. He shook his head to clear his vision. It couldn't be . . . "Aurelio?" He wondered if he was in some sort of redux from the Bermuda triangle or an episode from that old TV show *The Twilight Zone*, which Elda used to tell him about. What was Elda's half brother doing here? Yuri would have placed a bet that Aurelio would have long ago killed himself with drugs and drink.

Aurelio's nose was dripping onto his shirt. His face was pasty white. He sniffled and pleaded, "Yuri, man, I need some coke."

Yuri shook his head. "I don't deliver drugs anymore, Aurelio. What on earth are you doing here?"

"The man with the black truck is still chasing me. Now there are new people, sent by my half sister, watching me. But I am leaving here to see the goddess. She will protect me." He shoved into Yuri's hand a crumpled newspaper folded to the article.

"Who are the new people, Aurelio?"

"The man told me to stop watching them, so Stanislav and Yevgeni are taking turns." Aurelio scratched his crotch. "They are eating dinner in the restaurant."

"Did the man have a name?"

"Dmitri."

Interesting . . . a coincidence? *Don't believe in coincidences*, Elda and Tosh always said.

"I know this man, Aurelio. I can talk to him for you. Elda did not send him."

"Are you sure, Yuri? My half sister and brother are out to get me. I have been too smart for them and evaded all their traps so far." Aurelio looked past Yuri and screamed, "It's the man with the knife! Help me, Yuri!"

Yuri turned and saw Anatoly, who was shaking his head in disgust. "Go to your room, Aurelio. It will be all right. This man will not hurt you."

Aurelio ran on tiptoes, making a wide berth around Anatoly.

Anatoly growled at him as he passed, earning an "Eek" in response.

Yuri shook his finger at Anatoly in mock disapproval. "You shouldn't torture the mentally disabled."

"I should have killed him when I had a chance. Elda

would be better off."

"He was useful. He ran into Dmitri. Dmitri's with Murka, eating in the restaurant."

"Let's go have dessert with them," Anatoly offered with a big grin.

———

A large man pulled out a chair and sat opposite Dmitri. A shapely woman inserted herself between Dmitri and Murka. Another sizable Russian-looking man stood leaning against a nearby support beam.

Dmitri reached for his gun.

"I wouldn't, if you value your balls," the man opposite him growled.

Dmitri observed the man's hand was out of sight and assumed he aimed a weapon at Dmitri's genitals. He put both his hands on the table. Murka did the same.

"You have the advantage of us." Murka narrowed her eyes and moved one hand slightly toward her side.

"Don't try it," the woman warned her. "We're here for a chat, and I'd hate to have to blast a hole in your side."

Aware they did not have a clear advantage, Dmitri said, "We're reasonable beings. What do you want?"

"Are you Dmitri Smirnov and Murka Mikhailov?"

Murka spit onto her plate. "You know who we are. Who are you?" she stated in her melodic contralto voice,

"I am Anatoly Petrov. And you just ruined good food," Anatoly admonished, putting down the fork he'd held poised in the air, apparently planning to stab a hash brown from her plate.

Murka winked at him. He growled back at her.

The female backed her pistol off from Murka's ribs and put it in her holster. "Snezhana Chelovek." She held out her hand to Murka.

"Chelovek?" Murka inquired. "As in Toshchiy Chelovek? The ghost?" Murka gave Snezhana's hand an assertive shake.

Snezhana grimaced and wiggled her fingers.

"His niece. He sent us here. And if you leave my hand intact, I think we can help each other out here."

"Just evening the score." Murka winced and rubbed her side. "How?"

"You obviously don't want to return to work for Boris Siderov. Do you?"

"You *obviously* know a lot about us. I suspect if Boris sent you to kill us, you would have already done so. If we are having a reasonable discussion, could you direct your pistol away from my privates?" Dmitri requested.

Anatoly made a show of holstering his gun.

The other man came over and sat at the table. "Yuri. Just Yuri," he said.

"Actually, Boris *did* send us to find you and kill you," Snezhana continued, "but we believe you are of more use alive than dead. Except perhaps Nyoka. Would you like to hear more?"

Dmitri leaned forward. "Definitely yes."

Murka nodded her agreement.

"Let's order coffee and pastries first." Anatoly raised his hand for a waiter. "Can we get two pots of coffee and a plate of mixed pastries: cuerno with jam, orejas, plain and chocolate-filled churros, please?"

Snezhana looked at Anatoly with amusement. "Going native on us?"

"It's good to always know the local delicacies."

Dmitri looked Snezhana up and down. "And the non-local ones too."

She sneered at him. "Not in your lifetime."

Murka snapped to attention and smiled at Snezhana. "Not in yours either."

In the rickety old bus, Yevgeni piled Aurelio's belongings onto his lap and then secured his own seat behind Aurelio. Yevgeni motioned to Stanislav to sit in front of Aurelio. Aurelio reached forward and tapped Stanislav on the shoulder. "How much longer?"

"We haven't left yet."

The rough roads to Calakmul jostled everyone. Dust blew in through the opened windows. Aurelio's suitcase fell off onto the floor. Yevgeni stooped, picked it up, and returned it to Aurelio. He noticed Aurelio was wiggling and adjusting himself.

Aurelio looked at Yevgeni. "How much longer?"

"Five minutes less than the last time you asked, Aurelio. Go to sleep. We will be there soon."

Yevgeni rummaged in his own bag, reached over the back of the seat, and handed Aurelio a pill and a water bottle. Without question Aurelio popped the pill into his mouth and glugged down some water. The rest of the trip went quietly, as Aurelio slept under the influence of the strong sedative Yevgeni had given him.

Arriving at the Hotel Casa Las Lolas, Yevgeni and Stanislav dragged Aurelio to his hut and threw him onto his bed. He had peed himself.

"What now, Ruler of the World?" Yevgeni asked Stanislav.

"I have deemed there will be a full moon tonight, so we will find a way to get to the ceremonies at the ruins. First, we have a bottle of scotch to drink, and I scored some coke before we left the Cancun resort. Let's awaken Aurelio and partake." He rummaged for three glasses.

Yevgeni untied and removed Aurelio's shoes, took him under his arms, and pulled him to the shower, propping him up against the wall. He turned the water on and slapped Aurelio on his face.

"Is it raining?"

Yevgeni shut off the water and tossed a towel to Aurelio. "Come on—we have coke to do."

"I have hash in my bag." Aurelio, dragging the towel, dripped his way out into the main room and sat on the end of his bed.

Stanislav handed him a double scotch, followed by a bong. He laid out three lines of coke onto the coffee table and snorted one. Yevgeni dropped a black beauty in front of Aurelio. Aurelio snatched it up and tossed it into his mouth, refilled his glass, then snorted the second line. The third soon went up Aurelio's nose.

Aurelio stripped off his wet clothes and put on a dry pair of dingy tighty-whities that hung loosely on him. He started to the door. "Let's go to the ruins and await the goddess. The moon will be rising soon."

Stanislav tossed Aurelio a shirt and pants. "Put clothes on first."

The full moon shone over the ruins of Calakmul, Mexico, far into the jungles of the greater Petén Basin region, near the Guatemalan border. The huge stone ruins grew out of the surrounding green lushness. A bat flew over the heads of the assemblage crouched nearby.

Nyoka wore a headdress of snakeskins, woven into her black hair tresses, that stood out from her head, as if electrified. As she stood and stated "*Q'alajinik*," the crossed bones tied into her long skirt clattered. She ran out into the clearing. The gathering, chanting "*Ixchel*," danced around her. She held her hands up to the sky, the moonlight shining off her long, pointed nails.

"Goddess!" a man screamed. "Save me from those who persecute me." He stripped off his shirt, displaying his pudgy belly and flabby chest. He danced around her, hands on his hips.

Nyoka grinned, displaying her blunted canines with applied tips of gleaming gold. She took out a knife and slashed his belt and pants, which fell to his ankles. The man fell on his face, still writhing in dance. He thrashed until he freed himself from his ruined clothing, and he stood, swaying, his flaccid dick bumping against his loose briefs.

Nyoka retrieved a bowl of steaming liquid and held it to his mouth, "Drink thissss," she hissed.

The man did and watched in amazement as his penis rose. She reached for it and manipulated him until she could capture his cum into the bowl. She smeared his face and chest with it. He laughed and looked at her with adoration. She placed a studded collar around his neck and attached a leash to him.

A tour guide held high a closed umbrella and advised, "Keep closely together. There are many different animals in these jungles. In the clearing ahead of us, you will see the ruins of Calakmul, Mexico."

The tour group gasped in unison at the decayed beauty of the stone artifact. One woman looked over to the side and screamed, "There are feet there."

The guide motioned for his tour to stay put, drew his weapon, and approached the pair of bare feet sticking out of the underbrush. As he inched closer, he could see a naked man who was either dead, passed out, or asleep. He poked him with his umbrella. No response.

He called the local authorities and ushered his group away.

A uniformed policeman marched up to the desk at the Cancun resort and stood next to Yuri. "Do you have an Aurelio Ainsworth registered here?"

Yuri, who'd intended to obtain directions to the ruins of Calakmul, Mexico, perked up his ears.

"Yes, sir. May I ask what this is in regards to?" the desk clerk responded.

"We found a body at the ruins in Calakmul and ran the prints. A receipt in his pocket was from the restaurant here."

"Oh my." The clerk handed over the key. "Does he have next of kin?"

"We don't have that information, sir."

Yuri took out his phone and texted Tosh. WE NEED TO GET AHOLD OF ELDA. HER HALF BROTHER IS DEAD HERE.

Chapter Ten

WHY DID HE CALL?

Elda looked out over the Tuscan landscape. She never tired of the green and gold mix undulating over the rolling hills. She inhaled the odors of olive, combined with rosemary, sage, and tarragon. She paced around the living room, glancing every few seconds at her watch. At the exact moment she decided to go for a run, a Ducati Scrambler Nextgen Nightshift motorcycle roared into the driveway and spun to a stop in an impressive cloud of dust.

"About time." Elda coughed as she wafted away the dust from her face.

Tosh hopped off the bike and undid his helmet. "Thanks for meeting me. Shall we pop out for a run before we talk?"

"The news is that bad, hey?"

Tosh shrugged. "I'm not sure. You can let me know."

Tosh had asked Elda to meet him at a villa they called Gools. Elda owned the villa, but its lineage was well hidden. When the two of them had been hiding out and living at the villa, Elda had explained the concept of Gools to Tosh. When you reached Gools, you couldn't be made *it*—as in *tag, you're it*—tackled, hit, stolen from, or touched at all. It was a safe space. They'd agreed at this villa in Tuscany that they were safe with each other, and any warring agenda was dropped.

They raced into their rooms and darted back out in jogging gear. Heading out the door, they fell naturally into a comfortable running cadence, their footsteps in sync. The day was warm, with a slight breeze offsetting the heat of the sun on its way toward the undulating hills.

"What's up, Tosh?"

"I don't know how close you were to your half brother. I do know from Yuri he was quite the drug addict and hateful toward you."

"That sums it up, Tosh. You said 'were' and 'was.' Is he dead?"

"Yes."

Elda stopped as a wave of hurt rolled through her. She took a few deep breaths, releasing the pain. "Wow, that was surprising. I thought I'd mourned him long ago when he lost his brain, but I guess there's more in there. How did he die? Overdose?"

"Although blood tests showed recreational drugs in his system, they also found traces of persin, which could have contributed to his death. They are saying he died from heart failure during some ceremony in Mexico. According to others at the ceremony, the goddess repeatedly stimulated him so he could ejaculate. This was smeared all over his body. His heart could have been weakened to begin with, from lack of exercise, bad diet, and lots of cocaine."

Elda turned so she could read Tosh's face. Brown eyes bored into gray ones. "What are you *not* telling me?"

"He had marks on his body consistent with fingernail scratches and bite marks that correspond with human incisors, except they found traces of gold in one of the bites where the tooth hit bone."

Elda's eyes narrowed. She clenched her fists. "Nyoka."

"Yes. Are you okay?"

Elda breathed in, held her breath, and then exhaled. She massaged her forehead. "My sadness for my brother is more of lost potential. He was a bright man who could have done many things, but he pissed it all away. He was a drunk and an addict. He was vicious to his siblings. He would make fun behind the backs of each one: his brother's lack of ambition, his sister's weight and her penchant for going out to *meat night*, and his other sister's lack of motivation and tendency to steal. When he rotted his brain out on drugs, he became paranoid, and he verbally attacked me and his brother, claiming we spied on him for the FBI. He was in a miserable marriage and only stayed because his father had married so many times. To prove himself to his deceased father, he felt he needed to stick out this second marriage of his. God knows he doesn't deserve being avenged. But at one point I loved him."

Tosh nodded. "If you want to go after her, I will help you."

Elda stared out over the olive grove, her breathing shallow and angry. She inhaled deeply three times to kick in the vagus nerve's parasympathetic response to relax her. "Thanks, Tosh. I do. I'll ask Charlie to help with the hunt too."

"Excellent. I'll have Yuri book your flights and rooms. I'll come down too."

"So, Tosh, while we're here, shall we talk business?"

"*Cin cin.*"

Tosh and Elda clinked glasses. They sat across from each other at a small outdoor table at the Osteria del Conte restaurant in Montepulciano, Italy. A fine *Vino Nobile di Montepulchiano* and *Pecorino grigliato con prosciutto,* as an antipasto, perched in front of them. The aroma of berry and leather wafted up as they swirled their glasses. Elda turned her glass in the light, admiring the legs of the wine, clear against the glass. The bouquet of tomato sauce and meats cooking floated by their table from the kitchen.

Elda had decided that it was up to Tosh to open the conversation up to business. She sighed as she perused the menu. "Pecorino cheese from Pienza. I'm in heaven."

Frowning, Tosh glanced up from his menu. "What are you ordering, Elda?"

Elda flashed him a smile. Although Tosh could run major spy operations and make rapid-fire decisions, restaurant menus stymied him. "I can't eat all the traditional courses of a Tuscan meal, so I plan on ordering the hand-made pasta with a Tuscan meat sauce."

"You just want to save room for the chocolate lava cake," Tosh deadpanned. He scanned the menu again and closed it.

Elda cocked her head. "So what did you decide?"

"Sliced beef steak, with a side of flat pasta with a Tuscan red sauce and a salad. If I order the *tiramisu* for dessert, are you going to grab part of it?"

"Of course I will." Elda winked. "But I'll let you have some of my chocolate lava cake."

Tosh regarded Elda with his steely-gray eyes. "Can we talk business at *Gools*?"

"Yes, as long as it doesn't result in violence."

"*Khorosho.*" Tosh pushed his menu to one side. "I've made a deal with Boris to go out on my own with my folks. As part of the deal, however, I have to continue to make him look good and deliver on some jobs he needs done."

Elda nearly spit out her wine. Her eyes watered as she struggled to swallow. How similar their lives were.

"Did I say something funny?" Tosh inquired with knitted brow.

Elda held out her hand, palm forward, while shaking her head. She took out a Kleenex, blew her nose, and took a sip of water. "No, no. It's just that I made a comparable deal with Ed. Or rather, I and my team needed to cease to exist, since the Oversight Committee discovered us. To make sure I was gone, they sent someone to eliminate me. All the assassin has is an old picture from my BUPERS file, so he'll take a while to find me. A lot of people still believe I'm dead. Can you discuss what mission you're on?"

Tosh narrowed his eyes. "What is said in Gools stays in Gools, right?"

Elda held up her hands in surrender and leaned in. "Right."

Tosh looked around and lowered his voice. "There is a leak or multiple leaks causing many of our disinformation cyber farms to be destroyed or impaired."

"Interesting. The cyber farms are causing a lot of chaos in the United States." Elda struggled to not blurt out that she was most likely working against him. She wanted to find out more from Tosh before she confessed. "So what are you supposed to do about it?"

"Find the leaks and plug them. We found one potential informant in Moscow." Tosh stared into Elda's eyes as he continued, "A sniper killed the man before we could extract anything from him."

Elda held one hand over her mouth to keep silent and peered at Tosh from under her brows. "How unfortunate."

Tosh's gray eyes bore into Elda. "Really?"

"For you, that is." Elda's eyes twinkled.

Tosh tapped his fingers on the table. "Snezhana only

got a fleeting glance of the sniper. *She* jumped into a blue Marusia B2 sports car. A woman was driving."

Elda's eyes widened. "Oooo! Nice set of wheels there. Did you catch them?" She winked at Tosh. She figured Snezhana had suspected them and that Tosh had already put it all together.

Tosh sighed. "I think you know the answer to that, Elda."

"Well, let's suppose I've been tasked to stop the disinformation from Russia."

"Not from China too?"

Elda shook her head. "There are groups to handle that. No one is focused on Russia anymore. That gives Russia free rein to wreak havoc by discrediting what is real, pitting groups against one another and even dividing loyalties. It needs to be shut down."

Tosh sat back in his chair and took a sip of his wine. "Well, the lines are drawn. We could make a deal . . ."

Elda leaned in. "A deal, Tosh? That's unlike you. What do you propose?"

"We don't kill each other."

Elda chuckled and raised her glass. She didn't want to kill Tosh unless she had to. "I like that deal."

"*Cin cin.*"

They clinked glasses.

Charlie pulled up to the Dulles airport curb in a red Mustang convertible.

Elda flung her pack into the backseat and jumped in the front, barely getting the door closed as the car accelerated out of the airport. She clicked her seat belt closed. "If it's all right with you, I'd like to keep alive a bit longer." She reached back into her pack and drew out her gun and holster.

"Charlie raised an eyebrow. "Gunning for something?"

"Yes." Elda picked up a cardboard box from under her feet. "Chary Ellsworth, care of UPS. What did you order?"

"Oh! Take a look. I've been working with Ashok to disguise myself in the digital world. He recommended I read these books."

Elda lifted the first book out of the box. "*Extreme Privacy: What It Takes To Disappear.*" She read the title of the next book. "*Ten Arguments for Deleting Your Social Media Account.*"

Elda deposited the books back in the box and the box in the back seat. "I'd like to borrow them once you're done. I'll trade you a couple of mine."

"Sure. No problem. What ones are you thinking of lending me? That dusty *The Art of War*?"

"It would serve you well to read it. Although at this moment I embrace winning through fighting, which flies in the face of the book's teachings." Elda ran her hand over the leather interior. "I see we're keeping a low profile today."

"A wise mentor of mine once told me one of the best ways to be invisible is to be bright and flashy."

"What a wise woman she was."

"Who said it was a woman?"

Elda hit Charlie in the shoulder. "Smartass. I'm delighted you have learned so much from this mentor. You have grown well, Grasshopper. Now, what's the scoop on Mark?"

"Ashok has additional videos of Mark picking up shipments for the arms dealer. He also traced back all the accounts connected to Mark's and sent those numbers on to the FBI. The FBI managed to nab the warehouse guys and Mark and are working on rounding up the rest of that network."

"Not the brightest bulb in the pack. Very glad he's

gone, but that means they'll just send in another assassin, who may be more talented. How did Ashok find all this?"

"You will have to ask Ashok. *It is sure to delight you* if you can follow all the numbers and accounts and technical jargon."

Elda chuckled at Charlie's imitation of Ashok. "Good. We'll deal with any Mark remnants when we get back."

"Get back?"

"Pack a bag, Grasshopper. We're going to Cancun."

"Cancun? What's up, Master?"

"We're going to find Nyoka and kill her."

The wheels screeched, and the chartered plane bounced once as it came to a stop at the end of the runway in Cancun. The pilot turned the plane around and taxied to the gate at Terminal 1.

Elda, dressed as a male tourist with a wide-brimmed cameo hat, a bright Hawaiian shirt, large red-rimmed mirrored sunglasses, and a Nikon Coolpix P600 camera, exited the airport. A similarly garbed and accessorized Charlie cleared customs and immigration. Yuri stood by a black sedan at the curb, with his chauffeur's cap on, scanning the arrivals.

They strolled up to him. Elda opened the back door.

"So sorry, sir, but this car is reserved."

"Yes, we know, Yuri." Elda threw her pack in the backseat and hopped into the passenger's seat. Charlie tossed her gear on Elda's, paced to the driver's side, and jumped into the back.

Yuri peered in at his passengers. "New disguise, Elda? Well done. I assume that's Charlie?"

"Yup. Now where are we going?" Elda took off her sunglasses and rubbed the bridge of her nose, where they had made an indentation.

Yuri slipped in behind the steering wheel and drove away from the passenger pickup zone. "We all have rooms at the Grand Cancun resort. We will stay there for a few days and go to Calakmul for the full-moon ceremony and see if she shows up. I've booked a van to take us there and reserved rooms for an overnight stay."

Elda jabbed a finger at Yuri. "She's *mine*."

"Yes, she's yours, Elda, but we are all going to ensure she doesn't escape. And if she's a no-show, we'll help hunt her down."

"She'll show."

Dmitri sat studying the others in the group. He had heard many stories about Elda and Tosh and thought they were over-embellished fables. To him they looked like two older people who had outlived their usefulness.

Murka sat beside him and nudged him. "You're quiet, Dmitri."

Dmitri shook his head and sneered. "I don't get these people at all. They have all these rules. They act like friends right now but could be killing each other tomorrow. That doesn't make sense to me. There should be a monetary transaction and a contract that defines the action and the enemy. If need be, you torture them to get information. Then you kill them. And collect your pay. That's it."

Murka drew away from him. "So it's all about the money?"

Dmitri shrugged. "In a way. The more you kill, the better your reputation is, and the more money you're worth. There's no sides. This loyalty to country is bullshit."

Aghast, Murka looked at Dmitri wide eyed. "What about relationships?"

"Ha! That girly emotional stuff. I thought you had more sense than that, Murka. You screw before you get screwed. Sex is scratching an itch. And sometimes conquering another."

Murka stood and stared down at him. "You may learn, Dmitri, that there is more to this job, and more to life, than that."

"You're contracting out your services, Murka."

"I am. But I am also picky about what I accept as a job. There are ethics involved."

Dmitri snorted, "Ethics! Ha! You'll learn that no one has your back. That there's no right and wrong or truth. We live in a world of inconsistencies and backstabbing. Everyone is out for themselves, money, and power. And I intend to be there too."

"I think, Dmitri, that you better not move in with me. I don't trust you."

"You shouldn't."

The ruins of Calakmul looked like a 2-D faked movie set under the glow of the full moon. The clouds strung across in wide bands, allowing the moon to peek in and out. Elda and Tosh and their people spread out, waiting for Nyoka to appear. Elda moved forward through the crowd to be closer to the front. Tosh positioned himself behind her. Anatoly moved to an open spot to their left, giving him a clear entry to dash in. Charlie stood next to him. The rest were dispersed in the throng.

The clatter of bones announced her arrival. Nyoka howled and ran into the clearing. A group circled her and danced around, chanting.

Seething with rage, Elda held her hands in her pockets, each finger strapped to a short, sharp stiletto. The tips of her shoes had a knife-point inserted. Her face was sprinkled with gold glitter. She wore a long blond wig with bones woven in, using glow in the dark thread. Her smile displayed gold caps on all her teeth. She wore a cape made of ocelot skins draped over her shoulders, a silver glowing skull clasp holding it together.

Elda jumped into the center of the circle with Nyoka and shouted, "This woman is an imposter. I am the true goddess." She raised her hands in the air, knife tips sparkling in the moonlight.

The crowd emitted a collective, "Oh, goddess."

The two women circled each other, hissing, bones clicking.

Elda saw Anatoly, Charlie, Murka, and Tosh leaning forward, with their hands on their weapons.

Nyoka swung her arm, her red nails reaching for Elda's face. Elda ducked and danced to Nyoka's side. She stood there, swaying side to side, a guttural growl emanating from her throat.

Enraged, Nyoka shrieked and lunged at Elda, who sidestepped her. Elda swiped her hands across Nyoka's face as she passed. Blood dripping down her face, Nyoka turned and ran with her head down to butt Elda, only to be met by air. Elda kicked out and slashed Nyoka's leg with her shoe knife. Nyoka stumbled but spun around to charge again. Blood oozed from a gash on the back of her leg.

Elda stood and motioned for Nyoka to come and get her.

Nyoka started toward Elda, wobbled, and fell to her knees.

Elda stepped to Nyoka, and using the thumb side of her folded hand, threw a powerful uppercut to Nyoka's chin.

Nyoka fell onto her back.

Elda sat on Nyoka's chest. "You may wonder why you can't move. The gash in your leg was made by the knife in my shoe, which was covered in a paralytic drug. As it sets in, you will have increasing difficulty breathing."

Nyoka gasped and glared at Elda.

Elda caressed Nyoka's cheek with her stiletto nails, drawing blood. "You may be puzzled about what you have done to deserve this death. It *will* be long and painful. You can use the time to atone for your sins. But in the end you'll be saved."

Nyoka's eyes pleaded with Elda.

Elda squashed any hope of salvation Nyoka might have. "Your heart, for the first time in your life, will be merciful. It will stop your anguish in one last *painful* seizure."

Nyoka's eyes grew wide.

"You may ask why I am doing this to you."

Nyoka coughed and wheezed.

"You made a mistake. You killed my brother, you *bitch*."

Elda rose, removed her cape and wig, took off the stilettos, and careful not to touch the tips, pulled the knives from her shoes. She wrapped her paraphernalia into the cape, shouldered it, and strode away.

The group sat around the table outside the huts, picking at a dinner Yuri had procured for them. Only Dmitri and Anatoly had their appetites.

Murka sat herself next to Charlie. "I'm glad to see you when we don't have to kill each other." She leaned into Charlie for a moment.

Charlie didn't pull away.

Tosh sat across from Elda. Elda could read her fatigue in his eyes. He poured her a glass of Clayhouse Estate Argentinian Malbec. "Drink this. Revenge is best served with room-temperature wine."

Elda gave a halfhearted chuckle at Tosh's lame attempt

to lighten up the situation.

Yuri handed her an unopened bottle of water and cracked the top for her. She lifted her eyebrows. He shrugged. "Elda always told me to hydrate when drinking alcohol."

Anatoly looked at Elda with admiration. "*Der'mo*. You are one badass, Elda. And can I have your dessert?" He reached over and snagged her plate.

"Remind me never to piss you off," Charlie added.

Snezhana contemplated Elda for a while. "May I ask something, Elda?"

"Of course, Snez."

"Does it feel good to have killed Nyoka in that way?"

"Good?" Elda sat silent for a while. All eyes watched her. "No, that's not the right term. She was evil and had to be put down, so I feel justified. I also needed closure for my brother's death, and in fact, his horrible waste of life. So I feel satisfied. But I also feel empty and less of who I was. I think every kill takes some bit of humanity away." She looked at the quiet, sad-looking group and added, "However, I may keep one or two of the gold caps." She grinned widely, and a back tooth glinted gold.

Tosh put his hand on her arm and left it there for a few minutes, then raised his glass to hers.

"*Cin cin.*"

CHAPTER ELEVEN

ELDA LAY ON THE COUCH IN THE HOTEL IN DC. She draped one arm over her eyes. The other hand lay at her side, clutching her Smith & Wesson revolver. She heard the door open and a gentle cough.

"Miss Elda, ma'am?"

Without changing position, Elda answered, "Yes, Ashok?"

He pulled up a chair next to the couch.

Damn, this was serious. Elda sat up and looked at him.

He cleared his throat. "I have made a mistake, ma'am."

Elda looked at Ashok. He was rubbing his chin. His eyebrows threatened to fly off his face. "What type of mistake did you make? Would you like to tell me more?"

"Yes, Miss Elda. I am hoping you will understand. You see, I also have a half brother."

"You do? I never knew that. He didn't show up in your background checks." Elda wondered where this was going but sat back and let him continue.

"He has a different last name, and I don't mention him.

The family is most ashamed of him. He has a much bad gambling problem and owes money to some very bad people."

"I see why that would be a problem, Ashok, but how does it pertain to you?"

Ashok shifted in his seat and hesitated a moment before answering. "I had been ignoring him with the rest of the family, but somehow he found my email address and contacted me. In a moment of weakness, I replied. He swore that he was done with gambling. So I asked him over for dinner."

This was *such* a familiar family story. Drugs, gambling, sex, stealing . . . just fill in the addiction. She prompted him to continue.

He cleared his throat. "He saw that I owned some valuable items, and the day I was leaving, some men came by and broke into my apartment. I had already moved everything out and was visiting Miss Florence to say goodbye. So I left her place via the fire escape."

Ashok's brown eyes bored into Elda's. She could almost hear him pleading with her to not think less of him. She patted his arm. "And . . ."

"And, Miss Elda, I am afraid that they may find me again."

Elda wrinkled her forehead. "Do you still have that email address?"

"No, ma'am. I got rid of it. There is no trace left."

"Good. Is there any trace of your identity on the dark web?"

"No, ma'am."

"Do you have filters and protection from intrusions on all your devices?"

"Yes, Miss Elda, ma'am."

"Well done. Are you in touch with any of your family members?"

"I only chat with my mother in India once a week, but I do that from an untraceable IP address over VPN and monitor the call for anyone trying to tap in or trace it. It is most certainly secure. My mother thinks I live in California."

Elda's shoulders relaxed. He was covered. He only had to control his compassion. *Only.* How many times had she been caught in that familial trap? "Well done, Ashok. No more softheartedness toward your half brother, okay? Addicts will lie, cheat, steal, whatever they need to do for themselves. Trust no one. Not even your mother."

"Thank you, Miss Elda. It has been weighing heavily on my mind."

"And, Ashok?"

Ashok whirled around to face her. "Yes, Miss Elda?"

Elda brandished her fists. "If they come after you, they will have to go through me. Okay?"

"That is most excellent, Miss Elda. Thank you."

Knock, knock. A rugged, athletic-looking man, wearing dark-blue jeans, white T-shirt, and a tan jacket, stood in Ed's office doorway.

Ed sighed. This must stop *now.* "And who might you be?"

"Dmitri Smirnov at your service, *ser.*"

Ed startled at the accent. "You're Russian?"

Dmitri shrugged. "It's of no matter, but yes, I am. I have been hired by Senator Ronald Glass of the Oversight Committee. He informed me you required some rogue operatives taken out and that you would give me further instructions."

Ed searched in his database. There was no data on this man. "What's your background?"

Dmitri rattled off in a bored tone. "I'm twenty-eight years old, ex-military, a boxer. I worked at a security firm before being hired by the Kremlin as an assassin. I am now a freelancer operating out of Mexico."

Ed thought perhaps he could buy him off. "How much did the senator pay you, Dmitri?"

"Two hundred thousand US dollars. Half up front, the other half when I deliver."

Ed visualized his budget spreadsheet and did some quick mental calculations. "What if I pay you double that to tell Ronnie the job has been done?"

Dmitri shook his head. "That would be not right, *ser.*"

Not right?! This man is an assassin. Ed put his head in his hands and massaged his temples. The headache was starting again. "Look, Dmitri, this guy, Glass, has put the hit out on one of my best operatives. There's no upside for the United States to do this assassination. She has already removed the first two whom the committee sent after her. Although you look capable, she has taken down much more seasoned agents from Russia."

Dmitri snorted and waved his hand to one side. "I have a new job offer after this. I'm sure Tosh would be glad I removed her."

Ed scorned him. "Are you sure? Go call Tosh and ask him if you should kill Elda as part of a paid hit by an unscrupulous senator. See what he says about *your* future."

"Elda?"

Ed swore that he could see the hint of a smile in Dmitri's eyes. "Yes, take a moment and call Tosh now." Tosh would warn him off this job.

Dmitri gave a half bow and turned. "Excuse me, *ser.* I will return."

Ed sighed, sat at his desk, and typed a secure message to Elda.

Dmitri marched into Ed's office without knocking. "I called him."

"What did he say?"

"He told me not to."

"And . . ." Ed was curious. Dmitri didn't appear as if he was backing down.

"I told him I'd accepted the contract."

What the hell was going on here? Was this man going to go against Tosh's wishes?

"And . . ."

"He rescinded the job offer."

Good for Tosh. It sounded like there was more. Dmitri was a man of few words. "And . . ." Ed was irritated at Dmitri's lack of forthcoming.

"He also told me he'd kill me, starting by ripping my balls off and shoving them down my throat. I told him I considered his threat a challenge."

Ed's head felt like it was in a vise. "What? Good God, man. Don't you understand the rules of the game?"

Dmitri snickered. "There are no rules anymore. Only accepting contracts and earning money. The more I kill, the more valuable I am and the more I can charge."

"So take what I offered you and forget it." Ed's voice cracked from his attempts to not yell at this moron.

Dmitri sneered. "No . . . no . . . you see, I have met Elda and Tosh. They are old and old school. They play by old rules. I am the future. I consider this a challenge and a way to hone my skills and enhance my reputation. By killing them, I enhance my worth. The senator is the type to understand that."

Ed stood there, mute.

"I'll let you know when it's done." Dmitri tossed his card onto Ed's desk. "In case you ever need something done."

CHAPTER TWELVE

THE C-17 GLOBEMASTER III, CARRYING EQUIP-
ment for a joint NATO exercise to a Finland base,
rode rough. Its movements jostled Charlie and Elda
in their seats in the back section. Once in Finland, they
would travel on to St. Petersburg, using Russian identification that Ashok had created for them.

Charlie reviewed her passport. Oleg Baryshev, a Russian businessman who sold nickel byproducts to Finland.
She was traveling with another Russian businessman,
Pyotr Pavlov, who exported wood (sawn, plywood, rough,
and fuel) from Russia to Finland.

Their contacts in Finland had detained both the real
businessmen Russians, with visa issues. While they were
held, facial scans had allowed the Finnish intelligence to
make masks, duplicating the two businessmen's features.

The Finns also supplied the two Americans with bio-
metrically identical contact lenses and latex fingerprint
overlays. Shoe lifts helped match the men's heights. Their
hair color and style, down to the length of their beards and

mustaches, were copied. Layers of clothing helped duplicate their bulk.

Charlie glimpsed Elda studying her phone, shaking her head and muttering something Charlie couldn't hear over the sound of the engines. Straining, she caught the phrase "Crap, that's all I need."

She yelled over the sound of the four large Pratt & Whitney F117-PW-100 engines. "What's up, Master?"

Elda held up her phone. She projected her voice. "Ed texted me. There's another assassin after me."

"Just you?"

"Apparently."

Charlie was feeling put out that they didn't feel she warranted elimination. "Well, we got rid of the last two. What's the problem?"

Elda handed Charlie her phone.

Charlie read the text. "It's Dmitri."

"Yes, it's Dmitri." Elda took her phone back.

"Damn."

"My God, that bed was lumpy. I think the mattress was only two inches thick."

Charlie and Elda loped from their Sunpark Hotel in St. Petersburg, Russia, to the Neva manufacturing area. Charlie was rubbing her lower back as she walked.

Elda chuckled at Charlie's discomfort. She was glad of the distraction from her worry about being pursued by Dmitri. "My goodness, Grasshopper, you have gotten soft. Didn't you sometimes sleep on the ground in the military?"

"Yes," Charlie grumbled, "but that was to be expected. These were five-star lodgings!"

"It's why vodka is so popular here." Elda pantomimed throwing back a shot of vodka.

Charlie groaned and rubbed the small of her back. "So what do we know?"

Elda shrugged. "Not much. We know that there is a cyber farm operating out of this locale, but we are not entirely sure where."

"Great," Charlie said in a tone that implied it wasn't great. "So now what?"

Elda increased the pace. "We get there and we locate it using Ashok to help guide us. He's tapped into the satellites and should be able to get us within fifty feet or so."

"Then what?" Charlie struggled to keep up. "If the buildings are nested together, there's significant room for error."

"Ashok will send more intelligence, and we'll figure it out as we go. We do the same drill as before: We get our informant out, clear the building, and destroy the servers. Get the lead out, Charlie. We're in enemy territory."

Charlie picked up her pace. "Why this farm?"

"It's associated with a scientific research organization and targets its disinformation against science and fact by using a small amount of real information and then turning it to falsehood. It's helping to discredit what are facts and what is real science." Elda examined her phone for a message from Ashok. She stopped and turned in a full circle to scan her surroundings. No one was around. Elda didn't feel settled, however.

Charlie tapped Elda on the arm. "The coffee at the hotel was abysmal. Could we stop and pick up a cup here?"

"You may need a twelve-step program, but yes. There is no one tailing us." Elda examined her surroundings to verify that statement, and lunged at Charlie. "Down. Now." She threw herself on Charlie, and they crashed to the ground behind a parked car.

"Ooomph. You're solid muscle and heavy for a small woman."

"Shhhh." Elda rolled off Charlie to present a lower profile.

Anatoly and Snezhana crossed the street in front of them. Elda prayed they would not look back. She heard Anatoly complaining loudly. "No *snochniki*! They only made bagels. We're in Russia, not New York City."

Snezhana slapped him on his arm. "Focus, Anatoly. Tosh's intelligence said there was a spy at this server farm and the Americans were coming to take it down. Our job is to get there first and intercept them, as well as eliminate the rat. Keep an eye out."

"I could do better if I had decent food in my stomach," Anatoly grumbled as they walked away.

Elda tapped Charlie's back and whispered, "All clear."

The two of them stood, brushing the dirt off their clothing.

"Let's go this way." Elda led Charlie around the opposite side of the Novartis Neva pharmaceutical plant.

They ran to get ahead of the Russians, careful to run lightly to minimize any noise. When they stopped, they viewed the two Russians passing Farmasintez-Nord manufacturing.

"Once they're behind that tree"—Elda pointed—"run this way." She motioned again. "Use that small blue building for cover." She glanced at her phone. "Ashok's program indicates that the research building, *Institut Elektrofiziki I Electroenergetiki Ran*, may house the server farm. If he's right, it's a large tan-colored building in the direction we're heading. If we go fast enough, we may get there before they do."

They ran past the blue building, and after ensuring they were ahead of the Russians, dashed into the thick stand of trees and bushes by the research institute. They emerged by a small five-story building, which Elda assumed housed the workers for the nearby government agencies, including the institute. She looked down the road with binoculars and saw their two nemeses turning the corner, heading toward them.

Elda signaled to Charlie to drop to a crouch and follow her. They scuttled under the cover of a line of bushes to their destination.

"The black metal gates in front of the door are ajar," Elda said. "There's a bicycle there and a few cars in the driveway on the left, but there aren't many people there."

"Good. Let's go." Charlie sprinted to the large fir tree by the door and vanished behind it.

Elda heard Anatoly crashing through the trees in back of her. "*Der'mo*, Snezhana. We could have taken the road."

She bolted after Charlie, who moved through the gates and was trying the door handle.

"Damn, locked," Charlie whispered,

Elda spotted a card key reader and held a device Ashok had designed to it. The doors clicked open. Elda followed Charlie inside.

"Clear the building. Find the fire alarm and pull it. Then go upstairs to find the servers. I'll head downstairs and see if that's where they are keeping the servers. This floor looks like offices. Ensure everyone is out." Elda snapped out the orders to Charlie.

Charlie grabbed a white lab coat hanging on a coat rack by the door and threw one at Elda, who donned it as she rushed to the stairs. "Good thinking, Grasshopper." Halfway down, she heard the shrieking blare of the fire alarm system and footsteps running out the door. She came face to face with a shocked employee. The informant.

"Are you the Americans?"

"If I weren't, you'd be dead now. Show me which one is the administrator's machine and get the hell out of here. Meet me at the Bronze Horseman tomorrow morning at 0900 and I'll have your papers for you."

He showed her a machine at the head of the table. Elda nodded and aimed a finger toward at the stairs. "Go quickly."

He ran.

Elda plugged in a thumb drive to a USB port on the administrator's machine, and once it loaded, spun up a special program Ashok had written. She watched as the Percent Done meter kicked off. Ashok's instructions stated she must ensure the indicator reached 100 percent done before she removed the drive. At that point, the worm to destroy the server software would be well on its way.

1 percent, 2 percent, 3 percent, 4 percent . . . Agonizingly slow.

"They beat us to the server farm." Anatoly sprinted to the open front door, with Snezhana on his heels. He bowled over two employees trying to escape the fire alarm.

Snezhana jumped over the prone, groaning bodies. "I'll go upstairs, and you go down. The boy scouts are probably clearing the building. It's impossible to determine who is the spy with all this chaos. We're dealing with professionals. My money is on Elda again."

"*Da.* It's her style." Anatoly took the stairs two at a time, thudding into the basement.

Elda crouched down low behind the machines, where she could view the progress. *55 percent, 56 percent, 57 percent* . . . There would be no way to avoid Anatoly. She remotely kicked off a program of her own that she had also installed. All the servers beeped at once.

"*Der'mo.* I know you're in here, Elda."

She did not answer.

78 percent, 79 percent . . .

"There's no way out except to go by me."

89 percent, 90 percent, 91 percent . . . No response.

"You're getting old, Elda. The past Elda would never allow herself to be trapped like this."

99 percent, 100!

Elda jumped up, snatched the drive from the computer, and dove for the floor again. Bullets rang out as Anatoly peppered the room.

"You're no spring chicken yourself, Anatoly. The Anatoly I knew wouldn't have missed." She kicked off another program, and "Moscow Nights," played by the Russian Red Army orchestra, blared over the beeping.

Anatoly shot in the direction of her voice.

Elda shot at the ceiling above Anatoly's head. Plaster and pieces of wooden slats poured down on him.

"*Chert!*" The grit in his eyes blinded him. He shook his head to get rid of the dust, when he felt the prick of a needle in his neck. He thrashed out, his movements slowing. He felt his gun being removed from his hand and a chair pushed beneath his knees. He sat.

He heard Elda call down to him. "You'll only snooze for a short time. I didn't give you a full knockout dose for your size."

The room darkened.

Snezhana ran up to the third-floor laboratory. She couldn't think. She had to stop that fire alarm. It hit her. Kill the power to the building. She ran back downstairs.

She bolted down the basement stairs and crashed into Anatoly, tipping him off his chair with a thud. He lay there unmoving.

She felt for a pulse. He had a strong and steady one. She inspected him for bullet holes, cuts, bruises. Except for the nasty shiner he'd most likely have on his cheek from his fall, he appeared unharmed.

She slapped his face. "Anatoly!"

The din down here was horrible. All the machines beeped in different cadences. Over that noise "Moscow Nights" played on. The fire alarm still screamed. She had to find the power and stop the noise so she could hear any movement from the Americans.

Anatoly stirred. "Whaaa . . ." He passed out again.

Snezhana stepped over him and traversed to the back of the basement, searching for an electrical box. There! She gripped the large lever and pulled it down. Everything went black and silent. She listened. She could hear only her own breathing and Anatoly snoring.

"*Chert*!"

Having checked out of the Sunpark Hotel, Elda ambled southwest on the Admiralty Embankment next to the Neva River. Her spidey sense was tingling. She had ample time before she was to meet the man from the cyber farm. She would make some turns and see if she was being followed. She took a sharp left toward Palace Square. It would be wide open there. Although there would be tourists, it was a difficult area for someone to hide.

Elda wore a cap low over her forehead, a large-sized dark-blue windbreaker over a black Mother Russia skull T-shirt, blue jeans, black sneakers, and two cameras crisscrossed over her chest. She wore a black wig and carried her ever-present reversible backpack of goodies.

Elda caught sight of a large man cutting through the crowds and speaking on his cell. He would stop and snap a picture, but of the people around him, not the Hermitage. He turned and she recognized him—Anatoly.

Elda figured he had not identified her yet, and she didn't plan to let him do so. She held a camera to her face, snapping pictures of the Alexander Column and the Hermitage. Blending in with a group of tourists already scanned, she passed by him and took a right, back to where she'd entered the square. As she passed him, she heard, "*Net*, Snezhana. *Da*, I know she could be in disguise. But I see no one close to her. I have sent you all the pictures of any possible match. *Da. Da.*"

Elda needed to get rid of Anatoly before she reached the *Bronze Horseman*.

There he was. The informant was pacing by the *Horseman* statue. Elda glanced around. No Anatoly.

She jogged up to the man and reached inside her jacket, pulling out an envelope with his new documents and money. "Quick, take this and go. Grab a plane out of Russia. Do not tarry. Go to Germany and on to America. These papers will get you through the Russian border inspection."

The man grabbed the papers. His eyes widened. A shot rang out, missing both Elda and him.

"Run," Elda commanded, then faced Anatoly, her own weapon drawn.

Anatoly swiveled his gun in her direction and hesitated. She turned and dashed away in the opposite direction from the informant.

"*Der'mo.*"

Elda heard Anatoly's footsteps behind her. Good. The cyber farm spy was safe. At least for now.

She accelerated but knew she could never outrun Anatoly. She hooked a right onto the Admiralty Embankment and ran down to a short pier, where a small boat was pulling in. She leapt onto the boat and rolled across the bottom. The man piloting it stared at her and swung the wheel over, to not hit the pier.

She threw a wad of money onto his lap and yelled, "*Idi bystreye!*" She repeated in English, "Go quickly!" The man slammed the throttle into high gear. The boat roared away.

Elda stood with her hands on the pilot's shoulders. She slipped him an envelope with one thousand US dollars in it. "Take me to the Gutuyevskiy Kovsh inlet and let me out there. You will tell no one of this. *Ponimat'*?"

He nodded. "*YA ponimayu.*"

Elda hopped off onto the pier. She texted Charlie: Meet me at airport. Wear original disguise.

She popped up Google Maps. The Admiral Makarov State University of Maritime and Inland Shipping were nearby. She could hire a car, find somewhere to change, and also search for transportation to the airport.

Pyotr Pavlov walked out of a closet in the university. A student passing by asked, "*Vy zabludilis'?*"

Pyotr nodded at the student. "Yes, I am lost. I am looking for the exit and also somewhere I can hire a car to the airport."

The student clapped him on the back. "You are in luck. I have two hours off between classes and will take you to the airport for less than others would charge."

Pyotr sighed in relief. "You are most kind."

"No, just a starving student looking to make some extra money."

Elda examined the teen. His hands were callused, and he walked with the sway of someone who spent a good amount of time at sea.

"Have you been at this school long?"

"I have completed my first year. That was hard. My uncle is in the Russian navy, and he obtained my appointment for me. We are a seafaring family. If it wasn't for this, I'd be on a fishing boat as an apprentice."

As they strolled to his car, Elda found out more about this kid's life story. His accent meshed with the region he claimed he came from. She didn't believe in helpful coincidences, but perhaps, just this once, the mission was going as planned.

The rattling in the plane had Elda wondering what era the craft was from. The first C-17s were minted in the early 1990s. This thing could be up to thirty years old! Boeing did make planes better in those days. She hadn't heard of any landing gear falling off these ships.

She looked over at Charlie, who'd fallen asleep right after takeoff from the NATO base in Finland, despite the roar of the engines. She unbuckled her seat belt, pulled a blanket from a stack on the floor, and put it over Charlie. She took off her jacket and slipped it under the side of Charlie's neck to support her head. Charlie snored through it all.

Elda smiled ruefully. Youth. She remembered when she could fall asleep at the drop of a pin. Now her brain conspired with her bladder to keep waking her up. She stood and found the head, then took a blanket for herself and lay down across two seats, strapping herself in. She'd barely shut her eyes when one of her phones buzzed—the one she now reserved for Tosh. She kept a second burner for Ed and had her own phone. She had purchased all different brands and colors so she could keep them straight.

She knew she wouldn't sleep until she read what he sent her. She hoped she could sleep after.

DMITRI IS AFTER YOU.

WHERE IS HE?

AS OF TODAY, DC.

THANKS.

Damn. Elda shouldn't have read Tosh's text. Dmitri was a killer and in her locale. So much for trying to sleep.

Chapter Thirteen

Almost there. Ashok's fingers flew across his keyboard. He located the source of the fake messages on X and was about to take them down. First he had to breach the location's firewall and wreak havoc on their servers. From what he could see so far, someone without a lot of cybersecurity knowledge set up this server farm. He should have them destroyed within the hour.

Bleep. An alarm went off on one of Ashok's monitors. What was that? Someone was trying to kick Ashok off, only it wasn't from within the network he was penetrating—it was another external invader.

Ashok kicked off a macro to keep his work going and turned his attention to the intruder. His keyboard hummed as he pulled together and executed his program. There. That should keep him away for now. Interesting code stream. Where had he seen that coding style before?

Bleep. Another alarm went off. The other hacker was now trying to sneak into Ashok's network. Ashok went after him with a vengeance, locating the source and attacking, putting the other on the defense.

The two developers parried tit for tat. A green success box was displayed on Ashok's first monitor. Fantastic. He was through the server farm's firewall. He took seconds to access root-level clearance and kick off his program to bring those servers down. In those seconds the other breached Ashok's first firewall.

Not a huge problem. Ashok had a series of four different firewalls. Each one took a different approach. The first one was supplied by the vendor. It would lull anyone trying to attack Ashok's servers into a sense of complacency that it would be an easy job. The next one was Windows based, the next Linux, and the final one Apple. It would take a lot to get around all four firewalls.

Ashok attacked back. The other's first firewall fell. Interesting . . . Another firewall lay behind it. Ashok took a closer look at the code attacking him. He would bet his Linux laptop Stas Garin was behind the attacks.

Ashok booted four more computers and increased the velocity of his counterattacks. He would teach Stas a lesson.

Ashok attacked Stas's system from all his computers. One computer kept at Stas's first firewall to keep the entryway through it open. A second computer attacked the second firewall in the same way Ashok vanquished the first, in case they were both Windows based. The third computer attacked as if the firewall was Apple based, which would be Ashok's guess for Stas's MO. But he also might have a Linux firewall. Using that theory, Ashok made some rapid changes to his Linux program and fired it off on the fourth computer. He flooded the bandwidth with attacks.

Ashok typed at breakneck speed on his main computer, countering each line of code that came at him. He was advancing and not falling back. He thrust and parried and feinted to distract the other with false attacks.

There! Ashok found a crack to wiggle through on Stas's second firewall.

Was he undetected?

He roamed as far as he could, mapping out the internal network, then backed out. There was one more network behind it all. He left enough traces that he could return to where he left off at any time. For now he was ready to end this round.

He spiked the network traffic. Then sent his Linux firewall basher in. He came crashing through. He spun off a small program that halted the hacker's entire network.

Game won. He looked forward to the next match. Stas, or whomever it was, was a good adversary.

CHAPTER FOURTEEN

CCOMPANIED BY THE CONTRACTOR, KORINNA inspected every inch of the new space in DC. She spotted a missing cover on the electrical outlet in one room, plus wires not cable-tied together in the overhead of another. A dent marred the side of a piece of modular furniture. Korinna ordered it replaced. The gym equipment was backordered. Korinna requested they research other vendors to source it from, as long as the price didn't change by more than 10 percent. She watched the contractor to ensure he made notes of each discrepancy. She kept her own running list.

She was irritated that they still had work to do, but she was secretly pleased that it wasn't more. They should be able to finish this up within the month. And within budget. She smiled.

She sat at Elda's new wooden desk, an appropriately large one for the group's leader. It was the perfect height for Korinna. Perhaps she should order Elda a chair with more up-and-down range of motion? She added that to the furniture list.

Korinna then moved to the waiting room, across from the contractor, reviewing his schedule with him and ensuring their to-do lists matched, when a young, well-attired man marched up to them.

Korinna gave him a glare but said politely, "May I help you?" How did he get in? The door to this area was open for the workmen, but the rest of the building was locked up.

He stopped and looked down on her. "Yes, you may. I am looking for a Miss Elda Ainsworth."

The hairs on the back of Korinna's neck tingled. She detected a Russian accent and answered in that language. "There is no Ms. Ainsworth here. I am overseeing the buildout of this office space for a Mr. Edward Wilson."

"*Da.*" The man switched to English. "I was in Ed's office and saw this address. I'm following every lead. Do you know who the tenant is?"

"No, I don't. This is my last inspection, and then I'm moving on to the next piece of property the government is building out. May I ask who you are?"

"Dmitri Smirnov at your service, ma'am." He threw his card down on the table in front of where she was sitting.

Pompous *zhopa*. She stood, towering over him in her high heels, and glared at him.

"Well, as you see, I am trying to tie things up here so I can move on." Korinna gestured to the paperwork with an ease she did not feel inside.

He blinked. Korinna could stare down the strongest man. "No problem. I am sorry to have bothered you. If you do hear of her, please call that number."

"I certainly will." Korinna gave him a thin smile and pointed toward the open door.

Dmitri left.

Korinna shut the door behind him. She was glad she'd heeded Elda's advice and brought a change of disguise with her. She shook hands with the contractor, told him she would be back one more time to ensure he did all the changes, took her large tote, and headed to the restroom. On the way she texted Elda. WATCH OUT. A DMITRI SMIRNOV IS LOOKING FOR YOU.

Dmitri leaned against his car, watching the doorway of the building. He studied his fingernails as he waited for the woman to exit. He had his car parked at the curb and would take her to a secluded space to find out what she knew. Afterward he would dispose of the body.

He glanced up as a couple of male construction workers, chatting to each other, exited the building. His stomach rumbled and reminded him it was lunchtime. That bitch better come out soon.

More workers went by, leaving for lunch. Where was she?

After waiting an hour, Dmitri decided he would go get her and persuade her to leave with him. He slipped into the building behind a returning worker.

She was nowhere to be found.

Elda and Charlie landed in Dulles International from Budapest. Elda couldn't wait to shower and change. She'd slept little on the way back and had been traveling for fifteen hours. She hoped Charlie could drive herself home so Elda could go to her own apartment without stopping.

"You have your wheels here, Grasshopper?"

"Yes. See you tomorrow." Charlie jogged off through the garage.

Elda read her texts while wandering to her car. "Shit." She looked around to ensure no one heard her. That damn man had found her new office, and worst of all, Korinna. Her thumbs flew over the iPhone keyboard.

Go to Maine. Now! Satisfied that Korinna would follow her instructions without question, she responded to Ed's text.

U wrote the address dn?!!!

I know. Stupid. Sorry. but how did he get on base?

Ed rarely made a mistake like that. The political pressures must be getting to him. She was glad she was removed from all that.

NP. I will remove hm. othr missn accmplshd.

She texted Korinna again: shut dn wrk for 2 dys. I nd the ofc.

Korinna texted back: Argh n ugh. ok. @airpt.

Elda understood Korinna's anguish of having to delay the project. But she needed the office to lure Dmitri to and, if necessary, eliminate him.

She texted Ashok: plz resrch all lost DC Navy Yd IDs fm pst wk.

Her last text went to Charlie. cm 2 ofc, loaded 4 bear. b constr wkr

Elda swung by her Dupont Circle area apartment for her own weapons, a shower, and some extra-strong coffee.

Was that silver car following her?

She hoped so . . .

Elda had left enough traces around the city so that Dmitri would know she was around. She had planned to take 395 to 695 to the navy yard. However, it would be good to know if Dmitri was on her tail. She decided to pop onto Rhode Island Avenue Northwest and see who else made that turn.

The car was still there. About four cars back. He wasn't good at tailing. He swerved left and pulled back in, likely so he could see ahead better. To force him to move closer, Elda sped up and turned left onto New York Avenue. She had the advantage of knowing DC streets, which he didn't. She looked in her rearview mirror. There he was now, only two cars back. She could see Dmitri behind the wheel. Novice.

She swung onto 395 and floored it for a few minutes. He fell back and wove around the traffic, horn beeping, attempting to keep her in sight. Elda grimaced. Subtle. She hoped his shooting was as bad as his driving. She merged onto 695 East and took exit 1C for Eleventh Street SE. She took a sharp right to stay on Eleventh Street and an immediate right onto M Street SE. She drove to the navy yard gate and presented her ID.

Now to meet Charlie at the office . . . and wait.

The custodian opened his shed and wrinkled his nose at the smell. He propped the door open and went inside. And came running back out. Lying in the shed was a dead sailor. Or at least, he assumed the sailor was dead, from the smell, blood, and flies. He retched.

He closed and locked the door, ran to his car, and drove twenty miles over the speed limit to the administration building, getting pulled over by the base police when almost there.

"There's a dead body in my shed," he gasped after showing them his ID.

"Show us."

He led them back and unlocked the shed, stepping to one side to let them in.

One policeman walked in and spotted the body. He

came right out. "Let no one else come in here. We need to seal off the vicinity and not contaminate the crime scene further." He pointed to his partner. "Mack, call NIS. I'll search the guy and see if I can find his ID." He reached into his pocket for a small container of Vicks VapoRub, dabbed some under his nostrils, and marched back in.

Elda stashed her car in the back of the parking lot and jogged to the office. She ran up the stairs and peeked out each landing window. She saw Dmitri's car pull into a space. How did he get in through the gate? He must have stolen an ID. That would explain how both times he accessed the restricted area.

Bump-bump-de-bump-bump . . . bump-bump. She rapped on the door as she fumbled for her key. Charlie flung it open. Elda rushed in, shut, and locked the door. "Dmitri is behind me."

Charlie snapped to attention. "What do you want to do?"

Elda gestured to the wall that jutted out near the front entrance. "You know the secret passageway I installed? It leads around every room, plus has access to all the ceilings. Each ceiling has a sniper hole and a M110 semiautomatic sniper rifle with ammo stationed by it. I'm going to sit at my big desk in my office and wait for him to show. You get to that sniper position to take him out if need be. Okay?"

"Gotcha!" Charlie took off into the coat closet and shut the door behind her. Soon Elda could hear her moving up and toward the office ceiling. *Moving quietly* would be another checklist item for Charlie's training program. She also mentally added *more insulation* to Korinna's to-do list.

Elda jogged to her office and placed her Smith & Wesson M&P 380 SHIELD EZ pistol on her desk. She climbed up onto her chair with her feet dangling. The desk was far too big for her. But she accepted that it gave her status in some dealings, and she knew Korinna wouldn't change it out, so she'd requested foot rests installed for her feet. She'd also had a few more bells and whistles installed. One was a trigger that she could activate for the semi-automatic pistol hidden inside the desk drawer. She had designed the mechanisms to activate either by a physical trigger under her desktop or by a hidden button on top of her desk. It was all quite James Bond–like. A bulletproof screen could rise from the front of the desk. And the desk itself was a bulletproof shield. It was a monstrosity, but a functional one.

Korinna used different carpenters and contractors for various additions to the space so that none of these modifications existed in the original plans, and not one person, except Elda and Korinna, knew all the changes.

Elda texted Ashok: ANYI MISNG ID?

Ashok texted back: NIS FOUND DEAD SAILOR. No ID.

So *that* was how he had been accessing everything. She texted Charlie: D KLLD SLR 4 ID. X DNGR. KLL IST - ?? L8TR.

Damn. No way did Elda try this sniper position. Charlie put her eye to the scope on the M110 semiautomatic and sited through the peephole around the room below. There were too many blind spots. She didn't want to take out Elda by mistake and leave the asshole standing.

Charlie inspected her new weapon. She wished for time to field strip it and put it back together. Nothing like that for getting to know a piece. A trial run would have been helpful too. But that wouldn't happen now. No time. She made mental notes of what to modify before trying this again. She settled into position, feeling her hip bones against the metal piece covering the inside of the ceiling. She wished she had asked Elda if the ceiling below her was bulletproof.

Elda watched her security monitor. Dmitri entered the building by tailgating on a resident. She made note to offer to change that system into one that allowed only one person to enter at a time. He took the stairs two at a time and arrived in her hallway. Now she'd see how secure the door is.

Dmitri took out a lockpick set and worked on the lock. Fifteen minutes later he had not succeeded and was sweating and red faced. He stopped and pulled out two small plastic explosive bombs and affixed them to the hinge side of the door.

Elda nodded at his resourcefulness. That might work. She waited. A small bang and a puff of smoke later, the door still was in place. Dmitri took a short sledge hammer and a wrecking bar out of his pack. Five minutes later the door fell inward and Dmitri marched into the office waiting room.

If he wasn't trying to kill her, this prick could be useful. Elda picked up her automatic and trained it on her unlocked office door. It opened.

Dmitri stepped in. Almost engulfed by his hand was a Smith & Wesson M&P micro-compact pistol. Elda knew her Smith & Wessons. He had ten rounds to her eight. On second thought, he probably did the same trick she did: chamber one round and add a new round back to the clip. So that was eleven to her nine. She'd take those odds.

"So what brings you here, Dmitri?" What motivated Dmitri? Could she persuade him to lay his gun down, or would she have to kill him?

"I think you know that already, Elda. I am here to kill you." He raised his weapon.

"How come?" Elda asked with a lilt to her voice.

His brows knitted together and his hand lowered. "What?"

Elda shrugged, put her weapon down in front of her, and held her hands palms side up, with her elbows resting on her desk. "Why are you going to kill me?"

He shook his head in disbelief. "I have a contract."

"So?" Had she misjudged him? Did he have ethics after all? She lowered her hands onto the desk.

His eyes turned dark with rage. The gun raised. "*So?* Are you trying to fuck with my head? *So* they give me money. I kill you. They give me more money. That's it. Nice and clean and simple."

"Interesting." So he was just a dumb killer. Too bad. At first he'd looked like he had potential.

"Interesting! That's all you can say about it?" He put one hand to his head. The gun dropped to his side.

"Yes. You had a promising career, but you chose to throw it all away on this contract."

His face screwed up into a pout, and his leg moved, as if he were going to have a childlike tantrum. "No, no. That's not how it works."

"Explain to me how it works then."

Dmitri stamped his foot, and he waved his pistol around as he spoke. "It's like in the old Mafia, when you make your bones. Kill a person as ordered and you are accepted and a *made man*."

Elda kept her eyes on his weapon, hoping it wouldn't accidentally fire. "Except in this case you'll be shunned."

"No, no." He stamped again. "I will have taken out a legend."

"Point blank? For no reason except money? Because a crooked senator gave you a contract? You'll never work in a spy organization again. The military won't want you, not even as a contractor. Perhaps you could get a job as mercenary or a hit man for hire."

"That's what I want. Hit man for hire."

Elda sensed she was losing him. "And always be looking over your shoulder because no one will trust you? No one will work with you."

Dmitri snickered. "What will it matter? I will have money, women, fast cars, my own fame."

"It's a steep price, Dmitri." *Here it comes. If he's going to blow, it will be now.* Elda pressed the button for the bulletproof shield.

"One I'm willing to pay." Dmitri raised his arm and fired.

Elda grabbed her gun, dove to the side, firing and hitting him. He spun around from the force of the bullet. He fell backward, pushed by the momentum of a second bullet in the head. Elda rolled to the side of her desk and stood.

The bulletproof shield clicked into place. *Damn thing. Too slow.*

The ceiling clattered above as Charlie dashed to Elda's side. She ran to Elda, sitting on the floor. "You're bleeding."

Elda glanced at her upper arm. "He was a bad shot. I thought I defused him, but he blew. I must be losing my touch. That was some good shooting, Grasshopper. Thank you."

"You don't know the half of it. This place needs major modifications. I was impressed, Elda, at the way you almost had him. He wasn't going to stop for any reason. He wanted the reputation of having killed you. I suspect that he would have gone after Tosh next, had he succeeded here."

"Looking forward to chatting about it, but right now

let's patch me up until the medics get here. Don't let me forget to ask NIS for his weapon. That would be a nice addition to my Smith & Wesson collection."

Charlie dashed for the first-aid kit while Elda dialed NIS and called for a medic. Charlie returned and cut off Elda's sleeve halfway down the upper arm.

"Damn it, Charlie, that's one of my favorite shirts."

"Buy another, Elda. You can afford it." She sprayed antiseptic on Elda's arm while dabbing at the graze with gauze.

"Ouch!" Elda's eyes teared up.

"It's only a drive-by, whoosie girl."

That made Elda smile. "I see you took Olga to heart."

"I miss her. She was a great trainer, and fun."

"I'll engage her again to work with us soon. We need to sharpen up. After the medics finish with my arm, let's debrief. There's a lot that needs to be changed around here. We should try all the new systems and give the list to Korinna to get done before we move in."

Chapter Fifteen

"**T**'**FU TY.**"

Boris held the phone away from his ear. The Russian curses came fast and furious. Emil was upset about Nyoka's death, but there was no way Boris was paying Emil for that bitch.

Boris contemplated the scratches on his desk. Now that Nyoka was gone, he should have the desk refinished. In his musings, he almost missed Emil's next sentence. "*Chto?* Repeat that!"

"*Svoloch.* If you value your life, you will listen to me. You *will* pay me Nyoka's worth."

Boris laughed at Emil's gall. "She is worth nothing. I will pay you *nothing.*"

Emil sneered. "You forget, Boris—you have no more assassins left . . ."

Boris ended the conversation by slamming the phone down. Somehow Emil knew Boris had lost all his assassins. Emil could leak it out and have Boris removed or use it to blackmail Boris. In any case, it didn't bode well for Boris.

He stomped down the hallway to Gorky Krovopuskov's laboratory and strode into the lab. Gorky Krovopuskov was mixing steaming potions under a hood, with the air blower sucking the fumes up and out. Boris had the distinct impression of a cauldron with witches cackling over it.

Gorky did not disappoint. He was a wizened man with a slender bent-over body, wrinkled face, and beaked nose. He wrung his hands together as he spoke in a crackling voice. "You're lucky nothing in here is terribly poisonous today." Gorky chuckled, ending in a high pitch.

Boris emitted a faint "Ha-ha" at Gorky's old joke. He wanted to be out of the laboratory as quickly as possible. He didn't totally trust the blowers. Or Gorky, for that matter.

Boris cleared his throat, worried that he was breathing in the not so "terribly poisonous" fumes. "I need something easy to administer in someone's office, perhaps via chair arm or phone? Something that can't be detected and would mimic some natural event, such as a heart attack."

Gorky held a finger to one side of his nose and narrowed his eyes. He rocked from his waist, nodding.

Boris waited patiently. He would not do anything to disturb Gorky's equilibrium. There was less and less of it as the years went on.

"If you're looking hard enough, most anything could be detected . . ." Gorky drifted off into a high-pitched hum. He laughed in a nasally cackle. "How about a clear liquid that will dry onto a surface but still enter a person's skin if they come in contact with it? You'd have to be careful to wear gloves. Thick ones. And to take them off properly . . . hmmmm, hmmmm . . . Is it a woman? They have more skin exposed. Much easier."

Boris shook his head and croaked out, "N-n-no."

Gorky licked his lips. His fingers danced along his mouth. "Hmmmm." His eyes lit up. "Or I can make a powder that would dissolve into food or drink." He rubbed his hands together. "But you can't touch that either . . . or inhale it." He pointed a quivering finger at Boris. "Are you bringing him anything?"

"A check."

Gorky thrust his forefinger in the air. "*Otlichnyy.* Excellent. We can imprint it with a poison. Once he accepts it, within four hours, lights out! The poison will decay over time and be mostly gone from the paper in a few days. Anyone else handling it will, at most, get ill. Rather like a cold. Yes . . . yes . . . yes." He cackled. "How wonderful."

Boris frowned. "What about me, when I hand him the check?"

Humming, Gorky wiped the drool from the side of his mouth. He clasped his hands together. "Oh, how delightful. I can protect your fingers in a thin latex formulated to be impervious to this poison. Quite invisible to any observer too." He chortled. "Yes. Yes."

"But if I do that, my check may be used as evidence."

"Ha! And who would think that way? Most people wouldn't suspect. And if they do, who will they ask to test for poisons?"

Boris snickered. "You, of course."

Cackle.

Boris marched into Emil's office.

"And you are here because?" Emil held his fingers together over his mouth, partially hiding his smirk.

"You win. I will pay for her." Boris took out a pen from a pocket protector and opened his checkbook. "How much do you want?"

Emil leaned back in his chair and clasped his hands behind his head. "I would say that one million rubles a year for the next ten years would be more than fair."

Boris startled. Emil was giving him a good deal, but he should protest. "What! How would she bring you ten thousand dollars a year? The damage she causes puts her in the debit column."

Emil sneered. "That is why, my dear friend, I am only charging you that much. If it had been another of my agents that you lost, I would be charging you ten times that."

"*Svoloch'.*"

"Call me a bastard again and the price will go up."

Boris clicked the pen and was relieved to see the point stick out. He did not want to have to borrow a pen from Emil. Who knew what it could do to him.

The check had everything filled out except the amount. He scribbled the price, careful not to touch any part of the paper. He didn't totally trust the latex film on his hands. Using his fingertips, he tore off the check with a flourish and threw it in front of Emil.

Emil smirked. He picked up the check and ran his fingers lightly over the figures. He chuckled, folded the slip of paper, and inserted it into his shirt pocket. "Always a pleasure doing business with you, Boris."

"Spend it quickly, Emil." Boris stomped out of Emil's office.

Chapter Sixteen

ELDA FLINCHED AS SHE VIEWED THE EXPRESsion on Korinna's face.

"Geesh. How did you trash the place in *one* day?" Korinna, having stepped over the broken front door, stood frowning, with her hands on her hips, surveying the bullet holes in the new office.

Elda hung her head and tried to sound apologetic. "Sorry, Korinna, but we learned a lot through it."

"Like not to shoot up a brand-new office?" Korinna poked at a hole with her finger.

"Ah, no . . . sorry, but we have a list of things that need to be changed. For example, the metal crawl space is far too noisy. The sniper hideouts are uncomfortable and need a greater line-of-sight range. The main door is vulnerable since the hinges can be blown off. There aren't enough entryways into the inner corridor and crawl space. And although it's not our system, a person can enter the building by tailgating another. Oh, and the bulletproof shield on the desk is *far* too slow."

"Is that all?" Korinna was jotting everything down on a notepad.

Elda's burner rang. She looked at Korinna. "Excuse me. It's Tosh. I have to answer. Charlie may have a few more things."

She walked away to take the call. "*Privet*, Tosh."

"Snezhana and Anatoly are ready to fly over. I have a favor in return."

"Yes . . ." Elda tensed.

"There is an American here in Moscow who has been working with the GRU to help spread disinformation. They suspect he is double-crossing them by sending particulars about Russian intelligence to China. It would be helpful to entrap him and send him to Siberia for a long winter's stay. We thought that an American, acting as CIA, could get the information a lot quicker than we could. Would you like to be in on taking the American down?"

Elda's shoulders relaxed, and she exhaled the breath she hadn't realized she was holding. She was relieved she could get behind his request. "Yes, of course."

"Good. You fly over and help me here, and I will send Anatoly and Snezhana over to complete Operation Take Down. *Khorosho?*"

"It would be my pleasure."

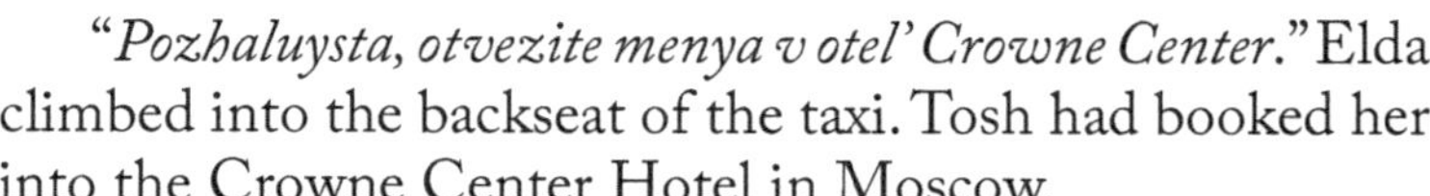

"*Pozhaluysta, otvezite menya v otel' Crowne Center.*" Elda climbed into the backseat of the taxi. Tosh had booked her into the Crowne Center Hotel in Moscow.

"*Izvinite, vy imeyete v vidu Hotel Plaza Garden?*"

"*Da.*" That was right. The old name of the hotel had slipped out.

The taxi pulled up in front. Elda reached back for her backpack. She turned and switched arms to get the bag.

Even though the wound on her arm was small, the newly formed scab pulled and hurt when she stretched.

She checked in and wandered to the elevators. Pausing, she looked up at the balconies. It was too early in the day for the women to be hanging out on the upper floors, soliciting foreigners and setting them up for the government.

Elda studied the elevators. The three cars followed the same pattern as before. One car stayed on the floor where the women were. Another stayed on the ground floor, ready to be summoned, and switched with the first one as needed, and the third one took guests to their rooms.

Elda examined the area. The old Crowne Center had been revamped and had new carpet. The garish reds had been toned down to sedate browns and grays. The brown clock with a rooster on top still stood tall in the lobby.

Entering her room, she spied a small, stuffed brown bear propped against the pillows, reading *The House at Pooh Corner*. She chuckled. Somehow Tosh knew she always traveled to Russia with the book *Winnie the Pooh*, to confuse immigration.

She reached for the book, and a shard of paper fell out, with the alphanumeric code II-10, followed by 3-43/44, on it. She opened the book to the Roman numerals for the table of contents, found the II section and counted in ten words: Breakfast

She leafed to page 3 and counted in for words forty-three and forty-four: eleven o'clock. Great. She could use some caffeine. She had time to shower, change, and head to the restaurant.

Hair still wet, she compared her makeup job with the picture Tosh had sent her. Marilyn Hunter looked back at her. It was a good match. She had confidence that Ashok had added her to the CIA database as an agent. Now she'd see how leaky that file was.

She looked at the time. Eight minutes before eleven.

She headed out to meet Tosh.

Elda arrived at the hotel restaurant, but Tosh was not there. The restaurant manager was the same as from her last visit. She met Elda with a flurry of Russian. She ushered Elda to a table and unfolded the napkin with a flourish and placed it on Elda's lap.

"*Spasibo.*"

"*Pozhaluysta.*" The manager turned and left.

Elda lifted the menu from her plate and spotted a white folded paper under it. She unfolded it to read: OUTSIDE PICKUP 11:45.

Plenty of time. Elda flagged down a waiter and ordered bacon and eggs and explained she had to leave by 11:30.

By 11:42 Elda had her hat, coat, gloves, and boots on and was standing outside. A black sedan drove up, and the driver waved her over. She strode to the car and recognized Yuri behind the wheel. He jumped out and opened the door for her.

"*Spasibo.*"

They drove to Tosh's new office in silence. Elda was surprised at the age of the building and the lack of security.

"It was affordable."

Elda startled. Tosh had materialized behind her. He was masterful at reading minds. She looked around the room and recognized a series of cameras embedded in the ceiling molding. She assumed the room was also miked. "Is this on or off record?"

"The microphones are off," Tosh replied.

"And the guns?"

Anatoly wandered in from the other room and patted his jacket pocket. "Here."

"Ah, hello, Anatoly. Long time no see."

Anatoly growled. "I now have an aversion to the song 'Moscow Nights,' Elda."

"I'm sorry, Anatoly. It's a beautiful song. But it can be

haunting. If it helps any, I'm not overly fond of beeping computers."

Anatoly snorted.

Elda threw him a paper bag.

"*Snochniki.* That helps take the sting out of losing to you. What else do you have?"

She presented a box about fifteen inches long by four and one-half inches wide by five-eights of an inch thick. He opened it and stared at the Merlin throwing knife.

"*Krasivyy. Spasibo.* A beautiful weapon. *That's* more like it."

Tosh held up his hand. "You will not try it out inside the office, Anatoly."

Anatoly growled and speared one of his *sochniki* pastries with the end of his knife and chomped into the soft dough.

Elda turned to Tosh. "What's the scoop?"

Tosh handed her a pen. "This is a recording device."

Elda twirled it around in her fingers. "When did you guys get all James Bond–like?"

"In the 1950s."

"Does the pen still work?"

Tosh glared at Elda. "It's a fine point. Black. Like you always use. Rotate the clip to turn it on."

Elda nodded and waited. It was time to get to the nub of the operation.

Tosh passed her a passport. "Here's your new identification. We have leaked that the United States is willing to pay vast sums for the right information and is sending Marilyn Hunter, CIA, to Moscow to negotiate the deals."

Elda opened the passport to view her face as Marilyn Hunter.

"The traitor, Richard Dingle—"

"Who?!" Elda's lips quivered and her eyes crinkled. "That *cannot* be the man's real name."

Tosh shrugged. "It's an unfortunate handle, but his

parents named him that."

Elda chuckled. "Please go on."

"We believe that Dick D. is selling sensitive Russian intelligence to the Chinese. He's also selling Chinese information to the Russians, but most of it's useless. We need his confession on tape. He'll be more likely to spill his guts to a fellow American, especially one as skilled as you in interrogations. Once you obtain the info, we'll move in and arrest him."

Elda nodded. "Okay. How do I meet Mr. D?"

"We have taken the liberty of arranging a meeting with him tonight at your hotel bar."

"Perfect. A straightforward op. This should be fun." Elda stood.

Tosh frowned.

"I'm going to play tourist. Shopping and the sights. Marilyn is only here for a few days, and she's going to make the best of it."

"Well played. Anatoly will cover you."

Anatoly growled.

After a shopping spree, Elda sat at a table in the bar of the Plaza Garden with a water and a shot of vodka. The noise from around the elevators filtered in, but she couldn't make out any distinct words.

A tall man with a graying crew cut trudged into the bar and looked around. Elda waved at him. He came over to her table.

"Miss Hunter?"

"Yes, and you must be . . . Mr. Dingle?" Elda had a hard time keeping a straight face when she said his name. She rose and held out her hand. The handshake was weak and his palm was clammy. The man must be nervous.

"Please call me Dick." He pulled out a chair and sat across from her.

"Dick, then. Please call me Marilyn."

"Well, Marilyn, I was intrigued when you contacted me. Your message was vague. What is so important that it can't wait to be discussed in my office?"

Elda gave him a smile. "I know your time is valuable, and I am willing to pay for it. That envelope is the tip of the iceberg." She slid a fat envelope across the table.

Dick pocketed it without looking inside.

Elda had gleaned from his files he was motivated by money and recognition. He was living far above his means and had bought an expensive piece of property in the Cayman Islands. She picked her words. "Your office would not be a good place to talk. Nor is this bar. Too many people know you. Shall we take a stroll and return here for a drink to celebrate your good fortune?"

"Celebrate? Good fortune? Now you have my attention. I am willing to listen."

Elda motioned to the waiter to put her drink on her tab and pulled her brown leather jacket off the back of her chair.

They strolled along the bank of the Moskva River via the Presnenskaya Naberezhnaya Road.

"I can't tell you my company, but you may know of it." Elda knew someone had accessed the CIA database the night before and the IP address had been traced back to Russia.

"Well, let me guess. You are an American, and being quite cagey. Could it be *the Company?*"

Elda winked. "Perhaps. *If* we assume you are correct in that guess, then you might also surmise what we know about you."

He held up his hands. "I'm a legitimate businessman operating out of Russia."

Elda raised her eyebrows. "With the full support of the Russian government and the GRU." She cocked her head.

He shrugged. "Perhaps, but there is nothing America

can do about that."

Elda waved her hand to one side. "We're not looking to prosecute you. We need you to work with us." That should bait the hook.

Dick leaned forward. "No prosecution? I am interested. Go on."

Elda leaned in and lowered her voice. "We are wondering if Russia is your only client or if you're willing to work with other governments."

He laughed. "It depends. Money talks, you know?"

"How would a quarter of a million tax-free dollars sound to start?"

His pupils dilated. He tapped his mouth with his forefinger.

Elda could imagine the wheels spinning in his head. She leaned back, as if ready to leave and pull out of the impending deal.

Dick held up his hand, palm forward. "That *is* intriguing."

"It's a limited-time offer. Do you have the bandwidth? We know you're already on another payroll besides Russia's. Does that country know about your work for Russia?"

Elda could see the sweat forming on his upper lip. She started to turn back to the hotel.

His response was quick. "No, and I'd like to keep it that way. Don't leave. I can do this."

He fell feet first into her trap. He was working for a second government.

Elda frowned. "You would be in a powerful position. And the money would accumulate rapidly. Can you take on a third allegiance? It's a lot of money for us to risk if you can't. Plus, we don't want to have Russia find out about this." *Keep him talking and he'll hang himself. Ego talks.*

He nodded with such force that Elda was afraid he'd hurt himself. "I can definitely do this. It would be helpful to cover the material I'm sending, if it ends up in multiple countries. Don't worry. Russia will never find out." He wiped drool from the corner of his mouth.

"Not many people can juggle that number of false alliances."

He chuckled.

Now to hit the home run. She angled in, her eyes bright with admiration and curiosity. "Does it matter that you would be betraying Russia to the United States?"

Dick snorted. "I'm already sending information about them to China. What does it matter if I send it also to another country?"

Tosh appeared at their side.

Dick startled. "Where did you come from?"

Tosh held firmly onto Dick's upper arm. "That is of no matter. Normally this would be your funeral, but you're in luck—Russia likes to have Americans to trade. You will come with me. I think a long winter in the correction colony will set your priorities straight."

A black car skidded to a stop at the curb. Anatoly hopped out. In minutes he had zip-tied Dick's wrists and thrown him in the trunk. Anatoly sped away with his new passenger screaming from the trunk.

Tosh faced Elda. "Thank you. We have it all recorded. He won't be released except in a trade."

Elda shrugged. "Who would want that trash?"

"I'll call you and let you know when I can send Snezhana and Anatoly over."

Elda frowned. "Send them back with me."

"I will send them shortly afterward. I have a couple of things to tie up here first."

Elda glared at Tosh. "Make it soon. I fulfilled my part of the bargain. I need you to come through on your promise. This senator is not stopping."

"Dyadya?"

"Yes, Snezhana." Tosh looked up from the pile of folders on his desk in their Moscow office.

Snezhana sauntered over from her desk and sat in a chair, Tosh's printouts in her hand. She ran her other hand down the back of her head and over the ponytail that once was there. "I've been thinking about Boris's request to find Kevin Ball's offshore accounts. I think it may be time we removed the money from the accounts we hid from Elda, now that we are no longer being paid by the Kremlin."

Tosh looked at his niece from under his reading glasses and gave a thin smile. "You're a step ahead of me, Snezhana. We found three accounts, correct?"

Snezhana laid the papers onto Tosh's desk, facing him. "Yes. And all were about equal in size. We told Elda about only one of them."

Tosh flipped through the papers. "Although I hate to give good money to Boris, I think we should let him have part of one account. Giving him that money will satisfy his need to find Kevin Ball's offshore accounts and we can move on. The accounts are in no way linked to each other. I did tap one to establish this office, but there is plenty left in that account to keep us going for many years to come."

Snezhana bit her thumbnail. "If Boris gets the money, will he let go of looking for the rest?"

Tosh took her hand, opened his desk drawer, and placed a nail trimmer in her palm. She chuckled. He winked at her and consulted his ceiling for his answer. "He will be enraged that there is so little in the account, but we could have Stas plant data bolstering the impression that's all there is."

"Excellent." Snezhana grabbed one of the papers and

scribbled calculations. "*Da*. That will work. There have been major losses in the worth of cybercurrency. If Stas shows that the money was laundered during these dips, it could account for a smaller amount in the end. Add transaction fees, and also imply that he skimmed off the top but show that's in a bank in the United States, where we can't touch it . . ."

Tosh sat back in his chair and stared at Snezhana. "You have a head for finance, niece."

Anatoly plodded over from his desk. "You could let him know the Americans found some of the money before Kevin could transfer it. It would be in the United States Treasury by now. We know Elda's ethics."

Snezhana studied her nails. "Perhaps now that she's on her own, she won't be as ready to turn away found money."

Tosh raised an eyebrow. "Perhaps . . ."

Chapter Seventeen

"**W**HERE ARE MY LAZY WINKIES?" OLGA Sokolov bounced into the waiting room with gym bags over each shoulder.

Elda came running out of her office and threw her arms around Olga.

"Ugh. No touchy-feely." Olga brushed Elda away but let a twinkle show in her eye. "Where is gym? You do have gym for Olga, right?" Olga spun around, taking in the area she was in. "Oh, nice place. Do you know how far Olga has come today? There better be tea and biscuits for Olga when she's done."

Elda's smile threatened to split her face in two. "Don't worry, Olga. I'd never forget your tea and biscuits."

"Olga knows. We have worked together for many years now." Olga bounced on her toes. "We better get going." She squeezed Elda's bicep. "Oooooh. That could be better. You know Olga told you to work out every day. You working out every day? How can Olga help you if you don't help yourself?"

Elda hung her head. "Ah . . ."

"No need to answer. Olga knows. You can't fool Olga."

"I never could fool Olga. The gym is over this way. It's small, but I think you'll like it. There's TRX straps, mats, weights, bands . . . most anything you'd need. The team is waiting for you there." Elda checked her phone. "And I will do extra pushups for being late. Someone is in the lobby for me."

"You make it quick. You need more muscles."

"Don't worry, Olga. I will ask for extra sessions with you, *khorosho?*"

"*Khorosho*. Olga work you out." She loped into the company's gym and threw her bags down with a clunk.

Korinna, Ashok, and Charlie sat on the weight bench and rower, chatting. They leapt up. "Olga!"

Olga beamed at them. "There you are! Olga now see how you really are. This gym smells good, hey? That means you are not in here working out yet. Olga change that."

The three looked terrified.

Olga laughed. "No need to be scared. Olga starts slow. Now, grab a mat. We do pushups." Olga took out her stopwatch and let them push up until exhaustion. She noted the results for each on the sheet attached to her clipboard.

"*Khorosho*. Not too bad. Now we do chest presses. Pick your weights."

They ran through the chest presses, bicep curls, kettlebell snatches, squats, running, agility, sit to stand, pull-ups, march in place with ankle weights, sit and reach, backscratch test, and balance on the Bosu balls. Olga zipped around correcting form and recording weights, flexibility, and endurance. When done the group sat panting and sweating.

"Not too shabby, but Olga wants you to do much more. That was evaluation session. Now let's start workout." Olga guffawed at the looks on each of their faces. "Olga kidding.

You go shower and meet Elda in the conference room. Olga see you in two days. Now Olga go get tea and biscuits."

Elda stopped short when she saw who was waiting for her in the lobby. She addressed the tall blue-eyed blond. "Murka. What are you doing here? How did you find this place? I thought you were happily settled in Mexico. Didn't things pan out for you?"

Murka held her hands out, palms up. She opened her jacket to show she had no weapons.

Elda nodded to acknowledge the openness that Murka was displaying. She also knew Murka, as a good operative, most likely had a pistol at the back of her waist and probably a knife in a calf sleeve.

"It wasn't easy," Murka replied, her sexy contralto voice reminding Elda why Charlie found Murka so attractive. "I've been scouring DC for you. Finally I spotted Charlie and trailed her to this building. I wasn't able to determine if you worked here or not, but I took a gamble and asked the receptionist here to tell Elda Ainsworth I was in the lobby. She played coy and said there was no one here by that name. I said I'd wait. And then you appeared."

"That was a nice bit of spy work. Let's take a walk."

Elda motioned for Murka to leave in front of her, placing her hand on the small of Murka's back. Yes, she had a gun. Now, at least, Murka would know that Elda knew Murka was armed.

They exited the lobby and onto the sidewalk. Elda came abreast of Murka. "What do you want, Murka? And just so you know, I can outdraw you."

"I come in peace. I want to work for you."

Elda turned and looked into Murka's eyes. She was serious. "Why?"

"I sense you are ethical with a solid sense of what's right and what's wrong." Murka's tone was sincere. "And that you and your team have the ability to correct the wrongs. I want in on *that*. And, to be totally truthful, Mexico didn't pan out for me. I am not ready to work for myself."

Elda narrowed her eyes. "How do I know you're not a plant sent by Tosh or someone else in the Kremlin?"

"You don't. You have to trust me and trust your instincts."

Elda paced around in the conference room of their new office, waiting for the team to settle in. The space felt sterile and unwelcoming. She mused on painting at least one wall a different color. The white walls, whiteboards, and metal equipment and chair arms shouted at her. She glanced around the table. Korinna, Ashok, and Charlie sat watching.

Charlie broke the silence. "What's next, Master?"

"Who else thinks the walls need painting?"

Korinna and Charlie raised their hands. Ashok shrugged. Korinna spoke. "But that's not why you called this meeting, right?"

"Correct. I'd like to discuss our next mission and staffing issues. There's so much to do. We have to prioritize, and we need help."

Charlie glanced at Ashok and back at Elda. "*What?* You don't think the three of us can change the world?"

Korinna cleared her throat.

Charlie blushed. "Oh, sorry, Korinna. Four."

"On the contrary," Elda replied, "I know the three of us can change the world. Ooops, four, that is. However, we might need some additional resources at times. Let's brainstorm on the potential projects and look at what skills we'd like to bring on." Elda paused and wrote on the whiteboard that covered the entire wall. "Here's some of my ideas. I'd like our operations to be targeted with results that have impact on bringing peace and stability to the world. Feel free to chime in with your own."

- FINISH INVESTIGATING WHAT WAS GOING ON WITH THE REAL ESTATE DEALS IN WALES AND THE UNITED STATES

- BLOW UP THE YELABUGA DRONE FACTORY

"The Yelabuga drone factory is in Russia. Its drones are being used against Ukraine. I did extensive on the ground research there for Ed, but I never had the chance to turn it over to him. This is Russia's main factory. If we can disable the production there, we can slow their advances against Ukraine and, potentially, also against NATO allied countries."

- STOP THE BIOWEAPONS PLANT IN RUSSIA.

"Bio weapons scare me. They should not be used by any country for warfare." Elda pointed her marker at Korinna. "For this one we'd need to consult with a bioscientist. Can you find us someone?"

Korinna made a note. "*Da*."

- TRIP UP THE NEW KOREAN RECRUITS IN THE UKRAINE

"If these new recruits get slaughtered, it would send a message back to North Korea. They can listen . . . or send more recruits to be slaughtered. That will weaken them. Either way is a win."

- FIGHT BACK ON THE CYBER INFRASTRUCTURE WAR

"This is a tricky one. It's been like whacking a mole. China, Iran, Russia, North Korea, and who knows what other countries, are behind this. However, it's within the United States where the propaganda gets distributed, often through right-wing, unregulated platforms. I'd like to find a way to cut them off from redistribution."

- Undermine the United States oligarchs who are working with Russia and China to weaponize space

"Space lasers are not a good thing. Neither is filling up the atmosphere with satellites that are not under impartial oversight and control."

- Bring back solid news media networks and free the media from single-point ownership

"Those who are exposed to real—i.e., curated and fact checked—news tend to exercise critical thinking and are less likely to be brainwashed. There's a campaign to eliminate traditional media sources and also to bankrupt certain colleges and universities where critical thinking is encouraged. Russia has done this with their population. Step one in any dictator's handbook is to discredit the media."

- Free Conrad Ferguson of the Boston Globe from Russian prison.

"Being an avid reader of the *Boston Globe*, I'm particularly invested in bringing this guy back. His *Globe* Spotlight exposé on Russian tampering in our elections was spot on. The Russians got him when he was over there, reporting on their treatment of Alexei Navalny. And last but not least . . ."

- Get rid of Senator Glass before he gets rid of me.

Elda put down the markers and sat.

Korinna looked at the list and laughed. "Really? Are we qualified to tackle *any* of that?"

Ashok raised his hand. "Miss Elda, ma'am. I would

like to research the cyber-information war. I think I could make great progress there. It would be most helpful if I had a second programmer to work with."

Elda gave him a thumbs-up. "Fantastic, Ashok. Write up what you need for qualifications, and we'll search for him or her."

Korinna cleared her throat.

Elda corrected herself. "Ah, that would be Korinna who would be sourcing your hire, Ashok."

"I have someone in mind, if you don't mind me looking first, Miss Korinna. Using my contacts will be a lot cheaper than sourcing through headhunters."

"As Elda would say, *knock your socks off*, Ashok. Please let me know if you need any help."

Charlie spoke up. "We can always reach out to Sophia to work on the real estate transactions again, but I'm intrigued by the man who's in a Russian prison. Who is he?"

Elda rose. She stood with her feet shoulder-width apart and emphasized her words with the marker she held in her right hand. "Conrad is a hard-hitting journalist who worked with *The Washington Post* for years, but he left them when their owner lost his spine. The gutsy *Boston Globe* snatched him up. He was writing about Alexei Anatolyevich Navalny and the Anti-Corruption Foundation and had gone to Moscow to write about the resistance movement there, when they arrested him as a spy. They tried him in the typical kangaroo court and sentenced him to twenty years in jail. He's being moved next month from Lefortovo Prison to Corrective Colony Number Six of the UFSIN of Russia for Vladimir Oblast."

Charlie narrowed her eyes. "Where's that?"

"West of Moscow. It's also known simply as IK-6 Melekhovo or Melekhovo correctional colony. It's a strict-regime corrective colony located on the outskirts of the town of Melekhovo, in Vladimir Oblast, Russia. There are some opportunities along the route where we could hit his transport.”

“With a third agent, we could hit the transfer and smuggle him out.”

Elda drew a checkmark in the air with her forefinger. “My thoughts exactly, Charlie. And we have someone who would like to work with us.”

“Who?”

“Murka.”

***

“Charlie. I need to speak with you alone.” A sweaty Elda grabbed a towel to wipe her face and hands and leaned against the doorjamb to Charlie’s office. Olga had apparently worked her pretty hard.

Charlie figured this would be a conversation about Murka. She hadn’t had time to sort her feelings out about that woman. She was so attractive.

Elda threw her towel the seat of the guest chair and plopped herself down with a groan. “I’m thinking of hiring Murka.”

There it was. Charlie needed to delay this to give herself time to discover what was true for her. She tossed a bottle of Excedrin and a water bottle to Elda, who snatched each out of the air. “I was surprised when you said she wanted to join our team.”

Elda shook out and consumed two pills, and gulped down half the water bottle. She cut to the chase. “It would pose a problem for you.”

“Me? Why?” Charlie wondered if Elda knew how attracted she was to Murka.

Elda rolled her eyes. “Oh, don’t try to pull that over on me. You know why. If I hire her, there can be no relation-ship between the two of you. If I don’t hire her, she may go work for the Russians, and then there can be nothing between you two."

It appeared that Elda knew. "So damned if you do, damned if you don't."

"Exactly."

Charlie spit out how she felt. "She's professional at her job, Elda. And she's good hearted. Her voice warms me and sends shivers up my spine at the same time. She's great to look at."

Elda raised her eyebrow, prompting for Charlie's conclusion.

"Would I like to pursue her? In a second. But if it didn't work out, things could be messy at work, whereas she could be a solid asset to us and perhaps a good friend to me. Bring her on. I'll gird my loins."

"She could be hard to resist . . ."

"I know."

"Okay. 'Nuf said. Let's get Korinna and inspect the new modifications to the office."

Korinna and Elda stood in the center of the lobby, looking up at the ceiling. "Are you all set there, Charlie?" Elda yelled.

Charlie's muffled voice floated down from the ceiling. "All set."

Korinna seized Elda's arm. "Do you have to shoot with real bullets?"

Elda analyzed Korinna's worried face. "It's the only way we're going to tell if the bulletproof ceiling works."

Korinna looked close to tears. "What if it's doesn't?"

Elda patted Korinna's hand to reassure her. "It will be okay. Charlie has a vest and a helmet on. That should protect all the important parts."

Korinna sighed and released Elda's arm. "Try to not wreck more than one ceiling panel. *Khorosho?* The contractor is ready to move on from this job. We're already over budget too."

In response, Elda shot the ceiling. The bullet embedded in the tile, but it went no farther. Immediately afterward, Elda was riddled with red paint-bullet splashes. She moved and was hit with blue paint spots. She continued to move around the room until she was decorated all colors of the rainbow.

"It's good," Charlie yelled down.

Elda looked around for Korinna and found her hiding under a table. "Thank you so much for doing this, Korinna. It *is* good."

Korinna crawled out from under the table and shook her head at the mess. "Geesh. It *better be*, after all the money you've spent. You should think about getting some income. The government could cut you off at any time."

"We're working on that one, Korinna. Charlie, come down." Hearing the muted sounds of Charlie maneuvering, Elda reached into a satchel and brought out a large paint submachine gun. Charlie came through the door. Elda fired. Charlie dripped red paint from head to toe. Elda did a war dance, holding her gun high.

"That was cheating!" Charlie wiped the paint off her eyes with the back of her hand.

Elda licked the paint off the back of her own hand. "It's all organic paint. It washes right off. It won't harm you."

Charlie suppressed a grin. "Not what I meant, Elda."

"I know." Elda grew serious. "You need to be able to check if anyone is waiting for you. Let's add a spy hole to the modifications list." She threw Charlie a towel. "Next, we're going to try to blow the front door."

"Seriously?" Korinna ducked back under her table.

Elda hoisted the table onto its side so it better protected Korinna from the door.

"Of course." Elda walked to the supply cabinet and took out two small plastic explosive bombs and chucked them at Charlie, who fielded them, one in each hand.

She took out two more and left with Charlie, shutting and locking the door behind them.

CHAPTER EIGHTEEN

Ashok's adrenaline was spiking at the thought of a rematch. Careful not to spill the cup of tea he had just situated on the table, Ashok reached over to a power strip and turned it on. A rack of five Dell PowerEdge R760 servers hummed to life. He placed his Linux laptop on his desk. That one shouldn't be needed right now. He powered up two Dell U3225QE Ultrasharp thirty-two-inch 4K Thunderbolt HUB monitors sitting side by side and daisy-chained together. Through them he could interact with all five servers.

"Most excellent." He patted the rack of servers. He then fired off a series of AI programs to search for cyber farms. Examining his watch, he decided to have some fun while waiting for the results. He powered up a third monitor and the Windows machine that he used to lure hackers into his network. He then built a series of different firewalls to keep any intruder out of the core of his network. He wondered if Stas was out there and if he'd take the bait. Ashok had enjoyed their last duel.

While waiting, Ashok labeled his cords and bundled them together out of the way. He felt it was important to have a neat work space. Functional was number one, but the way it looked spoke volumes about professionalism.

Ping.

Aha! Someone was attacking his system. Game on. Ashok typed furiously on his keyboard. He would locate this hacker before he breached the third firewall. If he was correct, about it being Stas, then the attacks should be coming from Moscow. The exact source would be obscured through connections to different hubs.

Ashok figured he'd systematically take down and then restore the Russian power grid, sector by sector. If he selected the correct grid, the attacks would cease while Ashok had that grid in the dark. There was a slim possibility that the VPN hub was in Moscow, but that would defeat the true value of having a VPN. He would only cause a hiccup in the power supply, but it would result in booting the intruder out.

There! Most excellent. Ashok had successfully booted him out. From the sector data he saw the intruder was from Moscow itself, not from Moscow Oblast. That left a lot of territory to search. Well, he best get started.

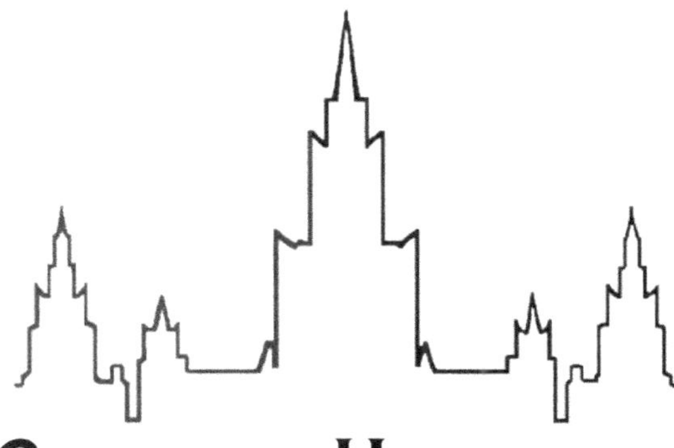

CHAPTER NINETEEN

"THIS MISSION IS TO BE CONSIDERED TOP Secret Eyes Only. You will tell no one about it or where you are going. Our lives depend on no details of this operation leaking." Elda closed and locked the DC office conference room door.

Korinna finished her electronic bug sweep and nodded at Elda. Ashok inspected the Cone of Silence machine and turned it on. This was a machine of Ashok's invention, which prevented any conversation of electronic signals from exiting the area.

Korinna, Charlie, and Murka sat around the large table. Ashok and Korinna joined them. Elda stood in front of the wall length whiteboard.

Elda took the lead. "I think you all have met Murka by now. If not, Murka, this is the team. Team, this is Murka. She's our new operative." Elda waited through the pleasantries and introductions, and started in. "Okay, troops, this is Operation Boston Globe.

"This is one of our most dangerous operations. It takes

place deep in Russia: in Moscow, west of Moscow, and south to Kazakhstan. Korinna, Murka. I have reached out to our contacts to supply us weapons and stage pickups for our various vehicles. I talked to Ed to see if he could arrange the entry into Kazakhstan, but he informed me we are on our own in this. The United States will disavow any knowledge of us or our operation. Ashok . . ."

Ashok gave out four passports, each from a different country, to each person.

Elda continued the briefing. "These are your identities. We'll switch IDs and disguises, as well as trucks or cars, at regular intervals. Murka . . ."

Murka walked to the map of Russia projected onto the whiteboard. "This is where Lefortovo Prison is located." She circled the location. "It's heavily armed and the electronic surveillance is comprehensive. The weak point is their transport of prisoners, which is done in an armored van, with two armed escorts."

"I've researched the armored vans," Charlie said, "and they have a vulnerability in the undercarriage of the back portion of the vehicle, as well as by the hinges on the doors. They also are top heavy and can be tipped."

Murka went back to the map. "IK-6 Melekhovo is located here." She circled a point west of Moscow along M7. "The drivers most often take the route due east from Lefortovo via E22 and M7 to Corrective Colony Number Six. It's about a three-and-one-half-hour drive, on a non-toll road, so we can move faster with less choke points."

Elda marched up beside Murka and circled another area on the map, west of the correctional colony. "This is a deserted portion of the M7 road, a stone's throw west of Lakinsk. We will take out the guards and van and grab the prisoner there."

Korinna pointed to leather carry-ons that she had positioned by Elda's, Charlie's, and Murka's seats. "These are your go-bags. I designed a schedule for the operation. It needs to be perfectly timed in order to intercept the van at the right spot and get away." She passed out a paper schedule to each person. "I will also securely send you this information. Memorize it. Then destroy it." She projected the timeline onto the whiteboard and used a laser pointer to highlight what she was referring to. "On this plan I have notated the times of the satellite passes overhead and the timing for the drones around Lefortovo and IK-6. The one thing working in our favor is the Russians tend to be slaves to routine. They have not been taught independent thinking."

"Where are we bringing Conrad?" Charlie asked.

Korinna consulted her notes. "We fly from Atyrau in Kazakhstan to DC, and from DC, catch a shuttle up to Boston. His home is in Cambridge, Massachusetts."

"That's the easy part," Elda added.

Elda took three deep breaths as she deplaned at Sheremetyevo International Airport in Moscow. Her hair was a short helmet of brassy copper. She sported a waist-length black leather jacket and a nose ring. She was loudly chewing gum with her mouth open. She wore blue jeans with a large silver belt buckle with a horse on it and carried a red-sequined cowboy hat in one hand, a large leather handbag over her arm, and pulled an overstuffed roller tote with her other hand. She wore black leather cowboy boots with red embroidery of flowers on the sides. She willed herself not to look at any of the hidden cameras tracking her movements to immigration and customs.

The immigration officer greeted her. "*Privet*, Miss Melinda Miller. Your passport, please."

She handed him her passport and answered, "Preeveyet.

Did I get that right? Your language is so hard to learn. I bought those Pimsler tapes to try and learn enough to get by—"

"Thank you, Miss Miller. And what is the nature of your visit to Moscow today?"

"I want to see *everything*. And to taste that lovely cavee-ar you have. When my husband, may he rest in peace, died, he left me a tidy little sum. I thought, *Melinda, do I squirrel this away for a rainy day? Or do I go and see the world with it?* Well—"

The immigration officer gave Elda her passport back and motioned her on.

"Well, thank you kindly, sir. Spahseeboo."

He sighed and waved her on again.

Elda swayed her hips as she rolled her bag to the exit. She strode to the limos, where a driver sat smoking a cigarette. "Excuse me." Elda referenced her translation guide. "Isvaneetee. I would like a ride to . . ." She referenced her dictionary. "Yakhat . . . to hotel."

The driver stubbed out his cigarette on the ground with his foot and motioned for Elda to get in the back seat of the sedan.

Elda stood by her luggage. She referenced the book again. "Bagza?"

He held his hand over his mouth and stared at her. She peered at him over her round red-rimmed glasses. "Vy Pooh-voh-write Englazy?"

He grabbed the handle of her luggage, looked down at the ground, rolled it to the trunk, and threw it in. Returning, he looked at her. "*Da*. I speak some English. Get in. We must go."

Elda hopped into the backseat.

The driver started the car and drove away from the curb. "The car has been swept."

Elda looked around and said in a heavy twang, "It does look pretty clean to me."

The driver glanced at her wide eyed in the rearview mirror.

Elda reached for her handbag and pulled out a pair of scissors. "Thanks, Charlie, for the lift. I'm going to transform now.

"Whew. You had me worried for a moment, Elda."

Elda positioned a small towel on her lap to catch stray hairs and propped a mirror up in the back of the seat and scissored the shape of her hairstyle. She opened the window and shook the towel out, letting the hair cuttings fly away. She reached for a small bottle of black hair dye and combed it in. She turned the cowboy hat inside out and ripped off part of the brim to make a smaller hat. She lay down on the backseat, took her jeans off, turned them inside out, and put them back on as black jeans. She cut the boots down to ankle high and died the stitched flowers with the hair dye so they blended in. She turned her jacket inside out and let down the hem and now wore a plaid hip-length jacket. Using the mirror, she applied prosthetic movie makeup, transforming the length of her nose and the shape of her face. She popped out her contacts and put in new ones. For the final change, she peeled off the latex appliqués from her fingers and applied new fingerprints.

All in ten minutes.

Charlie took a sharp left into a garage in Moscow. Murka greeted them and pointed toward the garage owner. "He tells us there's no vehicles available."

A jet-black Marussia B2 sports car sat gleaming under the lights. Elda popped the hood and spied a small slice of uncovered dark-blue paint. She looked around the engine block for the serial number. It was the same. This car got around. The owner strolled over to where Elda stood.

He looked her up and down with distaste. "This car is much too expensive for you."

Elda glared at him. "I had arranged for two cars to be available, as well as some gear stashed in them. The money we paid you more than covers a few hours ride in this one."

He snickered. "Perhaps you called the wrong garage, hey?"

Elda stepped in close to him and held a G10 glass fiber stiletto into his ribs. "If I push in and up, this blade will enter your abdomen under your ribs and tear you open. I will reach in and rip your heart out. Do you understand?"

The garage owner started shaking.

"You have picked the wrong people to cross. Now, where is my gear and the keys to our vehicles?" Elda pressed the blade of the knife through his shirt and into his skin.

"No, no. I have it all. It was just a misunderstanding." He pointed to a large metal box. "It has a combination lock. We couldn't open it."

Elda snarled. "That was the plan. Now give us the keys."

He reached into his pocket and handed her the keys to the Marussia and a second vehicle. Elda flung the keys for the B2 to Murka. She strode to the locked box and keyed in the combo, lifting out three black canvas bags. She doled out one to Charlie, one to Murka, and threw the third over her shoulder.

Murka strode over to the B2 and got in.

"Ooooh! Lovely. It's the same type of car we had for such a short time." Charlie hopped into the passenger seat.

"It's the same car, but don't get used to it, Charlie. We have another stop to go to pick up your vehicle. This one's Murka's in case we need a quick getaway with the prisoner." Elda confronted the owner. "Where's my van?"

He motioned to the back of the garage, where a gray UAZ-450 panel van sat among a pile of spare parts and tools.

She narrowed her eyes. "Does it still run?"

He shrugged. "Quite well, actually. This one has been retrofitted with armored panels in preparation for the war in Ukraine. It's slow, but no one would suspect it as a getaway car."

"You're right on that count." Elda called to Murka, who was hanging out the car window, with a gun sited on the owner. "Are you all set on cash?"

"*Da.* Their palms have been well greased, as you Americans would say."

"Okay! Time to pick up the truck. Charlie, do you want to ride with me?"

In response, Charlie shut the passenger door of the B2.

Murka wheeled up to the gate of a junkyard where a sentry sat snoozing in the guard box. Elda pulled up behind the Marussia. The engine noise and exhaust fumes from the van woke the guard.

Elda marched up to him. "*YA El'da. U tebya yest' gruzovik dlya menya.*" She slammed an envelope down in front of him.

He peeked in the envelope and pocketed it. He closed his eyes again, opening them wide when Elda pressed the barrel of her P-96 against his forehead.

"I *said*, 'I am Elda. You have a truck for me.'"

"*Da. Tam.*" He nodded in that direction and handed her the keys.

Elda motioned for Charlie to join her. In the cab there lay three duffels. Elda took out two and tossed the keys to Charlie. "It's all yours, Grasshopper. There should be explosives, grenades, flash bangs, guns, and ammo in your kit. There's some duplication with the first set of gear from the garage, but I needed to ensure we had something, in case we were double-crossed. Disguises and IDs are in the bag from stash number one. I recommend you check it before we leave here."

She darted to Murka and tossed a bag into the passenger seat, with the directive, "Ensure you have everything you need."

Murka rummaged inside the duffel. "This will do nicely."

"Good. You'll lead out, so you'll be on the other side of the garbage truck when Charlie flips it. That will give us an alternative escape route. We have a short time frame. I hope my wheels can make it in time. If I don't, you have the marching orders." Elda ran, jumped into her van, and started the engine. She pressed a transmitter in her ear. "Comms check."

One click, two clicks. Good. The comms worked. "Only talk if there's an emergency need. Otherwise, we use clicks. Let's roll."

Charlie headed east on M7, toward Lakinsk, Russia. She checked her watch and the GPS longitude and latitude every five minutes. She had to be at 56.03988° N, 40.04733° W, just west of Lakinsk, no later than 0800. It was now 0730. Charlie tightened the straps holding her to her seat and pressed the accelerator to its maximum.

At 0742, Charlie was there. She threw the truck into a sharp spin and pushed down hard on the lever that dropped a steel bar, assisting toppling the truck on its side.

Crash!

Charlie fell hard against her restraints, gravity pulling her toward the passenger side and ground. She wrestled to pull her body around to face upward and the open driver's-side window. She grabbed the sill with one hand and, after ensuring she could hold herself, unclipped the restraints. She muscled her body upward, reached out with her second hand, and pulled her upper body up and out the window.

The momentum moved her over the sill, and she tumbled down the side of the truck. *Thud.* She hit the ground, tucked and rolled, and lay there, wind knocked out of her.

That would hurt in the morning. She forced herself up. There was no time to lose. She reached into her pocket and withdrew a small bottle of blood. She smeared it on the side of her head and a hand, lay facedown, and poured the rest of it on the ground around her forehead. From a distance it all looked realistic.

Charlie reached into one of the deep leg pockets of her overalls, withdrew her loaded SR-1 Vektor pistol, and hid the hand holding it under her body. She lay waiting.

Elda looked at her watch: 0744. She verified her GPS coordinates. One more mile. She should be in position by 0755. The Russian spy satellite would fly over at 0830. They needed to be well down the road by then. The van with the prisoner should arrive at 0810, give or take a few minutes. Elda's team needed to be extremely efficient.

Elda pulled off the road and swept away her tire tracks. She threw a cameo cover over the van and ensured her P-96 pistol was loaded and she had spare magazines. She liked the feel of the ribbed grip in her hand and the ease of reaching the trigger through the larger trigger guard.

Elda ran up the road and flung herself down onto the ground in a shallow gully. From what she could see before she'd hid, Charlie had tipped the truck. She hoped Murka was also ready.

She wrapped herself in a dirt-and-grass printed camo tarp and waited.

"Olaf! What is that?"

Olaf, the driver of the prisoner transport van, squinted and shook his head. "What are you talking about, Ivan?"

Ivan slapped Olaf's arm. "You need glasses. You should not be driving with your vision problems."

"Shhh. Do not mention my eyesight issues. I need this job."

Ivan pointed ahead of them. "Look again. It's a large truck overturned on the highway. Slow down."

They slowed their speed. "Ah, I see it now. It's a garbage truck. They always drive those things too fast, and they are prone to tipping."

Ivan nudged Olaf. "Look. There's the driver on the side of the truck. He isn't moving and is injured. Stop and let me see if he's alive."

Olaf stopped the van. Ivan jumped out and ran toward the body, leaving his door open. Rapt at the scene unfolding in front of him, Olaf didn't notice anything else going on.

Elda scuttled up to the back of the van and affixed two small charges to the door hinges. She saw, out of the corner of her eye, Murka crawl under the van to slap a larger charge there. She waited until Murka was clear, and blew the door charges. She yanked the door open, grabbed the cuffed and bewildered prisoner, and dragged him with her at a run for her vehicle.

Once Elda was away, Murka exploded her bomb. At the same time, Charlie shot the guard who was leaning over her.

The police-van driver opened his door, flames licking at his running board. He fell out onto the ground, a large piece of shrapnel embedded in the back of his head. He took one last breath and lay still.

Murka helped Charlie drag the second guard back to the police van. They hefted him into the passenger side, then braved the flames to hurl the driver back into the driver's seat. They threw in two Molotov cocktail incendiaries to speed the destruction, and slammed the doors closed. They raced away to Murka's car.

A few minutes later, the B2, heading west toward Moscow, sped by the scene of the accident.

Charlie checked her watch. It was 0826. She nudged Murka. "Faster." The acceleration snapped Charlie's head back against her seat.

They flew by a gray van driving just under the speed limit, headed to Moscow.

Conrad had fallen asleep on Elda's shoulder. She spoke softly. "We're now on P158 South. Our professed destination, Nizhny Novgorod, is north on P158. If stopped, we claim we must have taken a wrong turn. We have two more stops. At the next stop in Saransk, we will switch into two vehicles."

"Can we get another Marussia?" Charlie pleaded.

Elda chuckled. "That was a great car, but I'm afraid, Charlie, you'll have to settle for a Lada Granta. It's small, cheap, but best of all, a common car."

"And then what, Master?"

Murka chortled. "I may like this *master* bit."

Elda glared at Murka's back. "Mind out of the gutter, Murka. It's not what you think. In answer to your question, Charlie, we will stop at a welding shop in Saratov Oblast and head into Kazakhstan."

"How do we get into Kazakhstan?" Charlie asked.

"Murka will drive the truck since she speaks Russian natively. We'll be hidden inside."

Murka frowned. "What type of truck am I driving?"

"An oil tanker."

"*Chert.* That's a big rig to drive."

"Can you handle it, Murka?"

"*Da.*"

Charlie scratched her head. "Damn, Elda. Where's there space to hide in a tanker?"

"Under the oil, of course."

"Damn."

Chapter Twenty

ELDA DREW HER GUN. SHE WOULD NOT BE double-crossed. She strode across the chop shop garage in Moscow. The B2 was already painted a dark blue. Elda's "loaf" van was being sprayed a military green. Conrad rubbed his wrists, where the handcuffs had cut in. Charlie wiped the blood off her head with a paper towel. Murka had run to the restroom.

Elda marched up to the garage owner and displayed a wad of cash. "No games this time. We have another car here."

"*Da.*" He pointed out a drab olive-colored Lada Niva Legend SUV. "Manual transmission. Four-wheel drive." He gave her the keys.

Elda reached inside and withdrew a new set of gear, only this time there was a fourth bag included. She handed the duffels out and said to Conrad, "I will help you with your disguise."

He stared open mouthed at her. "Who are you people?"

"It'll all become clear when you are sitting back home

in Cambridge, Massachusetts, with your wife and kids. Until then, we don't have time for small talk. Do as I say and we will get you out of here." Elda started applying his face makeup. "In that kit are new clothes. Put them on, and the guys here at the shop will burn your old ones. Oh wait . . ." She reached into his bag and pulled out a wig to cover his close-shaven skull.

Ten minutes later Charlie climbed behind the steering wheel, Murka hopped into the passenger seat, Conrad pulled himself up into the backseat behind her, and Elda positioned herself behind Charlie. "You all need to take a moment to look at your new identities." Elda wore a snazzy wide-brimmed brown hat and a dark-blue cloth coat. She had ringlets falling down over her forehead, and her hair was shoulder length. "The mister and I"—she smiled at Conrad—"my beloved Cheslav, are off on holidays with our most wonderful friends, Chary, who is driving, and his wife, Masha. We are going to Arzamas to see the beautiful cathedral and the paintings there. That will cover us until we pick up 158."

They drove onto M7 east to take the M12 south. About five miles away from Moscow, they heard sirens and pulled over to the side of the road to let the convoy pass. They watched as a combination of military GAZ Tigrs, emergency vehicles, and police and unmarked cars sped past them. A collective exhale sounded in the SUV.

"Uh-oh. It's showtime. Slow it down, Chary. Cheslav, let's hold hands."

They moved into the line behind two other cars going through the makeshift checkpoint.

"*Dokumenty, pozhaluysta.*"

They passed their passports to Charlie, who handed

them over. The officer in turn transferred them to another official, who scanned them into his computer.

Elda held her breath. She prayed their quickly applied disguises matched their photos and hoped Ashok had managed to enter them into Russia's database. Four minutes passed. Five. Six, . . .

The first officer marched back to the car with their papers in his hand. He gave them to Charlie. "You are all set. Enjoy your travels." He waved them on.

Charlie put the car in gear. Elda reminded her, "Remember, Chary, the backseat gets car sick, so please, no zero to sixty."

They drove into the garage, and the doors shut behind them. Elda loosened her jacket to ensure she had ready access to her P-96. She noted that Charlie and Murka had their weapons ready for any conflict.

The four travelers climbed out of the car, and a man jumped into the front seat and drove it out of an opened back door. Charlie moved to Conrad's right, with Elda standing on his left. Murka stood facing the other way.

A man in grease-stained coveralls sauntered up to them. "Your vehicles are out back. They are not fancy, but they will get you wherever you need to go. Follow me."

Elda nodded to the others to keep Conrad covered while she inspected the vehicles. She used her guide as a shield for one side while she scanned the area. They emerged from the garage into a large parking lot. He led her to two vehicles, a dirty white 2019 Geely Monjaro and a dark-blue beat-up 2016 GAZ-2705 panel van, and handed her the keys.

Seeing that Elda was still alive, the other three trotted over to join her. Murka and Charlie had their weapons drawn. The man in coveralls backed up with his hands in the air.

"It's okay. Stand down. You two have new identities as electrical workers. The papers and outfits are in your van, as well as signs to slap on the sides. We'll meet you at the welding shop in Saratov Oblast. Look for the Perm refinery tanker truck."

Elda shook the man's hand, slipping him some extra cash for the discomfort they may have caused him.

Elda and Conrad drove into the yard at the Weinmar's Welders welding shop in Saratov Oblast and parked next to the GAZ-2705 panel van. A large man worked in the back of the shop, with a welder's helmet on. Sparks flew as he applied his torch. The acrid smell of burning metal filled the air.

Charlie and Murka slid out and removed their gear. Elda cleared the contents of the Geely. Two men came out of the office. Elda moved her hand, ensuring she could reach their weapons. She saw Charlie doing the same. Good.

The men held out their hands. "*Klyuchi pozhaluysta.*"

Elda took Charlie's keys from her and dropped both sets into one of the hands.

The men jumped in, gunned the engines, and left with the two vehicles.

"That makes me feel a tad insecure," Charlie muttered.

"Don't worry, Grasshopper—the best is yet to come." Elda marched to Murka. "Are you confident that my instructions have been carried out without error?"

"The owner of this shop is a cousin. And he has been paid well."

"That helps." Elda strode inside the garage, where a Perm Oil tanker loomed outside the back door.

The large man came jogging across the room and hugged Murka. "It has been far too long, cousin!"

"Everyone, this is my favorite cousin, Matvey. Matvey,

show us the wonderful things you have done here."

Matvey led them out the back door and held out both hands. "You see before you an empty tanker, which we will fill up. After we come back, the three of you will climb in, thusly." He invited each of them to lie on a wheeled pallet, and they all slid under the truck. He opened the round hatch underneath. Inside was a panel of knobs and switches. He removed the false panel and revealed the opening into the tanker.

Matvey slid to one side and let Elda look inside. Welded in the inside of the tanker was a second container that would fit three to four people. She counted four oxygen tanks and masks attached to the walls. "I threw in an extra O2, for good measure."

"May I have a flashlight?" Elda requested.

Matvey handed her a flashlight and a headlamp. Elda climbed inside. She inspected the welds and tapped the metal on the container. She read the meters on the oxygen tanks to ensure they were full and tested the airflow on each one. She dropped back out of the hatch.

"Good job, Matvey."

He beamed. "We are the best welders around. I pride myself in my work and my team's work."

Elda winked at Murka. "I like your cousin."

Each person in the group took a look at their home for the next six and a half hours. After their inspection, they stood, not speaking, next to the tanker.

Elda stood feeling her heart beating in her chest after her viewing of their space. Visions of oil pouring over her head flooded her, and she could almost taste the thick fluid as it flew into her mouth and nose, cutting off any air. She gasped. Inhaling the pungent smell of the fossil fuel, she wanted to throw up. She shook herself out of her thoughts. "Go fill her up, guys. We'll get changed. Murka speaks native Russian, so she'll drive. No smoking, Murka."

Murka turned onto A298 SE. She wasn't a religious woman, but she was praying she and the tanker would pass inspection at the border. She also prayed the weight of their cargo would not crush the small container and that all the welds would hold. She didn't know which would be worse—dying by inhaling oil or being crushed to death. Neither way appealed. She was glad she was driving.

A hiss of air swooshed as Murka, approaching the border, applied the brakes. She would need to pass the Russian inspection and then the Kazakhstan guards.

A Russian border patrolman strolled up to her window, an unlit cigarette hanging from his mouth. Murka prayed he wouldn't light it. She held out her passport, the export papers, and most importantly, an envelope with cash.

He glanced at the papers and passport and returned them. "So Kazakhstan is getting our oil again?"

"We give them the dregs and keep the best for ourself. And they pay well for what we deliver to them."

He chuckled at the deception and waved her on to the next checkpoint.

"So what was the joke?" the Kazakhstan border guard inquired.

"I told him he was too handsome a man to be working the border. He should be in the movies."

The guard laughed. "Good one. I must check your oil level."

Murka climbed out and pointed to the ladder on the side of the truck. "You know where it is?"

"I've done this once or twice." He climbed the external ladder and unscrewed the cap, pulling out the attached dipstick. It dripped with a yellowish-brown liquid. "Nice, clean crude this time. They often bring in the bottom of the barrels." He screwed the cover back on and climbed down.

"Kazakhstan pays Perm well for the imports. There's no need to cheat." She held out her hand with the trifecta.

He handed back her papers and passport. "Have a good day. You're cleared to go."

Murka drove down A29 S, hoping the air was holding. She motored into the Tir Parking Dal'noboy truck stop in Uralsk Opan. She secured the parking brake and turned off the truck. Climbing out of the cab, she squared her shoulders, preparing for whatever she found inside. She crawled under the truck, unlocked the hatch, and removed the false panel.

"Man, I have to pee!" Charlie dropped out of the container and slithered out under the truck and ran for the restroom. Conrad fell out next. Murka helped him out from under the truck. Elda's feet dropped down, followed by the rest of her. She rolled out from under the truck, stood, and rubbed her face, which had grooves in it from the tight air mask.

She squinted and blinked against the light. "Wow. That's bright."

Murka offered sunglasses and a bottle of water. Elda slipped on the sunglasses and chugged the water.

Murka pointed across the street. "Our next vehicles are there."

"Another cousin?"

"Brother-in-law."

Murka strode over the dirt parking lot and into the garage. The smell of oil and transmission fluid wafted over her. The concrete floor was spattered with remnants of engine liquids and coffee stains. "Is Ali here?" she called out.

A tall man in greasy overalls ran over. "Murka! Is that you? It's been *far* too long! I have a vehicle that may suit your purpose. It's a canvas-sided farm truck that has had the backseat modified to carry more than farm implements, if you know what I mean? What trouble are you in now? Do you have time to come to the house and see your sister? I didn't tell her you were coming, in case you can't. You know how angry she can get, and she'll take it out on me. Have you eaten?"

Murka stood there laughing. "Ali, you should be my Jewish grandmother instead of my *shurin*. Elda, this is my brother-in-law, Ali. Ali, this is Elda. We'll let her look over the vehicle while we catch up. But no, we don't have time to visit. I am so sorry."

Elda had been standing next to Murka, looking around. She held out her hand with an envelope in it. "Hello. Ali. Thank you for your help."

"*Elda*. I am pleased to meet you." Ali took the envelope and shook her hand vigorously. "I will send out for some food. How many of you are there?" He accompanied Elda and Murka to the back of the garage, where a technician in filthy, torn, jeans was working on a farm truck.

Charlie walked through the garage doors, leading a squinting Conrad.

"There are four of us." Elda shifted her weight to her other foot. She looked around and spotted a door. "Is that a *tualet*?"

"Oh . . . by all means."

A few minutes later, Elda started up the old farm truck. The engine purred. At least this vehicle had been well maintained. Kudos to that technician.

Elda was dressed in baggy, dirt-stained, farmhand clothes, consisting of a brown shirt, brown trousers, brown socks, and brown dirt-encrusted leather boots. A brown cap topped the outfit. The others were dressed similarly.

The backseat had been raised about eight inches, and the hump, normally in the center of the back floor, was missing. The truck's axle had been lowered and the leaf springs reconfigured. Conrad lay across the backseat floor, covered by manure-smelling burlap bags, farm implements, and a toolbox. Charlie and Murka rested their feet on him.

Elda swiveled in her seat to examine her farmhands. They would pass. "Are we ready, everyone?"

"*Da.*"

"Yes."

"Mrrph."

"I'll take that last one as a yes." Elda pulled out onto the road. They were met by a bone-jarring pothole. She hoped the next road was smoother. The engine might run well, but either the shocks weren't in the best condition, or lowering the axle had affected the ride.

Elda turned onto A28 S. That was better. She didn't need to be distracted by truck issues. They were on the last leg of their mission. She needed to be prepared for anything. The only thing that could sabotage them now would be a betrayal. Elda knew she could trust Charlie with her life. Murka was still an unknown.

"Murka?"

"Yes?"

Elda scowled. She couldn't very well ask Murka if she was trustworthy. "Can we trust your brother-in-law?"

"Yes. For two reasons."

Elda lifted a hand off the wheel and gestured for Murka to continue. "And they are?"

"I paid him a year's worth of his salary for all this."

That earned a thumbs-up from Elda. "And the second reason?"

"He has to live with listening to my sister for the rest of his life if he fucks me over, and he knows that."

Elda chuckled. She'd trust her gut instinct that had led her to bring Murka onto the team. "Excellent. No need to stop and change disguises and vehicles again. Next stop,

Atyrau. And the airport."

The truck responded with a clunk and a puff of smoke.

"I thought you said this thing was well maintained, Elda."

"I thought it was, Charlie. Pray we make it to Atyau."

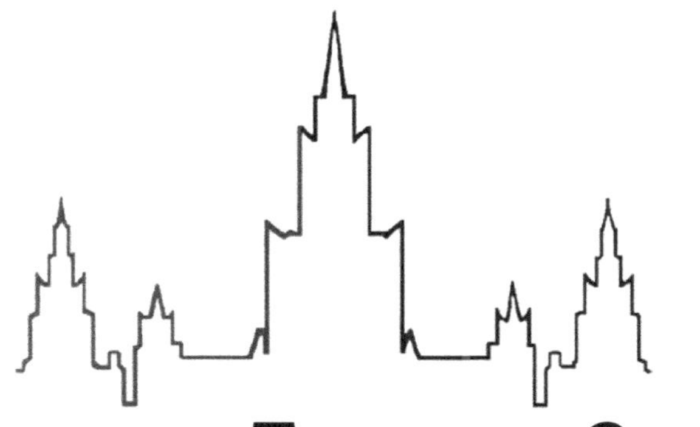

CHAPTER TWENTY-ONE

MY NEMESIS—PAPERWORK. ELDA SAT IN HER office, writing up a paper report on their last mission. She had her air purifier on to clean out the remaining odor of fresh paint, and the hum threatened to put her to sleep. She shook her fist at her desk.

A timid knock sounded on her half-opened door. She looked up and spied Ashok standing there, shifting from one foot to the other and wringing his hands. She had never seen him so nervous. Welcoming the interruption, she beckoned him in.

"Miss Elda, ma'am?"

"Yes, Ashok?"

"May I please take two weeks off?"

That couldn't be why he was so nervous. "When do you need it?"

"As soon as I'm able."

"You deserve it. Are you going somewhere?"

Ashok inhaled and rattled off, "I am going back home to India to get married. I would be most gratified if you would attend the ceremony." He stood there out of breath.

Elda's widened her eyes. "What?! I didn't know you had a girlfriend."

Ashok nodded, then shook his head. "I didn't, Miss Elda."

Elda held her hands out, palms up. "So what changed?"

"Well, you see, Miss Elda, when we talked about needing more staff, I reached out to Preyanka. She and I went to school together. She is most amazingly wonderful at computers. She has her masters in mechanical engineering now and wishes to keep working. Her parents, however, wish that she would marry and are setting up a most terrible arranged marriage. She does not like this man at all, and he would not let her keep working. After we talked, we agreed I would ask for her hand in marriage. She and I are both Hindu, which is a plus for the parents. So we will marry, and she will come to America with me and work here." Ashok stood, arms at his sides, smiling broadly.

"Work where?" Elda was still catching up with the conversation.

Ashok gestured around the room. "Here with us, Miss Elda. You will find that her work will delight you. She is most amazing. And she is small. We could fit her desk almost anywhere."

Elda held her hand to her forehead and forced herself to close her gaping mouth. "When is all this happening, Ashok?"

Ashok shrugged. "I would like for it to happen as soon as possible, before her parents change their minds. Perhaps next month."

Elda blew out a breath. "Whew." She stood. "Let's go get Korinna. We need to get Preyanka a work visa."

"Oh, and Miss Elda?"

She was afraid to ask what was next. In therapy, the client would always handle the smallest issue first. By the time they were leaving and had their hand on the door-knob, something huge would be disclosed. And then they'd walk out. "Yes, Ashok . . ."

He smiled and bounced on his toes. "Can she bring her brother over? He is also most amazing with his talents. It would complete my group."

Elda shook her head, and Ashok looked dismayed. "No, no, Ashok. I mean yes. I'm just thinking on how to pull all this off. Let's go see Korinna and our budget."

Tosh looked at his ringing phone. *Chert.* Boris. Tosh had hoped he'd be rid of that man for a while.

"*Prevet*, Boris."

"Did you hear they lost a prisoner on the way to IK-6 Melekhovo from Lefortovo Prison?" Boris's voice was flat, giving no hint of how he might feel about that fact.

Tosh was deliberately cautious. "*Interesnyy.* How did that happen?" Why was Boris sharing this? Did he suspect Tosh in some way? Tosh pumped up his blood pressure cuff.

"The job was professional and well coordinated. There are no prints at the scene, and they pulled it off between satellite passes, so whomever did it had access to high-level files."

Was that a trace of admiration in Boris's voice? From his description, it was a well-done extraction. Who could have done it, and what were their motives? Tosh looked at the BP meter. His pressure was within range. He removed the cuff. "What do they know?" For someone who had initiated the conversation, Boris wasn't forthcoming.

"Nothing. They appeared out of nowhere and vanished. We are assuming there was more than one person involved, and therefore they would have needed a car to get away. All we have are the bullets we retrieved from the charred bodies. They all come from Russian weapons."

That was a good amount of information. Much better. The perpetrators were not afraid to kill. They were armed and dangerous. "Charred?" Tosh probed for clarification.

"*Da*. They used a garbage truck to block the highway. They torched the transport van. We're assuming they burned it after they killed the escorts and took the prisoner. The guards' bodies were inside the van. But there are marks from one of the guard's shoes that suggest he was dragged to the van and thrown in. The positioning of the bodies would support that theory."

Tosh still didn't understand why Boris was telling him this story. "Idiots. Why on earth did they leave the van unattended?"

"Exactly. Not a smart move. All of this has the fingerprints of a Russian mob hit. But I can't think of why *they'd* be interested."

That was it. Boris was hoping that Tosh would solve this mystery for him. Tosh stared up at his ceiling and frowned. He was missing something. "Who was the prisoner?"

"Conrad Ferguson. He was an American journalist working with the Human Rights Foundation to expose corruption in Russia. So of course we arrested him as a spy."

Tosh looked out his window at a parking lot. He liked his view from the Kremlin better, but not the price tag it came with. He brought his focus back to the tale. He figured that the mob would only be interested if a lot of money was involved. "Would anyone pay to free him?"

Boris dismissed that possibility. "*Net*. He was small potatoes. *Melkiy kartofel'*."

Perhaps Boris's runaway assassins were in on this? That could be another reason Boris was interested in it. Tosh decided not to mention that to Boris but instead would probe to see why Boris cared. "The attack could have been politically motivated. Are you going to look into it?"

"*Net*. There's too little to go on. And from what we know about this type of vigilante reporter, he will show up again. *Then* we'll kill him. I thought it was an interesting incident that you might like to hear about and keep your ears and eyes open, in case you run across any clues in your travels."

That did sound as if Boris suspected his lost agents. "*Spasibo, ser*. I will keep it in mind if I pick up on anything that might shed light on it. You will be the first to know."

"*Spasibo*."

Tosh hung up. That was it. Boris wanted his ass covered. As usual. Tosh drummed his fingers on his desk. Professional. No collateral damage. Not done for money. That didn't equal the MOs of Boris's folks. An American journalist. Might it have been Elda and her team? But why would she have an interest in this journalist? Not her MO. He had promised to help her with her senator problem. Perhaps he could find out from her then. If *she* did it, he wouldn't rat on her to Boris. But Boris would kill Tosh if he found out Tosh had hidden information from him.

"This one's for freedom of press!" Elda passed out glasses of Veuve Clicquot champagne to her team members, who had gathered in their conference room. "Congratulations, gang, on the successful completion of our first op as a team. Well done, everyone."

The group sat around the oval table that could seat fourteen. The LED lights shone off the well-polished wooden tabletop. Korinna took her napkin and removed a handprint from the spot in front of her. "This is a solid walnut table, with no harmful chemicals. Your chairs are covered in organic cotton. The overhead lights are full-spectrum LED to mimic natural sunlight. The all-natural linoleum flooring is antibacterial and has limited seams, to cut down on places dirt and dust can hide. Let's have some respect for the healthy environment I've worked hard to create."

Elda patted her on the back. "You've done a great job setting up this office, Korinna. I think it's had a positive impact on my asthma."

"Yes, Miss Korinna," Ashok added. "Thank you so very much. I also feel as if I have much, much better energy than I did working under fluorescent lights. And I can see my screen with better clarity."

The cloth-backed roller chairs were unevenly spaced throughout the room. They slid well on the linoleum floor. Elda envisioned chair races in their future.

She set her glass down and sighed. "Freeing one journalist is like throwing a stone onto a rocky coast and expecting sand."

"Is that a New England saying?" Korinna took a large sip of her champagne.

Elda snorted. "No, I made it up, but I thought it fit." Her smile did not reach her eyes.

"There's more there. What are you thinking, Elda?" Korinna rested her champagne glass next to Elda's.

Murka refilled them.

Elda nodded a thanks to Murka and shrugged her answer to Korinna. "I think we're in for a rocky future and need to get together with like-minded individuals and protect America's infrastructure, freedoms, and intelligence."

Charlie grimaced. "That's a tall order."

Elda's mind raced. "Maybe not so tall, if we can chat with a few people I know. I'm thinking a collection of servers, offline, holding the secrets of the government that we don't want to fall into Russian hands. If the election goes the wrong way, we purge sensitive information from the federal servers, protecting our assets in the field and our military secrets. Those who are in line with us will most likely resign anyway. We can build a secret agency, unknown to the president or Congress. We can use this new group to protect those who are targeted for elimination or imprisonment. There are some black sites, known only to a few, that we should be able to hide from the new administration. And with the right financial folks and computer hackers, we can siphon enough money for our endeavors from the government, before it gets stripped to nothing." She drank, emptying her glass.

Charlie held up her hands in surrender. "Man, Elda. When you get going, you get going! Is this even possible?"

"We won't know until we start. I'm going to make some phone calls and visit some friends. Keep the home fires burning."

Chapter Twenty-Two

ELDA—IN DISGUISE WITH A SHOULDER-LENGTH brown wig, dark-green contacts, thick-rimmed round glasses, shoes with heel lifts, and a pockmarked face—climbed up the stairs to the Learjet, parked at the Schiphol Airport in Amsterdam. Once inside she was patted down for weapons and scanned for a wire.

"She's clean, Boss."

Elda advanced to the jet's owner and sat across from him. A balding, fit man, perhaps in his fifties, dressed in black slacks and a white shirt.

Elda took a deep breath. She hated asking for money, but without the US government's backing, she would need to find enough funds to support her initiatives. She also wanted to ensure those moneys would come without strings attached. "Thank you for meeting with me."

He leaned forward. "There can be no record of this conversation. We will have no contract. If asked, I will disavow ever meeting you."

Elda nodded. Obviously this man was used to having

the upper hand. It made sense. He was a successful businessman who owned a number of companies. He had the background and resources to help her achieve her objectives. From her research, he was bored and had money to waste. It was time to show him he didn't control her and to tweak his interest in investing in her, instead of buying a sports team. "Fair enough. I was never here. However, *you* are the one who sent out feelers, looking for a way to fight the gaslighting, misinformation, and disinformation and lead our country back to a democracy. For your safety, I have taken the liberty of erasing any trace of those messages. You should be more cautious in the future. If we go forward, I can arrange more secure ways to communicate."

The man sat tapping his electronic pen on the armrest. His eyes never left Elda.

Elda handed him a thumb drive. "The data on this drive will self-destruct in three hours. It cannot be copied. Any attempt to screen shot the pages will result in a blank page."

He crossed his arms. "And what do you want from me?"

Elda squared her shoulders. His asking was a good sign. Her pitch must be clear and succinct. "My ideas are outlined with a proposal for a business to execute them. You will form a small nonprofit, which will receive news blasts from various sources. It can be a small operation with a wide reach. We both know it won't drain your finances. You have enough money that this company will be a rounding error on your books."

He nodded and waited for Elda to finish.

"I have listed the names of the people you need to hire. Feel free to write them down. This company will be the true source of information, using the same tactics that have been used by others spreading the lies, only in reverse. You use enough of the propaganda to allow the believers to feel that they are towing the party line. Then you let them dig for the truth under the lies."

He took the drive from Elda, plugged it into his computer, and scanned the files. He nodded. "I can see some flaws in this, but nothing that I can't correct. We can hide our connection to your organization."

Elda stood. "Excellent. When should I check back with you?"

He rose and squeezed her hand. "Give me a quarter."

"Okay. See you in three months. By the way, my father taught me that a handshake was as good as a contract."

He offered his first smile. "I also believe that. Do you have a name and a contact?"

Elda shook her head. "Don't worry. I'll find you. Thank you."

Later that afternoon, Elda sat sipping a beer at the bar of the Mövenpick Hotel Amsterdam City Centre, Piet Heinkade 11. She may have just acquired funding and resources for helping reset the brainwashing flooding into the United States, but she also must expand into cybersecurity and electronic spying.

A man strode up to her and pointed to the seat next to her. "Is this seat taken?"

She glanced at him and at the chair. "I was about to take a walk."

He looked outside at the rain coming down in sheets. "It is a lovely day for one. May I join you?"

"I'd much rather bike ride."

"May I have a blue one?"

"Only on Tuesdays."

"Well then, I guess it's roller skates for us."

Elda stood and strode out the bar. She waited for him at the door, and they marched side by side.

Elda snorted as the rain pelted her head and poured down her face. "Too bad it's *not* a lovely day for a walk."

He tipped his fedora to let the rain run down his raincoat. "You never know what the weather will be when the password exchange is made up."

Elda silently cursed as she stepped into a large puddle, feeling the water seep into her socks. She wiped her eyes with her hand and looked at the man beside her. "So you're the money guy?"

His foot splashed down into a puddle and he groaned. "Yes. You have a concept for a software and hardware security firm?"

"I do." Elda passed the man a thumb drive. "I have developers, prototypes, and I'm hiring a CEO to run it and complete the staffing."

"What will you do?"

Elda wiggled her finger at him. "That's best for you not to know. However, I've heard that you have an interest in turning some things in the world more positive. That side of the business will be invisible but will require money and staffing. The development company will cover it. For the dark side, you won't get an accounting of where the money went or who works there."

He took off his hat, tipped it to drain the water off it, and replaced it on his head. "That sounds like a risk for me."

"Not really. Nothing can be traced back to you. You'll have to decide whether you can trust me or not."

He stopped and stared at her. "How will I figure *that* out?"

Elda gave him a folder, wrapped in plastic. "When you're somewhere dry, read the news articles in this folder. If you approve, call the enclosed number. If you don't, we part ways now. By the way, the contents of the drive I gave you cannot be copied and will delete themselves in two days. Decide quickly."

"And you are?"

"It's best you don't know."

Elda strode away in the heavy rain.

The early morning sun flickered in through the storefront windows, displaying the dots of dust stirred up by the humans within.

Elda sat, drinking tea, on a pile of rugs in a store in Goa. She inhaled the clean smell of woven wool. "It's good to see you again, Vharvik. How is your tribe?"

"Ah yes, I remember so well our conversation about our tribes. That was many years ago. And here you are back again. It is *good*." Vharvik, the store owner, poured more tea into Elda's cup before continuing. "My tribe has grown. It reaches far and wide now. Very good for business."

Elda stroked the rug at the top of the pile she was sitting on. "I'm sure you have no problems obtaining your inventory."

"Yes, and we have managed to branch out. My brother, Prajay, has opened a store in town. He sells tea and many other assorted items. You must visit him. In fact, have dinner with us tonight. Our distributor, Kushal Gupta, is in town. His reach is in every major tea-drinking country. I'm sure we can discuss how, as fellow tribesmen, we can help each other out."

"I don't have to fly out until tomorrow, so I would be honored to join you."

"Most wonderful."

Elda hopped down and placed her teacup on the tray. She sorted through the pile of rugs, examining the patterns and weaving.

He came and stood next to her. "This pile is all hand made. The one you have looked at twice has wool and silk in it and very fine weaving. I can give you a deep discount on it."

Elda turned her mouth down and shook her head in

regret. "I couldn't afford it. This rug is beautifully made. It must be expensive."

He pulled the rug out and laid it on top. "It is. But you are the first visitor the shop has had today. Therefore, a sale to you would be my lucky sale. And you are tribe too. So I can give you . . . what do you Americans call that discount?"

Elda chuckled. "Friends and family?"

"Yes. Very much so. A wonderful discount." He wrote down a number and passed it to Elda.

Elda took a pen out, crossed his number out, wrote down a new one, and handed the paper back.

His eyes grew large. "You have learned much since your last visit here."

They parried, the paper filling with counteroffers.

Vharvik laughed and agreed on Elda's final bid. "I will have it shipped to you." He rolled the rug up and tied it with twine.

Elda wrote down a UPS store address. "They will keep it for me until I get back to my office."

"Most excellent."

Elda paced to the door, and turned. "Until tonight."

That evening, Elda strolled to the Adlem Goi restaurant, playing tourist and glancing around for anyone who might be following her. She was uncomfortable without a disguise, but her visit here was to rekindle old connections and those connections had previously seen her without a disguise. The chances of an American assassin searching for her here were extremely slim. But unless any probability was at zero, it could still happen. Elda could not afford to relax.

Vharvik had told her to look for the statue of a man rowing a flat-bottom boat outside the restaurant. Sure enough . . . She scanned the dark street for familiar faces. All clear. She ducked into the restaurant.

She was to find Vharvik at a table under the mural

of the Mangueshi Temple. Elda was on edge. The room was cluttered with many interesting artifacts—a vintage scooter and two motorcycles tucked under the stairs, a collection of old typewriters, clay pots lined up on edges of stairs, a small wooden bar at the end of the room. It was the perfect place for an ambush.

Vharvik stood up and waved. She rushed forward. Part of her mind took in how well the mural was rendered. It also helped break up the monotony and oppressiveness of the mustard-yellow walls. A man darted out from under the stairs and nearly bowled her over. "So, so sorry, ma'am." He put a hand on her arm and stared into her face before dashing off. Elda willed her overtired and overactive nerves to calm.

Vharvik pointed to the man standing on the other side of the table for four. "This is my American friend Elda. Elda, this is Mr. Kushal Gupta." He pulled out a chair for Elda.

Elda judged Kushal Gupta as a handsome man in his late forties or early fifties. His eyes spoke of having seen many things. He was fit and exuded confidence. Elda sensed he did more than just export tea. She wondered if his import-export business included moving weapons across borders. That could be useful.

He held out his hand. "Call me Kushal."

Elda shook it. "I am pleased to meet you, Kushal. Are you from this area?"

Kushal shook his head, "No, I am from Calcutta."

"I've been there." And Kushal's accent matched that region. So far he was being truthful.

Vharvik cocked his head. "You have been many places, Elda."

Elda hefted the thick menu. "Yes, I have." She pointed to the fourth chair. "Are we expecting anyone else?"

Vharvik hung his head. Kushal spoke. "Yes. It was

unfortunate that he was unable to join us."

Elda glanced at each of them. From Vharvik's obvious shame and Kushal's vague answer, she guessed that their invitee would not dine with a woman. "Aha. All for the best. What's good to eat here?"

Crash. Elda instinctively reached for the weapon she didn't have. She looked over, and Kushal was staring at her.

"The kitchen staff can be clumsy here." Kushal waved the waiter over. "I confess I took the liberty of ordering for us. I hope you don't mind. You do get to select your drink, however." He gave a boyish grin.

Elda set down her menu. She liked Kushal. He reminded her somehow of Ashok. She kicked herself for stereotyping. "I don't mind at all, Kushal. What are we having?"

"Spicy fish curry with coconut milk, chicken vindaloo, steamed rice, naan, and for dessert, *dodol*, which is like a coconut pudding."

Elda looked skyward and held up her palms in praise. "That sounds delicious."

Elda startled as the waiter materialized by their table. "Perhaps you would like a coconut *feni* with orange juice?" he suggested.

Elda declined. "That's an acquired taste. I'll take the King's beer instead." It would not do for her to get drunk. She suspected Kashal had an inkling that Elda was more than just an innocent starting a company. She wanted to get to know him more before jumping into a business proposition.

Kushal deposited his menu over Elda's. "A most excellent selection. May we please have three King's beers."

The waiter collected the menus and left for the kitchen.

Kashal turned to Elda. "Elda, what do you do for work?"

And there it was. Elda wished she had the beer to sip to give her more time to think of her answers. "I'm in the middle of establishing a new company and the accompanying logistics."

Vharvik leaned forward. "So will you need to move things around?"

Elda nodded. "There is a strong possibility. The company is a combination of various organizations with different missions. We are looking for external partners."

Kushal tapped his fingers on his mouth. "Interesting. It sounds a bit covert."

Ah yes. Smart man. Elda grinned. "Aren't the best ideas ones with a touch of mystery surrounding them? And you, Kushal? What do you import and export, aside from tea?"

He winked at Elda. "That would be a conversation to be had in a more secure place. Let me just say for now, I handle a wide range of items for a diverse population of customers."

A hand reached in front of Elda. She stiffened, glad she didn't have a fork or knife. She might have stabbed the poor waiter. The waiter placed a plate with a napkin in Elda's place. Another reached into the center of the table and set down the main course with the sides. One waiter held the dish of rice and a serving spoon. Elda nodded at her plate. He added the rice to it. Next came the waiter with the spicy fish. Again, Elda nodded and was rewarded with a serving. She reached out with her right hand and selected a naan. Using the fingers of her right hand, she tore off a chunk of naan and collected some rice and chicken vindaloo from her plate.

Her eyes watered as she chewed. This was the real deal. She took a sip of beer to cool her digestive track.

Kushal's eyes brightened. "Good?"

Elda blinked back her tears. "Superb. We don't get food this authentic in the States."

Kushal was quick to follow up. "Will your companies be based in the United States?"

"Initially yes, but we hope to be worldwide in reach." *Careful, Elda. This man is sharp. I wonder what he really does.* Elda took another bite of food.

Kushal leaned in. "I would like to know more about this. How can I reach you?"

"You can't. I will contact you."

Kushal passed his business card to Elda. "Until then . . ."

Elda raised her beer. "We've never had this conversation."

Chapter Twenty-Three

TEN DAYS LATER ELDA BOUNDED INTO HER office and threw her pack into a corner. She buzzed the intercom. "Let's get everyone in the conference room."

The team assembled and had barely settled in, when Elda started. "I had a lot of thinking time when I was traveling. I realized that we're growing our organization, and until now we've been a close-knit, hand-sourced group. But as we bring more people on board, there'll be more room for errors and misunderstandings. In the Cold War we had a spy's code of ethics and Moscow Rules to go by. In today's world everything has shades of gray. Guardrails are missing. Ethics is an archaic concept followed by few."

Korinna brightened. "So we need a mission statement? To determine our North Star?"

Elda sliced the air with her forefinger. "Yes, exactly! As well as a code of ethics. We need to define our values and operating principles. As agents, we often find ourselves in unclear situations in which we have to act immediately.

How will we decide as independent operators? How do we work together?"

Elda paused and snagged a cup of coffee from the omnipresent urn on the side table. Some wag had labeled the urn CHARLIE'S COFFEE CUP. Elda chuckled.

Murka leaned forward. "I wanted to join this team because I felt Elda was ethical, had a solid sense of what was right and wrong, and we would be empowered to correct the wrongs."

All murmured agreement.

Elda whirled to Murka and emphasized with her coffee-cup hand. "Yes!" Liquid sloshed onto the floor. She bent and wiped up the spill with her napkin. "My point exactly. What is right and what is wrong? What does correcting the wrongs look like? What are ethics? Where are our boundaries? How will we know when we overstep them?"

Charlie held her head. "This is a bigger problem than I imagined."

Elda set her cup of black coffee in front of her. "Don't worry, Charlie. I think we can add caffeine to one of the things we value."

Elda handed out a typed sheet and projected an expanded list from her laptop onto the blank wall. "Look at the Cold War Espionage Act. The originators designed it to crack down on activities considered dangerous or disloyal to the United States of America. It further classifies those activities."

She scrolled. "The CIA has a code of ethics, although I think they have often violated them. But look at this one: respecting others and the diversity of professional opinions. Isn't that nice! So what are ethics?"

The group volunteered answers, and she scribbled them on the whiteboard, adding her own as she went:

- HONESTY
- INTEGRITY
- TRUSTWORTHINESS
- LOYALTY
- FAIRNESS
- EMPATHY
- RESPECT
- COMPLIANCE TO THE LAW
- PURSUIT OF EXCELLENCE
- LEADERSHIP
- DON'T SHOOT SOMEONE IN THE BACK
- BE GENTLE WITH ANIMALS, CHILDREN, AND THE ELDERLY
- REPORT MISCONDUCT
- TEAMWORK
- SPEAK UP, CONTRIBUTE

The group wound down. Elda considered the list. "Fantastic! Many of these are also in the US Navy Code of Ethics. Some date back to the cowboy code of ethics."

"Compliance to the law could be a tough one. As a black-ops unit, we often break laws," Charlie noted.

Elda nodded. "Yes. We'll have to refine these as we go. We also will need to develop operating rules. These will help us in our decision-making when operating alone and needing to make a decision quickly. This list is of the often-cited Moscow Rules. Keep the handouts and think about what *we* need."

Moscow Rules

Assume nothing.

Never go against your gut.

Everyone is potentially under opposition control. Trust no one.

Do not look back. You are never completely alone.

Go with the flow. Blend in. Keep moving.

Vary your pattern and stay in your corner.

Lull them into a sense of complacency.

Pick the time and place of action.

Keep your options open.

"Enough work on this for now. We'll also need to come up with an operating budget and an org chart. I'll do some strawman work, but I'll be talking to each one of you about equipment and personnel needs. Ugh. I hate bureaucratic organizations, more so when they are my own. Let's take a break and catch up on ops and staffing."

They scattered to their respective offices.

Feeling her jet lag, Elda slid down in her chair, when the smell of fresh coffee wafted into the conference room with Charlie. "So what happened while I was gone?" Charlie was returning from the break room, with a fresh-brewed cup of coffee and a new pot for the assemblage.

Elda took the coffee pot and refilled the urn. She breathed in the aroma, hoping that the scent would help perk her up. Her limbs felt heavy. She poured herself a large cup and added sugar. She opened a small can of Coca-Cola and downed that before she sipped her coffee. She looked at Charlie for the answer.

Charlie frowned. "Despite all Ashok's efforts, the disinformation and misinformation have ramped up."

Elda waved a hand in dismissal. "Forget it. We won't be able to stop that without a lot more help. That'll be coming in the future. I've been chatting with a well-heeled acquaintance who, if all goes well, will fund and supply a division to create a new source of news. This site will be under the guise of *the only legitimate place* to get the *real* scoop. They'll relay the crap that is being broadcasted and sneak in the real news in a way that the readers will think they have discovered a hidden message. The junk they are fed and currently believe in will pull the readers in. Over time these folks will be reset and reprogrammed through exposure to the facts. It's the exact reverse of how they were turned to believe that reality is fake news. Many a dictator has used this method to turn the populus. Feed them half-truths with tidbits of real news in it, so as they dig, they find more things that imply what they are reading is truth and not the gaslighting lies it really is. Now as they dig down into the tidbits buried in their world of false truth, they will discover more and more about the real new—thus shaking their beliefs. It will take a while to build and roll out into the mainstream, but this guy knows how to do that."

"Wow. Score!" Charlie pumped her fist and scratched her head. "What does that leave for us to do?"

"Don't worry, Grasshopper. There's plenty to do. We'll need money. Lots of it. I envision us cobbling together many different efforts into one. I always loved the Japanese Kanji symbol for cooperation." She drew a big *T* on the board with a small *h* stacked on top of two other *h* letters. "Many (the T) powers (the h letters) equal a big power. Perhaps we can adopt it as our symbol."

Elda waved down Ashok, who was in search of a break room snack.

"Ashok, if I give you a list of criminal portfolios, can you find a way to siphon a dollar here and a dollar there?"

Ashok frowned. "I would need a financial analyst, Miss

Elda, but I would think it isn't that hard. If the sums are large enough, and there are enough pockets to pick, we could siphon off a reasonable amount of money. However, you do remember, ma'am, that the real estate funds are sitting without an owner?"

"Good point, Ashok. I'll consider those funds. Tapping them may be more legal than stealing from the thieves. We'll have to see where all this lands on our ethics scale. Korinna, can you snag us a loyal financial analyst? We may need more cover businesses too. Software development may not be enough for all our activities. Import-export, real estate, financial management . . . Something that doesn't need to report a lot or show a product."

"Geesh. Is that all?"

Elda frowned, looked up and back at Korinna. "No. I think we may need a second office in another country, in case it gets too hot here for us. Something with an underground bunker and a fail-safe backup office."

"Geesh." Korinna hit her head with the palm of her hand.

Charlie spit out her coffee, laughing.

"And I think you'll need to hire some full-time staff so you can get back to working part time," Elda said to Korinna. "Agree?"

"*Da*. I am enjoying this immensely, but I do want to spend more time in Maine with Egor and get back to my art classes."

"Great. Draw up a plan to clone you. We'll need three to four more people. What does everyone think of Yuri? He's not well suited to be a spy, nor an assassin, but he'd make a great logistical coordinator and project manager."

"Will Tosh let him go?" Korinna inquired.

"I can ask."

"Would he want to work for us?"

"I do think so. Korinna, can you reach out to Yuri on

the QT. If he does want to explore the job, arrange an interview, and I'll clear it with Tosh. Tosh owes me for being late in helping with the senator issue."

Murka wandered in from her office. "What's up?"

"We all need to recruit more spies. Ones who are leaving the administration and also some who are staying. That will be the difficult part, since the new guy will surround himself with loyalists and yes men, but he will most likely ignore the low-level folks like cooks, waiters, cleaning staff. Also, they'll have to vet their contract hires. They can't vet everyone at once. They will reclassify all the GS jobs so they can randomly fire folks. We need to target positions they will overlook."

"Whew." Charlie mopped her brow.

"Funny, Grasshopper. I'd like each one of you to make suggestions about people you know that we might want to hire. Ashok, you already have suggested Preyanka and her brother, but I'm sure you know more developers and testers."

"Will we be working with Sophia's and Tosh's teams again?"

Elda drew her brows together. "Perhaps Sophia. It's been *far* too quiet on Tosh's side of the fence. Let's kick off this stuff in the background and, after that, see what he's up to. Tosh may be an asset at times, but he is one hundred percent loyal to his country."

As if he had been a fly on the wall, Elda's "Ed" burner phone buzzed. She put Ed on speaker as she strode to her office. "Hello, Mr. Ed. You're on speaker."

"No whinny, Elda?"

She leaned against her desk and rubbed her hand across her eyes. "All whinnied out. Running and doing this operation is wearing me down."

"I wish I could help, but I think I'm much more useful to you as long as I can stay here."

Elda was concerned that Ed's voice was flat. "Things bad there?"

"Tolerable, for now." Elda could imagine Ed polishing his shoes on the back of his pant legs. "But that's not why I called. The grapevine says there's another assassin after you. Again, hired by the Oversight Committee, but they didn't go through me, so I suspect they are suspicious that I may have tipped you off."

Elda made a fist and stamped her foot. She was *so* sick of having to put away these killers. "Damn. Do you know who he is?"

"I have no other information."

Elda held the back of her neck and looked down at her desk. She sighed. "Thank you, Ed. It's better than nothing."

"I've asked him to stop, but he laughed in my face."

Elda knew to whom Ed was referring—that bastard Senator Glass. "No worries. I have it under control. Thanks."

"If I hear anything . . ."

"I know."

Elda hung up and switched to her "Tosh" burner phone.

She said to his answering machine, "I can't wait any longer. You owe me."

She hung up.

Chapter Twenty-Four

"Okay, it's time that Senator Glass got dealt with." Elda accented her words by slamming her fist into the palm of her other hand.

Charlie, sitting at her desk, glanced up at Elda, who had been pacing in her new office. "What are you thinking of doing?"

Without answering, Elda took her burner phone out of her pocket, put it on speaker, and dialed.

"*Privet*, Elda."

Charlie leaned forward, her chin in her hand. This should be interesting. What was Elda doing now?

"*Privet*, Tosh. You're on speaker with myself and Charlie. I wanted to let you know that I have dispatched with Dmitri."

"*Interesnyy.*"

"He had taken a contract with a senator to kill me. By the way, I guess you were next on his list. He was after fame and fortune by killing the legends."

Tosh snorted.

Elda's jaw was set and her words clipped. "He was the third one the senator had sent. And he's got a *fourth* coming. I'm tired of fighting off assassins. I need to borrow Snezhana *now*."

Charlie sat at attention. She had never seen Elda so assertive with Tosh.

"*Da*. I'm sorry for the delay. We'll come right over. Let me go get her."

"*Khorosho*." Elda tapped her foot while Tosh fetched Snezhana.

Charlie refilled her coffee cup and sat back, ready to learn from a master.

Snezhana's voice came over the line. "*Privet*, Elda."

"*Privet*, Snezhana. Am I on speaker?"

"*Da*."

"Good. I need you and Tosh to hear this together. I need to set up a senator here. I would like him to be put in a compromising position. I figure that sex with a woman who is not his wife would not be enough to discredit him in today's political climate. However, sex with a Russian spy, drugs, money laundering, which I will fake through Ashok, and the threat of death might be enough to persuade him to back off."

Snezhana giggled. "What fun, Elda. Can I bring Anatoly too? He will grumble, but he would look good with his shirt off and holding a naked senator."

Elda pumped her fist in the air. "Excellent addition! I knew I was making the right call. *Yes*. Thanks, guys. Let me know when you can make it over here, and we'll do Operation Take Down. But make it soon. And, Tosh . . ."

"*Da?*"

"Can you bring Yuri too?"

"Are you thinking of stealing him?"

"Perhaps."

"*Da.*"
Elda hung up.
Charlie was laughing so hard that she was crying.

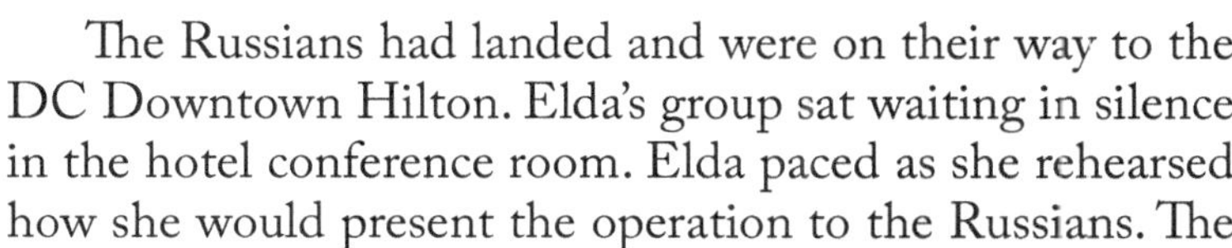

The Russians had landed and were on their way to the DC Downtown Hilton. Elda's group sat waiting in silence in the hotel conference room. Elda paced as she rehearsed how she would present the operation to the Russians. The tough sell would be Anatoly. Ashok circled the perimeter of the room with a metered gadget.

"The room is cleared, Miss Elda."

"Thank you, Ashok. You can stay, or go back to your work at headquarters. I will text or call if I need you today."

He centered the Cone of Silence on the table. "I have a program I'm a bit stuck on."

Elda waved in dismissal. "By all means, go. But check your texts."

"Yes, Miss Elda."

The Russian contingency burst into the room.

Ashok bowed his head to them on the way out. "Hello, Miss Snezhana and Mister Anatoly. Good to see you again."

Anatoly growled.

"Always good to see you, Ashok," Snezhana answered. "Feel free to ask Stas for anything you need to complete this operation."

"Thank you, Miss Snezhana." Ashok gathered up his equipment, powered up the Cone of Silence, and left the room.

To keep the location of the new office, and her apartment secret from the Russians, Elda had rented a large meeting room and five rooms, one each for the three visitors, for herself, and for Charlie.

She motioned for the group to sit. Before she could start, Anatoly groused, "*Der'mo.* I refuse."

Elda held up a hand to silence him as a hotel staff member came in with a tray of pastries, teas, a pot of hot water, and coffee.

"I am not bribable," Anatoly professed, as he jumped up to be first at the pastries.

"I know, Anatoly. Please hear me out."

Anatoly growled at her through a mouthful of food, though he leaned in as Elda explained the sting.

Snezhana bustled along the corridor to the cafeteria in the Dirkson Senate Office building. She held a stack of papers that she was rustling through as she moved forward.

Whap. She ran full force into Senator Glass, who was leaving the cafeteria.

"Oh! I am so sorry. This is all my fault." The two of them crawled on hands and knees to pick up the papers. Snezhana put her hand on his while reaching for the same page. She blushed and looked into his eyes. Their faces were inches apart. She parted her lips and licked them. "How can I make it up to you?"

He stood and held out his hand to help her up. She accepted his hand and rose, swinging into his body as she did. She paused a moment before moving away.

He looked her up and down. "Perhaps you would be free for dinner tonight?"

She looked at him from under her eyelashes. "Oh, that would be lovely. Shall we leave from here?"

He was still holding her hand. He stroked it with his fingers. "Perhaps we might start with dessert?"

She took her hand away, placed it low on her abdomen, and drew it up her body and lifted it off an inch shy of her breast. "Perhaps. Shall we say five p.m.?"

"I can be free by four p.m. I'll meet you by the front door." He took her hand again and kissed it. She brought it back to cradle the papers against her body, turned, and paraded away, accentuating her hip movements.

Once out of his view, she texted, IT'S ON. 4PM.

"That was quick! Let's go, gang." Anatoly, Ashok, Charlie, and Elda tugged on gloves and swarmed the senator's hotel room, placing cameras and secreting drugs in places where they could quickly pull them out and display them. As a final touch, Elda added felt-padded handcuffs to the bedside table drawer.

Once done, they retreated down the hall to the living room in Elda's suite, where Ashok operated the monitors and headphones.

"Charlie, can you pop back to the room and we'll test the video and audio?"

Charlie returned to the staged room and started speaking, "Oh, Senator. That is *so* good, Senator."

Holding back laughter, Elda spoke into Charlie's earpiece. "Okay, Charlie, you're coming in loud and clear."

Anatoly played with his noose and ran a finger over each of his knives.

Elda frowned. "And what are you thinking, Anatoly?"

"I am thinking, Elda, that if all goes south, I will silence the man another way." He placed a knife into a holder on his calf and another into a sheath on his belt. He slipped the noose into his pocket. "So when do I go in?"

"Snezhana will give us the go-ahead once he is out cold, with a little help from Snez and modern medicine, and we will all go in. We'll take a quick picture with Snezhana on one side and you, shirtless, on the other. We can position it so both of you are seen from the back and the senator's face is clearly visible. We clear the room, after which Snezhana will call for room service. I will intercept the waiter and bribe him to let me take the champagne into the room."

Anatoly frowned and reached into a white paper bag and took a chomp out of his Greek yogurt cherry danish.

"Where did you get that?"

"I bought some early this morning, in case the food here was bad. There's a pretty decent bakery down the road a bit. It's the Tous Les Jours Bakery and Café. You might want to order our snacks from there next time"

"It looks yummy, Anatoly," Elda said. "Ashok? Did you get the illegal financial transactions between Russia and the United States traced back to the senator?"

"Yes, Miss Elda."

"What's next?" Anatoly growled.

"Watch and learn."

Elda tromped to the senator's hotel room door with a bottle of champagne on ice. She felt her anger for the man tighten her jaw.

Anatoly clomped by her with a large trash cart. "Why do I always get the garbage?"

Elda glared at him. "After I enter, I'll drop the room key. I'll contact you when we're ready for your photo." Elda rapped on the door and used her duplicate passkey to enter.

Snezhana was removing the handcuffs after taking pictures. The senator lay naked on the bed.

Elda bet his body had never seen a gym. "Ugh, Snezhana. I can't unsee that. Ready for the photo shoot with Anatoly?"

"Yes. Let's get this done. He should be waking up in about ten minutes or so."

Anatoly stomped into the room and took his shirt off. He sneered at the body on the bed. Snezhana took her top off, and Elda positioned them on either side of the senator and draped the senator's arm over Anatoly. "*Der'mo!*"

Elda snapped the pictures. Both agents then jumped off the bed and dressed.

"Stay close outside, Anatoly, in case I need you," Elda ordered. "If you hear two clicks in your comms, dash in."

He left.

Elda turned to Snezhana. "Thanks much. Can you put on gloves, lay the drugs out, snap a few more pictures, run to my room, and get the printouts and put them inside the door here for me? Also, sanitize any place your hands may have touched."

"*Da.*"

Elda dashed into the bathroom and grabbed a facecloth, which she put over the senator's genitalia. "There. No one needs to see your junk."

She pulled a chair up by the bed and waited. A few minutes later he stirred.

Senator Glass blinked his eyes and rubbed them in an attempt to see clearly. He started to sit up, when Elda advised, "You may want to stay lying down. You're only wearing a towel, and it's covering a pretty ugly part of you."

He turned his head and stared at Elda. "Who are you?"

"Elda Ainsworth, at your service. I understand you've been trying to find me." She aimed her Smith & Wesson at him. "Here's the deal—"

He opened his mouth, and she held up her other hand. "Stay quiet and listen . . ."

Elda marched to the door. She picked up a small pile of photos and returned to drop them on the senator's chest.

His jaw dropped as he rifled through them.

"Unless you back off Ed, his teams, and those who worked for him, these pictures, which of course these are only copies of, will go public. If you obey, they will not see the light of day."

His eyes flashed. "You can't get away with this."

Elda sneered. "But I already have." She dropped another paper on the pile of pictures. It contained all his bank accounts and a financial trail of Russian money funneling into them and offshore. "It would be an easy matter to also publicize that information."

"Sex with a known Russian agent . . ." She dropped Snezhana's picture in front of him. ". . . and . . . you like men too, hey?" She dropped a picture of him in bed with a man and a woman. "And what are all these illicit drugs?" She flung the last picture at him.

"You'll ruin me."

"That's the plan, Ronnie boy. You will resign from all your committees and as a senator. I will keep these pictures as my insurance policy."

The senator had turned white. "There's one problem."

Elda's eyes narrowed. She didn't trust this man. "And what's that?"

There was a faint trace of a smile on his face. "I spun up another assassin to go after you."

Elda wanted to wipe that smirk off his face. "Who is he?"

"I don't know."

Elda raised her Smith & Wesson.

"I never met him. Believe me . . ."

Elda put her gun against his groin.

His eyes grew large. "R-R-Really. I'm telling the truth. We communicated via telegram."

Elda glared at him. "Damn you. Did you pay him?" She pressed the muzzle in harder.

The senator gulped and whispered, "Yes. A retainer fee of one million dollars. I owe him more when he starts looking for you."

"How much total?"

Silence.

Elda ratcheted her gun. A round flew out. She picked it up and brushed his face with it. "The next one comes out the barrel. How much?"

Sweat broke out on his forehead. "Ten million. One on agreement, three on commencement, six when the kill is verified."

"And what happens to you if the man doesn't get his payments?"

"N-N-o. You can't do that to me."

"I can, and if you step out of line, I will." Elda scribbled an account number and a bank name on a sticky and stuck it on his forehead. "You will transfer the funds to this account. I will expect twenty million to be deposited by tomorrow morning."

"Twenty million! The contract is only ten."

"Yes. I know that. And I also know that you have allocated twenty million for it. I assume the rest of that money was going to your own account."

Sweat beaded up on his upper lip and dripped off the side of his face. Elda put the barrel of her pistol against his cheek. "What's his username?"

"Wolfkiller666."

She removed the barrel and held out her left hand. "Give me your phone."

He handed it to Elda.

She pocketed it. "You'll get it back tomorrow."

He nodded, his eyes following her every move.

"Don't get complacent. I can always find you. And I have *no* reason to let you live. Understand?" Elda wheeled and stormed out the door.

Elda marched into Ashok's office, where he and Charlie huddled over a keyboard. "What do we have on this assassin?"

Ashok looked up from his typing. "It was very clever of you taking Mister Glass's phone, Miss Elda. I have cloned it and altered the telegram app on the senator's phone so that anything he tries to send from there comes here instead. He will not be able to communicate to the assassin, but we will. I will receive an alert if he attempts to contact WolfKiller666."

"Excellent." Elda peered at his monitor. "Do you have anything that would lead us to this killer?"

Ashok continued typing. "Nothing yet, Miss Elda."

"Damn."

Chapter Twenty-Five

KORINNA WAS DEEP IN THOUGHT AND jumped at a knock on her hotel suite door. She opened it to see Yuri standing there. Her eyes filled with tears at the thought of having someone capable of helping her and being able to return to Maine to be with Egor and her dogs. "*Privet*, Yuri." She held out her hand.

Yuri took her hand and kissed it. He beamed at her. "*Privet*, Korinna."

They moved into the office area to sit across from each other. Yuri handed her a single-page résumé. "How are the Troodles?"

Korinna passed Yuri her phone, open to her album of her dog photos. "Would you like to see pictures of them? Egor took them to the groomers yesterday."

The phone was dwarfed by the size of Yuri's hand. He flipped through the pictures of the two little terrier-poodle mix dogs. He had helped smuggle them out of Russia for Korinna and had grown attached to them. His eyes filled with tears. He patted his chest. He smiled at Korinna as he gave her phone back. "I miss them."

Korinna was interviewing Yuri as her potential replacement. She pivoted to the matter at hand. "Why would you want this job, Yuri?"

Yuri put his chin on his hand. He furrowed his brow. "I like Elda." He stopped and started again. "I enjoyed working for Elda. The jobs spoke to my talents. I never had to be involved with killing anyone. My strengths are in logistics and connections. I can get anything from point A to point B, on time. I admit that I am not as organized as you are, Korinna, with schedules and project plans, but I can give you . . . *gonka za vashimi den'gami* . . . How do you say it in English? A run for your money."

Korinna laughed. "I bet you could. I know you somewhat from your help in getting us out of Moscow, but Elda speaks highly of you. That's a good reference."

Yuri nodded.

Korinna glanced at Yuri's résumé. In her mind, it didn't matter. She knew some of what he had done, and Elda and Tosh both believed in him. "No attachments back in Moscow? You can relocate?"

Yuri passed Korinna his phone, opened to a picture of two cats. "Only Katya and Koshka. I have few belongings, all of which I could leave behind, as long as this job includes a furnished apartment."

Korinna stood. "Let me see what the next steps are. However, Elda said I must insist you talk to Tosh."

Yuri grinned. "I already have. I wouldn't be here without his approval."

Elda absently watched as Korinna wandered into the hotel conference room after interviewing Yuri. The floral smell of her perfume mixed with the steam of the cup of tea she was carrying. She plunked the tea down on the table and planted her hands on her hips. "I want him."

Elda sat, feet up, on a second chair, an untouched cup of coffee cooling in front of her, and staring at the wall. Her mind was turning over scenarios of how to find this latest assassin. She forced aside her irritation at her thoughts being interrupted before she had a solution. One at a time she brought her feet down, stared at Korinna, and raised an eyebrow. "I'm not sure Egor will like that."

Korinna waggled her forefinger at Elda and scowled. "Geesh. You know what I mean."

Elda winked at Korinna. "I do. Let's go back to the office and start the paperwork to bring him over, pending Tosh's approval. Speak of the devil . . ."

Tosh traipsed in with his luggage. "The rest are gathering their stuff to leave."

Elda motioned to a chair. "Tosh, we'd like to talk to you about Yuri."

Tosh dropped one bag, waved his hand. "He's already spoken to me. I think your job is a much better fit for him, although we'll miss him."

Elda exhaled, relieved at not having to face conflict. "Thank you, Tosh."

Tosh threw his carry-on over his shoulder. "Thank you, Elda for a fun operation here. I think even Anatoly warmed to it."

Elda chuckled at the memory of Anatoly, shirtless, participating in the sting. "Hopefully, we can work together again."

Tosh walked out the door, his words trailing behind. "Perhaps."

Elda felt a wave of loss flow through her. She was comforted when they worked together. They were stronger standing back to back. And she felt challenged when they were pitted against each other. Somehow their lives were intertwined. She prayed that they were not destined to kill each other. Part of her needed Tosh alive, whether friend or foe. She sighed and glanced at Korinna, who was frowning.

"Are you okay, *moy drug*?"

"*Da*, Korinna. Let's go to the office and finish up our paperwork." Elda finished her sentence with a faked, teeth-clenched, smile.

Korinna patted her on the back. "*Da*. Your favorite activity."

Hours later, Elda groaned. She brandished her fist at her monitor. "Why can't I make this Excel data table work?"

Korinna took the keyboard from Elda and made a few changes. "*Tam*." She handed the keyboard back.

Elda shook her head in admiration of Korinna's Excel skill.

Korinna slid a printed spreadsheet across the desk. Elda picked it up with two fingers, as if it were contaminated.

Elda's Ed burner phone rang. She stared at it for a ring before answering it. She was praying he wouldn't be giving her bad news. But it beat doing the budget. "Hello, Ed. You're on speaker. I'm in my office, and Korinna is here with me."

Ed's voice boomed over the speaker. "Hello, Korinna. Elda, I wanted to let you know that I heard Senator Glass is retiring. He quit the Oversight Committee. Good news, hey?"

Elda could hear traffic in the background. She lowered the volume. Her voice was devoid of joy. "It would be if he hadn't spun up one last assassin before he decided to get out of town."

"Did you help with his career choices?"

"You never know, Ed."

Ed laughed, then his voice turned serious. "Is there any way I can help you?"

Elda rued that he couldn't help. She missed Ed's calm

strength. "No, but thanks. I'll be sure to call if there is. How are things going for you there?"

"The purges have started. I don't think I'm on a list yet. My current job is not high profile."

Elda could tell by the change in the background noise that Ed was on the move again. "I'll keep my fingers crossed for you. Let me know if you need anything."

"Will do." Ed hung up.

Elda tossed the burner phone in a drawer. "Well, that part is done. Now if we can finish the budget, I'll be happy."

Korinna stood and held out her hand for the papers that Elda had scribbled calculations on. "I'll take it. I'm heading back up to Maine for a few days. You've given me enough guidance and figures. I'll put the rest into Excel."

"Thank you, Korinna." Elda handed Korinna a collection of different-sized papers with pencil and pen calculations, doodles, and figures on them.

Korinna shook her head. "Geesh."

Elda stood and stretched. "Now I can go get Charlie and practice some kickboxing in the gym."

Charlie and Elda wrapped their hands, donned gloves and shin guards. Elda started the cameras that were safely positioned off the mat to catch the action for the debrief after training.

"Now remember, Charlie, the goal is to practice our moves, not to knock the other person out. Okay?"

Charlie danced around Elda, jabbing the air like a boxer. "Yes, Master."

The two warriors squared off in fighter stances. Elda held both hands in front of her chin. She recognized Charlie held her arms at a ninety-degree angle by her side, thus signaling a potential intent to throw a hook at Elda.

They advanced.

As Elda predicted, Charlie threw a hook.

Prepared, Elda spun away and launched a glancing sidekick. She completed her spin, coming in toward Charlie, distracting her from Elda's feet, with a jab that missed, as Charlie drew back. Elda fed into Charlie's backward momentum with a forward kick.

Charlie's face reddened, and she came in fast with an uppercut. Elda spun to avoid it and pushed Charlie off balance with a side kick. She followed it with a heel thrust to Charlie's shins, and Charlie toppled to the mat.

"Ouch. Glad I have shin guards on." Rubbing her leg, Charlie rose to watch Elda position two dummies.

Elda punched one, and it rocked back and forth. "Let's practice on these guys. What you are doing is signaling your next move with your body position. You're also using either your hands or your feet, but not both at once. I'll demo the correct moves. You copy."

Elda talked through different scenarios and used the dummy to demonstrate her response. She had Charlie perform each movement and critiqued her as she went, not letting her move on until she had perfected the routine.

"Much better, Grasshopper. Tomorrow we will do some street-fighting techniques. When you are good enough, you'll be the trainer for the rest of the team."

Chapter Twenty-Six

"**I** DON'T LIKE THE DIRECTION THINGS ARE heading."

"What do you mean, *dyadya*?"

Tosh and Snezhana sat in his apartment in Moscow, finishing up a dinner of blinis and salmon. There was a small gas fire in a stove in the corner of the room, lending a warmth to the setting.

Tosh shifted a slice of raw salmon onto his pancake, spread some sour cream on that, and topped it with a dollop of black small-grained Beluga caviar. He rolled it up and cut off a piece with his fork. He took a bite, chewed, and swallowed. He pointed at Snezhana with his fork. "Russia has always admired strong men as leaders. Being told what to do is so much easier than having to fend for yourself. After the Soviet Union dissolved, the oligarchs took over, and money ruled. People were squashed down. We hated Lenin for what he did, but these new leaders destroyed people in a different way."

Tosh paused to take another bite. "In the world of

spies, however, there was order and reward. The Cold War served a purpose. It pitted strength against strength in a game that we knew no one would win. But the war took a twist. Much like Hitler demeaned the press and took away freedom of speech and any means of resistance, our government became more brutal and killed those who disagreed in a public way. And with the new social networking technology, the war became one of disinformation and tearing down the other countries from within, establishing the right wing, creating oligarchs, with the end goal of having one man here in Russia who ruled the world. A lofty goal, but one that he is winning. The Cold War is over. We have won. But at what cost to humanity? The Moscow we knew is lost to us. We don't value the lives of women or children. They are called collateral damage. We prize men, more so those who have white skin and fat wallets. There is no honor. Ethics are long gone. There is no respect for knowledge or skill, unless you consider cheating or being a con man and a liar, skills." Tosh downed his shot of vodka.

"So where does that leave us, *dyadya*?"

Tosh poured another shot for himself and one for Snezhana. "We have to decide which side we want to be on. The side of love of country and honor and pride. The side where our word is good. Where we kill only for a good reason. Or the side of cheating and randomly killing. I love my country, its rich history, its culture, its food, its music, its people. I would die for my country. But not necessarily for one man, who is potential evil."

"That's a dangerous position to take, *dyadya*."

"*Da*. Think carefully, niece, before you decide to join me . . . or not."

Tosh wondered if he should have said all he had to

Snezhana. His head was on overdrive. Despite his lack of sleep and the warmth of his gas fire, he could not relax. Was Moscow lost to him? Should he leave? The shrill ring of his phone broke through his contemplation.

Chert. Boris again. Tosh rolled his eyes but answered. "*Da?*"

"I have a job for you."

Tosh shook his head to clear out the alcohol and desire for sleep. He pumped up the cuff and read his blood pressure. "What is the job, and why me?" He realized he spoke abruptly and hoped Boris wouldn't take offense.

Boris answered without rancor. "I need an assassin, and I have none at this moment. There is a deeply planted mole in the United States government whom we tried to activate."

Tosh perked up. "What happened?"

Boris snorted. "He has been in Washington, DC, too many years. He enjoys his creature comforts there, has married an American, and has two teenagers with her. He knows that after he completes his mission, he will have to come back to Moscow, so he has refused the job."

Tosh was intrigued. "What mission?"

"We suspect the outgoing administration will delete information we need. We asked him to get all the data on existing American agents in Russia, and in other countries, who may be Russia's allies. He considered our request too risky because this intelligence is tightly guarded and access to it limited. His name will definitely come up if the leak is discovered."

Tosh's gray eyes narrowed. This man was a traitor. The Kremlin had enabled his cushy lifestyle and paid him well for his services. "That's valuable knowledge for us to have."

"Exactly. Killing him will send a message to others that we are not to be trifled with. There comes a time when the cost behind the luxury of living abroad *must* be paid back."

Tosh could get behind this request. "Deliver the files to my office. I will get my people on it." Tosh hung up. It was time to bring clear rules back for the Kremlin.

Elda's desk phone buzzed. She picked up in intercom mode. The team was enjoying using the old tech Korinna had installed. The intercom was much more secure than sending texts, plus it used far less electricity. Next, they'd be stringing together cans and string. Elda's eyes crinkled at the thought.

Ashok's voice came scratchy and tinny over the line. "Miss Elda, ma'am?"

Elda texted Korinna to have the intercom system repaired. "Yes?" She hoped he would get to the point.

Much to her surprise, he did. "I think we may be interested in two passengers who just landed at Dulles."

"Why?"

"My AI facial recognition, body type, and movement software calculates there's a seventy percent likelihood that they are Tosh and Snezhana."

Elda felt her heart race and her adrenaline spike. "Tosh and Snezhana?" She jumped up. "Let me see what you have. I'll be right there." Elda ran to Ashok's office. She peered at his monitor. "Well, hello there, my pretties. What are you up to in DC?" She patted Ashok's shoulder. "Good catch, Ashok. Let me know if you can track them any further."

Elda dashed out of Ashok's, paused at her office to grab a stun gun, and raced to Charlie's office. "Gear up. We're going hunting."

Charlie jumped up and saluted Elda. "Yeah! For what?" She snatched her weapon from her desk drawer and holstered it. "Ready, willing, and able, ma'am."

Elda grinned and shook her head at Charlie's antics.

"You'll need more gear than that. It's Tosh and Snezhana."

Charlie slipped a knife holder onto her forearm and loaded it with a knife with a four-inch blade. "Fantastic. Where are they?"

"DC." Elda pitched Charlie the taser. "We need to take them alive and find out why they're here."

Charlie fielded the weapon and placed it in her jacket pocket. "DC's a large area, Elda."

"I have a hunch. Follow me."

Charlie and Elda sat across from each other on the blue line train. They spoke softly, barely audible over the sound of the train car.

Elda leaned forward. "Charlie, the Russians usually stay at the Capital Hilton in downtown DC. Can you go check that out?"

Charlie nodded. It was an easy assignment. "Sure, Elda. What do I do if I find them?"

Elda stared into Charlie's eyes. "Detain only. Do not kill or seriously harm. Got it?"

Charlie frowned. That made the mission more difficult. But she knew better than to fight the Elda stare. "Got it. Where are *you* going?"

"I'm thinking that this may have something to do with our government. Perhaps contacting a high-level spy, since they've sent Tosh. I'm going to sniff around Congress."

Elda glanced at the vaulted concrete ceiling at the Federal Center SW station. They were so unimaginative compared to Moscow's marble-adorned metro stations.

She took a deep breath and stepped onto the steep

escalator, holding tight to the handrail, to the exit. She had not managed to completely vanquish her fear of heights. Near the end of the escalator, she noted the long, curved crack from side to side in the ceiling blocks. That wasn't reassuring. She jogged up and off the last few steps.

Elda continued running north on Third Street Southwest, until she reached Independence Avenue. She turned right toward the United States Capitol building and the House of Representatives office buildings. Her goal was to circle the Capitol building and also look around the three Senate office buildings along Constitution Avenue.

She snapped pictures as she strolled. Security was tight. Tosh would not be able to get at a member of Congress here, unless he had an ID and could access the tunnels and train. She ran on, scanning the passing cars and the pedestrians for views of Tosh or Snezhana.

There! Was that that Tosh? She had just turned south on Second Street Southeast. The man was heavier than Tosh and taller, but he moved the same way Tosh did. She headed in that direction. If he was done with his exploration, he would head for the Capitol South Metro station. There was no way she could get to the station before him. And if she boarded after him, she would draw his attention to her.

Elda scratched her head. What would she do if she were Tosh? Get off at the next station. That would be either Federal Center Southwest or Eastern Market. If she was looking for tails, she'd head away from the Capitol building.

She needed wheels. As if in answer to her thoughts, a middle-aged man walked out of a building and took a helmet out of the rear case on a beige Vespa GTS 300.

Elda approached the man. She noted his frayed cuffs and worn shoes. He might be open to earning some extra cash. "Excuse me, sir. How much did you pay for that Vespa?"

He patted the seat. "It's not new, but in great shape. I got it for sixty-five hundred, but they go for close to eight K now."

Elda held out an envelope with one-hundred-dollar bills sticking out. "May I borrow it for the day for ten thousand dollars? I have a friend coming to town, and I'm late meeting him. He has no idea of where to go in DC."

He furrowed his brow. His eyes didn't leave the envelope.

Elda stretched her arm out toward him. "It's a win-win. Give me your cell number, and I'll let you know where to pick up the bike. If I don't call, you have more than enough for a brand-new Vespa."

He squinted, nodded, took the envelope, and thumbed the contents. He scribbled his cell number on the envelope flap, tore it off, and gave Elda the piece, along with the keys.

Elda tapped his hand holding the helmet. "May I borrow your brain bucket too?"

"Oh. Sure." He handed it to her.

She put on the helmet. It was too large, so she strapped it tight. She hopped on the Vespa and motored away.

Tosh pressed his earpiece tighter into his ear to hear over the noise of the metro car. "Getting at him near the Capitol building may not be possible. There's a lot of security. We'll have to do more planning, Snezhana. Where does he live?" Tosh's train slowed for the Eastern Market station. He stood, noting who else on that car was preparing to disembark. "*Khorosho*. Have Stas text it to me when he gets it. I need to find quicker transportation."

He disconnected, strolled off the train, and stopped, miming consulting his phone. No one else stopped around him. He sprinted up the escalator. As far as he could see, he wasn't being tailed. He walked up Seventh Street Southeast, crossing Pennsylvania Avenue Southeast, until he reached the Eastern Market grounds on his left. Wandering around the market, he spotted a man holding a motorcycle helmet and exiting toward the back of the building. He ran to catch up with him.

"Excuse me, sir. I noticed you carrying a helmet. Do you ride a motorcycle?" Tosh hoped the bike owner was a Harley fan, but from the look of the man's red-and-yellow-colored sneakers, cloth jacket, and clean-shaven face, Tosh doubted it.

The bike owner brightened. "I do! Well, it's a Vespa Sprint 150. But I had to get a motorcycle license to drive it."

Tosh's smile faded. He forced one back. "So what's that? A six-thousand-dollar bike?"

The man puffed his chest out. "Plus tax."

Tosh pointed at the front of the bike. "Is your registration in the glove box?"

The Vespa owner frowned. "Yes. Why?"

"I'll give you eight grand for the keys and helmet." Tosh held out a large rolled wad of cash with a one-hundred-dollar bill on top.

The man shook his head. He stared at the money. "What? Ummmm . . . I don't know."

Tosh peeled off five hundred-dollar bills from the cash and pocketed them. "Here's your choice. Seven thousand five hundred and I get the bike." Tosh opened his jacket and displayed his gun. "Or I kill you and take it."

The scooter rider's eyes popped. He took a step backward. "You offered eight thousand before."

Tosh removed five more hundred-dollar bills from the roll. "It's now seven grand. When I take the bike, I'll have your registration information and know where you live. Don't call the police. You'll wait a day and then report the bike as stolen. You'll get it back and have some extra pocket change."

The man snatched the money. "O-O-O-kay . . ." He crammed the bills into his pocket.

"Thank you. Good choice." Tosh tore the keys from the man's hand and grabbed his helmet from the back of the bike. He shoved on the helmet. Good. It fit perfectly. He rocked the Vespa off its kickstand and walked it out of the parking space. He opened the throttle and roared forward to North Carolina Avenue Southeast. What a difference from his Harley.

Elda loved the familiar feel of the Vespa as she cut in and out of traffic. The GTS had great pickup and purred as she adjusted the throttle. She slowed the bike as she realized she couldn't get to the metro station in time to catch Tosh.

What would he do? He'd either turn around and get on the next train heading in the opposite direction or leave the station. If he left the station, the market would be a great place to lose a tail. She turned down Fourth Street Southeast. Should she go E Street Southeast-North Carolina Ave Southeast to the market and then down Seventh Avenue Southeast to the Metro station in case he hadn't reached there yet? Or continue down Fourth to D Street Southeast? She shivered. She wasn't dressed for scooter riding.

Deciding which way to go, she paused at the intersection of Fourth and E Street SE, when a Vespa 150 came speeding along from her left. She did a double take. Tosh?

Elda spun to the right and fell in a couple of cars behind. She coughed from the car's exhaust fumes.

Tosh turned right and caught New Jersey Ave SE.

Elda followed. Where was he going? He must know she was tailing him.

They sped by the eastern boundary of the Spirit of Justice Park and slowed down through the curves past the Cannon House Office Building, turning left on Independence Avenue. They passed the Smithsonian National Air and Space Museum, one of Elda's favorites. She mused that she needed to take a day off and play tourist. You never knew when it would come in handy. She decided to schedule a day to take the team on a field trip to the Spy Museum.

Tosh slowed and was tapping one of his gauges. Elda wondered if his scooter was acting up. At the Washington Monument Grounds, he pulled off the road, hopped off, jostled his Vespa onto its kickstand, and jogged north.

Elda pulled her Vespa next to his, rocked it onto the kickstand, and dashed after him, following him into a grove of trees in back of the Sylvan Theater. An arm caught her around her neck and pulled her backward. She felt the point of a knife against her neck. She had pulled her Smith & Wesson out of its holster and held it pressed hard into his groin.

"How lucky do you feel, Tosh?"

The knife pressure eased but remained stuck into her neck. Elda could feel the warmth of blood dripping down into her shirt. She could tell he had not hit a major artery, which meant that he was playing nice.

"Ah, Elda. I thought it was you. What do you mean?"

Elda remembered Gools, where they had agreed not to kill each other. She hoped it still stood and he would listen to reason. "Well, you could cut my neck, but if I'm quick, I can simultaneously shoot and get your femoral artery. We'd both bleed out together. And even if I'm slow, the death spasm could pull the trigger. It's set very lightly. For that matter, my nerves could cause my hand to shake and you'd be gone, even if we weren't trying to kill the other."

"I get your point, Elda. Shall we agree to back off?"

Elda moved her finger outside the trigger guard, leaving the gun in place. "Only if we can spend a few minutes talking before you dash off again."

Tosh snorted. "I won't be dashing anywhere. I need gas."

Elda backed her weapon off. Tosh was ready to negotiate. "Well, if you're nice to me, I could give you a lift to your hotel."

Tosh removed the knife from Elda's neck. "Or I could call a cab."

They stepped apart, pocketed their weapons, and faced each other like two gunslingers, their eyes searching the other's.

"Why are you here, Tosh?" Elda demanded.

Tosh shook his head. "It's none of your business, Elda."

Elda glared at him. "Yes, *it is*, Tosh. This is *my* country. What op are you running on US soil?"

Tosh raised an eyebrow. "Have you told me about the last mission you did in Russia?"

Elda put a finger up to her lips. "I don't know *what* you're referring to."

Tosh dropped the bantering tone. "My mission isn't anything you would object to, Elda."

He sounded sincere. Elda suspected they were done with the games and it was now time for truth-telling on both sides. "Then what is it?"

"We have a Russian spy to kill."

This was meaty. "Who? Why?"

Tosh glared at her.

Elda grimaced and held up her hands in surrender. "Okay. It was me in Russia. Now your turn."

Tosh sighed. "A senator who is a deeply planted mole. He refuses to activate. Life in America has been good to him.”

“Interesting.” Elda thought a moment. “Do you want help? I have a beta version of something from Ashok’s lab I’d like to try, and this may be the perfect moment to do so. We would most likely still need Snezhana to help deliver it.”

Tosh raised an eyebrow and relaxed his body language. “I’m listening.”

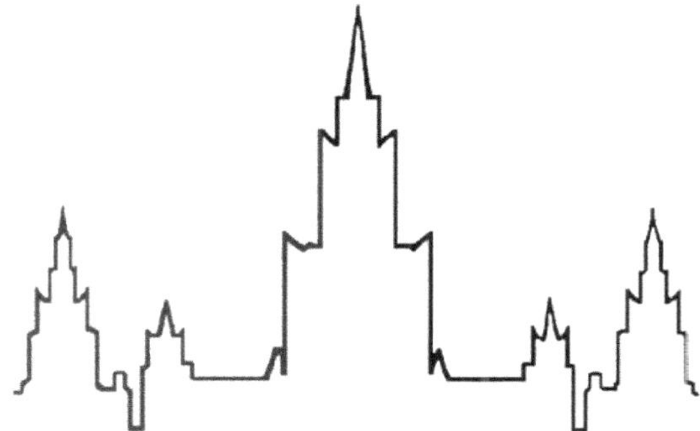

CHAPTER TWENTY-SEVEN

CLANG.

Snezhana looked around to ensure no one had heard the weight drop. She was reacquainting herself with the hotel layout and amenities, while waiting for Stas to get back to her with the senator's address. She moseyed into the gym to examine the Precor machine, when she spotted Charlie heading across the parking lot.

What was Charlie doing here? Snezhana sprinted out of the gym and down to a hallway where she could view what was going on in the lobby.

Charlie leaned onto the reception desk, holding what appeared to be a badge, speaking with a Hilton employee. He spoke and passed her an envelope. Charlie nodded and shook his hand.

What information did he hand out?

Charlie left the desk and headed for the stairs.

Snezhana followed the scents of toast, bacon, and scrambled eggs to the restaurant, where the staff was setting up a buffet. As they moved in and out of the kitchen,

Snezhana snagged a carving knife. Now armed, she ran back down the hallway to another set of stairs and raced up to the fifth floor, pausing at the top landing to catch her breath. She cracked the door and spied Charlie walking down the corridor toward Snezhana's and Tosh's adjoining rooms. She waited.

Charlie looked up and down the hallway and keyed herself into Tosh's room, slipping inside. Did the front desk give Charlie a passkey?

Snezhana ran on her toes to her own room and, without a sound, opened her door and went in. She crept to the door connecting the two rooms. Tosh and she hadn't locked it so they could have an additional exit route. She put her hand on the knob, ready to pounce.

The door was violently yanked inward, and Snezhana fell into Tosh's room. She somersaulted past Charlie, whose booted foot whizzed by her head. Springing up, knife in hand, she faced Charlie. The two women swayed, looking for an opening.

Snezhana, sure that she could take Charlie, sprang at her.

Charlie stepped back and whirled, landing a blow to Snezhana's back, continuing Snezhana's forward momentum.

Snezhana fell onto her face and rolled over. Perhaps this wouldn't be an easy takedown.

Charlie attacked.

Snezhana drove both feet into Charlie's legs, knocking her down. Charlie crashed onto her back with a grunt, and lay there.

Snezhana launched herself onto Charlie, knife ready to stab. Charlie brought her knees up to her chest, and Snezhana was met by two steel boots planted into her abs.

One part of Snezhana felt the pain and the other observed, while catapulting through the air. Interesting.

That was an Elda move. Snezhana landed with a crash against the side of the bed. She rubbed her stomach.

Breathing heavily, both women rose.

With a greater respect for her adversary, Snezhana warily advanced.

They wheeled to keep their eyes on each other, completing nearly a full circle. Snezhana lashed out with her knife. A steel-tipped boot propelled the knife from her hand. She dove to retrieve it and was kicked in the ribs in reward for her efforts. The breath was knocked out of her. She lay there facedown, panting.

She rolled onto her back. Charlie loomed over her, pointing a Makarov pistol at her.

Snezhana moved her hands over her head. "*Der'mo.* I should have expected that trick. And me without a gun. What did Elda always say? *Never bring a knife to a gunfight?* She was right."

Charlie motioned for Snezhana to get up and sit in the desk chair.

As she stood, Snezhana winced. Her ribs hurt. She scanned the room for the knife. She spotted it tucked into Charlie's belt. She was out of options. It was time to see what Charlie wanted. "What are you doing here, Charlie?"

"What am *I* doing here, Snezhana?" Charlie spat at Snezhana's feet. "You're the Russian spy in DC. That's *my* territory. What are *you* doing here?"

Snezhana wondered if Charlie would shoot her, but she didn't want to find out. "That's not for me to say. Tosh will be back soon. Perhaps you'd like to deal with him? Or you could leave now."

Charlie snickered. She threw a package of zip ties to Snezhana. "I would like you to zip-tie your ankles together and lash your right hand to the desk leg. You are right handed, correct?"

"*Da.*" Snezhana did as she was told. She had confidence that Elda wouldn't let Charlie kill her. Of course, Elda wasn't here . . . nor was Tosh. She wondered if her uncle was okay. He had been gone a long time. Snezhana began to sweat. "Now what?"

"Unless you're willing to talk, we sit and wait for Tosh." Charlie sat with her back to the wall and her gun aimed at the door.

"I'll warn him," Snezhana bluffed.

"I'll shoot you."

"I'm not sure who will open that door, Tosh. Charlie hasn't answered my text."

Elda, standing in the hallway, rapped on Tosh's hotel room door. Bump-bump-de bump-bump . . . bump-bump. She stepped to one side.

Tosh leaned over from the other side and swiped his key, pushing the door open with his foot.

Pistols drawn, Elda and Tosh jumped into the room.

Charlie lowered her gun.

"Charlie, you might want to check your phone more often."

Charlie glanced at her phone. STAND DOWN. "Oh crap. Sorry, Elda. You're right. I should have seen that earlier." Charlie took the knife from her belt and cut Snezhana's ties. "Sorry, Snez. You may want some ice on that side. I'll go get some." She ran out of the room with the ice bucket.

Snezhana stood and winced. She held her hand to her side.

Elda put an arm around her. "Let's pop into the bathroom. I'll examine those ribs for you. I assume they met with Charlie's boot tip?"

Snezhana flinched as Elda gently felt her ribs. "*Da.* My fault though. She beat me fair and square."

Charlie burst into the bathroom with the ice.

Elda took the bucket from Charlie and addressed Snezhana. "You're lucky. They're not broken and I suspect not cracked, but you'll have a nasty bone bruise that will hurt just as much. I recommend that you hold ice on it while we all chat." Elda reached into her backpack and came out with a vial of arnica pellets. She took Snezhana's hand and dropped five pellets into it. "Let these dissolve under your tongue."

Snezhana grimaced. "I'd rather a vodka." She popped the pellets.

"You can have that as a chaser. I'll call room service and have a bottle sent up. You're not going anywhere tonight." Elda wrapped the ice in a hand towel and gave it to Snezhana. "Hold that on your ribs up under your shirt for at least ten minutes. Once room service delivers the vodka, we'll powwow on how you and Tosh can best accomplish your mission."

The four spies sat around Tosh's hotel room, sharing the vodka bottle, with the lion's share going to Snezhana.

Tosh started the planning session. "Let's conference in Stas and Ashok. We need to find out this senator's schedule and determine the best place to intercept him. That may be difficult. The secretarial systems in Congress are a mishmash of isolated applications, some still only paper based." Tosh finished speaking and looked at Elda, who had one of her burner phones in her hand. "What are you doing, Elda?"

"Sometimes the old-fashioned way is the best. Let's see if this works." Elda plugged a device Ashok had devised into her phone and dialed. She put the phone on speaker.

A young female voice sounded through the phone.

"Senator Johnson's office. May I help you?"

A gravelly baritone answered the secretary's question. "I am hoping you can. I realize this is short notice and the holidays are coming up, but I'm only in town for a couple of days and I'd like to get on the senator's calendar. Are there any openings?"

"I am so sorry. I'm afraid not. The senator is taking tomorrow morning off to receive his Christmas tree. Every year he has had to take two mornings off, since the first delivery is never acceptable. I've blocked off tomorrow morning and also the next day. That's compressed his schedule. There are no openings available."

"Well, thank you for trying."

"May I tell him who called?"

"I'll call again." Elda hung up. She turned to the others and started laughing.

Tosh, Snezhana, and Charlie sat gaping at her.

"What was that voice?" Snezhana asked. "It wasn't one of yours."

Elda pointed at a small device plugged into her phone. "Clever, hey? It's a new toy Ashok developed. It changes the voice to obscure the voice print and speech patterns. Just in case the call was being recorded."

Charlie nodded. "I'll have to order one from him." She surmised, "Now all we have to do is find out what Christmas tree shop the senator orders his trees from."

"Small business systems are easy to break into," Tosh remarked, "although they could be paper based. I would bet it's a local shop and he uses the same one every year. He must like the power of rejecting the tree. Ashok should have better luck finding it, since it's most likely in the DC area, perhaps not far from the senator's house."

Elda dashed off a quick text to Ashok, siccing him on the problem. She addressed Tosh. "Tea? I'll call room service." She looked at Charlie. "Don't worry, Charlie. I'll get coffee too."

Tosh held his up his hands palms up, wrinkled his brow, and looked at Elda from under his eyelashes. "Do you have any biscuits? Olga got me addicted to those Bourbon Creams."

"The hotel won't have them, but I always keep them on hand for Olga. Charlie, how about you go bring back a package. Look in my room first. You have to perform your penance for not checking your phone and for beating up Snezhana."

"*Da.*" Snezhana rubbed her side and took a swig of vodka.

Charlie dashed out. The rest sat waiting for Ashok.

Room service came and left.

Charlie returned with Bourbon Creams. "Success!"

Snezhana glared at her.

Charlie scuttled over to a chair and sat, holding the package of biscuits.

"*Spasibo.*" Tosh took the biscuits from Charlie and poured tea for himself and Elda. He dipped his biscuits into his tea, smiling with each soggy bite.

Snezhana stuck with the vodka.

Elda could hear a clock ticking in the silence. She decided now would be a good time to explain how Ashok's ladybug worked. She held out a small case the size of a ring box.

"Aw, a ring. I have nothing for you in return, Elda," Tosh joked.

Elda kicked him with a gentle tap of her foot. "This is for Snezhana."

"I'm not your type, Elda. You'd be better off with Tosh."

"Oh my God. You *are* related. This is a ladybug for the mission." She opened the box and took out the bug. "Right now it's harmless. However, we will fill it with the poison before Snezhana takes it. Once you activate it"—

Elda turned it over and showed Snezhana the activation switch—"it will sting the right person."

Charlie held out her hand, and Elda put the bug in it. "How does it know who is the right person?

"It seeks out the DNA, much like the COVID vaccine did for the COVID virus. Tosh supplied Ashok with the senator's DNA from their database on the moles."

Charlie handed the bug back to Elda. "Does it have to sting to get the DNA?"

"No, it sweeps in sweat and skin flakes from the person it lands on. If there is a match, it stings and returns to where it was activated. If there isn't, it returns and waits for the next person. Quite clever, actually."

Elda's phone pinged. She read out loud a text from Ashok: Tree coming at 2pm tmrrw. Quality greens Xmas tree shop.

Sitting in the passenger seat of Tosh's rental, Snezhana checked her watch: 1:35 p.m. They were almost at the senator's neighborhood. The houses were huge, spread out, with fenced fields and horses in between. She inventoried her pain level. That witchcraft of Elda's worked well, as did the extra-strength Tylenol she'd popped an hour ago.

"Ready, niece?"

Snezhana glanced at the hollow ring she wore, compliments of Elda's tech lab, with the metal ladybug inside. "*Da, ser.*" She was grateful to see Tosh smile.

He pulled by the side of the road and stopped the car. Snezhana stepped out and trotted away in the direction of the senator's house. As she neared the driveway, she spotted a truck with a large Christmas tree overflowing the back and two men struggling to get the rope off. She stopped beside them as they pulled the tree down. The distinctive smell of fir filled the air.

"How beautiful." Snezhana reached out and touched a branch. She watched as the ladybug crawled into the tree. "And fresh too."

One man snorted. "The senator will hate it and send it back. He always rejects the first tree." The man shook his head and spat on the ground.

A sudden snow squall blew in, turning their surroundings into the insides of a shaken snow globe. Snezhana pointed up the street. "Do you gentleman know how far this road goes. I am visiting a friend, and this is my first run down here."

The workman shrugged. "This road? It goes on for miles."

"Then I'll expect, with this weather, I'll be turning around soon. Thank you." Snezhana waved and jogged off. She could feel their eyes watching. She pulled up the top of the ring, which had a small mirror the size of a dime on its underside. It magnified the view behind her. Slowing down, she saw the senator stomp out of his house. She turned and bent to tie her shoe, angling her head to watch the scene unfold.

The senator held the tree at arm's length. He turned it around and almost dropped it when he released one hand to swat at his neck. She could hear him yell at the delivery guys. They took the tree from him and tossed it back onto the truck. The senator stormed back into his house.

Snezhana ran back to the truck. "Can I have your card? That's a beautiful tree. I am sure my friends would like one like it." She reached up to touch the tree while they rummaged around for a card. One worker handed her a dogged-eared card.

"Thank you so much." Snezhana clicked the ring closed over the bug and dashed away.

Around the curve, and out of view from the senator's

house, Tosh was waiting with the car idling. She jumped in and turned on her heated seat.

Tosh looked at her. "*Sdelannyy?*"

Snezhana nodded and tapped the ring. "*Da.* All done."

"Now we wait for forty-eight hours."

Two days later the ring with the bug in it rested on Elda's desk. She had confirmed it was empty and had cleaned it out, to ensure no one got accidentally hurt from the dregs. Ashok would pick it up when he showed up to work today, and store it with the rest of his gadgets.

She scrolled through the intelligence reports. There it was. The senator had a massive heart attack that morning, while putting up his Christmas tree. How unfortunate. One more mole gone. Perhaps "hunting moles" should be added to their task list. She knew Tosh and she hadn't flushed them all out in their joint venture last year.

Elda took out her Tosh burner phone. She had another sitting in her drawer to replace it after this call.

"*Da?*"

"Congratulations. It worked. The next call will be from a new phone number."

"*Spasibo.*" He severed the connection.

Elda dialed him from the new phone and hung up before he answered. The new number would appear on his caller ID list. She pocketed the new phone, took the SIM card out of the old phone, and destroyed it. She inserted a SIM and dropped the burner phone into her desk drawer.

Lost in thought, Elda drummed her fingers on her desk. Was there a world in which she and Tosh could work together? The Cold War was over. Russia had won. But was Russia as it stood now the country Tosh wanted to keep defending? The Moscow of old was lost. Were Russia's leaders the ones Tosh wanted to defend? Or did he, like she, want a better world order, where each of their countries was strong but not evil? Where killing had a purpose and was selectively done. She made a mental note to invite Tosh to Gools in the not-too-distant future to discuss this further.

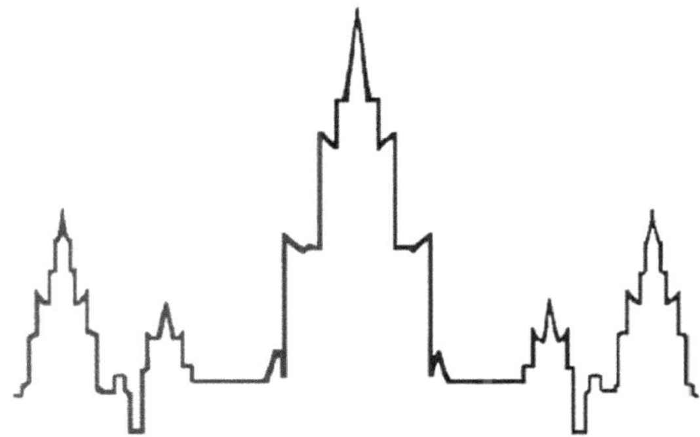

Chapter Twenty-Eight

DID IT ALL HAVE TO COME JUST TO DIE ON her desk?

Elda's neck hurt and her lips felt parched. Was her to-do pile any smaller? Elda was in her office doing her least loved chore, paperwork. She never believed in the concept of a paperless office. Just for one day, though, couldn't it be true?

Her inbox on her computer was filling up too. Email didn't live up to the hype of reducing the volume of forms and paperwork. In fact, Elda would swear email doubled the work.

Add messaging to the mix and social media to track, and each day was an overload of interruptions without blocks of time to get work done. And no wonder people lacked empathy. There was no time, nor reason, for face-to-face interactions anymore.

Elda didn't believe in handling anything sensitive via the internet. There would be a copy of it somewhere in the cloud, and once stored, it would be vulnerable. Any firewall could be breached with enough time and computing power. She didn't have Tosh's photographic memory. However, *even he* kept file cabinets with paper inside. Some considered the two of them dinosaurs. Elda considered herself and Tosh practical.

She had designed for her office a wall that slid open, behind which she locked the file cabinets, guns, other secured weapons, and sensitive equipment. She figured if someone wanted to get into it, they would have to invade her office physically, and she had installed various traps and obstacles to success there. Many wouldn't bother. Cyber-theft was the low-hanging fruit.

She remanded herself. Enough grousing. No wonder this stuff took her so long. *Get your work done.* Elda wrote, signed, filed her report, and closed the wall.

She reached into her shoulder holster and drew out her favorite gun, Smith & Wesson 380 Shield EZ pistol. It fit her hand so well, had a great weight, was easy to load, and reliable. With it, she felt strong and capable.

She popped out the magazine, flipped the field strip lever, and disassembled her pistol. Reaching into her top drawer, she lifted out the cleaning supplies. She hummed as she cleaned. Elda was sensitive to smells, so she had switched solvents to one that had a subtle oily smell and didn't overpower your nostrils, nor did it signal to everyone you walked by that *this woman's hiding a freshly cleaned gun.*

The new cleaner was a silicon spray that dissolved, leaving the weapon dry to the touch. Another positive. Who wanted a slippery gun? She laid out the cloth cleaning patches and the dental picks.

***

Charlie pulled out her Glock 19.

Elda sneered at the gun. "I didn't know you had a

femmie pistol."

"Watch it. It's still loaded," Charlie quipped. She had grabbed a coffee and joined Elda in the daily cleaning ritual.

Elda reached across and pressed the magazine-release button. "Not now." The mag clanked onto the desk.

Charlie stared at it and back at Elda. "How do you know I don't have one in the chamber?"

"That's your office gun. Even though you lock it up at night, you don't like to leave it here loaded."

Charlie bowed. "You're too observant, Master." She chuckled as she selected the forceps and a white cleaning pad.

Elda passed her a dental scaler. "Soon you will be more so, Grasshopper. Why did you come in here?"

Charlie laid the pieces of her gun in front of her. "I've been thinking. Before, if anyone asked what we did, I could say I worked for a boring government agency. What do I say now?" She held out her hand for the ONE Shot silicon spray.

Elda passed her the can. "Great question. I've been meaning to establish our cover identity. I have some of my own ideas, but let's see if Korinna's around. She was looking into this for me. Perhaps she has a suggestion."

Elda texted Korinna. While waiting, the two warriors put their pieces back together.

Charlie holstered her weapon. "Hey, Elda. What would you do if someone attacked while you were cleaning your gun?"

"That's easy. I have an automatic in each top drawer of my desk, as well as a machine gun that shoots out from the front of the desk."

Charlie held up her hands in mock surrender.

Elda's phone buzzed with an incoming message on the secure app. "Good. She's available. Let's conference her in." Elda typed on her computer and motioned for Charlie to come around that side of the desk to view the conference window.

Korinna's face popped up in the screen. She had a kerchief around her head and was holding a bottle of spray Clorox and a rag. "What's up? I was cleaning the bathroom, so let's make this a long conference."

Elda rolled her eyes. "You don't think we might be missing you?"

"Geesh." Korinna pantomimed putting her finger down her throat and gagging.

Elda put her hand over her mouth to hide her grin. "Okay. Okay. Remember when we had the conversation about incorporating into some sort of legitimate cover company?"

Korinna used the rag to clean her camera. "*Da.* I looked into what we'd have to do, but I'm stuck on what type of business."

"Import-export?" Charlie suggested.

Korinna shook her head. "*Net.* Might as well put *Spies Incorporated* on the sign. What about 'detective agency'?"

Elda gave a thumbs-down. "No. That's the same deal, Korinna. Plus, we'd get thrown in jail for how we resolve cases. I'd like us to come up with something that makes money on the side so we can support the rest of the business."

"An investment firm?" Charlie offered.

Elda grimaced. "I'm bad at that type of stuff. I doubt we'd be able to pull it off, unless you have some experience you left off your résumé. With Korinna's project management and language skills, we could handle an international business, but we need to be able to pass the sniff test. I'm thinking something to do with software development. That type of company can limp along for years without a real product, and if we added consulting work, we could bring in some decent cash. Let me bring Ashok in on the conversation."

Elda buzzed Ashok to join them and, when he arrived, brought him up to speed.

"Most excellent idea, Miss Elda. We would need more people to pull that off. My cousin does quality control. We might consider bringing him on board too."

Korinna laughed. "Geesh, Ashok. Soon we'll have your whole family here. Does your mother or father do software development?"

"No, Miss Korinna. They would not want to leave India."

Elda coughed to hide her chuckle. "Before we start bringing on new employees, let's draw up a business plan for this new company and a budget. Ashok, please work with Korinna and me on this. I do think cyber security is a field that would best fit us as a cover. Who knows, maybe we can dumb down some of Ashok's inventions and sell them as products in the future."

Meandering by Elda's office from the break room, Murka spotted the gathering and popped in. "What did I miss?"

"Not much. You wouldn't have any software development experience, would you?"

Murka wrinkled her forehead. "Software dev? Not since college, Elda."

"It was a reach. We're thinking of a cover company, but I'm not clear on how it might function or what our jobs will be." Elda rubbed her forehead. "Okay, let's meet in a couple of days as a full team and go over whatever Korinna and I map out. Until then, I've been thinking about the real estate scam that the Kremlin was running, and the money doesn't add up. I'd like to see if we can trace where the money went to and also if we can get our hands on the deeds of the real estate that they sold at a loss. I doubt if those transactions ever went through. Ashok, would it be possible to fit in looking at that too?"

"I can, Miss Elda, but I have a lot of projects right now. Can someone assist me?"

"Murka, could you possibly help Ashok in some way?"

Murka sighed and rolled her eyes. "Great. A desk jockey." She didn't join Elda's group to be stuck with administrative work.

As if reading her mind, Elda stated, "It's not secretarial work. It's real research. And only for a day or two. Don't worry, I'll get you out there again soon."

Elda handed Charlie a thick folder. "Charlie, can you please look at this information I brought back on the Yelabuga drone factory and see if there is any way we could blow it up and get away with it undetected?"

Charlie opened the folder. "Fun. I'll be glad to. Can I tap Murka for knowledge about escape routes?"

Murka raised her hand. "I'm right here, guys." She murmured, "They always ignore the secretarial help."

Elda snorted. "Do you have the bandwidth to also help Charlie, Murka?"

"*Da.*"

"Charlie *and* Murka, the route I took is in those reports too. That way may be burned now. While you're researching, I fear that Ukraine will not succeed in taking their country back. This may be our last window of opportunity to aid them in any way. I'd like everyone to noodle on how we might help. I had suggested taking out the Korean recruits, but they may now be too integrated with the Russian forces to do that."

"'Noodle on'?" Korinna's puzzled face stared from the

screen.

"Sorry, Korinna. Noodle with your noggin. You know, think with your head?"

"Geesh. You Americans and your sayings."

"And you think sayings such as 'The eyes are afraid, but the hands are doing' is clearer?"

"Works for me," Murka interjected.

"Definitely!" Korinna replied. "Much clearer, and encourages moving forward while figuring things out. I would think you'd like to adopt that as your mantra. I also always liked the saying 'A bad dancer blames his testicles.'" Korinna twirled her rag and smiled.

Charlie nearly fell off her chair, laughing.

"I told you, Charlie, you'd enjoy working with Korinna," Elda remarked. "Her mastery of languages and colloquialisms is remarkable." She turned back to the monitor. "I'll remember that saying, Korinna. Hopefully, I'll find the right time to use it. Now, everyone, scram and figure things out."

CHAPTER TWENTY-NINE

THE FOLLOWING WEEK, ELDA STOOD ONCE again in front of their whiteboard. She opened a blue marker and sniffed it. "Blueberry! Excellent. Korinna got us the fun markers."

Each operative had a thick folder in front of them. "Charlie and Murka did a solid job of consolidating a plan for blowing up the drone factory in Russia. Korinna has overlaid a timeline to it and added in any necessary background information. Take a moment to look at the pages inside those packets. You will have all day to memorize it. When we're done at the end of the day, we will destroy all traces of this op."

There was a rustling of papers as each agent browsed.

"Boy, I wish I had Snezhana's photographic memory." Charlie ran her finger over each line, her lips moving as she ingested the pertinent facts.

After about ten minutes, Elda clapped her hands. "Okay. Your attention back here please. The trip from Kostanay, Kazakhstan, to Yelabuga, up to Perm, and back to Kostanay is a minimum of thirty-two hours. We will use the same modified tanker that we had before. Murka's cousin, Matvey, was paid well to keep it under wraps in case we needed it again. Since going to get it in Saratov Oblast would increase the risk, by adding another fifteen or more hours of us being inside Russia, Matvey is going to deliver it to us in Zlatoust, Russia. The transfer should take minutes, since we are going to dry run it here."

"How?" Murka inquired.

"Ashok and I have built a wooden mockup of the tanker container, and we will practice getting up and into it."

Charlie shuddered. "Will we be sitting under a bunch of oil again?"

"Only for half the trip. We head out empty, which should allow us to make better time. We arrive near the drone factory after dark and leave Murka, our driver, and the truck in the Turgay truck stop north of Yelabuga on M7. Murka will gas up and buy some food for all of us. The drone factory is about an hour on foot from the rest area."

Elda projected a map of Russia and pointed out the places of interest.

"Murka, if we are not back in three hours, you are to assume we are dead or captured, and leave."

Murka started to object.

Elda held up her hand. "It does us no good if we are all captured. If Charlie and I are and you aren't, and you can get away, you might be able to find a way to spring us free."

Murka nodded.

Elda projected a picture of the drone factory and over-laid a blueprint of its structure. She circled six locations. "Charlie, we put the explosives in these places. After doing so, we'll activate them, starting the countdown clock. We'll have one hour to get away."

Charlie rubbed the sides of her head. Murka frowned.

Elda acknowledged their discomfort. "I know it's tight

timing, but we have to split the difference between the devices being discovered and them going off while we're still close enough to be caught. You'll note that everything we wear and use will be Russian, Chinese, or North Korean. We'll have nothing on us aside from accents, body types, and our faces that identify us as Americans. We'll disguise those as best we can."

Elda paused, letting it all sink in. "We have managed to enlist the help of a Lukoil employee. We'll pick him up just beyond Perm. He'll use his ID, along with the paperwork we supply him, for the tanker fill up. Bringing on an outsider is a risk, but he is Matvey's wife's cousin and we are paying him well. He has no incentive to turn us in. Anyway, he won't know about the hidden compartment in the tanker."

Charlie considered Murka. "Are you related to all of Russia?"

Murka winked. "I come from a highly sexed family."

Charlie blushed.

Elda groaned theatrically. She continued. "After the tanker is gassed up and filled, we'll be on our way back to Kostany. We'll drop the oversexed cousin-in-law off right after Perm, where he will have parked his car. We'll stay hidden until we reach Kazakhstan." She looked around the room. Ashok and Korinna stared back, wide eyed. Murka and Charlie flipped through their folders.

Elda pointed at the coffeepot and the muffins on the side table. "Korinna made us her extra-tasty, but healthy, dark chocolate muffins."

Korinna started to explain, when Charlie broke in. "Please. Don't tell me what's in them that makes them healthy, Korinna. I like to enjoy my chocolate. Now let's take a bio break and then start rehearsing. I want us to have the timing down to a second." Elda studied the projected map. What could go wrong?

A dense fog swirled around the pitch-black night when Murka pulled into the rest area on M7, northeast of Khlystovo, Russia. She parked at the far-end edge, ensuring no one could park to the south of her truck. She exited on the passenger side, slipped under the tanker, and in minutes opened up the inner compartment.

Charlie and Elda crawled out. The three spies synchronized their watches and set their alarms for three hours from now. Murka stood guard as Charlie and Elda ran off into the gloom. Murka sauntered to the lavatory (*damskaya komnata*), then browsed the store, buying a sizable hunk of *Rossiysky* cheese, a six-pack of Coke, and a large package of *ponchiki* donuts.

Returning to the truck, Murka crawled behind her seat, clutched her CZ-75 semiautomatic pistol, and lay hidden on the mattress there. Time to wait.

Dressed in gray and black, Charlie and Elda double-checked their directions and set out at a fast jog. Elda cinched her backpack straps tight, to ensure she wasn't jostling the explosives. They paused at the side of M7 and listened.

No lights, no sound.

They sprinted across. Surrounded by a world of gray, and limited in how far she could see, Elda felt like the fog highlighted her other senses. She could smell the diesel fuel from the truck stop. Sounds were muted but traveled farther. She could feel the dampness on her face and the resistance the ground made to her boots. Elda was grateful for the cover the fog provided, but also aware that it restricted her ability to see a threat far enough in advance to properly react to it.

They fell into a steady run, at the edge of Elda's breathing.

"Oomph . . . Shit!"

"Charlie, are you okay?"

Elda peered through the murk and spotted a body on the ground. She reached for her weapon and moved toward it.

"I'm okay. The only harm is to my self-image. I tripped."

Elda held out her hand and hoisted Charlie to her feet. After ensuring Charlie wasn't hurt, she instructed, "We have to get going. I want to take advantage of the fog and dark. Our schedule is tight." She took a hit from her inhaler, and they moved off at a fast pace.

The buildings stood closer together in this area. Elda felt her way to the factory, using her memories of the days she'd spent here scoping it out. She didn't want to take down the wrong building.

She stopped. "This is it," she whispered to Charlie, "You sure?"

Elda marched Charlie to the dumpster and shone her light on the wall behind it. There, low to the ground, was an *X* scratched into the foundation. "That's my *X*."

"Great. Let's get this done with. I'll meet you back at the *X* in fifteen minutes."

"Hustle and make it back here in ten minutes. This fog won't last forever."

Once Charlie returned, she and Elda trotted back to the oil tanker. About one-quarter of a mile away, they heard an explosion and the sky behind them lit up.

"Sprint! We're out of time."

The two flew the rest of the way, powered by adrenaline. They skidded to a stop by the truck.

Murka stood by the opened compartment, waiting.

"Get in. Quickly!" Elda pushed Charlie up and in and pulled herself in after her. The gloom they had been in was light by comparison to the blackness of the container. Elda reached around, and her hand fell on a bag. She felt inside. The familiar shape of soda cans answered her fingers. There was something else that could be cheese, and something softer . . . bread perhaps. No, pastry. She felt the truck start and pull out of the rest area. Confident they were on the road, she flashed on a light to further analyze her find. Donuts. *Not too shabby, Murka.*

She nudged Charlie. "Hungry?"

"Famished."

Elda spread the paper bag between them, took out her knife, and sliced off some cheese and opened the donuts. She handed Charlie a Coke and her oxygen mask and flicked off the light.

The truck slowed and stopped. It started again after two minutes.

"That must be the pickup before the refinery." Elda clicked on her watch light to read the time. "Right on schedule. Nice, steady driving, Murka." She checked the levels on the O2 tanks. They had enough.

Soon the truck slowed again and came to a full stop. Elda held her breath. Were they at the refinery? Would someone question the paperwork?

The truck started again, and after a short distance, stopped. That must be the fill-up point. She heard the fluid gushing in above their heads. Her heart raced. *Now* would be the time when the impact of the oil would break the weld. She ran her hand along the weld lines. All dry so far.

Charlie felt the motion beside her. "Everything okay?"

"So far. I don't know if it will sprout small leaks one at a time or engulf us in one go."

"Oh God."

The fill-up seemed to take forever, but the truck engine

started and they moved down the road.

"Uh-oh." Elda wiped a wet drop off her cheek. She massaged it between her thumb and her forefinger. The liquid felt viscous. She removed her oxygen mask and held her finger up to her nose. "Damn. Oil." Her heart thudded in her chest. Her breathing constricted.

"What! Is the weld letting go?" Charlie's voice cracked at the end of her sentence.

"Seems so. Even if it's a tiny spot, with the weight of the liquid above us, it might blow. What to do . . . What to do?" Elda breathed in through her nose and out through her mouth, to squash her panic and allow her brain room to think. "Where are you, you bugger?" Elda reached behind her and took a headlamp from its hanger. She shined it up and around the weld line.

"Can you see it?"

"Not yet."

"Shit."

Elda calculated the drop line from the weld to her cheek and focused the light in that spot. "Got it." She put her finger on a small drop forming. "At least it's slow right now. It looks as if I can dry it enough to repair it. I'll have to get it before it breaks through more."

"What do we do? We can't very well weld with all this combustible crude in the tanker."

"True. But I have the next best thing." Elda released a medium-sized box that was strapped to the wall. She opened it and pawed through the contents. She rejected using a bucket patch, since the leak wasn't big enough for it—and she wasn't going to widen it.

She selected a cleaning rag and wiped down the leak area. She removed a cleaning solvent and a fresh rag, which she used to wipe away the oil slick. Next, she gave Charlie a cloth mask to wear over her oxygen mask and put her own mask back on and covered it. "I'm not sure how this stuff will react to rubber, and we can't afford to lose our O2 supply. Also, we shouldn't breathe this stuff. Get on the comms, Charlie. Ask Murka if she can find a place to pull over and get some fresh air in here. Even without the epoxy smell, it's getting stuffy."

Charlie picked up her cell. "The signal is in and out, Elda."

"Go to the secure network."

Charlie spoke into her ear comm. "Murka, pull over when safe." She turned to Elda. "A lot of static, but she got the message."

With that, Elda took out a popsicle stick, a small piece of wood, and a double epoxy syringe and mixed the epoxy together. She placed a small fiberglass patch over the hole and slathered the mixture over the fiberglass.

"Will that fix it?"

Elda scratched her head. "I don't know. There's a lot of oil on the other side of that patch. I'm not sure if that pressure will end up widening the crack and cause it to spring a bigger leak."

"How long until we know if it works?"

"Twenty-five minutes or so." Elda felt the truck pull over. "Good, we have to do that air exchange."

"Do you think that's the only weak spot?"

"You better pray it is."

In the darkness, Elda felt along the weld line every ten minutes. It remained dry.

"I'll take over Elda. You need to rest."

"Thanks, Charlie."

Elda rolled onto her side in a fetal position, with her jacket and arm under her head.

An hour later she woke, refreshed.

Charlie's voice, muffled through her mask, came out of the blackness. "Murka stopped and let the guy out."

"Ah, I thought I dreamed that." Elda pressed the background-light option and checked her watch. She removed her mask, ate some cheese wrapped in a folded donut, and washed down with a glug of Coca-Cola.

"Go slowly on that. I think it's an hour before our next bathroom break."

"Damn. I wish you hadn't said that. Now I *have* to go."

"There's always the covered bucket over there."

"Damn. I'll hold it. I'm going to need Tosh's blood pressure cuff. The next mission will not involve being stuck in the dark, in close quarters. How's the weld doing?" Elda sniffed the air for an increase in oil, but all she could smell was the residual odor of the epoxy.

"Still dry."

"Thanks." Elda put her mask back on, sat against the wall of the container, and hugged her knees to her chest. She hoped the road would stay smooth. Hitting a bump would not help her full bladder.

Murka pulled the tanker over to the side of the road near a grove of trees. She slid off her seat and onto the ground and crawled under the truck. She opened the false panel and the hatch. Elda dropped out first and dashed to the woods. Charlie's feet hit the ground. She slithered her way out and ran after Elda.

So much for *Hello, Murka*... Murka leaned against the side of the tanker and looked up and down the road. There had been little traffic so far. The border would be tight. Her sources had notified her that the Russians had increased security precautions at the crossing. She watched as a smiling Elda jogged out of the trees.

Elda wiped her fingers across her forehead. "Whew. I thought I wouldn't make it. Contemplating using the bucket helped me hold it though. Thanks for avoiding the bumps."

Murka chuckled. "I'm glad I'm in my own suite. But that said, I'll let you take point while I use the facilities." She sprinted to the woods and passed Charlie coming back.

Despite dark sunglasses, Charlie and Elda both found themselves squinting and blinking back tears. Elda leaned back against the truck and sighed. "I'll never take sunshine for granted again."

Murka joined the two others. "Do you want the good news or the bad news?"

Elda put a finger to the side of her head and used it to point at Murka. "The bad news. I consider us being still alive the good news."

"The border is crawling with guards. Someone blew up a plant of some kind."

Elda rubbed the impressions the oxygen mask had left on her face. "Oh really? What a surprise. And the good news?"

"We're ahead of schedule."

"Alive and early. I'll take it. I'm worried about the weight of all that oil though. I'm thinking we could donate some of our load to a local monastery or nunnery."

"I know of a place in Yekaterinburg. It's run by the Congregation of Sisters Missionaries of Catholic Apostolate and is sizable. We're going to go right by it. Within spitting distance, as you Americans like to say."

Elda rolled her eyes. "You have a cousin there?"

Murka winked. "Great-aunt."

Elda clapped her palms to the sides of her head. "Let's go donate some oil. You can wangle a receipt for the border?"

"That won't be an issue at all. The order has been doing deals for centuries."

Elda high-fived Murka and gave Charlie a boost into the container. "Let's go."

With a lighter truck, after their stop in Yekaterinburg, Murka made good time. They'd be early to the border near Bugristoe, Russia, but that would be okay for their schedule, since they would experience some delay with the extra security checks. Murka patted the fully automatic, short-barreled, AK-12 Russian assault rifle resting next to her thigh. She figured if Kim Jong-un liked it, it was good enough for her needs.

She calculated that with the rifle she could take out at least four guards and drive like hell for the border. However, if the Russians had a well-armed squad at the checkpoint, there would be no way she could take them out. The team would be toast. Perhaps literally, if the tanker blew. She'd have to rely on her charm and good looks to get them through. She glanced in her rearview mirror and then applied some makeup during the next straightaway. She was pretty good at steering this rig with her knees by now.

"Uh-oh."

They weren't shitting about the increased security at the border. A squad of soldiers milled about, plus the line of traffic where there usually was none. Murka downshifted, braked, and joined the queue's glacial movement.

She slipped the AK onto the floor beneath her feet. A car was waved through. She moved the tanker forward and examined the troops. They looked green. The experienced ones were all in Ukraine or dead. She hoped these novices weren't trigger happy.

Her turn.

"*Privet, krasavitsa.*"

She smiled at his flirting hello and returned the compliment. "*Privet, krasavchik.*" It was easy to say. He was a handsome man.

"Please show me the oil level and paperwork for delivery."

She collected her paperwork and slid out of the cab, landing close to him. "You will like the level and paperwork." She winked at him.

He brushed against her as he took the paperwork. "I will? Why?"

"We are screwing our neighbors on this delivery."

"That sounds delightful. And how, may I ask, does that work?"

"You'll see in the paperwork that we gave away some of our cargo to the Catholic missionaries. The Kazakhstanis paid for a full tank, but that order has been modified to show they paid for the amount we are delivering to them. The manifest never lies."

"Beautiful and clever. Do you think your tanker might be late for its delivery?" He winked at Murka.

Murka beamed at him. "I wish it could be so. That would add a bad start to our negotiations."

"But a good one for you and me."

"Next time." She pressed against him as she gathered back her papers.

He brushed his hand down her back. "Ah, with regret, my lady."

Two cars behind her, she heard a scuffle, and shots rang out. Keeping in character, Murka screamed and hung on to her guard's arm. He held her close, and they ducked behind a car. The soldiers fired more shots at a car that had pulled out of line and gunned for the border. Bullets flew as the recruits chased after the vehicle on foot. The car wavered and stopped.

"Unfortunate." The guard helped Murka up. "You're shaking. Can you drive."

Murka wiped a tear off her cheek. "That was so scary. But I *do* need to get going. I'll be late as it is."

He helped her up into her cab with his hand on her butt. She started her engine and rolled down the window. "*Spasibo*." She blew him a kiss.

Elda could hear the shouting and the shots. She prayed they wouldn't be discovered. She hoped that Murka was okay and wasn't in the line of fire. She hadn't realized she was holding her breath, until she started breathing again when the tanker started up and they rolled along.

Relieved, she shifted her weight and put her hand down next to her . . . into a puddle. *Puddle?* "I'm turning on the light. I think we may have been hit."

Silence.

Elda's chest constricted. "Charlie?"

She flicked on her headlamp and saw Charlie out cold with oil running down onto her from a hole in the tank. *Damn.* She switched into crisis-control mode. Okay. Triage it. First, help Charlie. Then, stop the leak. Next, tell Murka to pull over when she can.

Elda examined Charlie. Her pulse was strong and even. Her color was good. She had a bloody gash on her head, where she was either hit by the bullet or hit her head on the bracket that held her oxygen tank. Her oxygen tank was still attached, and her mask held secure to her face. Good.

Elda turned her light above Charlie to the puncture in the metal. The liquid was rapidly pouring in for such a small hole. Not good.

Elda reached into her repair kit and removed a tiny bucket patch. If it was good enough to repair ships taking on water at sea, it should work here. She thrust the metal end through the hole and shook it until it swiveled into a T shape on the other side. She positioned the bucket, with a rubber gasket on its edge, over the hole and screwed it down until it sealed.

Murka hit a pothole, and Elda slipped down into the oil. The viscous glop seeped up her sleeve, into her hair, and onto side of her face. "My God. This sucks." She wiped the slick off her headlamp and examined the container for the shot's exit. *Aha! There it is.* She repeated her magic and sealed hole number two. She didn't see any others.

She slid her way to the medical kit and removed two gauze pads, a sterile saline solution, and tape. She patted the blood from Charlie's wound and sprayed it, covering it with a clean pad and tape. Charlie stirred. Elda held Charlie's head so she wouldn't tip over into the spill.

Charlie reached up to touch her head, but Elda caught her arm. "Elda? What the fuck? Ouch! I have a headache."

"Stay still, Charlie, and stay as upright as you can. We've taken on some oil. You have a slight head wound, but it's not bad."

"Easy for you to say. It's pounding." Charlie put a hand down to steady herself and picked it right back up, holding it in Elda's light and staring at the brown ooze dripping from her fingers. "This is gross. Where did all this goop come from?"

Elda held Charlie by a shoulder. She was anxious that they might hit another bump and send both of them into the growing puddle. "Please be careful not to fall into the oil. We got hit by a bullet and have a leak. We're moving, so I assume the truck's okay. I'm going to have Murka stop so we can relocate to inside the cab. Now that we're over the border, it should be okay for us to be out. We'll stash you on the mattress behind the seats, and I'll ride shotgun. There also has to be a leak on the outside where the bullet entered. That will need to be repaired. Luckily, I have some more of these cute little bucket patches."

Elda wiped her hand on a rag and took out her cell. No signal.

Having anticipated that, Elda clicked the mike for the two-way radio. Less secure, but a reliable backup system. "Fearless driver. Emergency pitstop needed. I repeat. Emergency."

"Roger that," Murka answered.

In five minutes the truck rolled to a stop. Elda heard Murka opening the hatch.

"*Gryaznyy*!" The oil poured around the edges of the hatch and onto the ground. A greasy Elda and a black-and-red-splashed Charlie flowed out with it. Elda slammed the hatch shut and crawled out from under the truck, pulling Charlie. She handed a bucket device to Murka. "There should be a leak on the passenger side."

Murka turned the tiny bucket over in her hand, staring at it. "What is this?"

Elda rolled her eyes and frowned. "My God. A stint in the navy should be required for everyone. It's a bucket patch. Never mind. Just look after Charlie. Get some clean clothes on her and settle her down on the bunk." Elda looked at Murka and touched her lips. "I like that shade on you."

Murka turned bright red.

Elda snorted. "OMG. I have two that blush. Let's get going. We don't want to draw attention to us."

On M-36 near Ozernoye in Kazakhstan, Elda pointed at the Quazaq Oil gas station. "Let's stop here and see if they need any crude, plus I can clean up a bit in the restroom." Murka brought the truck to a stop.

Elda slipped out, returning cleaner and sopping wet. She was holding a large paper bag. "I bought soap, wet wipes, and towels, but I need a shower. Unfortunately, they don't have one, and they aren't interested in any free oil today."

After passing by Ozernoye, Elda sighted a pond on the right side of the road. "Stop here!" Murka pulled the truck over, and Elda ran out with her soap and dove into the ice-covered pond. In a few minutes she had washed her hair and clothes. She ran back out and shook herself off like a dog.

"You're not thinking of getting back in the truck like that?" Murka pointed at a still-dripping, but clean, Elda.

Shivering, Elda grabbed dry clothes from her seat. She stripped off her wet ones, reached into the bag on the front floor of the cab, and pulled out two towels. She wiped off in rapid speed and pulled on her dry clothes. She wrapped the second towel around her still-wet head, tossed her wet clothes on the floor, and climbed in. "Can you please turn the heat to high for a while?"

A voice came out from behind the seats, "You know, Elda, that soap sucks for the environment."

Elda brought her knees up to her chest and hugged them close. "Yeah, I feel badly about that, Charlie, but I can't fly out looking like a ball of grease. How are you feeling?"

Charlie peeked from between the front seats. "I have a pounding headache, but I'll live."

Elda held up her fist. "How many fingers am I holding up."

Charlie threw her a finger, tossed a spare blanket at Elda's head, and lay back down.

Elda wrapped herself in the blanket. "Thanks, Charlie." Shivering, she focused on Murka. "So who's waiting for us at the next stop?"

Murka pulled the truck back onto the road. "Do you remember Cousin Matvey?"

Elda answered with chattering teeth. "Yes. Is he here?"

Murka turned the heat higher. "Yes. He's going to take possession of the tanker and take it back to his shop."

"Excellent, but that's back in Russia. How are we extracted? And is that as high as the heat will go?"

"It's like a sauna in here, Elda. You'll warm up soon. Cousin Matvey has a cousin Avian who works at the Airbus Helicopters Kazakhstan Engineering facility near the Astana International Airport. He likes to tinker."

Elda pulled the blanket over her head. Only her face showed. "Tinker, hey? I can't wait to see our ride out of here."

Murka pulled the tanker onto the grass at the Vertolonaya Ploshchadka helicopter pad. A stiff breeze blew across the open area.

"Is that a Mil M-4? I thought the last operational ones were in North Korea!" Elda threw off her blanket, shrugged on her coat, jumped out, and ran up to the rusted and aluminum-patched green vehicle. The four windows in the front curved downward at the ends, giving it a sad look. She climbed up using the hand and foot supports on the side and inspected the rotor. It was clean and well maintained. She peeked through the side window and glimpsed a glistening new instrument panel. She jumped down and looked at the rivets along the sides.

A man came around from the other side of the craft, wiping his hands on a rag. He held out a hand to Elda. "*Privet.* I am Avian. You are right. Many of the parts of this bird are from the Mil M-4. I have updated the key components to get it flying again. I was about to scrape and paint it, when Matvey called."

Matvey climbed out of the helicopter. "That was one wild ride." He ran to Murka and hugged her. "Hello, Elda and Charlie. So good to see you again."

Elda clapped him on the back. "Matvey, my genius

welder. I'm afraid we put a few holes in your truck. One of the welds inside is going too. I patched it. We removed some of the cargo weight, so it *should* make it back home."

"*Spasibo*, Elda. It's a long drive, so I will leave you now. Enjoy your flight."

Murka had been talking to Avian. She rejoined her cousin and her two teammates. "Avian will take us to Nur-sultan Nazarbayev International Airport in Astana. From there we can catch a flight to Frankfurt, Germany. From there we can fly directly into Dulles International Airport on United."

"Perfect. Thank you so much, Avian." Elda ran back to the tanker and pulled out their gear. "Our disguises and new papers are in here."

Chapter Thirty

BACK IN DC, ELDA SAT WITH CHARLIE AND Murka in their office lounge. Elda was wrapped in a blanket, sipping a hot chocolate, and had her feet up on the table. Charlie was drinking a large steaming cup of black coffee. Murka was letting her tea steep and munching on one of Olga's Bourbon Creams.

"You better make sure you leave some for Olga, Murka, or she'll make your life hell in the next group workout."

Murka chuckled. "Don't I know that!"

Elda noted Charlie looked worried and was playing with her bandage on her head.

"What's up, Grasshopper? And leave that alone. It's almost healed. You don't want it to get infected."

Charlie pulled up the camera app on her phone and turned it to selfie so she could view her head. "Do you think I'll have a scar there?"

"Most likely, especially if you keep playing with it."

Charlie dropped her hand to her lap.

"I think scars are sexy," Murka murmured.

Elda changed the subject, away from the two of them flirting. "Talk about sexy, Murka. What color was that lovely lipstick you had on while driving the tanker?"

Murka rolled her eyes.

"Seriously though, that was good spy craft. You had guard-dog boy wrapped around your little finger."

Murka smiled. "That was the intent."

"Bravo Zulu to both of you. I think, in the future, you'll be able to do the ops in Russia without me."

"Too cold for you, Master?"

"I may never be warm again. I think it's time we retired that tanker. I'm not a real fan of oil baths, or for that matter, ice baths."

Charlie smelled her hand. "I can still smell that stuff."

"My cousin would love to use the truck for smuggling. May I let Matvey lend it to him?"

Elda held her hand to her forehead. "Is this a new cousin or one we've met already?"

"He's a black sheep in the family. You haven't met him yet."

"Let's not bother to meet this guy, then. I would like a gig where we're not enclosed in a container of some sort. Feel free to give it away." Elda's burner phone vibrated. "It's Ed. I have to take this."

Trailing the blanket, she plodded to the other side of the lounge and plopped onto a counter. "Hey, Ed, what's up?"

"There was a drone factory blown up in Russia. Ukraine is taking credit for doing it. But I doubt they have that type of reach."

Elda's smile sneaked into her voice. "Gee, Ed. You just don't know what those guys can do. They have surprised me with their ingenuity and guts."

"I think that's what they want everyone to think. But I'm suspicious someone else did it."

Elda swung her legs and stretched her back. "Interesting. Well, if you find out, let me know."

"Well done, Elda."

"Thanks, Ed. But I'm sure you didn't call to give me a news update. Did you find out who is the latest assassin?"

"You're correct. This isn't a social call. And, I haven't any new info on the assassin. We have an issue here. An NSA employee absconded with highly sensitive data. We don't think he's left the United States yet, but we're pretty sure he'll be heading to Russia. There's an APB on him, and every agency we can activate is in the mix."

"So what do you need me for?"

"It's Blake Galkin."

Silence. Elda's breath stopped for a moment, while her mind caught up with the words Ed had uttered.

Ed filled in for Elda. "You can say I told you so. That you warned me he was a security risk. But nothing showed on the background check. I couldn't tell NSA that my agent's spidey sense said not to hire him."

Elda sighed. "Some days I hate it when I'm right."

"You served with him in the navy. You know him better than most."

Elda shook her head. "I doubt that. It's been a lot of years since the navy. He's been playing a long game."

"Will you help?"

Elda rubbed her face with her hand. Her eyes felt gritty and heavy. She inhaled, searching for some energy, finding none. "Man, I'd like to rest before jumping into this."

"It's time sensitive, as you are aware. We have to get him before he lands somewhere we can't extradite him."

Elda rubbed her jaw. She sighed. "Ouch. Okay, Ed. I'm going to need to start chugging a lot of coffee. This hot chocolate won't do the trick. I'll brief the team. Black ops, right?"

"Right."

Elda returned to the conference room. She texted Ashok and asked him to join them. With one look at Elda's face, Charlie dashed over to the break room and returned with two double espressos, a cup of tea, and a can of Coca-Cola.

Elda brought Korinna into the meeting via their secure chat.

"Geesh, you guys look a wreck."

"Thanks, Korinna. We mostly are. We need downtime. I most of all want to rack out right now, but Ed called with a priority mission. Can you add staffing for operations to the hiring lists?"

Ashok sauntered in, popped open his Coke, and took a sip. "Miss Elda, ma'am, I have the results from my program."

"Fantastic. Let's see what it came up with. All, Ashok has created a new AI app that will gather all available facts on someone, plus anything else we know about that person. You can ask it to predict an action. For example, Blake Galkin. Blake is an American of Russian descent. He served with me in the United States Navy in Wales. There was something off about him, and I never trusted him. It seems I was right in that. Blake most recently was an employee of the NSA and has absconded with some highly classified material."

Ashok nodded. "Very correct, Miss Elda. I have asked my program where it thinks Blake will head."

"Thanks, Ashok. I wrote down my choices where I think he will head. Ashok now holds my list. We'll have a runoff."

"Can we bet?" Charlie asked. "Ten bucks on Elda."

"I'll take Elda," Korinna replied.

Charlie high-fived the air. "I'm in with you, Korinna."

"Someone has to believe in technology," Murka offered. "I'll take Ashok's app."

"Thank you, Miss Murka, but I will also take Miss Elda."

"Guys, behave. This is serious."

Ashok laughed. Elda scowled at him and raised an eyebrow. He projected her choices onto the screen.

DC to NYC.

Private plane to Wales.

Chunnel to EU country.

Russia.

Next to it he popped up a window displaying the results of his AI program.

DC to NYC to Wales to EU to Russia

Charlie held out her hand. "Pay up, Murka."

Murka counted out 895 rubles into Charlie's hand. "Keep the change."

Charlie looked down at the stack that had overflowed onto the table. "What the fuck?"

"That's ten dollars, unless you want to be paid in a different type of currency."

Charlie blushed.

Elda rolled her eyes at the two of them. She refocused the meeting. "Your program shows potential, Ashok."

Ashok beamed at Elda's compliment.

Elda sat and addressed her team. "Here's why I made those decisions. Blake is a smart man who would figure that an APB would be out for him, so he would need to vanish. What's one of the best cities to disappear into? And he would also have to select his destination on an ability to get a charter plane out and not be on the manifest. NYC has a large Russian population, and he may have contacts there. If not, there are enough there whom he could bribe."

"Why Wales though?"

"Blake and I were stationed in Wales. It's not heavily populated, and not many people would think of it as an entryway into the continent. Most think of Ireland. If he heads for Wales, he would land at Cardiff Airport." Elda consulted her watch. "We may be too late. Let's get going. Grab your go-bags. Ed has a plane on standby for us." Elda chugged her double espresso and followed it with a half cup of black coffee.

"What about NYC?" Murka inquired.

"We have to get ahead of him. It would be like a needle in a haystack to find him in in NYC. But I've alerted Ed on that possibility."

"Should we contact Sophia?"

Elda flashed Charlie a thumbs-up. "Good thinking, Grasshopper. Already done."

The private charter jet rolled to a stop.

Charlie nudged Elda. "She's there on the tarmac."

Elda leaned across Charlie and glanced out the window at the other planes that had parked away from the terminal, where commercial jets lined up to take on and disperse passengers. The tarmac glistened from a recent rain. Sophia stood nearby with a car at her side.

"Roger that. Get ready to disembark." Elda stood, wrestled her backpack from the overhead, and moved forward. "Hustle and stick with me." Elda was the first one down the stairs.

Sophia strode to them and shook Elda's hand. "You are all cleared through customs and immigration and are remanded into my custody."

Recognizing that Sophia was in formal MI6 agent mode, Elda refrained from hugging her. "Thanks much for handling that, Sophia. Any news on our guy?"

Sophia checked her watch. "There's a cargo plane due in from NYC in about ten minutes. Could be him."

Elda nodded. "What's your guess on what mode of transportation he'll take?"

Sophia scratched her head. "I'm not sure. If he's arranged a car, it will meet him at the plane. Otherwise, I'd wager he'll take the train."

Elda handed Sophia an earpiece. Murka and Charlie signaled that they had theirs in already. "Comms check."

"Loud and clear."

"Right-o."

"*Da.*"

Elda surveyed the area to see what cars were parked nearby. "Sophia, how many vehicles do we have?"

Sophia pointed. "I have mine over there, and I snagged two for your lot."

Elda was pleased to be working with Sophia again. She was on top of things. "Excellent. Can we get a third for Murka, who will be stationed at the bus stop? Then she can help us follow him."

Sophia typed on her phone. "Not a problem. I'm on it."

"Okay. Thanks." Elda called to Murka. "Murka, pop over to the bus stop for the train. We'll buzz you if he's headed your way. If he's not taking public transportation, he's going via car on the M4. If he goes that way, grab your vehicle and join the chase."

Elda wheeled around to Charlie. "Charlie, take a car and wait for instructions at the BP Leigh Delamere service area. It should be in your GPS. You will assume the front tail there."

She addressed Sophia. "I'll lead out. You follow. I'll veer off into the rest area, and you assume the rear tail. Hand it off to Murka."

Rapidly planning, Elda ordered, "Murka, I'll need your race car–driving skills. If he's taking the M4, wait at the Shell station in Reading. It's five minutes off the M4 on Basingstoke Road. So you'll need to catch up and pass us."

Sophia added, "By that time, Elda, we should have a roadblock established. We're setting it up after the A329 interchange and after A321."

"Great, Sophia. Then you're well positioned, Murka. Follow behind him. The three of us will fall in behind you, in case he gets tricky and turns around when he sees the roadblock."

"But he'd be going the wrong way on a *motorway*."

Elda enjoyed Sophia's sense of British proper behavior being disturbed. "*Exactly*. If so, we take him out. Public safety and all that rot."

Sitting in her car on the other side of the charter, Elda watched the cargo plane roll to a stop. She thought back to her navy days and Blake's passive-aggressive behavior. She massaged her jaw.

The passengers and crew deplaned from the cargo plane. She could feel the bile rise in her throat when she spotted Blake. She clicked her earbud. "That's him. He's in his old United States Navy uniform. It still fits him well. Good disguise too. Who would suspect an aging foreign agent to be dressed as an ensign. But he still walks the same as he did so many years ago, and his face matches the photo we have from NSA."

Sophia chimed in. "There's a black sedan driving up to meet the plane."

Elda clenched and unclenched her hands. She massaged the back of her neck. After all these years, she was still angry at that misogynistic asshole. "Let's wait until he gets in the car, but get in your car, Murka, and start your engine, Charlie." Elda watched as the navy officer marched over to the sedan. *Traitor.*

The driver got out and waited. Blake threw his bag onto the passenger seat, handed an envelope to the driver, who peeked at the contents, nodded, and tossed him the car keys.

Elda notified the team. "It's on. He's getting into the car. It's a black sedan, license plate KY24 TXT." She received three single clicks in response.

Elda analyzed her disguise in the rearview mirror. He wouldn't recognize her. While waiting, she had applied a beard and mustache, which changed her image from anything Blake might recognize. She wore a black ball cap and a leather jacket. She planned on swapping out the black ball cap for a red one, the leather for a cloth suitcoat, and the beard and mustache for a goatee when she pulled in at the rest area. She would also swap out her plates. "Okay, you little bastard," she muttered. "It's time to pay the piper. I always thought you were slime." She started her engine and pulled up to the gate behind Blake.

Driving out of Wales into England, they passed over the River Severn. Elda was appalled at how low the water level was. It appeared the drought had also affected the UK. She felt attached to this land, having spent many years traveling through it. It was a second home to her.

Elda rubbed the back of her neck and rolled her shoulders. Her body was stiff after all the travel. Driving at the speed limit through familiar bucolic countryside threatened to lull her to sleep. She rolled down the window and turned on the radio. She tossed a couple of chocolate-covered espresso beans into her mouth and chewed, hoping the caffeine would kick in. "The years are starting to catch up with you, old girl."

"Hey, Master?" Charlie's voice came over Elda's comms.

Elda hoped no one had heard her talking to herself. "Yes, Grasshopper?"

"As much as I'm enjoying the scenic tour, there's enough of us. Why don't we force him off the road and be done with this?"

"I wish we could, but we're operating as black ops on this mission. We're not supposed to be here. We'll only intervene if necessary. Think of it as road surveillance training for the team."

"Gotcha. Thought I'd ask. Pretty landscape and all that, but this lacks action."

That was putting it mildly. Elda blinked the encroaching sleep out of her eyes. "Don't get complacent. We're nearly at the roadblock. There's the A329 interchange a half mile ahead. The roadblock should be a bit after that. Eyes open, reflexes ready." Taking her own advice, Elda chewed up two more espresso beans.

Murka's car was behind Blake's. She was swaying over the lane line, putting on eye makeup as she went. Murka was shaping up to be a solid operator with excellent disguise skills.

Sophia was stationed behind Murka. From what Elda could see, she was reading *The Times*. Elda cringed every time she picked the paper up, obscuring her forward vision. It was an effective camouflage though.

Charlie sped by Elda, cutting her off. She pumped her fist and yelled at Elda. Elda slammed on her brakes and accelerated around Charlie, throwing her the two-fingered salute. Elda keyed her comms. "Well done, Grasshopper. I needed waking up."

"I wanted to break up the monotony and keep us alert, as ordered."

As she passed the A329, Elda glanced in her rearview

mirror and saw a line of unmarked police vehicles enter the M4 and spread across the road, keeping any other traffic behind them.

She called the team. "We have a line of police behind us. Get ready to slow down. The roadblock should be in view in a few minutes."

"He's seen it and slammed on his brakes!" Murka called out. She swerved and missed hitting Blake's car by inches.

Sophia managed to stop before crashing into his bumper. She rolled down her window and started yelling at him. "You bloody pervert. What the fuck?"

Blake ignored the two cars and threw his car into gear and spun his steering wheel to the left.

"He's turning." Murka slammed her car in gear and pressed the accelerator to the floor while braking and turning, causing her car to almost flip as it made the tight turn. Elda pulled her car across the rightmost lane, ready to accelerate and ram him. She saw Charlie position her car in the leftmost lane to force him off the road.

They were ready.

Elda looked up the road, and Blake was coming at a high speed. She tightened her shoulder harness.

Murka was behind him, ramming his bumper.

Sophia was a car length behind Murka.

Charlie sped out and hit him on the left side, while Elda rammed him on the right.

The four cars welded together in one screaming metal mass as he kept his foot on the accelerator.

Elda felt the wind knocked out of her. She was surprised, but grateful, her airbag had not deployed. They were now heading at a high speed to the other police roadblock. They must stop Blake before they all became a fiery lump of car pieces.

She jumped on the comms. "If this thing still drives, I'm going to reverse. Press on with all that you have. It should send him into the guardrail. Get ready to jump if the whole mess starts to go over." With a metal screech and groan, Elda backed her car, minus its bumper, out of the wreck and slammed it to a stop. She jumped out, gun drawn. She watched as Blake's car was rammed into the rail, toppled over it, flipped, and landed on its roof.

Murka's left tire was half on the road, half off. Charlie's car had detached a foot away from going over.

Elda smelled a distinct smell of burnt rubber, gas, and oil. A plume of smoke rose from the wreck below her.

Charlie, Murka, and Elda ran down to the smoking wreck. The three operatives pulled an unconscious Blake from his car. Elda put two fingers on his pulse. He was alive.

A collection of police and MI6 agents soon joined them.

Elda showed them a false badge. "He's all yours. We were never here."

Sophia jogged up.

"Is your car functional?"

"Right as rain, Elda."

"Great. Can we get a ride back to Wales?"

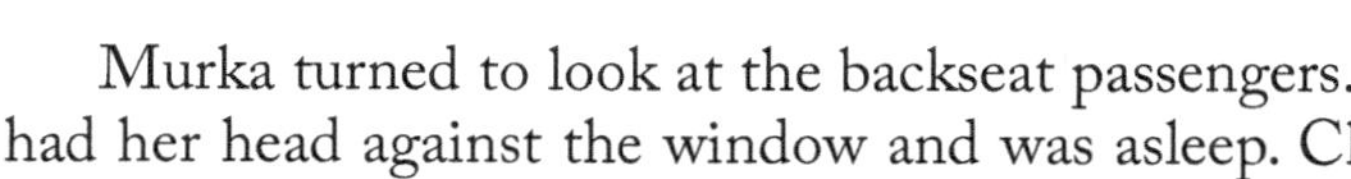

Murka turned to look at the backseat passengers. Elda had her head against the window and was asleep. Charlie shrugged out of her jacket, folded it, and slipped it between Elda's head and the window, then leaned back in her seat and dozed off.

Murka and Sophia spoke softly in the front seats while Sophia drove, within the speed limit, west on M4. "So, Murka, how did you get to join this motley bunch?"

"Ah . . . a long story, but as Elda might say, the Cliff-Note version is that I was an assassin for the Kremlin, working for Boris Sidorov. I didn't like his ethics nor our missions, so I defected."

Murka noticed the surprise in Sophia's sideways glance. "Wow. I didn't expect that one. How long had you been an assassin? And why?"

Murka scratched her neck, shifted in her seat, and looked out the window. She was not comfortable answering that question. "Not long at all, but long enough. I was at loose ends after the military. I left the service, since it was becoming too political and soft. The rules were no longer followed as they should be. I got a reputation for getting the job done and for being a *tverdaya zadnitsa*, or as you would say, hard ass. That endeared me to the Kremlin, who took me on for odd jobs. I was loyal to my country. I chalked up five kills, and when Boris had a full-time opening, I thought I'd take it."

Murka glanced back at Sophia, who nodded. "So what happened?"

Murka shrugged and went back to addressing the window. "The job sucked, *otstoy*. Boris was an ass. Elda bested us in our first mission. I took off for Mexico, where I was going to live and pick up freelance jobs. Elda came to Mexico, and I got to know her better. She is my idea of what this job should be about. So I went to the States and asked her for a job." She exhaled. It had taken a lot to share what she had with a relative stranger.

"It sounds as if there's a fair bit of subplots there. I look forward to hearing more at some point in time."

Murka gave a big sigh. "And you, Sophia? What's your story?"

"I fell in with Elda on a joint UK-US-Russian op to stop a plot against our three leaders. On that mission, my reckless husband, Oliver, was nearly killed." Sophia paused with the emotional impact of *that* memory. She took a deep breath and continued. "Elda helped me through that time and later went after those who had set him up, allowing me the kill."

"It sounds as if there is more to that story too."

Sophia nodded. Murka sensed she was lost in her memories. They drove on, the only sounds being the rhythmic breathing from the backseat and the sound of the tires on the pavement.

An hour later they drove into Cardiff Airport. Their charter was still there.

Charlie woke when the car stopped. Elda continued sleeping.

Sophia turned to view the sleeping Elda in the backseat. "Poor thing. She's just knackered."

Elda opened her eyes and sat up. "*Poor thing*?! *Really*, Sophia?"

"Sorry, Elda. I do wish I could let you all crash for a while."

"This part should be easy. Let's gather some more tools from the plane. Sophia, can you please see if you can get us a couple of rooms in St. Davids or somewhere along the way? We'll crash there tonight and start sleuthing tomorrow."

Sophia dialed a number. "No worries. What are we looking for?"

"In our last op together, many land deals went through before we arrived to stop the Russian money laundering scheme. most of these deals have been voided and the land returned to the rightful owners. The owners got to keep the money they had been paid, so it was a win-win for them. But there was more money floating around than the amount that ended up in the farmers' hands. I'd like a deeper look at the transactions and to speak to some of the players and see if we can suss out where it went. Plus, some of the land is still in limbo, so we should research who would inherit. It would be good to get that land back to the families."

Murka yawned. "Sorry, Elda. That wasn't a statement about the mission. I just didn't get a nap in."

Sophia hung up. "Don't worry, Elda. I heard it all. I snagged us the Boathouse in Little Haven. It's private and more secure, larger than Point Cottage, and is a stone's throw from St. Bride's Inn, which serves some lovely beef pies."

Elda patted her stomach. "Okay, everyone. A couple of pints and good meal at St. Bride's Inn in Little Haven. Then we follow the money in the morning."

Elda was amazed at the speed of the trip to Little Haven, Wales. The M4 had been continued from England through to the A40 to Haverfordwest. Gone was the white-knuckled drive along twisty narrow roads. She missed that.

They switched over to the B4341 in Haverfordwest. Elda felt more at home. The speeding cars on narrow, winding roads. The hedgerows and the green patchwork fields. This was *her* Wales.

They arrived at the Boathouse in Little Haven. Elda loved the place: The bright skylight-lit kitchen, with wooden table, and the living room with a small cherry-wood stove, leather chair, couch, and wooden coffee table.

They walked into one bedroom with a full-size bed. Elda referred to Sophia. "You drove and you got us this place. You can have dibs on the bedrooms. Let's check out the other room."

"Bunk beds!" Charlie vaulted up to the top bunk. "Dibs on this one!"

Sophia shook her head. "Elda, you can have the main bedroom. I'll keep tabs on the children here."

"I resent that, Sophia." Murka dropped her stuff on the bottom bunk.

Elda gave Sophia a pat on her shoulder. "Thanks,

Sophia. There's a beautiful view of the tidal bay and the rolling hills. Let's stretch our legs before the sun sets and grab a meal at one of the local pubs. I hope there's steak and kid."

The next morning, the four agents milled around the kitchen, waiting for the coffee to brew and the tea water to boil.

Elda sat at the wooden kitchen table and ran her hand over it. "Looks like ash. You don't see that much of it nowadays, because of the ash beetle infestation that wiped out so many of the ash trees."

Charlie rubbed her eyes. "Are we going to get a history-of-tea lesson next, Elda?"

Sophia chimed in. "Actually, the history of tea is fascinating."

Murka poured two cups of tea and brought them to the table for herself and Sophia. "Please, guys, I like tea, but it's too early for a history lesson."

Elda chuckled. "I'll second that. History was never my forte. I've invited Rhys Caddell to join us for breakfast. He was helpful to us when we worked to discover the Kremlin's real estate scam."

"Oh Rhys. I enjoyed him."

"Yes, he's quite the character, Charlie. You know him the best. I called him when we were on our way over the pond and hooked him up with Ashok to get some research done for us. He was more than willing to do it, since it means more of his family and friends will be taken care of. Ah, here he is now."

"Hal-lo, Charlie and Sophia. And Elda said she and Murka would also be 'ere, right. So who's who?"

Elda shook his hand. "Good morning, Rhys. We've made a pot of tea and bought some scones and jam for breakfast. I'm Elda. This here is Murka."

"And so you are, aren't you. All right. 'Tis good to make

your acquaintance. Now that we 've that sorted, I must say, right, that butty of yours, Ashok, is banging, you know? We did a tidy job on your research."

"Fantastic news, Rhys. We'll conference in Ashok and go over what the two of you dug up."

"Cracking. Do you mind if I rest and take off me leg?"

Elda pulled out a chair for him. "No worries. Go right ahead." She took off her gloves that she had on against the winter chill, sat at the kitchen table, and fired up her laptop.

Rhys took his leg off and propped it up against the table. Murka turned away and was shaking with laughter.

Ashok's face filled the screen, his eyeball close to his camera.

Elda pulled back from hers. "Good morning, Ashok. My apologies for the early hour for you. Are you having issues with your camera?"

Ashok retreated to a more acceptable distance. "My camera is fine, Miss Elda. I wasn't sure if we were on the air, as they say. This time works for me. I often work late into the night when I'm gnawing at a problem. Mister Rhys, it is most good to see you. We only were able to talk on the phone before."

Rhys touched the screen. "This is cracking."

Feeling cold, Elda pulled on her watch cap and replaced her gloves. "Run us through what you have found, Ashok."

"Yes, Miss Elda. You will be most delighted with this information. As you can see, there are twenty-two people who should be paid out more money from the transactions. I have initiated the transfers for them from the money that never quite made it to the United States Treasury."

Elda cleared her throat. "Never quite made it?"

"Yes, Miss Elda. That money was on hold, in case we had to return any of it. And in fact, I never told the treasury to expect it, since we didn't know if it was final or not."

"*Cwl* that. I can't wait to tell them, right?"

"Yes, very cool, Rhys. Ashok, did you have any luck tracing where the rest of the money went?"

"Yes, Miss Elda ma'am. I did."

Silence.

Elda's eyes watered and her lips twitched. Ashok was somewhat dramatic about his discoveries. "Excellent, Ashok. Would you like to share with us?"

"You will be most delighted, Miss Elda. The money was laundered through scores of shell accounts and transferred into Bitcoin and back."

Elda frowned in confusion. "I thought that wasn't traceable . . ."

"Nothing is infallible, Miss Elda. Anything in computers can be broken into with enough computing power, time, and brains."

"Well, Ashok, you have the time and brains, and if you need anything else for computing power, we'll find it for you."

"Thank you so much, Miss Elda."

Silence again.

Charlie held her hand over her mouth. Her eyes twinkled.

Murka looked perplexed.

Elda inhaled and blew out the air, before asking. "So where did it go, Ashok?"

"Well, Miss Elda. You will be most pleased with this. I have traced a portion of it to the Kremlin."

"And the rest?" Elda proactively prompted.

"And that is the problem. Despite my most excellent work so far, I have not yet nailed that down. I will need to take you up on that computing power offer, Miss Elda."

"Consider it yours. Just buy it and give me the receipts. You have done a fine job with your research, but if you had to guess, Ashok, where would it be?"

"Well, Miss Elda, that would be very difficult to say. I

am not in the business of guessing."

Elda looked to the ceiling and back to the screen. "When you get more computers and search, where would you start? That's a guess, Ashok."

"More like a data-backed theory, ma'am. If that's a guess, Miss Elda, I would guess that Tosh's team has it."

Chapter Thirty-One

LUKE SLAMMER DRANK A DOUBLE ESPRESSO
at the Lot 38 Espresso Bar. From his vantage point,
he could see down L Street and Second Street SE.
He sat with his long legs stretched out in front of him. He
looked at the application on his cell. No alerts. Searching
for this Elda Ainsworth character was like trying to find a
needle in a haystack. And he had heard that she might be
deceased. The million dollars in his offshore bank account
was a nice appetizer, but he wanted the entire ten million.

He checked his wolfkiller666 email. The additional cameras and monitors were arriving today. He'd go back to his
apartment and map out where he wanted to install the cameras. The application he had lifted on his way out of the CIA
did a fair job of facial recognition matching, given enough
data. The problem was that he only had Elda's BUPERs picture and a few others he had gleaned from the internet. Or
they were of someone that resembled the younger her.

Close enough for his needs.

Elda popped up her calendar on her monitor and scanned her schedule. An entire day of interviewing, starting in a few minutes.

All interviewees had already passed full background checks. Elda had arranged with her team that if she liked a candidate, she would pass them on with a thumbs-up emoji. If she had concerns but thought the candidate was a possibility, she would pass them on with a thumb sideways. At any point in the process, anyone could terminate the interview and escort the candidate out.

She brought up candidate number one's résumé and scanned it from back to front. Sandra Stewart. Sandra had done a tour in the air force and had been stationed as a liaison to the United Stated Navy in Rota, Spain. She'd also been stationed in Langley Air Force base in Virginia. She'd left after a four-year tour and gone back to school for her master's in computer science.

She'd worked for the CIA for a few years and then joined a fledgling hardware-software company in Seattle. From there she went to the San Francisco area, where she'd worked for different software development companies, rising through the ranks to CTO and CPO.

Sandra was now back in DC, and her goal on her résumé stated she was looking to parlay her military and government experience to gain a leadership position in software development. Elda figured that as a mature female, Sandra had aged out of startups. This was a wise move for her, and she seemed tailor made for the opening of CEO for the business side.

Elda strode out to where Sandra was sitting. She held out her hand. "Miss Stewart? I'm Elda Ainsworth." She stopped.

Sandra had risen and taken Elda's proffered hand. Elda

was now staring into eyes whose color defied definition. Blue? Blue with green tints? Blue with steel gray?

Sandra smiled. "Call me Sandy, please."

Elda guessed that Sandy was about two inches taller than herself. She had shoulder-length dark-brown hair and wore a tailored dark-blue jacket with black slacks that accented a trim figure.

Elda blinked and returned Sandy's smile. "Sandy then. Follow me into my office. Would you like coffee, tea, or water?"

"Coffee, black, please. That is, if you schedule in bathroom breaks during the interview process?"

Elda chuckled. "Of course." She liked this woman already.

A half hour later, Elda ended her interview with Sandy. "I have more candidates to interview today, but you're in the running."

She went on to interview two more CEO candidates, three for admin, and two operatives. She knew her team couldn't get through all the candidates in one day. She had scheduled two more days for their follow-up interviews. She'd ask them tomorrow morning if they required a fourth day. She desperately had to hire that administrative assistant.

After her interviews, Elda wanted to hire Sandra Stewart for CEO, but she wouldn't unless Sandy got all positive feedback from the interviewers. She had one candidate she was leaning toward for administrative assistant. She'd see how the others rated the three admin candidates. She did like one of the guys who had applied to be an operative. She had more candidates to go through tomorrow. Then she would rank them in her candidate spreadsheet.

She needed to make the offers on Sandra and Yuri, plus get Yuri brought over under the proper visa. She also had to move forward on filling out the software group with Ashok's relatives. She made a note to ask Murka if she had any other relatives who might fit any of the open positions. She hoped that blood ties would keep everyone loyal and trustworthy, but she knew from her own family that wasn't always true.

Tomorrow was another big day of interviewing and finalizing the arrangements for their India trip. Ashok's wedding was coming up fast.

Elda buzzed Korinna. "I need to go out for a jog to clear my head and then do you want to pick up some supper?"

"Can we eat in? I have a lot to tie up here before I can head back up to Maine."

"Sure. I can use the work time. Order whatever you want. I'll be back in an hour."

Elda never liked to take the same route twice in a row, but there were only so many permutations that she could run to get in her mileage. She had run this route a few days ago. She looked around as she fell into a comfortable rhythm. Her spidey sense felt as if something was off. She felt eyes watching her. From where? Was someone following her? She wove her way around, using some new side streets, searching. She stopped to tie her shoes. She dashed against the lights across traffic. No one appeared to be consistently around her.

Elda took a break and sat on a bench. A glint flashed in the tree across from her. She took out her cell and mimed reading a message while she took a picture. She sent it to Ashok. Can u plz resrch these?

Yes, Miss Elda, ma'am.

Thks. + bkup & del all info & photos of me fm my navy files. lv only dates of svc.

Yes, Miss Elda, ma'am.

Her reticular system attuned to these cameras, she spotted more of them along the way. Where did they come from?

Wearing a brown leather jacket, brown calfskin gloves, and a brown fedora, Luke strode along to pick up his Chinese takeout.

Ping.

Luke grabbed his cell phone from his pocket. His facial recognition program had discovered a potential match. He turned and jogged back to his apartment. Supper would have to wait.

Luke took his steps two at a time up to his floor. He dropped his keys onto a side table as he hurried to get to his computer. He always liked the excitement of the chase. Senator Glass had explained to him that this woman was a traitor to the United States. He wondered why they were asking for her to be eliminated instead of notifying the FBI to have her arrested. Something didn't make sense.

Luke pulled up the video feed from his cameras. The resolution wasn't the best and the woman was jogging. She fit the general specifications. It would be best to pull her medical file from the navy veteran database and see what her height and weight were, and add ten pounds or so for aging. He spun up another program he had obtained from his days in the CIA.

No records match.

How could that be? He went to retrieve her BUPERS files.

No records match.

That couldn't be right. He had pulled the picture from that database.

He ran everything again.

Same results.

He did a Google search.

No results found.

What the fuck was going on here?

Full of the Mexican food Korinna had ordered, and energized after a pep talk from her old friend, Elda returned to her office to find Ashok sitting on the floor outside her door, holding his laptop.

"Miss Elda, ma'am. I have found the source for these cameras."

Elda glanced at her watch. "Excellent, Ashok. But aren't you supposed to be getting on a plane to India?"

"Oh, I have plenty of time, Miss Elda, ma'am. My Uber doesn't arrive for ten minutes."

Elda rolled her eyes. Ashok always cut it close on travel. "We'll speak quickly then. What did you discover?"

"Whomever installed these computers used a Wi-Fi router with boosters along the way. Therefore he, or she, has a rudimentary knowledge of computers and the internet. He has a network with a VPN for his main computer, but none on the one that is connected to the cameras, so there is no protection for the IP address."

"So you have traced them to an IP address, and from that determined this person's physical location?"

"Exactly, Miss Elda. Most excellent of you to realize that. My program is delivering the name and address in just a few moments. I am sure of it. And since I now have unsecure access into his network, I will be able to deliver much more to you. I left me a back door in case he decides to lock down his security better."

"Wonderful sleuthing, Ashok."

Ashok's laptop binged, and he brought up a window. "He lives here in DC. His name is Luke Slammer."

"Luke Slammer? That sounds like a Marvel villain."

Ashok looked at Elda blankly.

"Never mind. Please send me that information, and we will handle Mr. Slammer when we return from India."

Ashok typed. "It is done, Miss Elda."

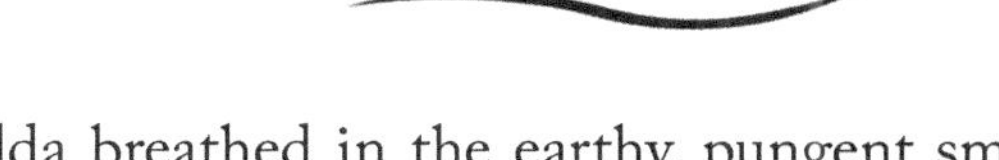

Elda breathed in the earthy, pungent smells of spices and humans. She dabbed at her eyes. She couldn't understand a word of what was going on, but she thought the ceremonies were beautiful. She looked at her hands. The henna designs on them were so intricate, but nothing compared to how they'd painted the bride.

Charlie came up to her. "How come you weren't at the turmeric food fight this morning? I couldn't understand it, but I had a lot of fun."

Elda eyed Charlie. Her face was splotched with yellow handprints.

In a yellow and multicolor blur, the bride's wedding party paraded by laughing and cleaning their faces with rags. They showed signs from the worst of the splashing.

"I've done it before. I figured it was your turn to experience it. I have no idea why they do that ritual. We need a translator."

The bride's father sat on the floor now, with the priest. He had clothing on either side of him and bowls of food in front of him.

An attractive man with graying temples walked up to Elda and Charlie. "You must be Ashok's coworkers from the States."

Elda stared for a second and held out her hand. "I'm Elda, and this is Charlie."

The man blinked and smiled. He shook Elda's hand. "So glad to meet you. I'm Ashok's uncle Kushal Gupta. Let me grab us some tea, and I can explain to you this lovely ceremony that is beginning." He forged off.

"How did he know who we were?" Charlie looked down at her dark-purple embroidered kurta set and sandals. She also sported a black bindi on her forehead. "Wait.

Wait. Let me figure it out." Charlie shook her head.

Elda knew Charlie was overwhelmed by the sound of so many people chatting, the smells of incense and turmeric, and the brightly colored garments. She watched as Charlie looked again. "Oh! You, me, Murka, and Korinna are the only white folks here."

Elda laughed. "Well done, Grasshopper."

Uncle Gupta returned with a tray of tea. He handed a cup to Charlie and one to Elda. He nodded at where the bride's father sat on the floor. "This is a very important ceremony that starts the marriage rituals. We pay our respect to our ancestors and every living creature that has brought us to this moment. We welcome them to join in, offering them food and drink and worship items, such as the flower petals you see on one plate. We offer them also clean clothes to put on. We ask for them to bless this ceremony and to grant forgiveness for any of our wrongdoings. The red powder you see there is tilak, and at the end the priest will make a paste of it with the ashes and sandalwood and place a red dot on the bride's and groom's foreheads, which will retain good energy in the body. The priest will bless the couple with a long life. The parents standing by the couple will signify their acceptance of this union. It goes on for quite a while, so please do enjoy your tea."

Elda took a sip. "This is wonderful tea. We don't get tea like this in the States."

Uncle Gupta agreed. "No, you don't. I run a tea import/export business. We do keep the best for ourselves. The UK gets the next best, followed by Canada. The consumers in the United States cannot tell the difference between teas, so we sweep up the discarded leaves from the floor and send them over."

Elda chuckled. "That may be a tall tale, but I believe you."

"You should. Now if you would please excuse me."

Elda took his hand and patted it. "Thank you for your

time. I look forward to chatting more."

He smiled at her. "I'm sure we will. I will ask Ashok for your office address and send you all some good tea."

Charlie took a big gulp of her tea. "I long for coffee, but I must say, this stuff is pretty good."

Elda tapped Charlie's cup. "Tea also has more caffeine in it than coffee."

Charlie chortled. "What don't you know?"

Elda beamed at Charlie. "I'm the Shell Answer Man."

Charlie shrugged. "Whatever that is, I am sure it was before my time."

Murka wandered over. She also had turmeric on her cheeks and forehead. "What did I miss? And did you know there's someone sleeping under the table? At first I thought he was dead."

Elda glanced over. "He's one of the help staff. They've been out straight preparing, and I'm guessing it's one of the few times he can grab some shut-eye. I'm going to wander off after Uncle Gupta and chat with him about getting Ashok's bride a visa. Then I'm going back to the hotel to catch some shut-eye myself. This party will be going on for days."

Elda walked up to the outdoor balcony, where Kushal Gupta was sipping his tea and looking out across the neighborhood. She leaned with one arm on the railing. "Uncle Gupta. It *is* a small world after all."

He laughed. "It certainly is, Elda. Now that I know that you are the one taking such good care of my nephew, I would be honored to participate in any endeavor that helps him succeed."

"Thank you. Your nephew will always be safe. He is a brilliant programmer and the core of our new cybersecurity company. We are hoping to add his wife, and perhaps some cousins too, as employees. That will mean we will need to bring them over on visas, which is a lengthy process."

Kushal looked Elda in the eyes. "I can assist with that problem and have them legally in the United States on any day you wish."

"That would be wonderful. There are too many deportations right now, and the processes for bringing people in are roadblocked."

"There is no need to worry. I will take care of the costs for this. In the future you will receive a deep discount."

"Then I'll owe you one."

Kushal grinned. "Yes. I find that is often an advantageous position to be in."

Elda returned his grin and nodded. "Yes it is. Our services are specialized, and we have ethical guidelines to follow in performing them."

"I will use them wisely."

"I'm sure you will."

Kushal sipped his tea. "Would you like another cup?"

"No thank you. I've had enough caffeine. I do need to catch up on my sleep." Elda added, "But there may be times where we will need to have certain supplies staged in a country and employees moved in and out without their presence being discovered. I'm wondering if it would be appropriate to call you?"

"I can help with that. You may need to assist me in sourcing these unique supplies, however."

"That should not be a problem. We hired an experienced logistics agent, Yuri, who has a vast network of connections. You would be tied into that through him."

"Most excellent. I can see where this will be a win-win."

Chapter Thirty-Two

Luke wondered if he should call Senator Glass and tell him Elda was nowhere to be found. He paced in his study in front of his camera monitors. He had spent enough days paralyzed. He needed to act, one way or another.

How badly did he want nine more million dollars? He had one already. Three would be a comfortable amount to squirrel away. He could collect his next three million for commencing the operation and then report her dead. No. He couldn't. That wouldn't be ethical. But was being judge, jury, and executioner ethical?

They said she was a traitor. But if she was a traitor, then there would be some evidence of that. Senator Glass never gave him proof, and Luke hadn't found any in his search. What if she wasn't a traitor? What story would Elda tell him? Luke needed to find her. He'd search where his cameras had alerted him to potential matches. Then he could follow her to a place where she would answer his questions.

He clipped on his belt holster and slipped a Glock 19

into it. That piece of equipment had also followed him out of the CIA. He grabbed his jacket and threw it on. He glanced in the mirror to ensure it covered the gun.

In a car outside Luke's apartment building, Elda watched as he jogged down the street. "Okay, Charlie, ten minutes max. This guy has training, so don't disturb anything. Your turn to key us in." Elda slipped out of the car and sprinted across the street with Charlie to the building. The front door was unlocked.

They sprinted upstairs. Elda watched Charlie use her lockpick set to open Luke's door. The knob turned. Elda clicked her stopwatch and showed it to Charlie. "Well done. However, I suggest you practice until you can get the time down to seconds, not minutes."

The two slipped into Luke's apartment. Elda wrinkled her nose at the stink of gym clothes thrown over a chair in the bedroom. She reached his study and nodded at the array of camera monitors. She spotted a wide-angle camera in the bookcase across from them. She resisted searching his drawers, theorizing he had tells in place. It didn't appear as if he had been living there long.

She circled back and met up with Charlie. "Anything?"

"Not that I can see. He's got a lot of tech straight out of the CIA lockers. But nothing that we could get him arrested for."

"Okay. It's been nine minutes since entry. Let's scram."

The following day Luke was back out roaming the streets in search of Elda. There had been no further hits from the cameras. He sat on a bench across from one of his cameras, hugging his arms around his body to ward off the chill of the wind on a cloudy day. He needed another layer of clothing. Maybe he should head back to the café?

Wait! Was that her?

Luke waited until a woman jogged past him, and he stood and looked around, consulting his watch. He noted her leisurely pace and set out after her. She turned left. He reached into his pocket and pulled out a bright-orange watch cap and put it on. He ran until he made it to where she had turned. He walked across the intersection and saw her turn right at the next corner.

Luke turned his cap inside out to the black inside. He sprinted to the next intersection and turned left. She was one block down, tying her shoe. He moseyed down the street at a casual pace. She started jogging again. He kept following.

The woman jogged into the navy yard. She stopped, chatted with the sentry, and went in. Obviously a regular.

Luke brazened it out and showed the gate guard his old CIA pass. If he got caught, Senator Glass had better get any charges dropped. To his surprise, the sailor didn't question it or call it in, just waved him through.

She was walking now and stretching her upper body. She stopped outside an office building and stretched on the stairs before going in.

Elda had instructed the gate guard to let the man following her through and also asked him to alert Charlie. She waited in the downstairs lobby with her back to the door. She could see whoever came in reflected in the shiny chrome of the elevators. She had told the lobby receptionist to let him proceed to the elevators.

He entered the lobby.

She strode to the elevator and rode up, knowing he would see what floor she stopped on. She left the door to the office open and sat in the lobby area.

Luke popped his head into the office. "Oh, excuse me. I'm a bit lost."

"Come on in. I'm sure we can help you."

He walked in.

Elda stood and held out her hand. "Before we chat, please hand over that Glock you have on your belt."

Luke's eyes widened.

"Come on, Luke. You didn't think you are that good at tailing after taking the CIA intro class, did you?"

His mouth opened and shut without a sound coming out. He handed her his gun, butt first.

Elda removed and pocketed the clip. "If you are thinking of doing anything funny, there is a sniper rifle aimed on you."

He glanced down at the red dot dancing around on his shirt and gulped.

"What was your goal in following me today?" Elda asked.

"I wanted to know if you are a traitor."

Elda cocked her head. "Would that have made a difference?"

"Yes, of course it would have."

"Why *of course?*"

"I defend our country from all enemies, foreign and domestic."

Elda raised an eyebrow. "Even as a civilian?"

"Yes."

"And if I were a traitor?"

"I'd be ten million dollars richer."

"Be happy with the one million they already paid you. I'm not a traitor, but the man who hired you could be called one."

"Senator Glass?"

"Is an ass."

Luke burst out laughing. "I didn't expect to like you."

"Does that mean you aren't going to continue to try and kill me?"

"Can you tell me who you are and why the United States Oversight Committee wants to see you dead."

"According to many, I'm already dead, and I'd like to keep it that way. Come with me to the break room and let's get coffee."

Murka wandered into the room with her gun drawn. "I'm more comfortable keeping him covered until we're one hundred percent sure of him."

"Good idea. Luke, this is Murka. She has a good aim." Elda texted Charlie that she could come down now. "Black or with cream and/or sugar?"

"Black please."

"You and Charlie will get along. Let's all go into the conference room to chat."

At the conference room table, Murka and Charlie sat on opposite ends and sides, with their guns trained on Luke. Elda sat across from him.

She put her hands on the table, palms down, and leaned forward. "I know your background, Luke, but how did you decide to freelance?"

"I hated working in the CIA. I felt they were too politically motivated. On hindsight, I should have gone with the FBI, but I rather liked the idea of being a spy. Macho and all that." Luke looked to Elda, who nodded for him to continue. "After I left the CIA, I was at loose ends. My father knew Senator Glass and suggested I see him to get some ideas about employment. The senator proposed I freelance, and he assigned me this job. For the good of country and freedom and all that. He knew which strings to pull, from what my father had already told him. Plus, I'm, at times, too transparent."

Elda narrowed her eyes. "You went to see him?"

Luke looked puzzled. "Yes I did."

Elda clenched a fist. "That lying bastard. I'll get him for that. He knew who you were."

"Yes. Why?"

"No matter right now. So he hired you to find and eliminate a traitor?" Elda concluded.

"Yes. You . . ." Luke trailed off. His tone questioning.

Elda looked him in the eyes. "Let me fill you in on my background, Luke. And I will ask my team to tell you what they wish to let you know at this time. When we're done, you can let me know what you think."

The four sat there, consuming many cups of coffee. Elda watched as Luke's body language changed from tense to relaxed and friendly.

"So, Luke. Am I a traitor?"

"No, Elda. I believe you. I would call you a patriot."

Elda shook her head. "Perhaps I was that, at one time. I would rather believe now that I am an upholder of values. Of democracy. Of truth and justice. However, I am fallible and therefore need good people surrounding me, to help in the decision-making and in determining our direction. Murka and Charlie, as well as Korinna and Ashok, are those people." Elda looked at Murka, who nodded. Elda's eyes consulted Charlie, who gave a thumbs-up.

"We are hiring operatives to join our firm," Elda continued. "Would you be interested in interviewing?"

Luke brightened. "Yes! Definitely."

"Good. Please take down the cameras and return what you stole from the CIA. Come back here tomorrow morning at nine a.m. sharp."

Luke cleared his throat. "The Glock is the CIA's."

"We'll keep it awhile."

"Damn."

Elda followed the sound of the cursing and found Charlie in the lab in front of an array of locks with a timer. "What's up, Grasshopper?"

Charlie leapt out of her chair and put her hand on her chest. "Damn, Elda. How do you sneak up like that?"

"It's all in the toes. Are you working on getting faster in lock picking?"

"I am, but some of these are devilish."

Elda sat next to Charlie and reached for one of the locksets. "Let's start with this one. Which picks would you use?"

Charlie pointed to two of the instruments.

"Good. Now show me."

Charlie inserted the picks.

Elda put her hand on Charlie's to halt her. "Start with one pick, like this." She took one pick and curled Charlie's fingers around it and brought it into the lock. She put the second pick in Charlie's other hand, and as she manipulated Charlie's first hand, brought the second tool into action. *Click.*

One by one they worked through the various locks. Elda sat back as Charlie started at the first one and unlocked it. Charlie reached out for the second one when Elda stopped her. "Again."

Charlie opened the first one again. And again. And again. Each time was faster than the time before. By the end, Charlie was sweating. "I didn't know lock picking was aerobic."

Elda chuckled and handed Charlie lock number two. "Let's get you good enough to help me train the rest of the team."

Chapter Thirty-Three

Elda, with the team's trainer Olga trotting behind her, ran through the office, clapping her hands. "Okay, everyone. Meet in the conference room now."

The group straggled in one by one and took their chairs. Elda conferenced in Korinna and Luke.

"I would like everyone to clear their calendars for next week and pack go-bags. This is a full-team operation. Luke, although your paperwork has not been completed, I would like for you to go with us."

Charlie raised her hand.

"Yes, Charlie."

"What's the mission?"

"You'll find out. This is a need-to-know basis."

"You want me to come down from Maine, Elda?"

"Yes, Korinna."

"Miss Elda, ma'am. Am I coming too? Preyanka is still in India awaiting her visa. I'd like to be here to support her."

"Sorry, Ashok. The *entire* team. I'll see you all Monday morning at 0800. The coffee will be on."

Monday morning dawned with the agents puzzled and fearful. Elda had never held them to a need-to-know standard.

Korinna walked out of her DC apartment, when a van pulled up next to her and the side panel door flew open. A masked operative grabbed her and her tote and pulled her in. The van sped away. Korinna was bound with zip ties and blindfolded.

"Be quiet, if you know what's good for you."

Charlie jogged into work, her bug-out bag over her shoulder. She stopped at a crosswalk, when she was tackled from behind and thrown into a van. A hood was pulled over her head and her wrists and ankles were zip-tied. She opened her mouth to scream, and a cloth was inserted and her mouth duct taped. Her bag thumped onto her body.

Luke, humming, bounded down the stairs from his apartment. When he reached street level, a gun was jabbed into his back and a needle into his neck. A masked operative supported his sagging body and heaved him into a white panel van.

Ashok was sleeping with his head on his desk. He was injected and carried down into the garage to the van.

Murka ran into the building and up to the office. She barged through the door. "Elda. I think someone is following me." A hand with a chemical smelling cloth covered her mouth. She was rolled onto a gurney and down to the van.

The driver looked at the person in the passenger seat. "All set?"

"*Da.*"

Charlie awoke with a dry mouth. She had a hood over her head, and when she moved to remove it, her hands were restricted by chains. She moved her feet. Chains there too. She felt a solid wall behind her, and the floor that she was sitting on felt like concrete. She pulled her body upright. She heard more clanking around her, and snoring.

"Who else is here?" she called out.

"I am," a woman answered. Korinna.

"Me too." Definitely Murka.

"So that's Murka and Korinna?"

"Yes, and you're Charlie?"

"Yes. Where are we? Why do we have hoods on? And who is snoring?"

A gravelly voice spoke out. "Good questions, Charlie Burlamachi. What do you remember?"

"I was grabbed from behind. I could hear a van door slide open. I was hog-tied and blindfolded before I could identify my assailants. The van drove about an hour, the first half of it on main roads, some highway. Then on smaller roads, perhaps unpaved. Who are you?"

"You will find out. Korinna Federov, what do you remember?"

"I had just left my building when a white van pulled up beside me. Someone jumped out and pulled me into the van."

"Anything else?"

"I heard one of the men answer the other in Russian."

"Are you sure both were men?"

"Yes. They both had deep voices. In fact, *you* were the non-Russian speaker."

Silence.

"Where are we?" Charlie called out.

Silence.

Korinna answered her. "I think the speaker left."

Murka clanked her chains. "Charlie, I'm on your left. Tip over, and I'll do the same. I might be able to grab your hood with my teeth and pull it off."

Charlie tipped toward Murka, who did the same, and they landed on their sides and found that they were closer than they thought. Charlie scooched down and brought her head in line with Murka's. She moved a touch more and though gagging from the cloth of her own hood, she grabbed Murka's hood with her teeth.

"Ouch! You have my hair too."

"Sorry, Murka. I'll try not to pull it out." Charlie manipulated Murka's hood off, ending with Murka's head resting next to her chest. She cleared her throat. "Can you take my hood off?"

Murka returned the favor, dropping the hood from her teeth and rolling away from Charlie.

Charlie looked around the room. Korinna sat with great posture against the wall. Luke was toppled over and still passed out. Ashok too. The room was entirely made of concrete, with a metal door on one side and a single window up high on the other.

Murka nodded at the window. "Do you think we can get out that way?"

Charlie looked around the room for anything to use as a pick. "Perhaps, but first we need to get out of these cuffs. Korinna?"

"Yes, Charlie."

"Do you have anything like a small pick, hairpin, or the like?"

"Hairpin? Geesh. No."

Charlie examined the floor around her. Was that a shard of metal wedged in that crack in the concrete? She turned and scooted her butt back toward the crack, feeling her way with her fingers. There!

"I may be able to get something. This is the one time I regret not having fingernails."

"How big is the crack, Charlie?" Murka inquired. "If I could remove your belt, could you use the prong to dig the metal piece out?"

"I can try. Move my way with your back to me."

Murka and Charlie positioned themselves into a spooning position. Charlie shuddered as she felt Murka's hands on her belt.

Murka chuckled, low and throaty. "Is it good for you?"

Charlie was glad Murka couldn't see her face.

Murka inched Charlie's belt off.

Charlie turned and took hold of the buckle from Murka. She slid on her back over to the crack. "Come on, you bugger . . . Yes!" She had the metal. She felt it. Perfect for a pick. "I have it."

They lay back to back while Charlie felt the cuffs' lock with her found object.

Click. The cuffs fell off Murka's right hand. She brought her hand around and massaged her wrist. "Well done, Charlie." She rolled over, took the pick from Charlie, and started working Charlie's lock. "I'm not as good at this as you are."

"Don't worry. Feel the lock. Be the lock."

Click.

Success.

Charlie rolled over and took the pick from Murka. In no time at all she had their remaining cuffs off and was working on Korinna's.

Murka walked over and removed everyone's hoods. Luke was stirring. She slapped his face. "Come on, Luke. We need you with us."

Luke sat up roaring and was pulled back by his chains. He glanced around. "What happened? Where are we?"

Murka paced the perimeter of the room. She tried the door. Locked. She examined the window, counted concrete blocks, and made measurements with her hands. "Korinna? How tall are you?"

"Just over six feet. Why?"

"Luke? How tall are you?"

"Five feet eleven inches."

"Perfect. If you lift Korinna up onto your shoulders, she will be able to reach both the top and bottom of the window. Any other combo of our heights would be a few inches shy."

Charlie, having freed everyone and awakened Ashok, returned to Murka. She scanned the wall. "Looks like you're right, Murka. There aren't any footholds on that wall. Our only other option is to try and overpower whoever comes in through that door."

"We have no weapons. One of us could get shot that way. Luke, Korinna? Are you game?"

Luke strode over. "Okay. You guys help get her on my shoulders and stabilize her. I'll squat down. I may need a little boost up from the squat though."

Charlie gave him a pat on the back. "You're a good man to admit that. I'll help lift you back to a standing position. Murka is taller and can reach higher to hold Korinna steady." She handed Korinna the piece of metal. "It should work as a screwdriver if you hold it this way." She demonstrated.

Korinna put the metal in her pocket so she wouldn't drop it.

Luke squatted. Charlie and Murka helped Korinna get her feet onto Luke's shoulders and waited until she had stood and had her hands against the wall. Murka moved in to hold her steady.

"Lean forward, not backward," Charlie directed Korinna. "Okay, Luke. On the count of three."

"Ready."

"One . . . two . . . three."

"Eeek!" Korinna rose up along the wall until she was in front of the window.

"Ashok, get on the other side of Luke and help hold him steady."

"Yes, Miss Charlie."

"There are four screws in this metal grid."

"Good. Don't worry if you drop them. Just don't drop the metal grid. I don't need another hole in my head. Slide the grid down by your side. Murka will grab it, and Ashok will take it from Murka."

Murka was on tiptoes holding on to Korinna's legs.

Ping. One screw bounced away, soon followed by three more. Korinna passed down the grid.

"Okay, Korinna. Does the window open?"

Korinna pried up the lock and turned the handle. The window opened. Fresh air blew in, carrying dust, dead leaves, and snowflakes. Korinna coughed.

"Can you pull yourself up and out?"

Korinna struggled to do so but didn't have the strength to lift herself up and over. "*Net.*"

"Bring her down and let's let Luke rest while we strategize our next steps."

Luke paced in a small circle. He reversed direction, then stopped. "I can pull myself out, but I'll be needed to hoist everyone up. Charlie and Murka, you look like you can pull yourselves out, right?"

"*Da.*"

"Yes, no problem with that part."

"Aside from me, I think you're the strongest, Charlie. What if we boosted you up and you pulled yourself out. Then we need pulling strength. So Murka would go next, followed by Ashok, and then Korinna. You and Murka will pull Ashok up and out, and he will hold your legs while you bring Korinna out. Now comes the tricky part. I haven't quite figured out how we get me out."

Charlie added. "I have. Murka and I lower Ashok down. He acts as a bridge. We hold his legs. Korinna lies across our legs to give us ballast."

Korinna rolled her eyes. "Geesh. First hairpins. Now ballast."

Luke's eyes lit up. "Yes! I grab on to Ashok's hands and start climbing up him as you three wiggle backward to pull us both up."

Charlie and Luke high-fived.

Murka held one finger to her lips and an arm across her waist and nodded, reciting each part of the plan. She looked up at them. "It might work."

"It better," Korinna said. "There's no other choice."

Charlie glanced around. The five team members lay on the ground panting. Charlie flexed her fingers to lessen the cramping that had set in.

Korinna sat up and looked around. "I hate to break the news to everyone, but this area is fenced in with barbed wire on the top."

"Fuck." Charlie raised herself up to a sitting position and assessed the yard.

Murka doubled into downward dog and stood. She held out a hand to Charlie.

Charlie took Murka's hand and stood. After a minute or so, she released it. "Okay, Murka, you go that way, but stay in sight. I'll go this way. Luke, can you make sure Ashok is all right?"

Luke looked at his torn pants and bloody knee that he had scraped on the way out the window. "No problem." He helped Korinna up, then the two of them hobbled to Ashok.

Ashok sat slumped. He rubbed his wrists, reddened from the cuffs and from Luke grabbing on to them. "My legs are cramped."

Luke hefted Ashok up.

"There's another building here," Charlie yelled from her side of the enclosed yard.

Murka, Korinna, and Luke, with Ashok over his shoulder, ran up to her.

Luke gently put Ashok down. "If you sit and massage your calves, they'll stop cramping." He leaned over and started in on Ashok's left leg.

Murka crept up to the building behind Charlie. Charlie scanned the perimeter for cameras but couldn't see any. "Murka, do you see any cameras?"

Murka turned in a 360. "*Net.*"

"Okay. I'm going for the door. Cover me."

Murka burst out laughing.

Charlie looked at her, puzzled. "What?"

"With what am I going to cover you? Do I spit at someone if they come out?"

Chagrined, Charlie chuckled. "You got me on that one. Okay, come with me. You'll be better able to reach someone with your spit."

The two reached the door. Charlie inched it open. The perfume of fresh-brewed coffee caressed her nostrils. "Did I die?" She opened the door all the way. The room was empty except for a conference table, comfortable-looking chairs, coffee and tea, soda, and pastries. There was also a first-aid kit on the table.

On the room's whiteboard was written: WELCOME. YOU HAVE MADE IT THROUGH THE FIRST TEST.

"What the fuck?" Charlie and Murka said in unison.

The rest straggled in. All sat. Murka poured tea for herself and Korinna. Charlie and Luke grabbed cups of black coffee. Ashok popped open a can of Coca-Cola.

They had barely started their drinks, when the large monitor at one end of the room turned itself on. A deep, hoarse, metallic voice floated down to them from the ceiling speakers.

"You all have been wondering why you are here."

"You're damn right we are," Charlie shouted back.

"This is a test of your skills, strength, flexibility, and teamwork. Should you pass all the tests we give you, you will be offered positions in my organization. You will be free to refuse, and if you do, I will let you go."

"We fucking already have jobs." Charlie threw a finger at the ceiling.

"Be patient and learn."

The monitor brightened, and a video of each one of them being captured was played.

"Tell me. Where did you go wrong?"

"Waking up this morning," Luke muttered.

"Aside from that, Mr. Slammer."

The video replayed his abduction.

Luke sighed. When the clip concluded, he confessed, "I wasn't paying attention. I was thinking of the day ahead and excited to be part of this team. I should have gone more slowly and scanned my surroundings."

"Exactly."

Charlie's video was replayed next.

"Fuck. Don't say anything, nameless voice. I can see where I went wrong. I wasn't listening to the sounds around me, nor was I doing a 360 scan of my surroundings."

The mysterious person guided each one through their capture.

"Murka?"

"I trusted that the office was safe."

"Ashok?"

"I didn't lock my office door when I went to sleep."

"Korinna?"

"I told Elda I would work for her."

"That could be so. You also walked by the street side of the sidewalk."

The monitor went blank.

Part of the other wall flopped over, turning into a counter. Korinna startled. Ashok went over and knelt to see how it had done that.

On the counter were five stations set up with a variety of locks and picks, as well as a timer and a blindfold for each person.

"There are locksets for you to unlock," the nameless voice instructed. "The first attempt not blindfolded. You are to time each effort. A green light will shine when you are to start, and a buzzer will ring when you have beaten the required time. You will unlock the lock blindfolded after you have met this time. When you have completed all the locks, you have completed the test."

"Why?" Luke blurted out. "What the fuck is this game?"

"Charlie, I hear that you are good at picking locks. Will you please have a contest with Luke on the first lock."

Charlie's eyes narrowed. "Get ready, Luke." She sat and waited for the green light and unlocked the first lock, got the buzzer, locked it, blindfolded herself, and unlocked it again. She glanced over at Luke, who was still working to unlock the lock the first time.

Murka sat next to Charlie, in front of her own locks. "Today taught me I could be better. I see that we have handcuffs in the mix. Being able to unlock them from behind my back would be useful."

Soon the entire team was engrossed in the exercise.

When they were done, a partition in the wall swung around with a buffet on it. Ashok ran his hands around the edges, trying to find the trigger.

A light blinked on and off over a door at the end of the room: "Restroom."

Korinna rose. "I, for one, could use the *tualet*."

"Who do you think is behind this?" Ashok asked as they ate.

"The Russians," Luke affirmed.

"Not our style," Murka responded.

"Oh, it could only be one person," Charlie exclaimed. "It has her fingerprints all over it."

Korinna returned from the lavatory and glared at Charlie. "Yes, and she will pay dearly for this."

Murka stood with her hands on hips and legs planted firmly. "What if you're wrong?"

Charlie looked up from her food. "What do you mean? It's got to be Elda. Look at the training we're getting. And she trained me on lock picking a few days before this. And who was positioned near the conveniently placed piece of metal? Me. It's Elda."

Murka pressed her point. "You want to think it's Elda, but where would she get the money for all of this? And there's more than one person behind the scenes here. She couldn't have moved us by herself."

Luke chimed in. "Elda visited a lot of people to raise money—"

"Yes. What if this is the result?"

Korinna broke in. "No, Charlie. There is no way all this could have been built in such a short time. Someone else owns these facilities."

"This is all very sophisticated," Ashok added. "It's beyond what we have at our office."

Charlie rubbed the buzz cut sides of her hair. "No, no. Look, guys. How would they know to go after us? Luke too. He was just added to the team. Only we knew that."

"What if they took Elda first?" Luke suggested.

The group sat in silence.

A door next to the restroom slid open.

Impatient with feeling powerless, Charlie stood. "Should we check it out?"

Korinna poured herself another cup of tea and sat back down. "What if it's a trap? The voice hasn't given us instructions. I'm staying here."

Murka pushed her chair back. "I'll accompany you, Charlie."

Luke rose and walked over to Charlie. "Mind if I come along? I'd rather action over inaction."

Charlie was feeling good about having Luke on the team. "Yes, please do join us."

The three turned and looked at Ashok and Korinna.

"Are you coming or staying?" Charlie asked.

"If you don't mind, Miss Charlie, ma'am, I'd rather stay here with Miss Korinna."

Korinna raised her cup of tea in a salute. "Come back alive."

A shiver went down Charlie's back. She wished she had a weapon. She stepped through the door into the darkness beyond.

The door behind the explorers slid shut. There was no light.

Charlie guessed the room had black, light-absorbing walls. "I'm going left along the wall to see how big this room is," she whispered.

"I'll go right." Murka replied. "I don't think we need to whisper, Charlie."

"I'll try to go straight down the middle," Luke added.

As they split up, Charlie was almost overwhelmed by a

deep feeling of loneliness and dread. She couldn't hear any footsteps. The room must be sound absorbing too.

"Argh."

"Murka?"

No answer.

"Luke, are you still here?"

"Yes, wherever here is. Was that Murka?"

Charlie turned around. "I think so. I'm going to go along the other wall to see if I can find her." She held her arm out, her fingers brushing the wall. She wasn't entirely sure why, but she didn't want to get too close to it.

Suddenly she felt a presence and a prick in her neck. "What th . . ."

Chapter Thirty-Four

CHARLIE AWOKE IN THE WOODS, WEARING A warm jacket, boots, gloves, and hat. All fit her but weren't hers. She looked up at the sky. The sun was coming up. She spied a zipped cloth duffel next to her and opened it. She inventoried a wide-mouthed stainless-steel water bottle, water tablets, a magnesium block fire starter, a length of rope, a fixed-blade Benchmark Bushcraft knife, a twenty-five-foot cord, a heavy-duty thirty-gallon plastic trash bag, and a folded eight-and-a-half by eleven-inch piece of paper. She shivered, despite the warmth of her clothing.

She unfolded the paper and read.

Your life, as well as your teammates', depends on how well you can perform this test. Due south of you is a van waiting to take you to civilization. It is the quickest way out. The other three directions lead you to days in the wilderness. Good luck.

Charlie snorted. Survival skills, hey? Not a problem. She took out the knife and tested it on a nearby tree. Nice and sharp. She'd get moving and find a place to stop for lunch. She'd search for a water source along the way. She looked up at the sky again. From the positioning of the sun, she figured it was around 7:00 a.m. It had risen in the east, but they weren't at the equator, nor was it the equinox. Therefore the sunrise was more east-southeast. She drew an imaginary arc over her head and bisected it. There. South. She headed off.

The going was slow, with dead leaves and fallen snow covering branches and threatening to topple her. She kept track of the height of the sun and calculated the approximate time. At around her 11:00 a.m., she heard the sounds of a stream and headed toward it. She inspected the bank to ensure she didn't slip into the stream. Hypothermia would not be a good thing out here. She didn't have a change of clothes either, so she had to keep her boots dry.

She couldn't reach far enough to dip the water bottle without stepping into the stream. She sat down, took out the garbage bag, and sliced off two boot-sized corners and slipped them over her boots, gathering the remaining material to tuck inside. She sat and regarded her invention. This would be slippery. If she had spare boots, she could put the plastic on the inside, but that was a moot point. She took off the plastic from one boot and left it on the other.

Charlie managed to get to the stream without falling, and with her non-covered boot on the bank, she planted her other foot in a shallow part of the stream. She could feel the cold seep in. She prayed that her foot was staying dry, scooped water into her bottle, and pulled herself back onto solid ground. She tore off the plastic. Her shoe was dry. Relieved, she tossed a water purification pill into the bottle, covered it, and shook it up.

She spoke to herself. "Okay, Charlie. Water is taken care of. Now food." She looked around and found a tree with a solid branch, straight enough to make a spear. She used the knife to hack it off and to sharpen one end. She looked around for tracks and found a rabbit trail leading to the stream. She sat down with her back against a nearby tree and waited. Where there was water, there would be animals. She wished she had never seen cute bunny movies as a child.

A half hour later, Charlie had a fire going and pieces of Bugsy skewered on sticks propped up over the flames. She had skinned the animal and cut off thin slices of meat in order to cook faster. She must get moving again. She had lost enough time and didn't want to be out in the woods after sundown. She gathered the cooked pieces into her shoe covering and stomped the fire out. In addition, she kicked dirt and snow over the fire. Water was too precious to waste putting it out. She watched the area for a few minutes, and the snow was not melting. Good. She didn't want to be responsible for starting a forest fire.

She took out one piece of meat to eat on the way and put everything else into her kit bag, which she slung over a shoulder. She looked back up at the sky. The sun wasn't visible through the grove of trees she was in. She detected a trail the animals had made that was roughly in the direction she needed to head, and started out at a slow jog.

Murka burst out of the trees into a field. A white van sat parked about one-quarter mile away. She staggered toward it. She hadn't been able to find any food or water during the twelve hours she had been in the woods and was feeling dehydrated. She slowed as she approached the van, and holding her knife and spear, she circled it. No sign of life. The front cab windows looked like a one-way mirror. As she came around the side of the van, the door slid open for the back. Weary, she climbed in.

There in the back of the van was a warm wool blanket, bottles of water, and granola bars. Murka grabbed at the food and water. She wrapped herself in the blanket and waited for whatever was next.

The van started moving, and the voice came through speakers in the back. "Congratulations, Murka. You made it. You should have no ill effects from this adventure once you hydrate. Aside from not looking hard enough for food and water, you finished this test well. We did have to reposition the van to intercept you, however. Your calculations of due south were three degrees off."

It was midnight when Luke stumbled out of the forest. He was cold. The sky was overcast, and his surroundings were dark. He had no idea where he was. He had managed to find water, but no food, and he was starving. He looked up from his feet, and there in front of him was a white van. "I'll kill the bastards." He grasped his knife tighter.

Luke staggered toward the van, when he felt something prick him in his neck. He brought his hand up and came back with a dart. "What the fu . . ."

Charlie settled down in the back of her van and put the wool blanket over her shoulders. The voice came over the speakers. "Congratulations. You completed the test. You were on course to find the van, you supplied yourself with fire, food, and water and kept warm and dry. You'll find food and water in the box near you. We are taking you back to the conference room for debriefing."

Charlie knew it was useless to ask questions, and being fresh for whatever was thrown at her next was important. She drank water and ate a granola bar, made a pillow out of her jacket, wrapped the blanket tight around her, and fell sound asleep.

The van stopped. Charlie sat up and shook herself awake.

The voice came through the speakers. "This is your stop, Charlie. Your mission is to return to your office without being intercepted. You are to identify and evade any tails."

The side door slid open. Charlie blinked and squinted as the daylight assaulted her eyes. She rubbed the tears away, threw two waters and three granola bars into her bag, and jumped out. The van peeled away. Where was she?

She oriented herself to direction and time, using the sun. She looked across the street. Salvation Army. Perfect!

A few minutes later, Charlie emerged with a yellow slicker on, a bright-orange watch cap, and neon-blue sneakers. Her boots and survival kit resided in a worn Victorinox backpack she had slung over her shoulder. In her pocket she stashed an old paper map of DC, with directions to a homeless shelter scribbled on it.

Charlie started her trek to the southeast. On the crowded sidewalk, she bumped into a man and wandered off muttering about space rays and saying she was sorry. She threw his wallet away after removing the cash. Now she had over $200. The next encounter provided her with an unlocked cell. A few more brushes and she had what she needed. She called an Uber.

Charlie exited the Uber three blocks away from the office. She figured anyone wanting to intercept her would be at the office. She consulted the watch on her wrist, another five-finger discount from an unwitting pedestrian. She could make it. She slipped into the UPS store.

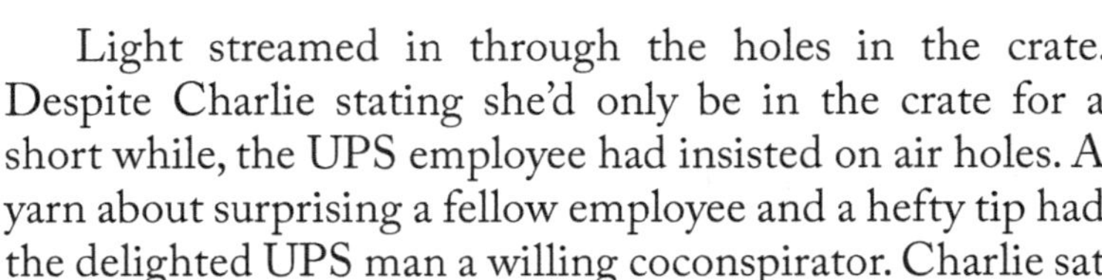

Light streamed in through the holes in the crate. Despite Charlie stating she'd only be in the crate for a short while, the UPS employee had insisted on air holes. A yarn about surprising a fellow employee and a hefty tip had the delighted UPS man a willing coconspirator. Charlie sat back to enjoy the ride.

The ride wasn't that enjoyable. It was bumpy and much longer than she'd anticipated. She figured they must be doing deliveries before heading to her office. There, the truck had stopped. She could feel the crate being moved onto a dolly. Once she was inside, she had a hammer and crowbar with her to pry her way out. She heard footsteps leaving and waited.

All was quiet. She went to work and soon fell out of the crate.

"Where the fuck am I?"

CHAPTER THIRTY-FIVE

CHARLIE ENTERED THE EMPTY CONFERENCE room and headed for the pot of coffee. Halfway through her cup, the voice sounded from the ceiling.

"Shipping yourself in a crate was quite creative, Charlie, but it's been done before. We had the UPS employees in our pockets, and we diverted your truck."

"Fuck."

"Well done though. You almost made it. Now, in the wall behind you, you will find a locked closet door. Unlock it. Inside will be a variety of pistols, rifles, and machine guns, but no ammo. Disassemble and assemble each weapon. When you feel you have it mastered, put on the blindfold from the locks exercise and start again."

The counter with the blindfolds, locks, and picks swung down.

Charlie attacked the test with gusto. She was humming as she took the weapons apart and reassembled them.

Two hours after Charlie had entered the room, Murka joined her.

Charlie smiled at Murka. "I am delighted to see you."

Murka nodded. "I'm happy to see you too, Charlie. I messed up on the direction and was three degrees off in the survival exercise. Much to my surprise, they dumped me off in DC. I got caught halfway back to the office."

Charlie frowned. "And the van was there when you emerged from the woods?"

"Yes, why wouldn't it be?"

"You were off. How did the van find you?"

"Good question . . ." Murka swiveled to look at what Charlie had been working on. "Are those guns?"

"Yes. No ammo though."

"*Chert.*"

"It's a fun challenge. We're to field strip each weapon and put it back together again. When we feel we have it, we do it blindfolded. Race you . . ."

"You're on."

The two had finished their race with five weapons, when Luke entered, looking disheveled and beat up. "They drugged me again, the bastards."

"Don't worry. If Elda is behind all this, there will be no ill effects, and it looks like you needed the sleep."

Luke pounced on a weapon. "Are these real guns?"

"Yes. No ammo though."

"Damn."

Murka looked around the room. "Where are Korinna and Ashok?"

The voice sounded again. "Korinna and Ashok were given a choice to participate or not in the survival skills exercise and the weapons. Since they don't desire to be agents, they opted out."

"Damn," Luke muttered. "No one told me I could opt out."

"That's correct, Luke. You need this training. Charlie, since you are done with your weapons, and you aced the survival test, please stow your guns back in the closet and walk out the door. Murka, please complete the test. Luke, the task here is to select one of each weapon and disassemble and reassemble each one until you are ready to do it blindfolded. You have three hours."

"Damn."

Charlie walked out of the conference room into the hallway. A blinking sign over a door said, Charlie enter here.

She opened the door to a small room with travel kits and gear. The voice floated down from the ceiling. "Pack a go-bag. The guns and other weapons in this room are real, as is the currency. Once you are done, go through the door opposite you."

This seemed straightforward. Charlie examined the weapons, the disguises, the passports, and the other equipment and devices. She selected her top-priority items and a second tier, packing in that order. She stopped when her pack was full but light enough to carry. She went through her head different scenarios and decided she was set. She shouldered the bag and left the room.

Chapter Thirty-Six

"I KNEW IT WAS YOU!" Elda high-fived Charlie. "We needed to keep you confused. These exercises had to simulate real-world experience. There's only so much you can learn in a classroom. We had eyes on you at all times, so you were never in any real danger. It's just that you didn't know that."

"So that's how you met everyone as they emerged from the woods, even when they were off course."

"Yup. You all had trackers in your clothing, and we had three drones up following you."

"Who's *we*?"

The other door to the room opened, and Olga bounced in. "Olga help!"

Charlie nodded. "Ah yes. It all is beginning to make sense. What's next?"

"First I will see what you selected to take in your go-bag and the weapons you secreted on your body. Then we'll play the game of *how can you use an everyday device as a weapon*. After that you go home and get a good meal and night's sleep. The contents of the go-bag are yours to keep. Tomorrow we do hand-to-hand combat and evasive driving."

Charlie pumped her fist. "Yes! Fun."

Elda went through Charlie's pack. "One suggestion is to grab reversible clothing, even if it's not your style. In fact, *especially* if it's not your style. And you could use a multitool as well as a wrecking bar. Other than that, you did well. Now . . ." Elda laid out in front of her a comb, fork, spoon, knife, credit card, pen, and fingernail clipper. "Describe the uses for each of these."

Charlie frowned. "Hair, eating, buying things, writing, clipping nails . . ."

Elda took the comb and broke off the teeth from half of the shaft and ran the toothless end on the rough concrete wall until she had a good shank. She took the credit card and ran one side back and forth over the wall. When she was done, the card had an edge that would cut paper. "With enough time I could sharpen the spoon. The fork can be used as is, and the knife could also be sharpened, since it's a dinner knife and not a steak knife. The pen can be used to make an airway for first aid, as a container for a recording device, or syringe, or in a pinch, a weapon. Aim for the eye with that one."

"Got it."

"Look at everything around you as potential weapons, lifesaving devices, or hiding places. Scoot now and I'll see you tomorrow. Your car is parked outside."

The following morning at 0800, Charlie, Korinna, Ashok, Murka, Luke, Olga, and Elda sat in the conference room. They spent the first hour critiquing their errors and helping teach one another.

"Okay, team. I know this has been hard on you. It was

necessary. You can't learn these skills sitting in a classroom. All of you made mistakes that you won't make again. A real mission, as you know, is no picnic. We have to be overprepared."

Elda looked at each participant to ensure they tracked with her. "Today, hopefully, will be fun. First, hand-to-hand combat-skills training by Olga in the gym. After lunch, it's off to a closed area for evasive driving techniques. My bet is on Murka for being tops in that one."

Murka smiled for the first time that day.

"Grab your morning break beverages and goodies. I'm going to teach Korinna and Ashok some basic defensive moves here, while the rest of you go with Olga. See you at lunch."

Korinna, carrying her omnipresent teacup and a blueberry scone, tiptoed back into the room, with Ashok hiding behind her.

Elda laughed at their antics. "Come on in, guys. I'm not going to hurt you. Help me move the table and chairs off to one side."

Korinna moved chairs, while Ashok and Elda muscled the table, leaving a decent-sized area to practice in.

Elda had the two of them stand facing each other. "Now, Ashok, reach to strangle Korinna."

"I don't want to hurt her, Miss Elda."

"Don't strangle her for real. Just put your hands around her neck. Let me show you."

"Geesh, can't we get a dummy to work on?"

Elda raised her eyebrow.

Korinna grinned. "*Khorosho.* I fell into *that* one."

Elda put her hands with her thumbs in the front and fingers to the sides of Korinna's neck. "Now, Korinna, lift your right hand up high and swing it down and to the left."

Korinna did as she was told, and she knocked off Elda's hands. Korinna pranced around in a circle.

"Nicely done."

The two practiced breaking a choke hold.

"You broke the hold. What next?"

"Run?" Korinna volunteered.

"Yes! Run away as fast as you can. If the assailant is small, you could slow them down by finishing your break of the choke hold with an elbow into the gut, or lower. Ashok, please show me your choke hold."

Elda broke the hold and swung her elbow down and low, stopping an inch away from Ashok's groin.

Ashok looked down, wide eyed. "Thank you for stopping, Miss Elda."

"Now let's see how to get out of someone trying to capture you from behind." Elda came up behind Korinna and wrapped her arm around her shoulder and across her body.

Korinna kicked back, connecting with Elda's shins.

"Yeow! I should have worn shin protection. Good one, Korinna. That's right. Go for the legs. If you can spin, you can bring your leg behind the assailant's knees and bring him or her to the ground. And then what do you do?"

"Run like hell."

"Yup, Korinna. Beat feet! Whoever attacked you might be pissed by now. See, you have some basics already. Let me go get some shin guards and we can practice this move."

The group reconvened at lunch. Elda examined the body language of each team member to see if any ill feelings remained from their bouts, but they looked excited. Their adrenaline flowed as they chatted and chowed down. Good. She'd get the debrief on how they did from Olga later.

She clapped her hands to get their attention. "While you guys are here, and lunch settles, Ashok is going to teach an intro to cybersecurity and how to use our secure communication applications. He's made some changes, so this should be new for everyone."

Charlie groaned. "Classroom lecture on cybersecurity?"

"Don't worry. It's brief and hands on."

Ashok brought up the applications one by one on his screen and instructed how they worked, while the team had dessert and coffee or tea.

Once Ashok was done, Elda sent them all a message, asking for a response.

Next, they practiced cloning a phone and inserting spyware on phones and computers.

"Elda, why can't I clone your phone?" Charlie asked.

"I have new security on my phone that Ashok will put on all your devices." Elda clapped. "Okay, guys! Grab your coats. Let's go play bumper cars."

The spies walked out of the building to an army-green beat-up bus waiting with its engine running. Elda marched up the steps and handed the paid receipt to the driver.

The driver put it in a cracked plastic storage bin next to his seat. "We're a little short on buses today. Hopefully, Old Faithful here will make it to the industrial park and back."

"And if she doesn't?"

The driver scratched his buzz cut. "We'll have to wait for a repair truck."

"I hope she at least will get us there."

The seats in Old Faithful were patched with duct tape and had no cushion to speak of. Aside from having engine problems, it appeared that Old Faithful was needing an updated suspension system. The ride was brain jarring.

A cloud of smoke followed them from the rear. Elda hoped the exhaust pipe was emitting the noxious plume and Old Faithful wasn't burning up. It was impossible to hold a conversation over the noise of the engine and bus body, so they all sat quietly.

They pulled into the parking lot of the Calvert County Government Office. Elda had arranged to have the junker cars delivered there. It was Sunday, so no one was working. The team piled off the bus.

Elda called them to her side. "Here's the exercise. I'm your target. You'll be in your cars when you spot me driving out of the lot. Your job is to capture me unharmed. I'll give you ten minutes now to strategize, and we will start. Check your comms."

Elda's car was parked at the entrance, facing Duke Street. The other cars were parked diagonally so they would have to back out, buying Elda a few minutes.

"On your mark, get set, *go*." Elda peeled out onto Duke Street and took a left onto Main Street.

"Oh no, you don't get away with *that*." Murka spoke to Elda's rapidly receding car. She floored the accelerator. Murka's car tires squealed as she whipped around and raced to catch Elda. She glanced in her rearview mirror. Charlie was right behind. Luke was behind Charlie.

Murka knew Korinna and Ashok had stayed on the bus, using laptops to monitor the event from above via drones. The debrief should be fun. But now *she* would catch Elda.

Murka turned left onto Main, Charlie still following her. Murka nodded in approval as Luke went right. Their strategy was to divide and conquer and come back together to encircle Elda once she was spotted.

Murka drove straight on Main. She saw Charlie turn left onto Church Street.

Murka took her first right onto Armory Road. Driving

at a breakneck speed, she held binoculars up and spotted what might be Elda turning right at the next intersection. She keyed her comms. "Charlie, Luke, head north. I think I have her on Armory Road." She took the right onto Fairground Road. Her theory was that Elda was trying to avoid being spotted on straightaways.

She found herself in a maze of dead ends, roundabouts, and curved streets. "*Chert.*" She pounded her steering wheel, got on the comms, and reported having lost Elda.

Charlie was driving north on Armory when Murka's message came in. She pulled into a driveway near the traffic circle of Armory and Dares Beach Road. From her vantage point, she wasn't easily seen, but she had a decent view of the roundabout. She spoke to the road. "Master will have to come back to roost in order to win. This looks like a choke point. I might get the jump on her. Or I'll be sitting here until they tell me the game's over. That would piss me off. I'll give it ten minutes, and if she doesn't come by, I'll go hunting for her."

Elda sped out of the maze area and to Fairbanks North. At the intersection of Fairbanks and Dares Beach Road, she turned left toward Armory. At the traffic circle, she continued south on Armory.

"Damn." Charlie was behind her. Where did she come from?

In front of her she spotted Murka heading at her, going close to ninety miles per hour. Elda wrenched her steering wheel left and spun off onto a small side road. In a cloud of dust and dirt, Murka was on her tail.

Elda turned left and left again two more times, heading in a circle.

Murka bumped Elda's car's rear.

Elda spun right and slammed on the brakes, whipping the wheel around to go into a spin around Murka, since Charlie had parked her car across the road, blocking the exit. She gunned her engine, speeding through backyards and two unpaved parking lots to exit onto Fairground Road.

No one followed.

Elda pulled into a parking space at the Calvert County Government Office. She bounded up the bus steps to Korinna and Ashok. "Where are they?"

"Miss Murka ran into the side of Miss Charlie's car. To her good fortune, Miss Charlie had exited the car prior to that. And Miss Murka was wise to have buckled her seat belt and lucky that her airbag deployed. But it appears both cars are not drivable. Miss Murka called Mister Luke, who is driving them back here."

Elda wiped the sweat off her forehead. "This team is good. They almost had me."

"But they didn't," Korinna pointed out with a smile. "I'll call the tow company."

"Thanks, Korinna."

Luke drove up with Murka and Charlie. As they filed out of Luke's car, a flatbed truck roared by to pick up the pieces of Murka's car.

Elda hustled down the steps of the bus to meet her warriors. She held out a scratched James Bond Matchbox car and handed it to Murka. "I confer on Murka the guts award. You are one hell of a driver. And you and Charlie came within seconds of beating me. You displayed good teamwork. And, Luke, you did a great job of covering the other ways I might have gone. Good thinking." Elda clapped him on the shoulder. "Get on the bus. Your cars will be collected. Oh, and, Luke, can you please help Ashok with the drones?"

Luke nodded and swiveled to a drone that landed near his feet. He reached out to pick it up, and it hopped away. "What the fuck?"

Ashok stood by the door of the bus. "Sorry, Mister Luke. I was trying to be humorous."

Luke shook his head, squatted, and hoisted the drone. He entered the bus with it. Ashok popped out, lifted the second drone, and brought it with him as he stepped into the bus.

Murka and Charlie hopped into the bus, followed by Elda. She tapped the driver on the shoulder. "We're ready to go when Old Faithful is."

The driver started the bus up. It rattled and roared and smoked but moved at a good pace.

Elda stood and faced her people. Each looked beat but elated. "You are an amazing team. I am proud to work with you. Tomorrow we will have more fun. Bring your weapons. We are going to do close-, medium-, and far-range shooting. Please move in close so we can hear. We'll use the ride to critique today's driving and share what was going through our minds. Ashok and Korinna, please start the video."

The next morning the team marched out to find Old Faithful waiting for them, with the same bus driver as before.

Elda raised an eyebrow and climbed up the stairs. She paused next to the bus driver and handed him the receipt for today. "Still a bus shortage?"

He grimaced. "Cost cutting."

Elda gave him a pat on the shoulder as she headed to her seat. "I hope you have plenty of duct tape and wire," she called back.

He laughed.

After another bumpy, smoky ride, they arrived at a bunch of abandoned buildings with a lot of space surrounding them. The sign on the gate said, PRIVATE PROPERTY. KEEP OUT. Another sign stated, INDUSTRIAL PARK COMING SOON.

Elda jumped off the bus, took out a bunch of keys, and opened the gate. She waved the bus in. The bus driver halted the bus inside the gate. Elda ran over and yelled into the bus, "Guys, there are two gun duffels near where I was sitting. Please bring them out."

The team gathered. Elda hefted one bag onto her shoulder. Luke took the other.

"Behind these buildings I've positioned targets for each one of you at fifty, seventy-five, and one hundred yards. Those are the pistol targets. Use your own weapons on these targets. Korinna and Ashok, I brought a couple of extra guns if you want to try. I'll gladly coach you through."

Elda pointed and started walking. "If we come over here to the right, I've set up targets for the snipers at three hundred, six hundred, seven hundred and fifty, one thousand, one thousand two hundred, one thousand four hundred, and one thousand seven hundred and fifty yards. For this part of the exercise, please pair up with a spotter." Elda set the bag down and motioned for Luke to do the same. "In these bags are a L115A3 sniper rifle, a Cheyenne Tactical M200 Intervention, an Accuracy International AXSR, and a Barrett Mk22 MRAD. There is ammunition to go with each of them."

The bus driver trotted over to Elda. "I was a pretty good shot in the army, and if you're helping those two, you'd be one spotter short. May I join in?"

"Do you have a weapon?"

"Always." He opened his jacket, and Elda could see his pistol on his hip.

Elda narrowed her eyes as she reassessed him. She shook his hand. "You're in." Elda clapped her hands. "Okay, gang, let's start. Remember your gun safety. Do *not* point a gun at anything you don't wish to destroy. Only put your finger on the trigger when you are ready and committed to shoot. Point down range at all times. Once you are done, lay your weapon down with the slide back and the cartridge ejected." Elda put down a smaller bag. "In here you'll find eye shields and ear protectors."

Elda put on her own, grabbed two extra pistols, and ran over to coach Korinna and Ashok.

The shooting began.

Wearing overalls covered in splotches of red paint, the team nosily climbed back onto the bus.

Korinna wiped her forehead with the towel Elda had thrown her. "Are you sure this stuff washes out?"

Elda shrugged. "The package claimed it does." She continued to distribute towels.

Charlie caught her arm. "Master, that was fantastic. Running through those abandoned buildings with paint guns, flushing out the enemy. It was as close to real life as you can get."

"Without the need for a medic," Elda added.

The driver had removed his coveralls and folded them, so the paint was inside the fabric. He handed them to Elda. "Thanks much for letting me join in. What was this all about?"

Elda accepted the clothing. "Stress relief and team building."

"You sure know how to do that. I feel great!" The driver

started the engine and Old Faithful snorted and blew out a puff of smoke as the engine engaged. "Old Faithful's doing pretty good too!"

Elda watch each person stagger into the conference room.

Luke slumped into a chair. "Fuck. Are we still going?"

Charlie marched in with the coffee pot.

When they were all assembled, Elda clapped her hands and pointed to the whiteboard where she had written:

<u>North Star</u>

To protect the United States' national security and democracy by gathering intelligence and neutralizing threats from abroad and within.

<u>Goals</u>

gather information on potential threats

protect the bill of rights, esp. first amendment freedoms

Prevent misinformation, terrorism, and cyber attacks

Disrupt the actions of hostiles and proactively neutralize.

<u>Core Values</u>

Integrity, Courage, Initiative, Respect, Teamwork, and Pursuit of Excellence

"These workshops are to ensure we are fully prepared to achieve the above. I expect each one of you to ace this training and to help each other achieve their goals."

Elda ran the team through two more days of training. In the office, they practiced dead drops, message passing, pickpocketing, and snatching IDs. Once she felt they were ready, she enlisted Olga's help to monitor each one as they practiced their skills in the city. They had to abide by the rule *you must take a picture of what you stole and put it back*, which added to the complexity of the exercise.

The following day they stayed in the classroom and learned the various aspects of disguises, practiced passport forgery, used an automated combo finder on doors and safes, and the pros and cons of different recording devices, ranging from pens to external audio scanners and where to best plant them.

At the end, Elda stood in front of the team. "Great job everyone. We will be refreshing these skills on a yearly basis, and I expect you to practice shooting every week at the range. Remember, complacency kills."

Chapter Thirty-Seven

BORIS PLAYED WITH THE SCRATCHES IN HIS desk. He was unhappy with Tosh's performance and regretted letting him go on his own. On the plus side, Tosh had delivered on the political assassination, and his team *did* get rid of the reluctant mole in the United States. But Tosh didn't get to Boris's assassins in Mexico before the drug lords killed them, and Boris had not seen any money from the Kevin Ball mission. Perhaps he could remove Tosh entirely? Could he pick up Tosh's group? Probably not. Those people possessed too much loyalty to Tosh to effectively work for anyone else. He tapped his fingers on his desk. Tosh still had many friends in high places. Perhaps if Tosh was terminated? How? Boris had no assassins. Whom could he tap?

Boris picked up his phone and dialed.

The man on the other end answered on the third ring. "*Prevet.*"

"*Prevet*, General Krovopuskov. I have need of your services. Would you be available to meet for dinner?"

Boris scanned the National Hotel's Grand Café Dr. Zhivago dining room for General Leonid Krovopuskov. He considered the red blindfolds on the white statues fitting. Many clandestine conversations went on in this place, in plain view of the Kremlin, often ending in a death. He hoped that the general would cooperate and this conversation would not merit his killing. Boris would not like to upset the general's brother, Gorky.

General Krovopuskov marched through the door, stopped, and stood ramrod straight. Boris stood and waved to him. Leonid marched over to Boris's table. Boris shook Leonid's hand, "General."

Leonid pulled out the chair across from Boris and sat. "Boris, how good to see you again. What are you drinking?"

"*Net*. This is on me." Boris flagged down the waiter. "*Dve vodki pozhaluysta*." Boris saw a flicker of distaste fly across Leonid's face. "Vodka is acceptable?"

"Of course. *Spasibo*. You mentioned on the phone that you had need for my services. I can't imagine what that could be."

Boris laughed. "Just like you to get right to the point. Very well. I have an issue that I cannot solve from within the Kremlin."

Leonid frowned. "But, Boris. You already owe me one for the time I burned some incriminating paperwork for you."

Boris showed his teeth in the approximation of a smile. "*Da*. I do. In the interest of being able to retire at the rank of general, perhaps you will make this two?" There was the stick. Boris would pull strings to rip Leonid of his rank before retirement if he did not comply.

Leonid nodded. "And if I do this?"

"I could see a promotion in your future."

"And what is this favor?"

Leonid's blank expression and flat tone confused Boris. He'd thought Leonid would be ecstatic about a promotion this close to retirement.

"There is a man in my organization who needs to disappear."

Leonid raised an eyebrow. "Who is this man?"

"Toshchiy Chelovek. Have you heard of him?"

The waiter placed Leonid's vodka on the table, his arm blocking Boris's view of Leonid's face.

Boris signaled for the waiter to leave the bottle.

Leonid looked at Boris. "Do you wish that he disappear from his job and view, or be eliminated?" he asked, as if inquiring about the weather forecast.

Boris shrugged. "Whichever you find more convenient. It's of no matter to me. I just want him gone. It would have to be sudden and swift with no trace back to me. Can you do that?"

Leonid put his fingertips together. "Is he the one they call the gray ghost?"

"*Da.* He is extremely talented and has too many friends in high places in the Kremlin for me to take action."

"That will be difficult."

"Difficult, but not impossible?"

Leonid paused and squinted. Boris figured he was calculating the odds of success. As Boris started to squirm, Leonid answered. "*Da.* However . . ."

Boris narrowed his eyes. "However . . ."

"You will owe me more than the promotion." Leonid grasped the menu, shaking it at Boris. "And more than the expensive dinner I am about to order."

Tosh wore a black hoodie under a leather jacket. He sported a mustache and goatee, and his hair was pulled back into a ponytail. His fingers were tattooed, and the flames of a dragon poked around his neck. His leather motorcycle boots displayed well-polished silver-colored toe protectors. He swaggered over to watch the skaters in Gorky Park while lighting up a cigarette.

Leonid, wearing a tattered greatcoat and worn leather shoes, staggered toward Tosh. "*Isvinite*. Do you have a spare cigarette?"

Tosh held out the package, and Leonid selected one. Under the cover of his hand putting the butt in his mouth, Leonid mentioned, "I'm supposed to get rid of you."

Tosh showed no reaction. He leaned forward to light the cigarette for Leonid. "*Razne?* For whom?"

Leonid inhaled and blew out. "Boris."

Tosh turned and viewed the skaters. "*Interesnyy.* When?"

Leonid inhaled and coughed out, "Soon."

Tosh swung the pack toward Leonid, who nodded and asked, "*Dve?*"

"*Da.*" Tosh shook out two cigarettes for Leonid. "May I help you in this endeavor?"

Leonid choked on the smoke. "Of course, my friend." He coughed.

"*Khorosho*. Unless you hear from me sooner, meet me back here in four days." Tosh strode away.

Elda stopped in mid-jog. That was a buzz in her left pocket. Tosh.

"*Privet*, Tosh."

"*Privet*, Elda. I need help. You and as many of your team as you can spare."

Elda didn't hesitate to answer. "Of course. Any hint why?"

"I am being eliminated."

Elda stared at her phone. Had she heard that right? What was going on in Russia? Tosh was in trouble. "We'll be on the next flight."

"*Spasibo*."

Elda pocketed the phone and dashed to the office. She ran panting through the door just as Charlie walked into the break room for coffee.

"Team," Elda wheezed, "conference room. Ten minutes. With go-bags."

In five minutes the team was assembled, travel kits at their sides. Elda strode in with a clean shirt, jeans, and hair still wet from the shower. She started without any preamble. "Tosh needs our help. We'll go to Moscow under cover. Make your new identity papers, don your disguises, and meet back here in two hours so I can ensure you'll pass any biometric scans. We leave tonight. Once we have our IDs, and Ashok has uploaded everything needed into the databases, I'll call Korinna to work with Yuri to make our reservations."

"Me too?" Ashok asked.

"Yes, Ashok. I'll need you to work with Stas. Olga, Murka, Charlie, and Luke will be operational. Korinna will stay in Maine. We can use Yuri in Moscow for any logistics. I have some ideas for the op, but we'll need all of Tosh's team too, to pull it off. Get ready to leave."

Thirty-two hours later, Elda, bleary eyed, stumbled out of Russian immigration and spotted Yuri in his chauffeur's uniform holding a sign that read, INTERNATIONAL CONFERENCE ON AMERICAN LITERATURE AND COMICS. She stomped over in her embroidered cowboy boots and bright-red cowboy hat. "Pree-vet. That's my conference,"

Elda declared with a Texas twang.

Yuri's lip twitched as he refused to look at her.

Luke strode over to join them. He had on a black T-shirt that displayed a picture of the Joker with yellowed teeth, red lips, and a white face. He wore a studded black leather motorcycle jacket and black leather boots. His hair was dyed green and spiked.

Yuri blinked and held his sign higher.

Murka sashayed over and stood next to Luke. She wore a tight red tank top, a gold belt, dark-blue jeans, and gold boots. She tossed her long black hair as she chewed gum. "This the conference?"

Luke smiled at her with a toothpick between his teeth. "You're in the right place."

Yuri rubbed one eye.

Charlie jogged up wearing a Captain America costume.

Murka chuckled. "My, my, Captain—you are well endowed."

Charlie put her hands on her belt and winked at Murka.

Yuri coughed. "Madam from Texas, are there more in your party?"

"You can call me Pearl. It means precious gemstone. And my gemstone is very precious."

Yuri brought his hand up to his mouth and coughed. His body was shaking. "Well, thank you, Pearl. Are you expecting anyone else?"

"Duh. Or is that, dah? Well, yes. There should be two more coming."

A large bald man, green faced, with red tattoos, stomped up. He sported a green-and-red uniform of some sort.

Elda greeted Olga. "Hello, Drax the Destroyer."

Olga grunted.

Something that looked like a tree with vines wrapped around ambled toward them. Ashok's hair stood straight up and had a green tint at the end.

Yuri blinked. "Is Mister Groot here the last?"

Elda clapped Yuri on the back. "You got that right, pardner!"

Yuri held his sign high and turned. "Will you all please follow me?" He led the motley crew through the noisy crowd to a black limo. He placed their bags in the trunk as the team claimed their seats. He slid into the driver's seat and pulled the limo away from the curb. "There's water in the cooler."

Elda grabbed one of the mini bottles and took a long drink, emptying half of it. "Thanks much, Yuri. What's on the agenda?"

"We'll go to the hotel, where you can clean up and grab some decent food. If you need to, take a short nap. We'll leave in an hour to go to an off-site location to plan the mission."

Tosh stared at everyone. "This meeting never happened. No one may know that your team is here, Elda."

"And where is here? You had the windows blacked out in the back of the van."

"We are in an abandoned warehouse in Russia, near Moscow."

"I figured that much out already, Tosh."

"My apologies, but we need to keep Leonid in the dark as much as possible. Plausible deniability, *ty zanayesh*?

"*Ya ponimayu.*"

Stas reached into his bag and pulled out a device with exposed circuit boards and blinking lights. "I made this to your specs, Ashok, but I didn't have time to make it pretty." He strung a wire from one of the boards in to a large circle in the center of the table.

Ashok examined the object. "That should work, Mister

Stas. Most excellent. We now have activated the Cone of Silence. The meeting may begin."

Leonid was gaping.

"Coming to this meeting in costume seemed the right thing to do," Elda explained. "If anyone asks, we can say we are preparing for the conference. I figured, as Americans, we might as well be outrageous. No one expects a spy to be dressed as Captain America or Groot. They all think black clothes and trench coats."

Tosh shook his head and chuckled. "And you brought the entire team. *Spasibo*."

Elda nodded. "Yes. I have an idea, but I don't know if it's feasible. If it is, we need both our teams to pull it off. There's a lot of moving parts. And for it, Luke needs to be able to speak pretty fluent Russian before we go into it."

Tosh waved the issue away. "That's not a problem. We have a way to accomplish that."

Charlie raised her hand. "If it doesn't hurt too much, can I volunteer for it too? I'd like to be able to speak Russian better."

"Good idea, Charlie. Tosh, can you wire her up tonight too?"

Tosh startled and stared at Elda. "How do you know about that?"

Elda smiled at him.

Tosh shrugged. "No worries. We will handle it. So what is your idea, Elda?"

"You have to die again, Tosh. Only this time Toshchiy Chelovek *cannot* come back."

"*Interesnyy*. Say more."

"We will need to involve your poison guy . . . what's his name?"

"Gorky."

"Ah yes, Gorky. Is he trustworthy?"

The general spoke up. "My brother, and Snezhana's

godfather, is trustworthy."

Elda's popped her eyes wide and eyebrows almost to her forehead. "Wow. I thought nothing would surprise me. Good. Thank you, General."

"Leonid."

"Leonid."

"So we will need Gorky to conjure up a couple of items—a sedative and a temporary paralytic that is good enough to have Tosh pronounced DOA at the hospital. We will need two ambulances and a hearse. Do we have a whiteboard? I can map it all out for you."

Tosh stared at Elda. She reached into her pack and pulled out a stack of folded large pieces of white paper and a set of markers. She unfolded them and laid them across the table, making a temporary writing area. "As you would say, Tosh, no problem."

At midnight two days from the meeting, Tosh lay fully dressed on his bed covers, reading a book. He heard his front door open and someone enter. He felt to ensure his gun was under his pillow, just in case the intruder was different from the visitors he was expecting, and had broken in. When he spotted Leonid at his bedroom door, he dropped his book onto his chest, closed his eyes, and snored. He felt his feet being zip-tied together, a hood pulled over his head, and a hypodermic needle prick in his neck. He went limp but could still hear what was going on. His body was rolled over and his hands brought behind his back and zip-tied together.

He was lifted onto what felt like a gurney and rolled out of his apartment. He heard the door lock behind them. Although he usually took the stairs, for once he was grateful the elevator was working. He didn't relish being dropped down a flight or two. He knew from the plans that he would be transported to Lefortovo Prison in Moscow for the rest of the night, with Luke as a Russian army soldier standing watch.

Tosh sat up after a restless cold night, on a hard bed with no blankets. The zip ties were gone. He heard keys clanging against his cell door and a soldier yelling for him to get up. *Bog, please do not let anyone of us get killed today*, he prayed to himself.

"*Davay, dvigaysya!*" Luke yelled at him.

To himself, Tosh praised Luke for a halfway decent accent as he yelled again for Tosh to get his ass going. Luke prodded Tosh with the end of his rifle to make the point. The Lefortovo Prison guard snickered as Tosh nearly fell on his face and had to be caught by Leonid.

Leonid held Tosh's arm firmly. "We are taking you to your final home. Say goodbye to the nice treatment you have had here." Leonid handed the prison guard the paperwork for Tosh's release. The jailer scanned it and nodded for them to leave.

Leonid pulled a bag over Tosh's head and led him out of the prison. "We have a car for you out back. It will be your last ride in luxury."

Luke followed, covering the two of them. They stopped outside the prison.

Tosh shivered in the cold. He heard Leonid order Luke to get the car. "*Voz'mi mashinu!*" The noise was deafening. Gunfire erupted all around. He fell to the ground. On the way down, he pounded his chest and the hidden pouches of blood burst.

Silence.

Tosh could feel his anxiety building and his blood

pressure rising. He heard sirens and a voice cry out, "*Doktor*, over here." A hand touched his neck to feel for a pulse, and he felt the now familiar prick of a hypodermic needle. The voice cried out again, "*Net*. He is gone." He felt himself being carried onto a gurney and rolled into an ambulance. His body was limp, and he felt himself slipping into darkness. His last thought was, *I hope that was our* doktor *and not an assassin.*

Elda, the *doktor*, trotted over to check on Tosh and nodded at Murka. "Deceased. Take him to the hospital. We will transport him to the Kremlin morgue from there." She moved over to where Leonid was lying and where Snezhana, dressed as an ambulance driver, was examining him. "*Doktor*, he is wounded in the arm."

Elda nodded. "Let's move him into the ambulance, and I will see if I can repair it here or if we need to transport him. What about the other one?"

Luke was sitting on the ground, holding a bloody thigh. He started to rise, using his arms and good leg, but Elda yelled at him. "*Zhdat'*!" She grabbed a medical kit and strode to him. She examined his leg. "You are lucky. It went straight through. I can stitch you up in the ambulance." She helped him up and over and into the ambulance.

Snezhana closed the door and drove off.

Inside the ambulance, Elda spoke to Luke and Leonid. "I'll need to do small incisions on both of you so when I stitch it up, it appears as if the bullets hit you. I'll apply antiseptic and bandages. Once at the hospital, I'll show them my credentials and tell them that since the wounds are small, I will be taking you two to the Kremlin for a debriefing. And I'll remind them that it's best if the hospital is not involved in this matter."

Elda took out a scalpel and sterilized it.

Luke turned pale. "Are you sure you are trained to do this?"

"No, but I have repaired worse in the field. Relax. You will have barely a scar." She handed him a small towel. "Bite on this."

The general shrugged. "Better that way, *doktor*. He won't squirm."

Elda patched up both patients. The general sat like a rock through his procedure.

Luke passed out.

It was a gray day in Moscow. Flakes of snow fell from the sky. The wind was brisk and cold. Snezhana stood crying next to an open grave in Novodevichy Cemetery in Moscow. Tosh's body had been cremated, since there was scant space left in the cemetery. Those high in government had bequeathed him the honor of internment with so many other famous Russians.

Boris stood off to one side. The DNA from the remains had matched Tosh's. He was rid of him. And yet, in some way, he felt sad at the end of a legend in the Kremlin's history.

After the interment, Boris strutted over to Snezhana. "I am so sorry about your uncle. He was a great man. What will you do now?"

She sniffled. "I don't know. He was my hero. I had wanted to be like him, but I do not want to end like him. I may travel while I figure out the rest of my life."

Boris patted her on the arm, turned, and left.

The two teams sat around the table in the abandoned warehouse with a bottle of vodka. Leonid turned to Tosh. "How did you get the DNA to match?"

Tosh chuckled. "It was an old trick. Anatoly found a body that was my height, weight, and ethnicity. We riddled the face with bullet holes to render it unrecognizable. Stas changed the Kremlin database to have the corpse's DNA and fingerprints instead of mine."

"I won't ask where Anatoly found the body."

"It's best that you don't," Tosh agreed.

Elda quaffed her shot of vodka and addressed Tosh. "So now that you're dead again and will have a new identity, what are you going to do?"

Tosh shrugged. "I was thinking of going to Gools for a while, if you don't mind."

"Feel free. We'll need to catch our flight, but I'd like a few minutes to talk to you in private before we go?"

Tosh downed his shot and stood. "Shall we chat over in the corner?" He led the way.

The team watched as their leaders chatted, stood, and shook hands.

Anatoly grumbled. "Much better than the last time they killed each other."

Chapter Thirty-Eight

CHARLIE POPPED INTO ELDA'S OFFICE. "So what's next, Boss?"

Elda's encrypted comms beeped. She opened the app. "Oh, I may have that answer for you soon. It's Ed. He wants to meet by the Lincoln Memorial. Asks me to come in disguise. Something's up. Let's call in Luke and Murka."

Charlie stuck her head out of Elda's office and bellowed, "Luke. Murka. Elda's office. Now."

"We do have an intercom system, you know . . ."

Charlie laughed. "This is their hearing test."

Luke trotted in, followed by Murka. "What's up?"

"Ed wants to meet with me. He's asked for a public, crowded place and for me to come in disguise. Something's wrong. I want each of you to go in disguise too, and see if you can spot anything out of the ordinary. Someone trying to listen in to our conversation. Someone following Ed. *Any* eyes on us."

Charlie saluted. "Gotcha, Master."

Elda shook her head at Charlie's antics. She was glad of

the break in her own apprehension. "Okay. Go suit up. We meet him at the Lincoln Memorial at ten hundred sharp."

Elda hobbled along, using her cane for support. She was white haired and bent with age. Her steps were short and hesitant. She stopped to consult a map in her hand and shuffled forward. By ten she had made it to the Lincoln Memorial. She looked up at it in awe.

Ed stood in front of her. She moved up next to him and said in a quavering voice, "Do you know, young man, that it took forty-eight years from when Congress designated the funds for this building for them to start building it in 1914? Our government moves at a glacial speed."

Ed looked down at her, and she winked at him.

"Sometimes I think our government follows the wrong people."

She squinted her eyes. "Do you know your facts, young man?"

"No, just suspicion."

She patted his arm. "I can give you knowledge. Do you know who?"

"I don't."

Elda nodded. "Well, architect Henry Bacon designed this memorial, and sculptor Daniel French created the statue of Lincoln."

Ed smiled down at her. "I appreciate all your help. This has been quite enlightening."

Elda held his arm. "I enjoyed talking to you, young man. I hope to see you again. I'm often here."

Ed patted her hand. "Thank you." He turned and lumbered away.

Charlie limped along with a trash bag suspended over her shoulder. She was picking up pieces of paper and assorted litter with a garbage stick. Her heavy coat and boots with lifts helped give the impression that she was a male. The applied mustache helped too. She looked toward the Lincoln Memorial and saw Elda approach Ed. She scanned the crowd and picked out a man dressed in a long black coat paying them attention. Whoever he was, he wasn't good at being covert.

She watched Murka, dressed in a wide-brimmed hat and long coat with leather high-heeled boots walk past the man and stare up at the monument. Murka turned, smiled at the man, came close to him, had a brief conversation, and sashayed away. The man took his eyes off Elda and Ed to watch her go, then returned to his surveillance.

Charlie spied Luke, dressed as a United States Army private, on the other side of the Memorial. She figured they both had Elda well covered and took her trash picking toward the Washington Monument. She spotted a man filming the area. His camera had an interference tube microphone connected on one side, and he had it headed in Ed's direction. He had a lanyard around his neck with News printed on it. She heard him grumble when she passed in front of him, looking at the ground for trash.

So they had put on Ed at least two people, who appeared to be novices at spying. Charlie couldn't wait to hear what Elda had gleaned.

"Okay, gang, whatcha got?" The team was seated around the conference room table in their office. The smell of fresh-brewed coffee filled the air.

"Ed is definitely under surveillance, and they are not too good at it," Charlie offered.

Elda gave a thumbs-up. "Good. I surmised that too. Ed asked for help, since he's suspicious someone is watching him and he doesn't know who is behind it. How many did you see, Charlie?"

"I detected two of them. One in a long black coat, and another with a camera and a shotgun microphone on it directed at Ed. He made no attempt to conceal the direction he was filming."

Murka spoke up. "I did a brush pass of the man in the long coat and managed to clone his phone, as well as RFID skim his wallet. Ashok is sorting through the data now and will join us shortly."

"I stopped to ask directions of the man with the camera, and did my own electronic pickpocketing. Ashok has that data too," Luke added.

"Did anyone see the third person?" Elda asked.

Charlie's eyes flew wide open. "No! Was there one?"

Elda chortled. "No, Charlie, there wasn't. Just checking that you only picked up on valid threats. Congrats everyone on a job well done."

Ashok strolled in, carrying his laptop. "Ah, Miss Murka and Mister Luke, that was the most wonderful data you gave me. And Miss Elda, per your request I have analyzed Ed's office equipment and disguised myself most cleverly as part of a cleaning crew and scanned Ed's apartment for bugs." He sat and smiled at the team.

"Thank you, Ashok. And what did you find?" Elda prompted.

"Everything was as we suspected. Wiretaps, cameras. They are most definitely spying on Mister Ed."

"Well, although that isn't great news, it's good to know. Do we have any clue who they are, Ashok?"

"Yes we do, Miss Elda. I happened to reverse trace the taps and also used the data we obtained on the people to discover the group behind it all. I did have to do some additional digging into a few databases."

The only sound in the room was of Ashok typing on his laptop. After a few minutes, Elda cleared her throat. "Ashok, that is wonderful information. Could you share with us?"

"Oh, most certainly, Miss Elda." Ashok projected his screen. He popped up one window. "Here's the info from their phones and credit cards." He brought up a second window. "And here is where the wiretaps are being sent from." He opened a third window. "And here is the signature on the wiretap order."

"Ah, Jack Stone. He's Ed's boss. But who are these other people? And the source isn't from Ed's area . . ."

"Exactly, Miss Elda. So I dug deeper." Ashok minimized the other windows and brought up a fourth one.

Elda leaned forward. "Black Force? What the heck is that? And how did you get this executive order?"

"It is better that you do not know that, Miss Elda. It appears, however, that the president has formed a new black-ops group under Jack Stone. Their first priority is to ensure the loyalty of Jack's other employees. I took the liberty of inserting some old digital information into Mister Ed's online history that shows he is a loyalist to the new regime. I also have obtained access to the black-ops team's server and have flags on anything that mentions Ed or Elda, and also myself and Charlie."

Elda tapped her fingers on her desk. "Excellent work, Ashok. Let's provide Ed with a spare set of ID, cards, and cash, which he can pick up from a secure location, whenever he needs to. I'll also pull together a disguise and escape route for him." She drummed her fingers again. "This new group looks well funded. We know they aren't experienced, but we should keep an eye on them. You never know what they'll be tasked to do."

Elda sat near the Lincoln Memorial, in a motorized wheelchair. She spotted Ed out for his lunchtime walk. "There you are again, young man."

Ed smiled and stopped and patted her shoulder. "You are in a wheelchair now? Is everything okay?"

She reached up and clasped his hand with hers, transferring a locker key into it.

Ed brought his hand down and into his pocket.

She looked up at him and said in her quavering voice, "I decided I'd be better off for long trips with some fancy wheels. These are rather fun. But"—she looked into Ed's eyes—"you never know what might interrupt our lives." Seemingly changing the subject, she went on, "Presidents are so powerful, you know? Nowadays all they have to do is sign an executive order and wheels are set in motion. Did you know how long it took to build the Lincoln Memorial?"

"No, I don't." Ed frowned.

"Eight years, from 1914 to 1922. They had many groups working on it. Some black. It got interrupted by the First World War."

"Black, you say?"

"Definitely." Elda pivoted again. "Do you have grandchildren?"

"No ma'am, I don't."

"My granddaughter is such a love. Her job is so hard. Her boss is always looking at what she is doing. She is okay for now, but I gave her a key to my house and told her, 'If you are ever in trouble, honey, come to grandma.'" Elda beamed at Ed.

Ed nodded. "You are a good grandmother."

"I try to be. Now watch me go, young man—this thing is speedy!" Elda putted away.

Elda sat at her desk with her feet up, drinking a double espresso. A waft of coffee bean smell floated in from her door, followed by Charlie, holding two cups of black coffee. "Wanna clean guns, Master?"

"I'm thinking, Grasshopper, of taking a few days off and wandering around the Maine woods. We've been going pretty hot and heavy on the ops and we have a bunch of hiring to finish. I'd like to be fresh for that. But sure, bring out that girly gun and let's race to take 'em apart and assemble them again."

"Blindfolded?"

"You're on."

The laughter from the doorway stopped their race. Elda took off her blindfold and waved Murka in.

"What's up, Boss?"

Elda knotted her brow and examined her crew. They all looked as tired as she felt. She decided. "Okay. We're going to do an off-site. I think everyone could use a break." She picked up the phone and dialed Korinna. "*Prevet*, Korinna. You're on speaker. You know that place in Maine almost at the Canadian border? The one that's ritzy but not too pricey?"

"*Da . . .*"

"Let's rent rooms there for the group for this upcoming long weekend. We can kick back, and there's also a paintball place nearby. That would be a fun outing . . ."

"I thought you were going to come up north and take time off, Elda."

"This is time off. Everyone's worked hard. We now have the core team that will be the leaders who will train the others we hire. We're ready. But we need some R and R recharge time."

By now Luke had joined the group, and he pumped his fist in the air. "I'm in!"

Olga wandered in. "Olga come? Olga bring snow-shoes."

Elda chuckled. "It's up north, Olga, but there won't be snow."

"Olga bring hiking boots."

Ashok, who had been standing behind Luke, popped his head in. "May I bring my laptop, Miss Elda?"

"Of course, Ashok. It's how you relax." She swung her feet down and stood. "Grab your go-bags, gang."